CAST OF CHARACTERS

Captain Jim Warnford. An engineer and former soldier with a score to settle.

John Marden. A burglar whom Warnford befriends in the course of a burglary.

Ashling. Formerly Warnford's batman, now his loyal and resourceful manservant.

Captain Rawson. The officer who testified against him at Warnford's court martial.

Percy and Stanley Johnson. Two sausage skin importers from Germany.

Henry Smith. Their manservant.

Thomas Elphinstone Hambledon. A British spy, recently returned from Germany.

Charles Denton. His friend and colleague, another British spy.

Alfred Reck. A wireless expert, who shares a flat with Hambledon.

Ludmilla Rademeyer. A motherly German woman who keeps house for them.

Mrs. Ferne. A large elderly woman who dotes upon her many cats.

Edward Palmer. A pork butcher from Hoxton and a receiver of stolen goods.

Chief Inspector William Bagshott. Hambledon's capable ally at Scotland Yard.

Victor Richten. A German with a black beard who keeps popping up everywhere.

Houys. A sympathetic Belgian hotel proprietor.

Captain Roger Kendal. An Army friend of Warnford's.

Jenny Kendal. His charming sister, who cares a great deal for Warnford.

Professor Quint. An elderly botanist.

Dr. Goddard. A psychiatrist who runs an exclusive insane asylum.

Plus assorted police officers, landlords, shopkeepers, servants, farmers, hotel staff, German agents, and mental patients.

Books by Manning Coles

The Tommy Hambledon Spy Novels

Drink to Yesterday, 1940
A Toast to Tomorrow (English title: *Pray Silence*), 1940
They Tell No Tales, 1941
Without Lawful Authority, 1943
Green Hazard, 1945
The Fifth Man, 1946
Let the Tiger Die, 1947
With Intent to Deceive (English title: *A Brother for Hugh*), 1947
Among Those Absent, 1948
Diamonds to Amsterdam, 1949
Not Negotiable, 1949
Dangerous by Nature, 1950
Now or Never, 1951
Alias Uncle Hugo (Reprint: *Operation Manhunt*), 1952
Night Train to Paris, 1952
A Knife for the Juggler (Reprint: *The Vengeance Man*), 1953
All that Glitters (English title: *Not for Export*;
Reprint: *The Mystery of the Stolen Plans*), 1954
The Man in the Green Hat, 1955
Basle Express, 1956
Birdwatcher's Quarry (English title: *The Three Beans*), 1956
Death of an Ambassador, 1957
No Entry, 1958
Concrete Crime (English title: *Crime in Concrete*), 1960
Search for a Sultan, 1961
The House at Pluck's Gutter, 1963

Ghost Books

Brief Candles, 1954
Happy Returns (English title: *A Family Matter*), 1955
The Far Traveller (non-series),1956
Come and Go, 1958

Non-Series

This Fortress, 1942
Duty Free, 1959

Short Story Collection

Nothing to Declare, 1960

Young Adult

Great Caesar's Ghost (English title: *The Emperor's Bracelet*), 1943

Without Lawful Authority

by Manning Coles

Rue Morgue Press
Boulder / Lyons

Without Lawful Authority

ISBN: 978-1-60187-027-8

Rue Morgue Press

87 Lone Tree Lane

Lyons CO 80540

Printed by Johnson Printing

Boulder, Colorado

PRINTED IN THE UNITED STATES OF AMERICA

About Manning Coles

Manning Coles was the pseudonym of two Hampshire neighbors who collaborated on a long series of entertaining spy novels featuring Thomas Elphinstone Hambledon, a modern-language instructor turned British secret agent. Hambledon was based on a teacher of Cyril Henry Coles (1895-1965). This same teacher encouraged the teenage Coles to study modern languages, German and French in particular, having recognized Coles' extraordinary ability to learn languages. When World War I broke out Coles lied about his age and enlisted. His native speaker ability in German prompted him to be pulled off the front lines and he soon became the youngest intelligence agent in British history and spent the rest of the war working behind enemy lines in Cologne. The books came to be written thanks to a fortuitous meeting in 1938. After Adelaide Frances Oke Manning (1891-1959), rented a flat from Cyril's father in East Meon, Hampshire, she and Cyril became neighbors and friends. Educated at the High School for Girls in Tunbridge Wells, Kent, Adelaide, who was eight years Cyril's senior, worked in a munitions factory and later at the War Office during World War I. She already had published one novel, *Half Valdez*, about a search for buried Spanish treasure. *Drink to Yesterday,* loosely based on Cyril's own adventures, was an immediate hit and the authors were besieged to write a sequel, no mean feat given the ending to that novel. That sequel, *A Toast to Tomorrow*, and its prequel were heralded as the birth of the modern espionage novel with Anthony Boucher terming them "a single long and magnificent novel of drama and intrigue and humor." The Manning Coles collaboration ended when Adelaide died of throat cancer in 1959. During those twenty years the two worked together almost daily, although Cyril's continuing activities with the Foreign Intelligence Branch, now known as the Secret Intelligence Service or, more commonly, MI6, often required that he be out of the country, especially during World War II. Cyril wrote *Concrete Crime* on his own but the final two books in the series were the work of a ghostwriter, Cyril not wanting to go on with the series without Adelaide. While earlier books had shown flashes of humor, the present volume, *Without Lawful Authority*, published in 1943 but set in 1938, marks the collaborators' first use of the almost farcical humor that would come to be their hallmark. For more details on their collaboration and Cyril's activities in British intelligence see Tom & Enid Schantz' introduction to the Rue Morgue Press edition of *Drink to Yesterday*.

TO

C.A.J.Y.

Although He (Remembering Old Days)

Still Likes the First One Best

1
On the Evidence

WARNFORD sat in an armchair before the fire in his flat in Pight's Mews, off Gloucester Place. He had on his knee a handbook, *Engineering Practice for Small Workshops*, but he was staring at the fire instead of reading. Nice little lathe, that 3½-inch Drummond, and the drilling machine wasn't too bad, considering it was secondhand; he'd always wanted a workshop of his own and now he'd got it. A set of milling cutters would be necessary if one were going to turn out anything worth doing; he would get them in the morning. Yes, and anything else he wanted, too; it was so very nice for him, wasn't it, to be able to buy himself anything within reason he wanted; anything, that is, except the one thing he really desired, reinstatement and the black mark wiped out. His mouth twisted and he moved uneasily in his comfortable lounge suit because it was too comfortable, no pressure from the strap on the shoulder, no constriction round the waist from a stiff Sam Browne belt, no more, no more. And Rawson had resigned his commission; why? Very queer. There was no reason why he should resign, nothing at all against Rawson, unless …

No use brooding like this; think about something else. It would be interesting to make a model steam locomotive, 2½-inch gauge; take up rather a lot of room, but it gives one more scope for detail than a smaller size. Steam-driven boats required a pond, but a scale-model Foden steam wagon would be interesting, or an exact model of one of the early steamcars; probably drawings were obtainable somewhere. Anything but a tank; no more scale-model tanks, no more. "Where's that model now?" he thought. "One of these days I'll ask Rawson, and if he doesn't want to be taken to pieces like a jointed doll I think he'll answer me." Warnford's jaw stuck out and his dark eyebrows met over his nose.

There was a dull thud from the room next door which attracted his attention. "Sounds as though Ashling's dropped the telephone directory, unless the poor chap's been taken ill himself." He listened intently and heard sounds of movement; evidently his servant was still capable of activity, and Warnford returned to his thoughts. Those engine parts advertised by Bassett-Lowke which only wanted some machining and assembling were rather nice; it might be as well to start with one of those; it would provide a lot of experience. He made a long arm for the Bassett-Lowke catalogue on the top of the bookcase beside the fire and stopped halfway at the sound of a peculiar dragging noise outside the room. The next moment the door was kicked open and Ashling came in, towing behind him the unconscious body of a man whose arms and legs trailed limply on the floor. Ashling himself had an air of quite unusual ferocity owing to the fact that he was carrying a heavy round ruler between his teeth, having no hand to spare. He dropped the body on the carpet, took the ruler out of his mouth, shut the door quietly, and explained himself.

"Look what I got, sir! Found 'im burgling your safe and dotted him one with this." He flourished the ruler.

"Good lord, man, you may have killed him!" said Warnford, getting up hastily.

"No fear, I didn't 'it 'im in the right place for that, only to put 'im to sleep. I didn't know but what 'e might be armed, sir."

"Quite true, he might have been," said Warnford, running his hands over the man, "but he isn't. He's breathing all right. Pour some water on his head."

This was done, and the burglar gasped once or twice, opened his eyes, and struggled to a sitting position, rubbing the back of his head. "What—?" he mumbled. "Who are you—?" Then in a clearer voice, "Which of you dotted me that one? My soul, what a clout. I shan't get a hat on for days when the bump comes up."

Warnford and Ashling looked at each other in surprise, for the voice was pleasant and cultured, nor did the burglar resemble in the least what one expects burglars to look like, now that he was in his senses again and no longer a crumpled heap on the floor. He was more like a Boat Race night reveller at Vine Street next morning, a little the worse for wear but unmistakably a gentleman.

"I did, sir," said Ashling gruffly, adding by way of excuse, "You didn't ought to've been burgling our safe."

"Believe me," said the burglar, still feeling his head tenderly, "I wish from my heart I'd left the damn thing alone."

"Have a drink," said Warnford, pouring him a stiff whisky and soda. "Not that this is going to stop me from telephoning for the police in a few minutes, but have this one first."

"Thanks awfully," said the burglar, struggling unsteadily to his feet, "awfully decent of you. Probably saved my life, if the idea appeals to you. Well, here's luck." He took a pull at the whisky, and the color began to return to his face.

"Sit down," said Warnford, turning a chair towards him, "and have a cigarette. Feeling better?"

"Much, thanks. I wonder if you'd mind—er—disarming your servant. That blunt instrument makes me nervous."

Warnford laughed. Ashling put the ruler down on the table and fidgeted a little. The burglar was so calm that he made the other two feel awkward. "Will you be wanting anything else, sir?"

"I don't think so, thanks," said Warnford, and Ashling withdrew. The uninvited guest lay back in his chair and closed his eyes. Probably his head was aching, thought Warnford, and took the opportunity to look him over. Not a young man, forty at least, but evidently very fit and active; rather on the small side, but strong and wiry. Rather shabby clothes, but one wouldn't put one's best suit on to go burgling. Queer case; wonder what made a man like that take to burglary in the first place. The visitor opened his eyes and smiled.

"Yours must be a pretty exciting sort of life," said Warnford as an opening.

"Interesting, in its way," agreed the burglar. "Lots of psychology in it, you know. After a certain amount of experience you can tell the moment you look round the house whether they're the sort of people who keep their money in the safe, leave it lying on the mantelpiece, or hide it away among their clothes. It's usually women who do that, middle-aged single women." He yawned suddenly. "Sorry. Must be the whisky acting on the clout."

"Have some more," said Warnford, who had suddenly been seized with an idea. "You've been at it some time, then."

"Since soon after the last war. I was demobbed, like everybody else; my people had died, and there wasn't any money worth mentioning. Nobody wanted to employ me. Why should they? I didn't know how to do anything except kill Germans, and nobody wanted anybody killed after November '18. Othello's occupation gone, what? So I drifted into this and I've been pretty lucky; only caught once, and then of course I got off lightly—first offender, you know. I don't know why I'm babbling to you like this; hope I don't bore you. Effect of ebony ruler on the brain, no doubt. I thought this job was going to be so easy, too, all nice and quiet till your batman drifts in and bangs me on the head," he went on in a comically pained voice. "Don't you people ever go to bed? It's past one o'clock now. Which reminds me, if you're going to send for the police—"

"I don't think I am," said Warnford. "I've got another idea. I am going to ask you to put me wise about this burglary business. Opening safes, particularly; are you an expert on safes? I suppose there are different methods for all the various different makes. I am a fair mechanic, used to handling tools."

The burglar had been regarding him with growing horror. "But, my dear good chap," he burst out, "are you bats? Here you are, apparently pretty well off, very comfortable flat, Bentley car in garage below, faithful devoted servant, and all that; why in the name of holy Mike throw it all away? Are you hard up? Why take up burglary, of all things? I suppose you're bored. Better be bored than jailed, believe me; I've tried both. You're sure to be caught sooner or later; think of the disgrace."

Warnford burst out laughing, but it was laughter of a nature to silence his guest completely; he merely sat and stared.

"I'm not doing it for money," explained Warnford, "and the disgrace doesn't frighten me, strange to say. I am doing it for a purely private reason."

His guest's face lit up with the gleam of sudden recollection and immediately darkened again with sympathy. "Of course," he said slowly, "I remember you now. I was wondering why your face was familiar; saw your photograph in the papers at the time the case was on. I never remember names." He lit another cigarette and stared thoughtfully into the fire.

"I haven't changed it," said Warnford harshly. "It is still Warnford."

"No business of mine to comment, but it struck me at the time you'd had a raw deal. In fact, I thought you'd been framed."

"Just fancy that," said Warnford sardonically. "Whatever made you think that?"

"I dunno, just an idea I picked up. But probably you'd rather not talk about it."

Warnford hesitated. It did seem absurd to talk about one's very private affairs to a total stranger and a burglar at that; on the other hand it is often easier to talk to a stranger, and this was a man of his own caste, burglar or no. It came over Warnford suddenly what an immense relief it would be to talk to someone about it again; he and Ashling had dropped the subject long ago, and there had been no one else. When you dive down a side turning every time you see an old friend coming you don't make new ones either. But this man was different; he also was outside the pale, and in spite of his profession there was something about those steady eyes which inspired confidence.

"I don't want to bore you with an old story," he began.

"It won't bore me."

"Well—I was in the Tank Corps, if you remember. I took a lot of interest in the experimental side—always been keen on engineering. Ultimately I came to have a lot to do with the new stuff; had one or two little ideas of my own adopted, as a matter of fact. Then we had down a complete set of plans for a new tank—very hush-hush. I had to get the hang of them and explain them to a selected few. It was a good design in many ways; I was very keen about it." He paused.

"The plans were in your charge, were they?"

"Yes. I had one key to the safe; the C.O. had the other. There were only two keys. The design was rather complicated, so I made a small scale model to make it easier to understand. As you probably know, it's not always easy to follow a design on paper if you're not used to engineers' drawings."

"I'll take your word for it," said the stranger. "I'm not an engineer myself."

"Of course I kept the model locked up too. Nobody saw it who wasn't entitled to, till one morning I opened the safe and found plans and model missing." He paused again, but his visitor merely lit another cigarette and waited.

"There isn't much more to tell. I was court-martialed of course; I expected that. What I didn't expect was that evidence would be forthcoming which suggested I'd sold the stuff to agents of a foreign power. Of course there's no doubt that such agents did get it."

"What I didn't understand at the time," said the burglar frankly, "was why, if the evidence was true, you weren't sent to the Tower."

"It wasn't very convincing evidence," said Warnford. "I was alleged to be hard up. I wasn't really, but I saw no sense in blueing good cash on the sort of damn follies most of our fellows go in for, you know. Then, two days before this happened, I bought the Bentley. Again, I was supposed to be in the habit of driving up to town and meeting mysterious people; I was seen in quiet restaurants with men of un-English appearance. That was pure invention, though I did run up to town pretty often. In point of fact, I went to see a lady, but one can't say so. They could not find any corroborative evidence about my mysterious friends, so they let that drop, but the suggestion had its effect. Left a nasty taste, you know."

The burglar nodded. "Who produced this evidence?"

"A brother officer, fellow named Rawson. Always been rather a friend of mine, too; that is, as much as he was a friend of anybody's. Not a very popular bloke, actually, but dashed keen on his job in the same way I was. On the engineering side, rather than tactics and field exercises."

"Know anything about his antecedents?"

"Not much. His people were dead, I gathered, and he didn't seem to have any near relations, but lots of chaps haven't. Told me once he'd been privately educated as he'd been considered delicate when he was a kid; I always put down any little differences to that."

"What sort of differences?"

"Oh, I don't know. Sort of lack of background, I think, as much as anything. If you've been to a big school it's always cropping up; old so-and-so out in Rangoon or somewhere, of course, he was in my form; that sort of thing, don't you know? Nothing of that about Rawson; you'd think he wasn't born till the day he joined us. Small differences in outlook, habit of mind—oh, I don't know. But there was something."

The burglar nodded. "Speak many languages?"

"I don't think so. Always said he was a fool at languages—and yet—"

"What?"

"I remember a little incident once. I came into the mess bar one day and Rawson was there. He didn't see me come in, and I smacked him on the back and made him spill his drink, you know."

"Well?"

"He swore, as anybody might. Only he said it in German."

"He did, did he? You speak German yourself, do you?"

"Oh yes. My father was with the Army of Occupation, and my mother went to live with him at Wiesbaden. I went too. I was quite a small kid at the time, about ten or so, and you pick up languages easily then. I went to a German school for some time."

"Rawson is still with the regiment, I suppose."

"No, he isn't," said Warnford in a puzzled voice. "I saw in the paper that he'd resigned his commission quite soon after I left. I've no idea why, and of course I don't hear any news now except occasionally through Ashling. He was my batman nearly all the time I was there, but he left, time-expired, about four months before my affair came on. He wrote to me after the case, and I came up to town and saw him. Then when I moved in here I took him on again. But of course Ashling's correspondents in the regiment wouldn't know anything except gossip. Ashling says Rawson was always very much disliked by the men, too much of a martinet. Hadn't quite the right manner, I always thought. Ashling did suggest that Rawson wasn't too happy with the other officers after I left, for what that's worth."

"Perhaps they resented his evidence," suggested the stranger.

"They may have done. In point of fact, his remarks weren't too well received at the court-martial, I thought; there was rather a purple silence, if you know what I mean. But the damage was done all the same."

"Wonder where he is now."

"So do I. I should like to know," said Warnford. "I should very much like to know. Then I should like to take him somewhere private, where no one could overhear us, however much noise we made, and talk to him."

"Better not, perhaps."

"Why ever not?"

"Don't you see? Suppose he came to pieces in your 'and, as the housemaids say; nobody would believe it wasn't murder. Look at your motive."

"Revenge, ha-ha? I suppose they would say that. I don't want to kill him; I want to—to unmask him is, I believe, the correct phrase."

"Is that why you want to study burglary?"

"Not only that, for it's quite on the cards I shall never see or hear of Rawson again. No. The point is this. Whether Rawson really had much to do with it or not, there's no doubt that they were spies of some sort who had my plans and the model. My idea was to keep my eyes open for what you might call suspicious characters; if we're as riddled with spies as they say, there must be plenty of them about. Then I propose to investigate them closely. It is possible that one thing might lead to another and eventually to Rawson, but if it doesn't I shan't be wasting my time."

"Sort of unofficial counterespionage?"

"Oh, I know it sounds mad, but—"

"If you find papers or things like that—maps—you send 'em to British Intelligence, I suppose?"

"To the Foreign Office, I think. I don't know where British Intelligence hangs out—does anybody? The F.O. will do."

"It's a hideous risk you're running," said the burglar thoughtfully.

"Not so much as you think. If a man loses papers he's no right to have he won't call the police, will he?"

"You might take quite innocent papers by mistake, or—"

"Then he can have 'em back by return of post."

"Or you might find yourself up against people compared with whom our police are doting aunts and indulgent grandmothers."

"Make life quite exciting, won't it?" said Warnford casually. "Have another spot?"

"No, thanks, I don't drink much. I still think—"

"Oh, for God's sake!" burst out Warnford furiously. "Think, man. I'm twenty-five and I may live to be seventy-five. Am I to spend the next fifty years of my life hiding in corners, dodging people I used to know, driving the Bentley to places where they don't know me, and using up the rest of my days making model engines in my workshop downstairs? I won't commit suicide. I expect Rawson thought I would, so I'm damned if I will. But I can't go on like this. I can't; I can't! I shall go mad; I've started talking to myself already." He paused, emptied his glass, and went on in a quieter tone: "Sorry to be so dramatic; frightful bad form. There's another point too. I used to hold the King's commission; now I don't. We shall be in for another war soon; it's coming. When it comes I can enlist, but there's no point in my doing so now; I'm a trained man already. If I do this I shall at least be doing something; if I'm successful at all I might be quite useful—with luck. At least I shall have something else to think about all the mornings, all the afternoons, all the evenings, nearly all the nights—I don't sleep much—"

"All right, all right," said his visitor soothingly. "I've made my protest; let it go at that. When you put it like that it's still crazy but not quite so mad. I will help you in any and every way I can."

"That's frightfully good of you."

"Not at all. On the contrary, I hope you'll let me in on this a bit. Two heads, you know, and all that."

"No," said Warnford decidedly. "This is too damn dangerous. It doesn't matter for me—I'm done for anyway—but you—"

"Don't make me laugh," said the burglar.

Warnford laughed himself. "I'd forgotten your career; I had, honestly. But anyway, it's not so—"

"Oh, dry up, do. If you come to that, I also held the King's commission once. It's true it was only a temporary one, but it was a good one while it lasted. If I can turn my talents to good account—"

"Well, we'll see—er—"

"Marden's my name. John Marden."

2

Johnson Brothers, Importers

THE SAFE looked like being a teaser, and Warnford knelt on the floor in front of it, listening in an agony of concentration. He was waiting for a faint clicking sound inside which would be the tumblers falling into place as he found the right letter, for this was a five-letter combination safe. He had a small box on the floor beside him from which one connection led, like a stethoscope, to his ears while another ran to a rubber suction disc on the safe door close to the little window which showed the five letters. There were five small dials also, one to each letter; when these were turned the letters changed.

With hands damp with nervousness Warnford turned one dial at a time, and number one clicked into place. Two also. Three. Four was a trouble. If there was any click at all it was too faint to be audible; he left it for the time being and went on to the last. His fingers felt stiff. What a time all this took; surely one couldn't expect to be unmolested all this time—number five went down with a click that was almost loud.

He sighed with relief and returned to four, pulling the door gently at every letter, not troubling to listen, till at last the safe swung slowly open. Warnford sat back on his heels, took his listening apparatus off the door and out of his ears, and wiped his forehead. He was surprised to find he was perspiring. Now the— A footstep sounded behind him, and he sprang to his feet and turned all in one movement. It was only Ashling with a stout metal box in his hands.

"I'm sorry, sir, if I startled you."

"It's all right, Ashling, come in. What is it?"

"Only this money box, sir. Been collecting threepenny bits in it for years, sir, I 'ave, till it's nearly full, and now I find I've lost the key and can't open it no 'ow. I was wondering, sir, whether you could open it for me while you was at it like."

"I'll have a shot at it," said Warnford.

"With a skeleton key, sir, or some such?"

"You don't want a skeleton key for a lock like this," said Marden, getting out of the long chair where he had been smoking in silence and watching Warnford's efforts with the safe. "Give it to me a minute. Got a bit of stiff wire anywhere? A hairpin'll do quite well."

"This is a bachelor establishment," said Warnford. "Here's a wire paper clip. Will that do?"

"Fine, if you'll pass me the pliers. Now we straighten it out—thus. And bend it over at one end, like this. Then at the other end, so; that's to make a handle to turn it with. Then we insert the wire into the keyhole after this fashion and feel for the pawls of the lock. This is where the long delicate fingers, like those of an artist, come in useful; all the best burglars have them—in books. Though personally the most expert lock wangler I ever met had hands like a bunch of bananas, which only goes to show— There. My soul, I didn't know there were so many threepenny bits."

"Thank you, sir, very much," said Ashling gratefully. "I'm much obliged, I'm sure." He went out, carrying his money box carefully.

"Ashling'll be able to have a real evening out now," said Warnford. "Well, how did I get on?"

"Oh, not too badly at all. You'll get quicker with practice."

Warnford had hired the safe on the pretext of having to store some valuables for a short time for an aunt who didn't believe in banks. When it came to experiments in boring holes in safe doors, sawing them open and generally manhandling them, he would have to buy one, and safes are expensive things.

"You'll improve with practice," repeated Marden. "I'll shut it up for you again in a minute, and then you can have another try. Safes which are locked with a combination of figures work in exactly the same way as this one, of course, and present no difficulties. You must try and be quieter. You let that box of yours slide off your knee twice before you decided to leave it on the floor. It's extraordinary how loud small noises sound at night, especially bumps on floors. Always remember never to leave anything where it can possibly fall down or roll off. Another thing, put your tools away the moment you've finished with them, then if you have to make a bolt for it you won't leave so much behind."

Warnford nodded eagerly, and Marden began to stroll up and down the room, talking as he went.

"You sprang to your feet when Ashling came in; you would probably have done better to sit perfectly still if you're fairly sure you haven't been heard. People who wander about houses in the middle of the night are probably looking for the bathroom, not the study or wherever the safe is kept. Or they might want a book or a drink of water. It's incredible how little people see if there's no movement at all. You want to keep perfectly still, hardly breathing at all, and think about something innocent and far away. Such as a frog hopping slowly round the edge of a pond or a cow lying in long grass, thoughtfully chewing the cud with its eyes half shut."

"For heaven's sake, why?"

"Because there is such a thing as telepathy. If you think intently about the person who comes, ninety-nine out of every hundred will feel it and know there's somebody there."

"I see."

"Continuing my general instructions," said Marden spaciously, "here is a tip if you're talking on the telephone. If the bird of either sex at the other end says he or she is alone and you wonder whether it's true, make some excuse to leave the phone for a moment. Put the receiver down on the table and instantly pick it up again and listen. Most people who have someone in the room with them will make some remark at that point when they think they are not overheard. After a moment, whatever the result, touch the table with the receiver again and go on talking."

"Continue, Machiavelli," said Warnford.

"What else? There are hundreds of tips, all useful. Tread on the front edges of stairs to avoid creaks; the riser will take your weight. Oh, if you're walking across a room in which someone is sleeping, take a step when they breathe out and wait while they breathe in."

"Even if they snore?"

"Even so. I'm told it's something to do with the pressure on the inside of the eardrums, but that may be all baloney; I'm not a doctor. Beware of the snorer; they sometimes wake themselves up with an extra-loud snort and, having their mouths open as a rule, they hear extra well in the ensuing hush."

"Especially as they're usually convinced somebody else has made the noise."

"Exactly. You know how to prevent a sneeze from fruiting, don't you? Press your finger firmly on your upper lip close below your nose; it's infallible."

"I had heard that one," admitted Warnford.

"It's fairly well known. If you're doing a bolt and you dash out of a gate or drop from a garden wall practically into the arms of a policeman, don't run away from him. Run towards him, avoiding, of course, the outstretched arm. He will then lose time turning round to pursue you instead of getting straight off the mark, and you will be several yards to the good."

"When I am standing on the extreme edge of a stair," said Warnford, "thinking of cowslips and pressing my finger on my lip so as not to awaken the snoring policeman on the top step, I'll remember your words."

"Splendid. Now, if you'll turn your back a minute I'll rearrange these letters for you and you can have another shot at safe opening."

Some days later Marden said, "You know, I've been thinking over your case, and the more I think, the more convinced I am that Rawson is at the bottom of it."

"Uh-ha," grunted Warnford.

"At the same time, there's no doubt Rawson is merely one part of a large piece of machinery. He may have liked you quite a lot personally, but that wouldn't stop him from doing his job."

"Well?"

"You had some idea of happening across some German spies at work and hoping they'd lead you to Rawson. I don't know whether it's occurred to you that if you could start with Rawson he might lead you on to something very much bigger."

Warnford looked at him.

"There's no doubt," went on Marden, "that there's a lot of espionage going on, if only one could get a start—find a door leading into it, as it were. You know one door: Rawson."

"Yes. But what could I do? There are professionals at this job; they'd have no use for enthusiastic amateurs."

"No. None whatever. But if you could prove your usefulness you might not always remain the amateur. What? Wouldn't that be better than spending the best years of your life on a personal vendetta?"

Warnford slowly colored to the hair, and a light came into his eyes which had not been there for a long time—not since he walked into a long room to see his sword lying on a table with the point towards him.

"Yes," he said thoughtfully, "that's just remotely possible, I suppose. I don't know anything about these matters—and anyway, I'm discredited," he added bitterly. "Besides, how do we find Rawson?"

"Private enquiry agency," said Marden promptly. "I can put you onto one. Not one of those ghastly divorce-a-specialty places, but a real good one."

"Why, what have you had to do with them?"

"Quite a lot. Hasn't it ever struck you that if you want to know all about a particular household, what hours they keep, how many servants they've got, who their friends are and when they call, there's nothing like a good private enquiry agency? They never ask why you want to know. They've saved me weeks of work many a time."

"It's an idea," said Warnford.

"Of course it'll cost you something, but you won't mind that. Got a photo of the late lamented? Good. Let's take it along."

But though Marden's favorite agency did their ingenious best for a matter of three months, nothing came of it. Captain Rawson had apparently ceased without trace.

Warnford made it clear at the outset that if Marden were to help him to carry out his rather nebulous ideas, the partnership must be on a business footing. A man of that type would not take up burglary as a profession if he had private means, though the younger man was surprised to find what a paying game it was "when intelligently conducted," said Marden, "which it seldom is. Why, the first thing the police do when a robbery has been committed is to look round and see who's throwing money about—I mean, of course, in circles where people don't usually have money to throw."

"I always thought of burglars as more or less starving between jobs," said Warnford, "and then having a glorious binge when they'd pulled something off."

"That is more or less the way they go on. I've always been frightfully careful not to do that; I just keep enough current cash to keep me going on a slowly rising scale and invest the rest. The Desmond diamonds—you read about them in the paper, I expect—were a great help. A few more windfalls like that and I shall retire to Kent and breed spaniels. Black cockers. Or Aberdeen terriers. There were always cocker spaniels and Aberdeens at home when I was a boy."

"You like Kent, do you?"

"I was brought up there. In fact, I've got a cottage there still, not far from Maidstone." Warnford learned by degrees through different conversations that Marden had married during the war, a marriage which consisted solely of a few wonderful leaves spent in hotels here and there, with much talk of the home they would have when the war was over. Then the young wife fell ill and it turned out to be pulmonary tuberculosis, it was one of those interminable lingering illnesses culminating in seven months at the Brompton Hospital, where she died. Money for doctors' bills, money for nurses, for special diets, for periods in nursing homes by the seaside, weekly payments to the hospital, presents of flowers and fruit, traveling expenses to go to see her, all these things swept away Marden's gratuity and a few hundreds he inherited from his parents, everything except Halvings, the cottage near Maidstone, which he could not bear to part with; besides, it was let and brought in something every quarter. "She might have got better; I had to have somewhere she could go to." It was at this point, Warnford gathered, that Marden took to burglary. "This was during the postwar slump, you know; there were no jobs to be had for an untrained man. I saw my late captain one day in Kensington High Street selling bootlaces. Burglary's better than that; if not so honest it's much more interesting. Occupies your mind. You've got to keep fit too; if you take to drink you're done. I reckon burglary has saved me from a lot, and I only rob those who can spare it. Profiteers' wives and suchlike."

Marden used to come up to the flat two or three evenings a week, sometimes oftener, to sit on a box in Warnford's workshop while he was boring out tiny steam-engine cylinders on the Drummond lathe or filing small parts to fit within extremely fine limits. At the end of a month or two it seemed like a bad dream that he had spent so long brooding alone with no one but Ashling who knew or cared who he was or what became of him, getting more morbid and bitter with every passing day. The blue devils retired into the background at once at the sound of Marden's knock on the door and his quiet voice talking about dogs and fly-fishing, dowagers and diamonds, night raids in no man's land, and what the corporal said to the mayor of Lessines.

One day while they were still hoping for news of Rawson from the enquiry agency Marden went to Hoxton on private business of his own, a little matter of a pearl necklace and a few other trinkets. When the affair was settled as satisfactorily as is possible with a receiver of stolen goods—which isn't saying much—Marden left the furtive-looking house with a sense of relief. He strolled down the street and had stopped at a corner to light a cigarette, when a small man who was crossing the road towards him glanced up with an expression of surprise.

"Well, well, if it isn't Marden! Quite a stranger; haven't seen you for a long time."

"Hullo, Collard. How's things?"

"Not too bad, you know. Not too good, either. It's a hard life, isn't it? Come and have one?"

Marden agreed. Collard was an ex-headmaster of a Council School who had involved himself in rather serious difficulties when he was asked to account for some Benefit Society funds of which he was treasurer. After that matter had been disposed of with some inconvenience to Collard he had not found it easy to find employment, and he had become a bookmaker's runner. He was not, however, very successful; he seemed to attract policemen as the jam pot attracts wasps. In places where no policemen should be, and at times when they ought to have been elsewhere, they always arrived at the wrong moment for Collard. Marden was sorry for him, not a bad chap really; at the moment he was pallid and grayish in complexion from a recent visit to Maidstone Jail.

"Come and have one with me," said Marden, and led the way. They talked about one thing and another in a quiet corner of the half-empty saloon bar, of the doings of Hitler, and of what he would do next. Collard said he thought perhaps the Germans would settle down now they were all one, as it were; didn't Marden agree?

Marden did not; he said he thought there would be trouble and England would be in it, as usual.

Collard said that no doubt Marden was right. "Probably you know more about international affairs than I do; you've traveled a lot, I expect. I did think the Russians were going to give us trouble at one time, but they've been minding their own business these last few years."

Marden said he thought the Russians had their hands full with their own affairs, and, anyway, their activities were more in the nature of people trying to spread a gospel. The Germans, on the other hand, when they went poking about, meant mischief.

"It's funny you should have said that," said Collard, dropping his voice. "There's been a little bit of funny business going on down here nobody seems to get to the bottom of. Know old George King, do you? P'raps you don't. Everyone who lives about here knows him. Decent old chap, keeps a cigarette-and-newspaper shop round the corner two—no, three turnings down the road. Accommodation address for advertisers, that sort of thing. Well, it seems somebody got in touch with some of the real toughs round here, you know, men who'd cut their grandmother's throat for twopence, you'd think. They wanted them to knock out poor old George on his way to the post one dark evening and take everything off him. They could have any money there was; what these other fellows who were trying to get 'em to do it wanted was the papers he carried."

"Queer," said Marden. "Very odd. What papers would a man like that be carrying, anyway?"

"I've no idea at all; it seems silly to me. Anyway, as I was saying, everyone likes old George, and I don't suppose he'd have much money on him really, so there was nothing doing."

"Very funny indeed," said Marden. "I say, miss! Same again, please. Who were these mysterious people? Any idea?"

"I was told—I don't know if it's right, mind you—that it was two gentlemen who come into the Spotted Cow fairly regularly. I don't know their names, but they're foreigners if I ever saw any."

Marden thought this story would interest Warnford; it did. He sat up in his chair and said, "What did I tell you? I knew we'd drop across something like this sometime, if we were patient. Do you know the Spotted Cow? Oh, you do, good. Have you ever seen the two foreign gentlemen there?"

"No," said Marden. "My connection with the Spotted Cow is rather peculiar. It is run by a retired C.I.D. sergeant whom I know and, strange to say, I rather like him. I don't mean to imply that sergeants in the C.I.D. are inherently unlikable; quite the contrary, so far as I know. I do not mingle—much. But this fellow was the man who caught me the only time I ever was caught—touch wood. He was very decent to me indeed, made things as easy as possible at the time, and kept in touch with me afterwards, not officially, just in a friendly way. I don't know why. I appreciated it, though. If I were a respectable law-abiding citizen now I should owe it to him."

"Does he know you're not?"

"I hope not, though he may have his doubts. I told him I was living on a legacy from an aunt; I don't know whether he believed it. Why shouldn't he? Most people have aunts, and they can't take their money with them when they die."

"No. D'you know what's-his-name—the man in the newspaper shop?"

"George King. I didn't until today, but I dropped in there after I got rid of Collard, and we had a chat about things in general. Nice old fellow, I thought; got a gammy leg in the South African War."

"But what's behind it all, Marden? Wouldn't Collard say any more, or didn't he know?"

"I should say he didn't know; he's not very intelligent, really. He's the bookish type—perhaps that's why he took up with bookies. He did say one odd thing, though I doubt if he noticed it himself; I think he was only quoting what he'd been told. He said King was to have been set on on his way to the post. These people are interested in King's correspondence, evidently."

"But if King keeps an accommodation address," said Warnford, "most of his letters would be other people's readdressed, wouldn't they? Not his own."

"I suppose so. I can't explain it."

"I think we drop into the Spotted Cow, don't we?"

There was nothing of the gin palace about the Spotted Cow. It was an old-established place of a better type than one would expect to find in that neighborhood and, of course, very well run, seeing who was in command there. Mr. Gunn was something of a martinet, so rowdies and troublemakers went elsewhere. The furniture and fittings were good solid stuff and so, said Marden, were the barmaids, steady middle-aged women who knew how to behave. The house was eminently respectable and attracted a clientele to match, quiet elderly men and their wives, small shopkeepers and army pensioners who all knew each other and went there to meet their friends. The place was divided into two, a large saloon bar with a small lounge leading out of it, with a wooden partition between them. There was a public bar also, of course, but it was somewhere round the other side, out of sight.

Marden led Warnford into the saloon, which was comfortably, if rather stuffily, furnished with settees along the walls, easy chairs set about a number of small tables, and the bar counter across the end. There were colored advertisements on the walls, and in each corner a tall plant stand upholding an aspidistra. There were two or three groups of people sitting about talking quietly and drinking, for the most part, a rather heavy port in thick glasses. Mr. Gunn himself was behind the bar; his face lit up with pleasure when Marden came in.

"I'm very glad to see you," said Gunn warmly, "very glad indeed. It's a long time since you've been in to see us."

"It's been too long," said Marden. "I've been meaning to come in many times, but somethings always cropped up to stop me. I've brought a friend of mine along with me tonight—Mr. Warnford."

Gunn transferred his interested attention to the younger man, but there was no suggestion in his manner that the name conveyed anything to him. "I am pleased to meet you, sir. Any friend of Mr. Marden's is very welcome here indeed; he knows that. What can I get you, gentlemen? This one is on the house."

Marden enquired after various mutual friends and eventually looked round the room, nodded to one or two acquaintances, and asked casually whether any new people of any interest had taken to coming in since he was last there.

Gunn looked at him and replied in the same tone that the house had made a few new friends lately. There was Captain Butler, now, very interesting man who had spent his life piloting ships up and down the Hooghly, a very treacherous river by all accounts. He wouldn't be in tonight; he was away, spending a week with a married daughter in the country somewhere. There was old Mr. Williams who, believe it or not, had spent forty-five years doing nothing but paint rocking horses. Funny, that; you'd think it was monotonous, but he said no, there was a lot of scope in that job if you were anything of an artist. Couldn't he sing, too; probably because he was Welsh. If he was in the mood and it was a night when there were all friends there, Mrs. Gunn would play for him on the piano in the lounge there and he'd sing "Just a song at twilight," and "Land of my fathers," that sort of thing. It was a real treat.

That old gentleman in the far corner with white hair, he's an undertaker. Gloomy sort of job, you'd think, but comic things happen in all trades; he'd make you roll up with laughing sometimes when he got talking. The worst job he ever had was boxing up the Sidney Street gang, what was left of 'em after the fire and all that. Not so good. Well, there's got to be undertakers.

The door opened and two men came in. They were short, fat, bald-headed, and rather obviously brothers. They sat down on a settee against the partition which separated the saloon from the lounge and nodded to Gunn, who turned and gave an order to one of the barmaids. She went away and returned at once with two tall glasses of lager on a tray, which she carried across the room to the newcomers. They greeted her in a friendly manner, lit cigars, and began to talk together.

"More habitués, evidently," said Marden.

"Mr. Percy and Mr. Stanley Johnson," said Gunn drily.

"Sounds very English," said Warnford.

"Yes, doesn't it?" said Gunn.

"There is a theory," said Marden, "that the English are descendants of the Lost Tribes of Israel. When you look at those two—Englishmen—you'd almost believe it."

Gunn laughed, and Warnford asked what they did for a living. Tailoring? So many Jews were tailors.

"Oh no," said Gunn, "at least I suppose you might say it is clothing of a sort. They are sausage-skin dealers; they import them from Germany. Most of our cats'-meat overcoats come from Germany, I understand."

"That's interesting," said Warnford. "Harmless imports anyway, sausage skins."

3

The Apple Row Incident

Warnford and Marden allowed a few days to elapse before they went again to the Spotted Cow; they did not want Gunn to wonder why they came back so soon, and it did not take much to start Gunn wondering. In the meantime they put the enquiry agency on the track of the Johnson brothers and received an interim report. Gunn was quite right; they were sausage-skin importers with a second-floor office in Leadenhall Street. Their home address was in Apple Row, Westminster, No. 23. Apple Row lies between Great Peter Street and the Horseferry Road, near the gasworks. They were brothers named, respectively,

Percy and Stanley; they kept one servant, a man named Henry Smith, who lived on the premises, and there was also a charwoman who worked there for two hours every morning except Sundays. Further particulars would follow.

"Let's have a look at Apple Row, shall we?" said Warnford.

Apple Row was a short street of narrow three-story houses without basements. The houses had even numbers on one side of the road and odd numbers opposite. Number twenty-three was five houses from the end and backed onto the gasworks.

"Twenty-three wants doing up," said Marden. "It hasn't been painted outside for years."

"So they make up for it by having expensive-looking curtains inside," said Warnford. "There's a bit showing at that window next the door. I know about curtains; I had to get some for the flat not long ago."

They strolled on past the house, glancing idly about them and not showing any particular interest in anything, and turned right at the end of the street. "Wonder what's behind these houses," said Warnford. "Nothing much. Only a back alley for the tradesmen's boys."

"Your shoelace is loose," said Marden; "at least it would be a help if it were. Tie it up at the end of the alley, will you?"

Warnford did so, and Marden waited for him. When they walked on Marden said it was a very short alley and only served four houses, counting bathroom wastepipes.

"So it doesn't reach twenty-three."

"No. Apparently not. The Johnson brothers' domestic lager will have to be brought to the front door. Very awkward."

Warnford waited till they reached a deserted stretch of pavement and then said, "So anyone who wanted to get into the house would have to operate from the street."

"Unless they dived in through the cellar flap," said Marden.

"The best way would be to get a key for the front door. I think the gasworks come right up to the back of number twenty-three, and gas companies have a mania for high walls."

"How d'you propose to get the key?"

"I was wondering whether Ashling would like to make friends with the useful Henry Smith. We'll go down to the Spotted Cow tonight; something helpful might occur."

When they walked into the Spotted Cow that night the Johnson brothers were already there in their usual seat against the partition, placidly consuming their usual lager. The room was rather fuller than usual, so it was quite natural for Marden and his friend to pick up their glasses and stroll past the Johnsons through the doorway into the lounge beyond. The door was standing open and screened from immediate view anyone sitting just behind it; that is, back to back with the

Johnsons. Marden led the way to this place, and Warnford, as he sat down, noticed that the bar in this room was merely a small serving hatch, and the door screened them from observation from that point also.

"Quite private in this corner, isn't it?" he remarked.

"It would be if the family party by the fireplace would go away," murmured Marden. "I want to try a little experiment."

"They are more than halfway through their drinks," said Warnford hopefully. "Of course they might order some more."

"Let's wish them away. If we both concentrate hard it might have some effect. Assemble your will power, direct it upon the fat woman, and wish hard."

The fat woman took another sip of her Guinness and said that though there was no doubt that Nellie was a nice girl, she did, nevertheless, make things trying for those who had to do with her.

The thin man who seemed likely to be her husband said, "Pink lino!" in a scornful voice and lit a short cigar.

"I wouldn't mind," said the girl in the party, "if it wasn't for the rabbit."

"It isn't the rabbit that worries me," said the soldier; "it's the poetry."

"Poetry!" said the thin man, and attended to his glass.

"The canary's the worst of the lot," said the fat woman.

"Oh, I don't mind the canary," said the girl. "It does sing rather a lot, but you needn't listen."

"What I want to know," said the soldier, "is why a harp?"

"Why, indeed?" said the thin man. "Have another, Lizzie?"

"You aren't concentrating hard enough," said Marden in a low tone.

"I can't," said Warnford distractedly. "Why a harp? Does the rabbit play it?"

"The rabbit's got pink eyes," said the soldier.

"Well, the poor thing can't help that, Bill," said the girl tolerantly.

"I wonder how long the Johnsons usually stay," said Marden.

"But she could help putting a pink ribbon round its neck," said the thin man.

"They were still here when we left the other night," said Warnford.

"I can't say I like that bamboo furniture," said the fat woman. "Easy to move, I daresay, but give me something solid."

"Come to that," said the thin man, "I don't suppose the bamboo furniture likes you either, Lizzie."

"I wonder if the fat lady's nervous about fires," said Marden. "I shouldn't wonder. Think of fires. Sparks on hearthrugs. Wires short-circuiting under floors. Flames running up curtains—red flames—yellow flames—picture them in your mind and thrust them upon the fat lady."

Warnford concentrated till he felt as though he were squinting, and the fat woman moved uneasily.

"Are you going to have another, Lizzie?" asked the thin man.

"I don't think so, not tonight. I think we'd best be getting back."

"Keep it up, keep it up," said Marden; "it's working."

"Oh, Mother," said the girl reproachfully, "it's ever so early yet."

"We can get a bottle of something and take it home with us," said the fat woman, "and all have a nice game of cards. Wouldn't you like that, Bill?"

"Anything you say," agreed the soldier amiably.

"What's the matter with you, Lizzie?" said the thin man. "Got a feeling the house is afire, or what?"

"There," breathed Marden triumphantly, "I told—" But the fat woman began to laugh.

"Funny you should say that. No, just the opposite. I can't remember turning off the scullery tap after I filled up the kettle, and it'll be all over the floor. Let's go back, Tom; I shan't be easy till I do."

The party picked up its belongings and reluctantly went. At last the two men had the room to themselves. Marden hastily emptied his tumbler and, saying, "Do you like parlor tricks? I'll show you one," held the top of the glass against the wooden partition and applied his ear to the other end. "They're not talking English," he said. "Yiddish, is it? I'm no linguist."

Warnford stared for a moment and then followed his example. The voices of the Johnson brothers came through the panel, muffled because they were speaking in low tones, but audible. One of them said, *"Wie viel uhr?"*

"It's German," whispered Warnford. "He said, 'What's the time?' and the other said, 'It's getting on for nine.' "

"Look out!" said Marden quickly, and they snatched their glasses into a more usual position as a barmaid came through a door at the end to clear the table by the fire. She filled her tray and went, and Warnford listened again, but there was no sound from the other side of the panel.

"They're either not talking or they've gone," he said.

"Sit still a minute," said Marden. "I'll go across to the serving hatch and get a fresh supply. I can see them from there. What's yours? Whisky again?"

When he came back with two glasses in one hand and a siphon in the other he said, "They're still there. Just placidly watching the company and not saying a word."

Warnford readjusted his tumbler and went on listening, but there arose a babble of talk and laughter from the other room, and when the Johnsons did say anything it was difficult to catch it. At last in a quieter moment he heard one of them say, "It really isn't much good having a man listening all the time; they don't usually say anything important till after nine."

The other grunted, and they relapsed into silence again. A man and a girl came through from the other room to sit at a table in the far corner and talk in tones too low to be audible; Warnford removed his glass just in time.

"Those two are too much interested in each other to look at us," said Marden, "but if we went on leaning our heads against tumblers they might notice something. Of course you could say your wife was spending the evening with your mother-in-law and you were doing that to cool your burning ears, but perhaps we'd better not. I think the seance is over for this evening; let's go and talk to Gunn."

But Gunn was too busy to give them much of his time, so they went home to Warnford's flat and called Ashling into consultation. Having told him the whole story as far as it went, Warnford added, "We thought it would be a help if you got to know this manservant of theirs. Goodness knows what he's like, but you might get something useful."

"I'd talk to the devil," said Ashling, "if it would get us somewhere. Wonder what he'd drink—green vitriol, I suppose. Leave it to me, gentlemen; I'll pick this bloke up somewhere."

"Look in the directory," suggested Marden, "for the name of the people at number twenty-three in the next road, and then go to 23 Apple Row and ask for them. It's easy to say, 'Ass that I am, this is the wrong street,' and if they are nasty, suspicious people they can turn it up and find it was so. Probably any old name would do, but we may as well use simple forethought."

"At least I can see the man," said Ashling.

He did not fail them. After ten days of Smith-culture on the part of Ashling, they had accumulated as much information as they seemed likely to get, since Smith would not talk about his masters. Ashling had very definite views about Smith.

"Oh, 'e was in the war all right, but I've got a feeling 'e was on the wrong side. 'Is battles is right enough, but they're the wrong way round if you get me, sir. Another little thing, 'e's got a real nasty scar on 'is forearm, and when I says something about it 'e says it wasn't so bad only for them crepe-paper bandages. Didn't bind, like, as a proper one should, an' stuck to the wound something 'orrid. Well, we didn't use crepe-paper bandages."

"No, but the Germans did," said Marden. "This is most interesting; please carry on."

"Digging trenches, 'e talks about long-'andled shovels. Ours was short-'andled jus' like a garden spade 'andle, you remember, sir. We used to think them German long-'andled ones was a good idea; 'e says no, they was that awkward in a confined space."

"Case proved to my mind," said Marden. "The fellow's a Jerry. Any news about the household?"

"Doesn't talk about that much. 'E can't meet me Friday 'cause the gentlemen are goin' to be out, and when they're out 'e's got to be in."

"Curious," said Marden. "I should have thought a manservant could more easily be spared for an hour or so when his masters were out."

"I suppose they've been at home more lately since Smith has been able to get out," said Warnford.

"I suppose so. They haven't been at the Spotted Cow the last twice we were there," said Marden.

"Smith did say they'd been more at 'ome lately, but I've never seen 'em."

"Does he ask you in, Ashling?"

"No, sir, never. If I 'ave called for 'im by arrangement 'e's always ready for me, and the twice I went too early a'purpose 'e said would I mind strolling on and 'e'd overtake me. 'E did apologize for not asking me in, said it was a awkward 'ouse, 'aving no back door, which no doubt is true, sir."

"Thanks, Ashling. I think you've done very well."

"'E might ask me in, sir, if I was to be took ill one night on the way 'ome."

"It's an idea; we'll think it over."

"Well, Warnford? What about it?"

"I think I'd like to have a look round the house, don't you?" said Warnford slowly.

"I think it might hold points of interest, even if they're only the points of automatics. Ashling?"

"Sir?"

"Does Smith carry a latchkey?"

"Yes, sir."

"An impression of it would be a help."

"Certainly, sir."

"Good man."

"Do we go," said Warnford, "when the masters are out and the man's in, or when the man's out and the masters are in?"

"When the masters are in, I think," said Marden slowly. "For two reasons. One is that if Smith is out with Ashling we shall know when to expect him back—at about ten past ten; we should have no such certainty about the Johnsons. The other reason is that if the two old boys are at their nefarious work, whatever it is, there might be more stuff lying about. I expect they put things away pretty tidily before they leave the house."

Warnford nodded and said, "I think we two should be a match for the sausage merchants."

"I think so, too, though if one man's got a gun and the other hasn't, their respective waist measurements don't come into it so much."

"Take your ebony ruler, sir," suggested Ashling with a grin. "A crack on the wrist with that and 'e won't 'old a gun for months."

"Don't remind me of it, Ashling," said Marden. "The sight of it gives me an inferiority complex."

"Number seventeen," said Warnford. "It's the third door from here."

"I've got the key," said Marden. "Nice quiet street this, isn't it? Don't step on the coalhole covers."

"You'd notice noises here."

"That's what I meant. We ought to have hired a barrel-organ to play 'I wonder who's under her balcony now?' Well, here goes."

The key slid in with very little reluctance, considering that Warnford had made it himself, and the door opened quietly. The two men went in; Marden shut the door silently, and they stood in the dark hall listening. There was no sound at all in the house, but there was a smell of cigar smoke, and presently someone coughed. The sound came from the room on their left. Marden touched Warnford's wrist, and they moved along the hall towards the kitchen premises at the back. That door was ajar; they pushed it open and went in. Marden switched on his torch and threw the beam round the room. It was a very ordinary London kitchen with a dresser at one side, a gas cooker on the other, and a table in the middle; on their right as they entered there was the matchboard partition masking the cellar stairs, with a door at the far end. Warnford went to this door and lifted the latch with his fingers; a straight flight of steps ran down.

"Coals or beer?" breathed Marden.

"Both, by the smell. Let's go and see."

"Why?" said Marden, but Warnford switched on his own torch and went down, Marden following.

"Quite a big place, isn't it?" whispered Warnford. "Runs the whole depth of the house, of course."

"And the coals fall into it through the hole in the pavement outside, at the far end. A few packing cases and an odd table. Beer this end. Are you thirsty, or making arrangements to blow up the house? If not, why are we here?"

"Just idle curiosity," said Warnford. "Besides, I always like to know what, if anything, is behind me. There's room for twenty men down here. I only thought that a cellar the full depth of the house might have something interesting in it."

"There's a wire running along the wall here, look," said Marden, shining his torch closely. "Thin wire, like piano wire, painted. Goes up the wall"—running the light up—"and through the ceiling into the room above, presumably. Whaffor, as they say?"

"Something to do with the house wiring?"

"I'm no electrician, but I never saw house wiring like that before. Where does it go to the other way?"

"Along the wall towards the front of the house," said Warnford, following it with his torch. "Right into the coal cellar. Not so easy to see here; it's so coal-dusty. It disappears here somewhere. Never mind, I don't suppose it concerns us unless it's a burglar alarm."

"Funny place for a burglar alarm unless they expect people to slither through the coalhole and pinch their kitchen cobbles. Of course you may be right. These bricks on which we stand may be flashing red and blue lights all over the house. Hidden eyes may be watching us through inverted periscopes. Presently a sinister voice, apparently coming from the wall, will—"

"You've been reading thrillers," said Warnford.

"Habitually. Well, now we've seen that, what next?"

"Go and call on the owners in that room upstairs? Or have a look round first?"

"Pay our call first, I think. We can look round the house more comfortably when they're trussed up."

"Suppose the room door's locked?"

"Bad mark to you," said Marden reproachfully. "The key was in the outside of the door, and you didn't notice it."

"Might be bolted inside."

"I withdraw the bad mark. I am only a simple burglar, unversed in the tortuous ways of spies. Then we will burst it in. Come on."

The whispered conversation ceased, and two silent shadows crept up the stairs, through the kitchen, and along the hall to the sitting-room door behind which someone coughed again. Marden threw a light on the door handle; Warnford grasped it, turned it, and flung the door open all in one movement.

The bright light within dazzled their eyes for a moment; all they saw was that one man was sitting in a chair while another man was kneeling on the floor, facing the wall opposite. The next instant the light went out and the man in the chair hurled himself straight at Warnford. Marden thoughtfully shut the door behind him and waited, amid the confused sounds of conflict, for somebody to try to bolt. Someone came towards him; he switched on his torch momentarily and landed his opponent an uppercut which lifted him off his feet. He crashed into something which broke and thumped to the floor.

Marden judged by the noises that the other man was still too busy with Warnford to shoot, so he turned his torch on the battle. The little bald man, fighting with astonishing ferocity for one so short and fat, had got hold of Warnford's hair with one hand, his collar with the other, and was apparently trying to kick him with both feet at once; Warnford had already hit him on the nose with copious results and was now hammering at his head with short jabs less effective for being at such close range. Helped by the light, the soldier pushed the man away with such violence that he cannoned into the wall and bounced back. Warnford hit him once more, and that finished it.

Marden found the switch, turned the lights on, and surveyed the battlefield. "Well, that's that," he said. "We will tie them up tidily before they come round, in order to save unnecessary argument. We will gag them, too, to obviate yells. We will park them in the kitchen, I think. Who'd ha' thought these City Magnates would have fought like that?"

When this was done they returned to the sitting room. Warnford began looking through the contents of an open rolltop desk, but Marden stared round with a puzzled look.

"What's the matter?"

"Where's the safe?"

"There's no safe in this room."

"Yes, there is," said Marden positively. "I heard it shut just as the lights went out. Hang it, man, if I don't know the sound of a closing safe, who does?"

4

Unofficial Subscriber

WARNFORD left off opening drawers and looked at him. "Are you sure? I didn't hear anything."

"My dear chap, you were much too busy with your boyfriend to notice a little thing like that, but I did. Hiss of escaping air, thud of closing door, followed by a clanging noise. Why the clang? And where's the safe?"

"Fellow was kneeling on the floor opposite the door, wasn't he?"

"He was, yes. In front of the electric fire, warming himself, presumably. No, by heck, this fire's stone cold. He wasn't warming himself, unless he's got an unusually strong imagination." Marden switched the fire on, and the elements began to warm up. "It's a real fire too; it works." He switched it off again and began to feel round it, pressing here and pulling there, while Warnford went back to his pigeonholes full of papers till an exclamation from Marden stopped him again.

"My soul! Now, what d'you know about that?"

The whole panel of the electric fire swung open on hinges, and behind it was the door of a safe. "Four-number lock; now we shan't be long."

Marden returned to the hall to fetch the small attaché case he had concealed on the coat stand, got out his listening apparatus, put the ends in his ears, and stuck the other end on the safe door.

"Warnford!"

"What?"

"There's somebody talking in that safe."

Warnford felt his nerves prick in his finger tips and his scalp tingle; Marden's face, turned half towards him, showed the whites of his eyes all round the pupils. The soldier pulled himself together.

"It isn't a real safe," he said. "It's a door leading somewhere. Better be careful."

"A door eighteen inches by twelve for those fat men! Don't believe it. Get the poker or something and stand by; I'm going to open it."

But electric fires have no pokers, so Warnford armed himself with a heavy ruler from the desk which made Marden smile when he saw it. In a matter of seconds Marden took the earpieces out of his ears, laid his hand on the handle of the safe door, and said, "Now for it." Warnford stood with the ruler poised for action, and the safe door swung slowly open.

Inside was nothing but a telephone receiver of the pedestal type with the earpiece lying on the bottom where Stanley Johnson had dropped it in his haste. Somebody at the other end of the wire was talking, for the earpiece was squeaking and gibbering to itself after the manner of earpieces when the line is good and the speaker has a resonant voice.

Warnford and Marden stared at the telephone and then at each other. Marden picked up the receiver and listened, but a moment later the receiver said, "Goodbye," quite audibly and followed it with a loud click, after which there was silence.

"He's rung off," said Warnford in such an aggrieved tone that Marden laughed. "Just as well, perhaps," he said. "We can have a look at it now; there may be something funny about it."

But the receiver presented no unusual features except that there was no bell that they could see anywhere. There was another perfectly normal telephone on a small table near the door; when Marden lifted the receiver of this a bell said, "Ting!" in the hall outside.

"Well, that's that one," he said, putting the receiver back. "No connection at all with the firm on the other stand. What shall we do, wait for Clarence Cholmondeley to ring up again, or give the house the once-over?"

"Let's wait just a few minutes," said Warnford.

"We haven't too much time; it's nearly nine now."

"I know, but let's give it a few minutes more. This may tell us more than anything else we can find."

"We might have a look round this room while we're waiting," said Marden. "Did you find anything interesting in that desk?"

"Not in the unlocked drawers; there's one locked one here I was just going to deal with. What's that you've found?"

"Portable wireless, rather a natty little set. I thought I'd look inside because, in a book I was reading the other day, there were papers concealed in a portable— Hullo, this is rather a funny wireless set, isn't it? I'm no expert, but it looks a bit unusual."

Warnford abandoned the rolltop desk and went to look.

"I know these sets; we have—they have them on tanks, or something very like this. They are receivers and transmitters. You listen in with headphones in a tank, of course; probably this one's got a loudspeaker—yes, it has. If they want a reply they say, 'Over to you, over,' and you turn that switch which brings the transmitter into action and then you can answer."

"I see. What shall I do with it, put it back where I found it? Or break it up?"

"Leave it for the moment," said Warnford. "It might be rather amusing to take it away with us and see if anyone wants to talk to us. I'll just look through—"

There was a click from the telephone receiver in the safe; Warnford made a dive at it and got it to his ear just as the squeaking started again.

In July 1938 Thomas Elphinstone Hambledon returned to London via Danzig from a very long visit to Germany and after a short period of leave was posted to the Foreign Office to pick up the threads of current affairs and make the acquaintance of men who had come there during his absence. His room was small, but he had it to himself except for his secretary, who occupied a desk facing his own. Both desks were austerely furnished with an inkpot, a glass pen tray, two trays labeled "In" and "Out" respectively, lots of blotting paper, a pile of narrow sheets of yellowish paper—the traditional "buff slips"—and twin receivers from the same telephone extension.

Tommy Hambledon did not really care about having a secretary at all; he said it made him feel old. The fact was that so many years of working underground in the dark, like a mole, had made secrecy second nature to him, and it fidgeted him to have a man there all the time hearing what he said and seeing what he wrote. He fell gradually into the habit of extending his lunch hour till it was nearly time for his secretary to leave, and then working far into the night when he had the place to himself.

This evening he had a visitor, a long lean man who was sitting in the secretary's chair with his feet on the secretary's desk and drawing cats on the secretary's blotting paper. He was filling up a few gaps in Hambledon's information about men and affairs; his name was Charles Denton.

"What worries me most at the moment," Hambledon was saying in rather an irritated tone, "is having to be so infernally law-abiding. I can't even have anyone brought here for questioning just as and when I want to, or they demand a solicitor or write letters to their M.P. about it, and as for going through a house—"

"I know," said Denton. "You have to get a search warrant signed by the local authorities—"

"Who want to know why, and you can't and won't tell 'em—"

"Does cramp your style more than somewhat, doesn't it?"

" 'As is well known to one and all,' " quoted Hambledon. "Unfortunately for us. Look at this fellow who's arriving tomorrow. D'you suppose he'd blow airily into Germany like that? Or Russia? Not on your life. Yet if I go through him and his goods with my customary thoroughness and fail to find what I'm looking for I shall just have to let him go. He will then go and take a room at the Carlton or somewhere and write letters to *The Times*, complaining about the hostile and suspicious attitude adopted towards friendly foreign visitors by the officious mutton-headed jacks-in-office here. 'What,' he will say, 'is England coming to? Once the door-ever-open to the by-inordinately-despotic-governments-oppressed stranger, now the loathsome trail of a more-than-Nazi-heel tyranny bars the entry of a—' "

"Can a trail bar an entry?"

"Of course it can. Look at ivy."

"Have it your own way," said the amused Denton. "What are you going to do about it?"

"Have him pulled in and chance it. You heard the report about him on the telephone just now, didn't you? I think that's good enough."

Hambledon picked up the telephone receiver and gave a number, waited a few moments, and began.

"Is that the Southampton police? Can I speak to the superintendent or inspector—whichever is on the premises at the moment? … Thank you. … Good evening. Hambledon, Foreign Office, speaking. I want you to send somebody aboard the Havre boat tomorrow as soon as she docks and collect a man calling himself Gray who is coming over on that boat. I want him brought to me here, by car, under escort. He is not to communicate with anyone, and no fuss will occur on the quayside or elsewhere."

"Don't forget his luggage," put in Denton.

"His luggage will accompany him," said Hambledon into the telephone. "Here is his description," and there followed a detailed catalogue of height, coloring, and physical characteristics. "Got that? … Good. I shall be much obliged if you will kindly attend to this little matter for me. Good-bye." Hambledon started to take the receiver away from his ear but hurriedly replaced it, an expression of extreme astonishment crossed his face, and he gestured to Charles Denton to pick up the other receiver. A perfectly strange voice had intruded upon the line.

"Excuse me," it said. "I do apologize for eavesdropping, Mr. Hambledon, and for butting in like this, but I think you ought to know that your line has been tapped."

"Dear me," said Hambledon blankly. "Who are you?"

"I am speaking from 23 Apple Row, Westminster," said the voice, and Denton snatched a pencil to write it down. "This telephone is in a safe concealed behind an electric fire in the front sitting room of this house, on the ground floor. Door left of the front door as you enter. The two owners, Percy and Stanley Johnson, are trussed up on the kitchen floor at the back of the house. I think they have regained consciousness; I hear mooing noises."

"How very interesting," said Hambledon.

"The servant—they keep one manservant—will be out until about ten minutes past ten; the time is now—er—nine-twenty. I will leave the safe standing open and the front door unlocked to save you trouble, as no doubt you will wish to take some action in the matter."

"You bet I will," said Hambledon, "but who are you? Here, half a minute—don't go. Dammit, he's rung off! Denton, put down that receiver; I'm going to ring Scotland Yard. What did you think of that, eh? … Is that Scotland Yard? … Special Branch, please, urgent; this is the Foreign Office. … Thank you. …

Please send some men At Once to 23 Apple Row, Westminster—"

Warnford put down the receiver and laughed. "How was that, Marden? All right? I think we'd better scram without a moment's delay. Got the tools? Good. We'll leave this light on, I think, put the front door on the latch. No, leave the wireless set for the police; perhaps it might amuse Mr. Hambledon, whoever he is, to play with it. He sounded an incisive sort of bloke. All ready? Well, shall we go?"

Charles Denton strolled into Hambledon's room at the Foreign Office the following evening and found him there together with a wizened little man who was examining a portable wireless set.

"Sorry to breeze in again like this," said Denton. "Fact is, I found your story last night so enthralling I had to come in and hear the next instalment. I'll come back later if you're busy."

"This is part of the next installment," said Hambledon. "You two know each other, I think; Denton—Reck. I believe you met in Köln at the end of the last unpleasantness."

"Lord, yes," said Denton as they shook hands. "I remember you quite well. How are the silkworms?"

"Silkworms I no longer cherish," said Reck, speaking with a strong German accent. "They were not at any time remarkable-for-sparkling-animation companions."

"This wireless set was found at 23 Apple Row," said Hambledon. "Reck is looking it over."

Reck gave much the same account of it as Warnford had given to Marden, adding that this set probably had a duplicate—or possibly more than one—tuned in with it. When the transmitter on the corresponding set was switched on, this bell—called the relay bell—would ring. By turning that switch the loudspeaker would be brought into action and the message received. If it was desired to reply, the loudspeaker was turned off and this switch put on instead, which awoke the transmitter to a sense of duty. Very neat little set, very. Made in Germany.

"That's very interesting, what?" drawled Denton. "Regular Demon Kings, these Germans, always popping up, aren't they?"

"Anything more you can tell us, Reck? How far would this thing send a message?" asked Hambledon.

"I can better decide," said Reck, "if the other correspondent speaks. Perhaps tonight, perhaps tomorrow; how can I know? This will not for a long distance carry; two—three miles perhaps, four at most, and that in the open."

"Oh. Well, we must hope for the best."

"What happened to the two birds trussed up in the kitchen?" asked Denton. "Have you grilled 'em yet?"

"The police started by making a few routine enquiries for me," said Hambledon. "The men are twin brothers, Percy and Stanley Johnson, born in Avenue Road, Chiswick, on September 22nd, 1890."

"And were they?"

"No. At least Somerset House never noticed it. They were privately educated and started life as office boys in Medstead & Higginbotham's, wholesale bacon merchants, in St. Mary Axe. They were then fifteen, so that was in 1905. Or '06."

"Was there such a firm?"

"Oh, certainly, and still is. Well known and deservedly respected. Unfortunately for our victims, Medstead & Higginbotham have kept all their records. They have, of course, had office boys named Johnson, but not between 1900 and 1910, and never two Johnsons at once. However, our Johnsons stayed on there, without the firm's noticing them, till 1914, when they joined the Army and served in France from 1915 to 1917 with the Middlesex Regiment. Percy was wounded in February 1917 and Stanley in August of the same year."

"And were they?"

"I haven't heard yet, but I shall. Confirmation is made more difficult by the fact that they can't remember which battalion they served in. Curious, isn't it?"

Denton laughed.

"After the war," went on Hambledon, "they inherited a couple of thousand pounds each from an uncle named Ebenezer Harris who lived in Castle Street, Wimbledon. He died in 1920."

"What does Somerset House know about that?"

"Nothing, strange to relate. The will of the late Ebenezer Harris also passed unnoticed."

"Curiously unobtrusive lives your friends have led."

"Yes, haven't they? With the proceeds of this legacy they started in a small way as importers of sausage skins from Germany in a tiny office in a turning off Leadenhall Street. This part is true. The business prospered and they moved, in 1926, into Leadenhall Street itself, where they still are, or were until yesterday."

"And their secret telephone?"

"The Foreign Office private line passes their front door. I don't know how they discovered that and I probably never shall. They dug through the front wall of their cellar till they met the cable—it runs nearly four feet below street level—and connected up. I had them in here this afternoon and asked them to tell me all about it." Hambledon paused and smiled reminiscently. "They were a sorry pair. Percy has a wonderful black eye and a nose about twice its normal size, which is saying something, believe me. He looked like Cyrano de Bergerac. Stanley's jaw hurt him; he had also bitten his tongue."

"The gentleman with the charming voice who spoke to us on the telephone last night," said Denton, "must have had a busy five minutes."

"According to the Johnson brothers, there were two of them. One was tall, black-haired, and quite young, the other much smaller and older too. The younger one looked like a soldier. The Johnsons would know them again; at least Percy would. They were kind enough to suggest that if I would let them go they would try and find our friends for us."

"Suffering from swollen cheek too," said Denton.

"I thanked them kindly," said Hambledon, "but said I thought I could find them some other little jobs to do in the immediate and prolonged future, such as picking oakum or sewing mailbags."

"How did they explain away the telephone?"

"They didn't. They knew nothing about it, they said. They didn't know there was a safe behind the electric fire. They thought it was just an ordinary fire; it worked all right. It did too; the police tried it. Yes, they'd seen a lot of wires in the cellar but thought they were part of the ordinary house wiring; they are not electricians. The secret telephone must have been installed by the previous owner, who died there; they bought the house from his executors. They didn't know anything about it, kind sir; really they didn't. Nor about an envelope found under a loose board in the front sitting room. It contained a transcript of the last four days' telephone calls from the Foreign Office, bless their little innocent hearts. When I brought that out they turned so green that I had them removed; I thought it wiser."

"Quite right," said Denton. "It's so disconcerting when one's guests are sick at a party. No luck with the wireless yet, Reck?"

"Not yet," said Reck. "Presently, perhaps."

"What about the blighter on the Southampton boat?" asked Denton.

"Oh, he's all right. We found what we were looking for wrapped up in a bit of oiled silk in the middle of a stick of shaving soap. Quite informative it was too. We are keeping him on ice for a few months while we deal with the matters arising, as they say on committees. He was foolish enough to assault the police in the execution of their duties—he really did—so that's easy. He'll go into the cooler for six months. He brought a list of information required from various people; one of them was that fellow at Newcastle—"

The electric bell in the wireless set rang suddenly and Hambledon stopped abruptly. Reck sat in the secretary's chair with the set on the desk before him, waiting for a voice to begin talking; when it did he turned the set about till the voice was at its loudest. It was speaking in German.

"Come to me at once, please. I want to speak with you," it said. A man's voice, not unpleasant to listen to, and not too peremptory; just calmly giving an order he knew would be obeyed. After a moment's pause the phrase was repeated, after another pause repeated again. "Reply, please," finished the voice.

"On the wings of a dove if only I knew where you live," said Hambledon thoughtfully. "You haven't turned over to transmitter, by any chance, have you?"

he added in an anxious whisper to Reck.

"I am not yet senile," said Reck acidly.

"No, no. I only thought—habit, don't you know—"

"Pity we can't ask him for his address," said Denton. " 'Sorry, old bean, where do you hang out? Slipped my memory.' "

Five minutes later the bell rang again, and the voice repeated its remarks in a rather less patient tone.

"Where d'you think he is, Reck?"

"Not more than two miles far, in that direction," said Reck, indicating a line passing directly over the inkpot. "In some house on that line, under two miles."

"There would be at least two thousand three hundred and fifty houses within two miles in that direction," said Denton gloomily. "That's practically due north."

"Perhaps a little less," said Reck in an encouraging tone.

"Two thousand three hundred and forty-nine houses," said Denton. "It's somewhere round Euston. Think of all those squares and terraces full of hotels and boardinghouses." He sighed audibly.

The bell rang again, and the message was repeated at intervals for the next two hours. The voice became by turns contemptuous, commanding, and finally infuriated, and wound up by calling the Johnson brothers "pig-faced imbeciles."

"He should see Percy now," said Hambledon. "Not so much pig as anteater."

"Or baby elephant?" suggested Denton.

"No. Elephants are comparatively refined. You haven't seen Percy."

"By the way," said Denton, "didn't they keep a servant?"

"Yes. He arrived at the house with a friend of his and walked straight into the arms of the police. We didn't get much out of them. The Johnson retainer didn't know anything, not even where he was born nor exactly how old he was; this may be perfectly true—or may not. The other fellow was merely a friend he'd spent the evening with and seemed to the police to be genuine enough except that he gave a false address, but quite a lot of people can't remember where they live when the police ask 'em suddenly. He said he'd never been inside the house and wouldn't know the Johnson brothers from a bar of soap. So we let them go, to see where they went to after that. I shall receive reports in due course, no doubt."

The bell rang again. "Come to me at once," said the voice. "I wish to speak to you."

5

The Lady Who Liked Cats

Marden was sitting in his usual armchair in Warnford's flat next evening, reading the paper, when he came across a paragraph which interested him. "Dope Traffic Discovery," said the headlines. "Cocaine Haul in Westminster." Marden read it aloud. " 'As a result of smart work by the metropolitan police, a large quantity of cocaine and other drugs was discovered in the cellars of a house in Apple Row, Westminster, last night. The tenants of the house, Percy and Stanley Johnson, sausage-skin importers of Leadenhall Street, E.C., were taken into custody and will be charged with unlawful possession of dangerous drugs. As a result of this discovery the police have come into possession of information which they hope will enable them to break up a powerful and dangerous drug ring which has been operating in this country for some time past.' There, what d'you know about that?"

He looked across at Warnford, whose jaw had dropped with astonishment. "Drugs?" he said incredulously. "Drugs? Am I batty, or are they, or what did we barge into?"

"Not a word," said Marden, "about unlawful possession of an unauthorized telephone. Of course that cellar may have been stocked with cocaine for all we know; there were some boxes down there and we didn't examine them. But I don't know that I believe it, somehow."

"Is this the kind of thing Hambledon does when he goes into action, d'you think? My hat, I wouldn't like to get the wrong side of him!"

"You said he sounded incisive on the telephone; I think you were more than right. Well, I suppose we shall never know the truth of the matter. Not a word, you notice, about their servant. Wonder whether they roped him in too."

"No mention of ours, either. I wish Ashling would come in," said Warnford uneasily.

"He'll be all right; he can look after himself."

"Yes. You don't follow me, evidently. The point is this. If Ashling has been caught and says he's a friend of Smith's, or if Smith says he is, and Ashling is traced back to us—I was accused of trading with the enemy before. What would they think now? If Hambledon gets his claws into this—" Warnford shivered.

Marden put the paper down. "If I may say so, I think you are letting that suggestion of Rawson's get on your nerves," he said. "You were never accused of that officially, and no independent evidence was forthcoming to support it. Unless Hambledon reads through the evidence in detail he will never hear of it, and I doubt if the record of a military court-martial will be available to any civilian, will it?"

"Hambledon would get it," said Warnford with conviction, "if he wanted it. And this business would be corroborative evidence, don't you see? At his old tricks again, they'd say," he went on with increasing bitterness. "Rawson is clever, you know; you can't deny that. I expect he thought I'd nose around and try to find out something about the people who took the plans. Well, any man would. So he took the trouble to discredit in advance any move I might make in that direction. Very clever, you must hand him that. It's more than I was, you know. It makes me laugh, looking back at all that. I made friends with him when nobody else would. I thought they were all just prejudiced against the poor chap. In fact, I thought it was rather nice of me. Funny, isn't it? I never asked what the other fellows had against him, and, being a friend of mine, of course they never said a word. I wasn't really frightfully interested in what they thought; I was only interested in tanks, and so was Rawson—damn him! So he and I rather ran in couples, and I thought I was doing him a good turn, whereas all the time I was being played with like a blasted rag doll. Thought I was such a bright boy and all the time I was being had for a mug." Warnford laughed unpleasantly. "Why don't you laugh too; can't you see a joke? Then I'm made use of; no doubt he had my key copied, and not only that, but he damns me in advance with his foul suggestions because he thinks I'll never dare go within a mile of anything that looks like espionage for fear the British authorities think I'm mixed up in it. They probably will too. Don't you see?" went on Warnford, hammering his knee with his fist. "If I do get on the track of anything he's only got to get the word round to Hambledon, and I'll go down for fifteen years for white-slave trading or something equally foul—"

"Stop that at once," said Marden authoritatively. "You're getting hysterical. Sorry, old man," he added in his usual gentle tone, "but you're letting this get on top of you. What makes you think your brother officers believed one word of Rawson's story? Especially as he didn't produce any evidence to prove it. That surprises me, you know. I should have thought he would. Some seedy waiter who'd seen you with a bullet-headed man talking guttural German at a corner table in some shoddy restaurant."

"It wasn't necessary," said Warnford obstinately. "The hint was enough. Far more artistic, you know."

"I thought you said," persisted Marden, "that the remarks were not well received. You said something about a purple silence, if I remember rightly."

"That won't make any difference to Hambledon. The suggestion is there if he likes to put two and two together."

"Very well," said Marden. "Give up the idea, then. I always thought it was hellishly risky—told you so at the outset, if you remember."

"Give up the idea!" blazed Warnford. "Will I hell! I'll get Rawson someday or get shot at dawn myself; it won't matter if I do. I've nothing more to lose."

Marden saw it was no use arguing and relapsed into silence; after a few minutes Warnford went on more calmly: "There is one thing I'm very sorry about, very sorry. We had practically fixed up about your coming to live here; that won't do now. I'm not dragging you into this."

"You're not keeping me out," said Marden bluntly.

"I won't have it."

"You'll have to. I am not leaving you alone to make a whole lot of damnfool mistakes and hand yourself to Rawson on a plate—"

"I'll see I don't, and if I do it's my own fault. But you aren't—"

"I am. If you've changed your mind about wanting me here that's O.K.; I can go on as I am, but I shall continue—"

"It's not that; you know that perfectly well. I want you here very much, and more than ever since this idea has dawned on me, but—"

"Very well. I move in tomorrow," said Marden calmly, and nothing Warnford said made the slightest difference. At last he gave it up. "I think you're mad," he said, "but have it your own way."

They waited two more days for news of Ashling, till Warnford was really anxious, and even the patient Marden admitted that things had gone on too long, whatever the "things" might be. "If Ashling doesn't turn up by midday today," said Warnford, frying eggs for breakfast, "I'm going to ring up all the hospitals I can think of. He must have come to grief somehow. If he'd been arrested, too, the papers would have said so, wouldn't they? Besides, why arrest Ashling?"

"They wouldn't arrest Ashling. They might have kept him overnight and questioned him in the morning, but no more than that. Is this toast brown enough for you?"

"Yes, quite. I shall ring up—"

The telephone bell rang, and Warnford went to answer it. "Ashling 'ere, sir," said the voice at the other end.

"Thank goodness. Where the hell have you been all this time? I was just going to hunt the hospitals for you."

"I'm very sorry, sir, but I thought it best," said Ashling in a mysterious tone.

"Oh? Why? Where are you now?"

"Reading, sir."

"Reading? Why Reading?"

"I don't know, sir; it just 'appens to be Reading if you get me."

"No, I'm hanged if I do. What are you doing there?"

"On my way 'ome, sir. Would it be possible, begging your pardon, for you to meet me with the car at Guildford?"

"Er—I could, I suppose. But why not come back by train?"

"I don't like railway stations, sir."

"What?"

"Not London ones, anyway."

"Ashling, have you been on the drink?"

"No, sir," said Ashling promptly, "though what I've 'ad 'as been enough to make me."

"Oh. Very well. I'll meet you outside Guildford Town Hall at—it's nine o'clock now—at twelve. Can you make it?"

"Yes, sir. Thank you, sir."

Ashling kept his story till they got home again; in fact, he slept in the car all the way from Guildford. He seemed tired.

"Now," said Warnford, when lunch was over and pipes were lit, "let's have it."

On the night when Warnford and Marden raided the house in Apple Row, Ashling and the Johnsons' servant spent some time in a cinema near Victoria, were bored with the second film and came out again, repaired to a house of refreshment where they were known, and stayed there till closing time, drinking a quiet glass or so of beer and talking to their friends. When the place closed Smith said it was time he went home, and Ashling said he'd see him as far as the door.

"I wish I 'adn't now, sir, but I always did, and I didn't like to do any different that night from usual. I thought you'd 'a' got 'em all trussed up quiet so things'ud seem jus' the same as always and I'd say good night at the door and walk on same as usual. But, oh dear, I did get a shock."

The two servants walked along Apple Row, which seemed as quiet and deserted as it always did; Ashling said good night as Smith put his key in the keyhole. The front door opened suddenly, and a policeman about seven feet high and four feet wide appeared in the doorway and said, "Come in 'ere, both of you."

Smith turned to bolt, but a long arm shot out and grabbed him and he passed inevitably into the house. Ashling also turned very promptly to leave and cannoned straight into another policeman who was standing just behind him. "And the dear knows where 'e came from, sir; 'e wasn't there the second before."

The servants were marched through the house into the kitchen and told to sit down on two hard chairs till somebody was ready for them. Ashling was completely fogged. He had no idea why the police were there unless Warnford and Marden had somehow been overpowered and arrested; even so, why arrest him and, particularly, why Smith? The Johnsons' servant sat beside him, tense but motionless and silent; eventually Ashling gathered that he was intently listening and also that Smith might have been horrified but that he was not surprised.

From where they sat they could see nothing of what was happening along the passage, but sounds came to them, heavy steps on the stairs, furniture being moved, and bumping noises. Smith was leaning slightly forward, his lips parted and his pale blue eyes darting quickly from one side to the other at every sound; on the other side of the kitchen a constable stood by the cellar door, watching. Presently voices sounded from another place and steps ascending; two men in plainclothes came up the cellar stairs, and their hands and faces were black with coaldust.

Smith relaxed suddenly with a sigh and leaned back in his chair. Ashling shot a glance at him and noticed that his usually pasty complexion had turned a greenish white and his eyes momentarily closed. Sounds of a car stopping outside the front door were followed by voices in the passage. An unmistakably

English voice said, "Come along, now. This way, please," and there were footsteps. A thick voice was raised in protest. "This is an inconceivable outrage. I will have a question asked in Parliament," to which the English voice merely replied, "Mind the step."

Ashling began to feel better; evidently it was the Johnsons who were being arrested and not his master, unless the police had arrived on the premises in time to catch them too. The car drove away.

"I couldn't let you know," said Warnford. "I didn't know where you were. We set the police onto those blighters and then left before they arrived. I'll tell you why presently. Carry on."

"I saw in the paper next morning, sir, as they'd been pinched for drug smuggling."

"Yes," said Warnford and smiled. "I'll tell you all about that later. What happened next?"

Ashling and Smith were taken to a police station, told they would be questioned next morning, and locked up in the cells for the night, Ashling not daring to protest because he did not want to bring Warnford's name into it and he wanted time to think up a story. He was not one of those from whom ingenious explanations flow naturally on the spur of the moment.

Next morning he gave the police the name of Allen which he had adopted for Smith's benefit, and a false address, told them that he was out of a job at the moment but was going to one in Liverpool in three days' time, that Smith was merely an acquaintance with whom he sometimes spent an evening, and that he didn't know the Johnsons at all, had never seen them and wasn't interested. After which they told him he could go; he was shown into another room where Smith was waiting, and they walked out together.

Smith looked better when they got outside in the fresh air; Ashling said little and waited for him to talk. The first thing he did was to buy a paper in which he read the paragraph about the drug charge.

"Drugs!" said Smith with a snort. "Ridiculous." He showed it to Ashling.

"Lumme," said Ashling tactfully, "what a thing to say!"

Smith looked at him carefully and said, after a moment's pause for thought, that drugs were disgusting and he wasn't going to be mixed up with it. "I shall leave that job," he said.

Ashling refrained from pointing out that the job seemed to have left him and merely remarked, "Quite right. I sh'd do the same."

"I think I shall go abroad for a spell till all this 'as blown over," said Smith.

"Abroad? Why? You'll get a job easy enough in England."

"If I stay in England maybe they'll call me up to give evidence in that case, and I won't be mixed up in it. I've got a brother lives in Ostend; I'll go to 'im for a few months."

"Ah," said Ashling wisely. "You'd be out o' reach there."

"Yeah. I'll get some money and go across today, I think."

"Going back to the house?"

"Oh—presently, perhaps. I suppose the police'ud let me in," said Smith casually, but Ashling did not believe him. "You could 'ear in 'is voice, sir, as 'e'd no intention of going." Warnford nodded and Ashling went on, "Then 'e asks me what I meant to do. I said I didn't rightly know; I expected I'd lost my job, being out all night without leave. 'E said, ''Ow much money 'ave you got?' and I counted up what I 'ad on me, which was four and three-pence."

"One moment," said Warnford, interrupting. "Smith said the drug charge was ridiculous, but he didn't seem to expect them to be acquitted of it."

"No, sir," said Ashling. "I noticed that myself, but I didn't feel called on to say so."

"No, quite. Please go on."

Smith very kindly said he didn't think four shillings and threepence was enough if Ashling was to be turned out on a cold world at a moment's notice. "Better come along with me; while I'm getting some money for myself I'll get some for you too."

"You've got some useful friends," said Ashling enviously.

"I have. They might be good friends to you, too, if things fitted in that way."

Ashling didn't quite like the way this was said for some reason; there was nothing offensive about it, but it made him wonder what he would be expected to do in return. However, said Ashling, money is always useful stuff to have about and, what is more, it would be interesting to see something of Smith's friends, so he agreed. Smith called a taxi and gave a number in Princes Square, Bayswater. This turned out to be one of a number of residential hotels; Smith told the taxi driver to wait, glanced at Ashling, hesitated a moment, glanced at Ashling again, and finally said, "You'd better come in too. Come on."

They walked up the steps into the usual hotel hall, with a red Turkey rug on the floor, a bamboo hatstand with an aspidistra in front of it, several framed announcements of current theatrical shows on the walls, and a staircase going up at the back. A porter in a striped linen jacket came to see what they wanted, and Ashling kept close enough to Smith to hear him ask if Mrs. Ferne was in. The porter said she was and showed them into a small room to wait.

"Mrs. Ferne is a very nice lady," said Smith, fidgeting about the room.

"Oh, yes?" said Ashling.

"Very fond of cats."

"Cats?"

"Cats. God about 'alf a dozen of 'em 'ere."

"Don't the 'otel people mind?"

"Don't seem to. Lovely cats, they are. Fact is," said Smith in a burst of confidence, "she 'ad one of 'er cats stolen once, and I got it back for 'er. She was grateful! Never been able to do enough for me since then."

"I see," said Ashling, who, as a matter of fact, was getting more puzzled every moment. Mysterious telephones are merely to be expected in a spy hunt, and even dangerous drugs fit in quite well; loaded automatics or a dagger or two only add to the local color, but why cats?

The door opened quietly, and a magnificent blue Persian trotted in, followed by a tawny Siamese with black muzzle and paws. A gentle voice outside said, "Come along, Elvira, then! Do make up your mind." A tortoiseshell cat stalked in with an elderly lady immediately behind. Smith bowed jerkily from the waist and said, "Good morning, Mrs. Ferne. I've brought a friend of mine to see you, name of Allen."

"Good morning, Mr. Allen. I am glad to meet any friend of Smith's. He found my lovely Heliogabala for me when she was stolen; did he tell you? So cruel. The loveliest gray Persian. I hope you like cats, Mr. Allen."

Ashling murmured something polite and felt a complete fool. Mrs. Ferne was a very charming old lady with soft blue eyes and a lovely complexion. She was stout and walked with a stick; she dressed in trailing black draperies which showed rents here and there from the impulsive affection of her pets. Altogether she was a model of harmlessness in Bayswater, and yet there was something about her which puzzled Ashling.

"She seemed such a nice person," he told Warnford. "One of those large soft old ladies you see by the dozen trailing off to St. Mary Abbotts Sunday mornings, each with 'er little prayer book. But there was something wrong about 'er, and not till I was sitting at Reading Station this morning waiting for a train did it strike me what it was. She 'adn't got enough wrinkles."

"Looked too young for her age," said Warnford.

"Not so much that, sir. But she 'ad not got enough wrinkles."

"Perhaps she'd had her face lifted," suggested Marden.

"Not she, sir; she wasn't that type."

After a little more casual conversation between Mrs. Ferne, Ashling, Smith, and the cats, Smith drew the lady apart into a window embrasure and said something to her in a low voice. She said, "Why, of course. I am very glad you came," and Smith said something else inaudible to Ashling. Presently Smith came across the room, gave Ashling a pound note, and said, "You go and pay off the taxi, will you? I'll be with you in a minute."

Ashling went out and found a little man in a bowler hat talking to the taxi driver. Apparently he was asking if the taxi was disengaged, for the driver merely jerked his thumb towards his flag, which was up, and made no other answer. The little man said in a flustered voice, "Oh dear! I beg your pardon; I do really," to Ashling and the driver collectively, and wandered off along the pavement, trailing his umbrella behind him. Ashling had a vague idea that he'd seen him before somewhere, but it did not seem important. He paid off the taxi driver, and the cab drove away, overtaking the little man. Ashling watched them idly, thinking, “The old gink can ’ave it now.” To his surprise the man made no attempt to hail the taxi.

Surprise awakened Ashling’s memory, and he remembered where he had seen the little man before. In the police station that morning, while he was waiting to be interviewed, the man in the bowler hat had passed through.

Ashling felt himself go cold. The police were trailing them. He was supposed to be a friend of Smith’s. Smith was mixed up with a gang of German spies if he wasn’t one himself. The police would follow Ashling and discover that he was Warnford’s servant; they would think he was the go-between if they remembered that—Rawson’s suggestion. They might even pull Warnford in to be questioned about it, and the whole wretched business would start again just when he was beginning to cheer up.

Ashling started violently as someone clapped him on the shoulder, but it was only Smith with a friendly smile, holding out a comfortable-looking wad of pound notes.

“Startled you, did I? Must ’ave something on your conscience. Cheer up, ’ere’s ten quid for you.”

Ashling thanked him confusedly and said something about paying it back when he got another job, but Smith dismissed the idea; what was ten pounds between friends? Besides, the lady would be offended; mustn’t do that. “She wants you to go in and see ’er any time you’re this way. I wish you would, too; she’s a nice lady and got nobody to do things for ’er, ’specially after I’m gone. Say you will.”

“Don’t know what I could do for the likes of ’er, but I’ll certainly go. I owe ’er something if she won’t let me pay this back,” said Ashling, who meant to avoid not only Princes Square in future but the whole Bayswater district if possible.

“That’s right. You stick to that. Now, I’m going to stop this taxi and go to Victoria; come and see me off? Oh, come on. I ’ates going off anywheres all on my own,” said Smith, grasping him in a friendly but firm manner by the arm with one hand and signaling a crawling taxi with the other. Ashling hesitated; after all, the man had just given him ten pounds; one could hardly rush off and leave him then and there.

Smith opened the door of the taxi, propelled Ashling gently inside, and told the driver to call at a Cook’s office on the way to Victoria. “Always get my ticket at Cook’s whenever I go abroad,” he said. “Saves trouble. Book you right through, trains, steamer, and all.” He chatted cheerfully on the way to Cook’s. “You’ll be all right, won’t you? Look, if you can’t find a job maybe I can ’elp you to one. I could, easy. Or Mrs. Ferne would. ’Ere’s Cook’s; I won’t be a minute.”

He dashed across the pavement and dived into the office. Ashling would have got out of the taxi and disappeared at once, only he could see Smith watching him through the glass panel of the door. Ashling gnawed his thumb as an aid to thought. Look such a fool bolting off without a word like a scared rabbit. Easy to slip off at Victoria in all that crowd.

Smith came out again, said, "Victoria!" to the driver in a commanding tone, and they drove off again.

"Better give you my address in Ostend," he said. "I'll write it down for you. 'Ere you are. 'Otel Malplaquet, Rue de la Chapelle—that's just Chapel Street in English. My brother, 'e's the manager there. Clever chap, my brother." He looked at his watch as the taxi swung into the station yard. "Quarter to eleven; just timed it nicely."

"What time's your train?"

"Eleven o'clock."

"Look," said Ashling as the cab stopped, "you go and get yourself a seat. I'll go and get you some papers at the bookstall and bring 'em to the train. See you in a minute." He dodged round two piles of luggage into the station and hid himself behind a notice board.

Smith came into the station and walked straight across to the departure platform for the Continental train. As he neared the gates two unobtrusive men stirred from their lounging positions and approached him, one on each side. They reached him at the same moment; one of them tapped him on the shoulder; Ashling saw his lips move. Smith glanced right and left, but the men closed in on him; they wheeled about, and all three walked back towards the entrance.

Ashling immediately dived into the underground station, took a ticket from the first automatic machine he saw, and jumped into the first train that came in, regardless of where it was going.

6

The Man with the Fur Collar

Ashling never had any very clear idea of where he went after leaving Victoria except that he seemed to have circumnavigated the London Underground Railway system. He changed trains repeatedly, leaping out at the last moment as the train was starting again to make sure no one jumped out after him, and being the last to enter a train after pretending he didn't want that one. After visiting places as mutually incompatible as Latimer Road and Moorgate Street without ever seeing the same man twice, he calmed down a little; when he reached King's Cross he remembered he was hungry. He came out in the main station and looked cautiously about him.

Nobody took the faintest interest in him, so he went into a refreshment room and ate meat pies, with beer. His spirits rose with returning energy and he diverted his mind by watching the people. There were a number of Americans there, men and women together; they wore badges pinned to their coats and were talking about boarding a train at this depot. They disapproved of the coffee and drank other things instead. Presently they all trooped out together, and Ashling sat still, trying to make up his mind that it was safe to go home. Something white on the ground caught his eye; it was a badge which one of the Americans had dropped. He picked it up and idly stuck it in his lapel.

There was a man leaning against the bar who appeared to Ashling to be watching him, and his budding peace of mind withered again. Refreshment rooms were not places where one expected to meet the police, but probably these plain-clothed fellows were different; they popped up all over the place; you'd think half the population of London was in the pay of Scotland Yard. Ashling got up slowly and walked out. The moment he put his head outside the door he was seized upon by a porter.

"This way, sir, quick; you'll lose your train. You'll 'ave to run, sir, come on."

"'Ere," began Ashling, but the porter took no notice. "Run!" he said, propelling him with a firm grip on his elbow. Ashling, feeling as though life had become a nightmare in which people incessantly pushed him into places he did not wish to enter, passed through the platform gates in a kind of dream and was expertly heaved into the already moving train. Several hands reached out and received him.

"You cert'nly do cut things fine, Mr. Harrison of—where is it?—of Winslow, Arizona. I'm very pleased to meet you, Mr. Harrison. I have never yet had the opportunity to visit your home town, but my dad knew Winslow when it was just a depot, a water tower, and a tin store, that's all. Now they tell me it's a real progressive town."

Certainly a dream. Ashling began to think that if he composed himself and kept quiet for a little while this torrent of events would die down and he would awake to find himself in bed at the flat. Another voice broke in.

"Say, Mr. Harrison cert'nly does look queer. It's running like that right after eating. Come and sit in this corner, Mr. Harrison, and stay quiet."

Kind hands deposited him in the corner; there followed glugging noises, and somebody thrust a flask cup into his hand. "Put that where it'll do most good, Mr. Harrison; it's the real stuff."

It had a curious flavor in Ashling's opinion, for he had never encountered rye whisky before, but it did revive him. This was no dream; he was in a train with kind people with American accents, but why on earth did they address him as Mr. Harrison? However, he had wanted to dodge the police and he was certainly doing so, so why worry? His new friends good-naturedly left him in peace for some time while they talked among themselves; he gathered after a time that he and they were the A.O.L.S.B.s, the American Order of Loyal Sons of Boston,

Lincs. As a general rule it is people from Boston, Massachusetts, who come to Boston on the River Witham, which once was the port of Boston on the North Sea, in that part of England which is justly called Holland. Mr. Leggatt from Connecticut, now in the corner opposite Ashling, explained that he had had a better idea. He had founded an association of those whose forefathers actually came from Boston, Lincs., and at long last he had been able to find a time when there would be enough of them in Europe all at the same time to make a joint expedition to the home town of their ancestors. "Yes, sir. Thirty-seven of us; I call that a very sizable party. And I consider that Boston in the old days must have been a sizable place, if you reckon up the number of residents that must have crossed the Atlantic to produce all the members of our association. No doubt there are many more who do not belong to it."

Ashling settled himself in his corner, and the movement brought into his line of sight the badge with two ribbon tails which was pinned on his own coat collar. He had forgotten all about it till then. Mr. Leggatt, opposite, also wore one, and Ashling could read it from where he sat. It said, "A.O.L.S.B. Mr. Morris P. Leggatt of Connecticut, a Loyal Son of Boston, Is Pleased to Meet All Other L.S.B.s." Light dawned on Ashling, who had not previously encountered this kind of thing. He was wearing the badge of Mr. Harrison of Winslow, Arizona, and had no business to be here at all. He was gate-crashing a party.

Embarrassment overcame him, for Ashling was not of the bumptious type. What is more, he was certain they would know he was an impostor by his accent the moment he opened his mouth to speak. Then, instead of being hauled in, he would be thrown out. Probably they would send for the guard, whom they called "conductor," and he would ask for Ashling's ticket and discover he hadn't got one. He could pay, of course, thanks to Mrs. Ferne's ten pounds, but it would look as if he'd tried not to. He sighed deeply and settled down to apparent slumber. Tracking down criminals had such unexpected difficulties.

Presently Mr. Leggatt got up and said he must now go and talk to some more Brothers in the other compartments; another man also rose and said he would like to introduce the president to his friend, Mr. Brewster of Wisconsin; yes, a descendant of *the* Brewsters. Ashling took advantage of the general stir to slip away down the corridor into a part of the train filled with quite ordinary people, not loyal sons of any particular place. He slipped his badge in his pocket and sat down with a sigh of relief.

Five minutes later the guard came along and said, "Tickets, please," in a tired voice. Ashling said that he had caught the train at the last moment at King's Cross and hadn't had time to buy a ticket and pulled out a pound note.

The guard looked mildly surprised and asked how he managed to get past the barrier.

"I was pushed past," said Ashling with perfect truth.

"Where to, please?"

"Er—" hesitated Ashling, who didn't know where the train was going to except Boston and didn't want to go there. He felt that, kind as the Americans were, there would be a certain awkwardness about meeting them. When Mr. Leggatt met the real Mr. Harrison of Winslow there would certainly be mention of a missing badge, and when Mr. Leggatt said that Mr. Harrison of Winslow was in his carriage farther back and not in the least like this Mr. Harrison to look at, enquiries would be made. Ashling felt he had had too many enquiries for one day already.

"Well?" said the guard impatiently.

"Er—I've forgotten its name."

One or two people smiled, and Ashling turned bright pink. The guard looked at him with the resigned expression of one who looks after mental deficients every day, only some are worse than others.

"'Aven't you got the address you're goin' to?"

"I'm not going to any particular address. I'm—I'm going on a walking tour."

"Oh. And where was you goin' to start from?"

"That's what I've forgotten."

One of the other passengers leaned forward and suggested that if the guard had a list of stations at which the train was going to stop it might help the gentleman to remember.

"The next stop," said the guard, disdaining printed lists, "is Peterborough, change for Boston; after that Grantham, Retford, Doncaster, Selby, York—"

"'Ere, stop," said Ashling. "I'm not going—"

A tall form obstructed the light from the corridor. "Excuse me, Conductor, I was looking for a— Ah, Mr. Harrison, there you are. We were afraid you were taken sick, so I said to Mr. Hawksworth of Michigan, who was sitting next to you, that I would just take a little walk down the corridor and see if I could hear any news of you."

"Thanks a lot," stammered Ashling, with the best American accent he could recall from the cinema. "That's real kind of you. I was just telling the conductor—"

"Does this gentleman belong to your party, sir?" asked the guard.

"Certainly he does," said Leggatt. "He's got a badge. Haven't you, Mr. Harrison? You were wearing it just now."

"I—it fell off," said Ashling, pulling it out of his pocket. "I'll pin it on again," which he did. The train began to slow down. Leggatt glanced out of the window and saw houses and streets approaching.

"What is this place, Conductor?"

"Peterborough."

"Do we stop here?"

"Yes, sir. Your carriage will be detached from this train and put onto the local for Boston, which leaves at three twenty-two."

"We'll have some time at Peterborough," said Leggatt, looking at his watch. "It's only five past three now."

"Four minutes past," said the guard, pulling out his. "That's when we're due in."

"I stand corrected," said the American good-naturedly, "but does it matter?"

"This is the Scotch Express," said the guard. "If you gentlemen will kindly return to your compartment—" He shepherded them firmly along the corridor to rejoin the other Loyal Sons of Boston.

"The first time ever I came across to Europe," said Leggatt, "my dad said to me, 'When you're in England, son, you'll find a lot of things that seem funny to you, but there's only two things you mustn't laugh at. One's the Scotch Express and the other is the Army and Navy Stores.' I must say I've always found he was perfectly correct."

"I'll say," said Ashling, and stood in the corridor with the others to review Peterborough Station. Three-four till three twenty-two; if he couldn't lose himself in eighteen minutes he'd know the reason why.

"Say, brother, d'you think they keep rye whisky in this refreshment bar? I want a flask of rye whisky."

"I should say," said Ashling. "If we don't find it in one bar we can try another, can't we? Come along, Mr. Waters of Chicago." For Mr. Waters came from another compartment and would not bother to cherish him like Mr. Leggatt of Connecticut. So the Brothers set out together, but of course there was no alcoholic refreshment of any sort being sold at that hour. Then Mr. Waters found he had mislaid his companion somehow. Ashling would have left the station altogether, only there was a policeman at the door who looked at him. Besides, he'd got to get back to London, and probably the train was the only way. So he went to ground and read a paper till three twenty-two, and a very long time it seemed.

He came out when he was sure the coast was clear and looked at a timetable pasted on a board. The next train to London was three forty-seven, just nice time to buy his ticket. He put his badge in his pocket again, but, as bad luck would have it, he sneezed and snatched out his handkerchief; the badge came, too, and fell to the ground and a ticket collector saw it.

"Excuse me, sir, this is yours, I think—Oh! You're one of that American party; 'ow did you come to get lef' be'ind?"

"I—I got out to buy a paper," said Ashling, losing his head.

"Well, you 'ad best part of 'alf an hour to do it," said the ticket collector reproachfully. "Still, I expect our ways do seem strange to you gentlemen from foreign parts. Now, what can we do for you? Let me think."

"It don't matter a bit," said Ashling. "I'd just as soon go straight back to town; in fact, I ought to; I've just remembered—"

"Oh no, you can't come all this way and jus' go back an' not see Boston at all; it's a lovely place, Boston, and you'd ought to climb up the Stump."

"Climb up the—"

"I 'ave it. There's a special going through at three-forty; it's stopping here to pick up someone. I'll put you in one of the extra coaches; we always puts an extra couple of coaches on to steady the train, like. I'll tell the guard; 'e'll see you right. Come this way, sir."

"But I don't want—"

"No trouble, sir, at all. After all, if you American gentlemen come all this way to 'ave a look at the old country, we'd ought to 'elp you. Pin your badge on again, sir; you'll lose it else."

Ashling gave way. His one idea that day had been to remain as inconspicuous as possible, and never before in all his life had he attracted so much attention. It was very disheartening. He and the ticket collector waited on a platform otherwise only occupied by the distinguished guest for whom the special was stopping, one porter in attendance, and the station cat. The train came in, a short train of three coaches, and only the middle one was occupied. The ticket collector explained matters to the guard while the distinguished guest was being welcomed and handed in.

"O' course," said the guard, "the gentleman can come an' welcome. If 'e won't mind George they can travel together an' I can get 'im out of the van where 'e's no business to be."

"What, old George?"

"Ah, old George."

The ticket collector smiled, opened a door for Ashling, and said perhaps he wouldn't mind if another gentleman traveled with him. Ashling said, "Of course not"; the other gentleman arrived suddenly; the door was slammed, and the train started off again.

The other gentleman was a tall thin man curiously dressed for August in a long overcoat with a fur collar, striped trousers, a bowler hat, and brown boots. He said, "Good afternoon, sir. I am glad to travel with a fellow guest."

"Fellow guest," said Ashling. "I don't think I am anybody's guest, not as I know of."

"Aren't you going to the wedding?"

"Wedding? No. What wedding?"

"The one I'm going to, o' course. Be a sport and come, I'm sure you'll enjoy yourself. Nice wedding."

Ashling came to the correct conclusion that George had been toasting the happy pair, but it didn't matter. It was only as far as Boston.

"Is that what the special's for?" he asked.

"Lord bless you, no. That's for Lord What's-his-name—can't get it for the moment—going to open a flower show or a swimming pool or something. He doesn't know he's taking me to a wedding. Does he?"

"Doesn't 'e?"

"He doesn't, does he?"

Ashling thought he'd better change the subject. "Know the bridegroom, do you?"

The thin man burst into peals of laughter. "Do I know the bridegroom? That's a good one. Do I know the bridegroom. I must tell him that one. I says to you, 'I'm going to a wedding.' Didn't I? Yes. And you says, 'Do you know the bridegroom!' " He rolled about in his seat.

Ashling began to see why the guard had not wanted to keep George in the guard's van; a little of this would go a long way. He wandered into the corridor, found a compartment as far from George as possible, and sat down to read the paper. It was some little time before he was discovered again.

"If you aren't going to wedding," said George, "what you going to Boston for?"

"Business," said Ashling shortly.

"No. Can't be. Nobody does business in Boston on Saturday evening. Today's Saturday. Ain't it? Must be, 'less they've altered the wedding. There you are, then. No business. Ever been in Boston before?"

"Never."

"I'll show you round. Take you Guildhall. Take you climb up Stump."

"Listen 'ere," said Ashling. "I'm not climbing up any stumps. What is it, anyway, custom o' the natives, or what?"

George looked out of the window. "Come 'ere," he said, and pointed to a tall tower soaring into the air above the houses and the flat plain beyond. "See that? That's Boston Stump. Eve'ybody climb Boston Stump. Three hundred and sixty-five steps, same as the years in a day. Ain't it?"

"Some climb," said Ashling. He removed his badge from his coat lapel, meaning to throw it out of the window, and then put it back, remembering that it served him as a railway ticket to Boston.

"What for?"

"What?"

"Your prize."

"That wasn't a prize."

"Looks like prize. Seen some like that at agricutter—agriculture shows. On pigs and cows and sheep and lambs and horses and dogs and—"

"Oh, put a sock in it," said Ashling. When the train came to a stop he leaped out of the compartment and ran for it, meaning to leave his companion behind, but the ticket collector at the door had a word with him about his party having arrived earlier, and the thin man caught him up.

"This way," he said.

"Where to?"

"Boston Stump, o' course."

"Listen," said Ashling. "I am Not Going to Boston Stump. Got that?" He pulled his badge off and tossed it over a wall. The thin man grabbed him by the arm, but Ashling freed himself roughly and turned back. Directly behind him was a group of five Americans which included Mr. Waters of Chicago. Ashling turned hastily away, and the thin man fell into step alongside.

"Look 'ere," said Ashling desperately, "what time's this wedding of yours?"

"Half-past two."

"It's five o'clock now; if you run you'll just get there in time."

"Round this corner," said the infuriating George, taking no notice. Ashling jibbed again, but at that moment Mr. Leggatt of Connecticut came out of an antique shop and Ashling fairly dived round the corner, dragging the thin man with him.

"You do change your mind a lot, don't you?" said George plaintively. "First you will and then you won't and then you will and then you won't and then you—"

"Oh, cheese it," said Ashling.

The next event which made any real impression upon his mind was finding himself in a church and being urged to ascend a winding stair. He would have refused but for the sound of a feminine American voice behind him saying in a loud whisper that three hundred and sixty-five stairs was not what the doctor ordered for her insteps and a masculine voice saying he guessed that went for him, too, only it wasn't insteps; it was figure. Ashling went up the stairs like a startled rabbit dashing into its burrow. He went round and round until it seemed as though he were marking time in the same place upon a revolving tower; behind him he heard the persevering steps of George, who must have been a much fitter man than he looked, especially when one remembered the overcoat with the fur collar. At last the stairs came to an end and they emerged at the top, glad to find somewhere level to stand upon and plenty of air to draw into their laboring lungs. Ashling drew a long breath, blinked once or twice, and found himself looking straight into the face of Mr. Hawksworth of Michigan.

Ashling never remembered going down those stairs. He had some recollection of passing through the streets of Boston, because somebody shouted at him when he cut it rather fine across the nose of a car. When he really came to himself he was trotting steadily along a country road with no idea where he was going.

He sat down on the bank by the roadside and lit a cigarette. How pleasant, how soothing to be all alone. The few motors which passed took no notice of him, and there were no pedestrians in sight till a tramp came along from the direction of Boston.

Ashling waited till the man drew level with him and then said, "Say, mate! Where's this road go to?"

The tramp stopped and said it depended how far you went along it; he had heard it said that you could get to the Land's End if you kept on long enough.

Ashling said that he didn't think he wanted to go quite as far as that tonight, thank you; all he wanted was a quiet, decent place where he could get a bed for the night—and a shave, he added, fingering his scratchy chin.

"Somewhere where they'd make you pay for it, I suppose?" said the tramp.

"I wouldn't mind," said Ashling, secure in the possession of Mrs. Ferne's ten pounds. The tramp recommended Swineshead about six miles farther on, and Ashling sighed and rose to his feet. The tramp said there would be a bus along presently; in the meantime the two walked along together, speaking of this and that. Later on they passed through a small village where the tramp suddenly crossed the road for a reason which only became obvious when Ashling saw a neat cottage standing by itself in a garden. Near the gate was a notice board with notices pinned on it headed "Lost" and "Swine-Fever" and "Stolen" in large black capitals. It was a police cottage. There was a man in shirt sleeves leaning over the gate, enjoying the evening air; the tramp shot a sideways glance at him and quickened his pace slightly. The man in shirt sleeves straightened up suddenly, took his pipe out of his mouth, and said "Oy!" in a loud voice. "Here! I want you!"

The tramp went off as though someone had fired a pistol to start the hundred-yards race, and Ashling instinctively did the same. But the policeman was young and active, and flying footsteps behind steadily gained on them. Presently an arm came forward and grabbed the tramp, who stopped at once, and so did Ashling.

"'Ere," said the tramp between gasps, "you can't arrest me like that. You ain't got your armlet on."

"Tell that to the magistrate in the morning," said the constable, "while you're telling him what you did with those blankets you pinched off the line at the Red Lion six months back. You," to Ashling, "what were you running for?"

"Because I thought you didn't want me," said Ashling with pained dignity. At that moment a bus came along the road going towards Swineshead; he boarded it with a sigh of relief and left the tramp behind.

Next day he made his way southward by stages, still shying at the railway, and slept the night at Oxford. When he got to Reading the following morning he thought it safe to ring up Warnford.

"You know," said the amused Marden, "you must have led a singularly unspotted life until now."

"Why, sir?"

"You've had so little experience in running away."

7
The Desmond Diamonds

TOMMY HAMBLEDON sat in his room at the Foreign Office with a letter upon the table before him. He was reading it aloud, with marginal comments, to Denton, who was occupying the secretary's chair during that gentleman's absence for lunch.

"Tell me what you think of this," said Hambledon. "It begins in stately and measured prose, '— Hambledon, Esq. Sir: I am writing to express to you in a fuller and more adequate manner than was possible in the few moments at my disposal the other night my sincere apologies for eavesdropping upon your telephone conversation with the Southampton police.' "

"Oho," said Denton. "That fellow."

"Yes. He goes on, 'Please believe me that no consideration on earth other than the welfare of the country would have induced me to take so distasteful a course.' I like his rolling Georgian periods, don't you?"

"Very much. I don't know why a burglar shouldn't be literary."

"Burglar my foot," said Hambledon energetically. "Listen to the rest of it. 'I was very interested to read in the paper of the large amount of dope you found in the cellar. I must be very unobservant; I didn't see any during my little stroll round the property. Perhaps it was under the coal.' Is that sarcasm or humility?"

"Ask me another."

"I hope it isn't sarcasm; it reminds me of Goebbels, and I don't like Goebbels. To continue: 'Probably you already know it, but in case you don't, the so-called Smith whom you arrested at Victoria was on his way to Ostend to stay with a brother of his. At least he said it was his brother. According to him, he is the manager of the Hotel Malplaquet in the Rue de la Chapelle.' D'you know the Hotel Malplaquet at Ostend, Denton? No. Then I'm afraid you soon will."

"I hope they can cook," said Denton gloomily.

"Take some bicarbonate of soda with you. He goes on, 'I think you heard that Smith called at a private hotel in Princes Square, Bayswater, because you had one of your men outside, the little man with a bowler hat and an umbrella. Smith—' "

"I think the little man in the bowler hat wants the sack," said Denton.

"He seems to have slipped up somewhere, doesn't he? I am informing Scotland Yard; I won't have this kind of thing. These men will be coming home with chalk marks on their backs next: 'I am X 37 of Scotland Yard, watch your step.' However, to return to the letter: 'Smith went to call on a Mrs. Ferne who lives there. She keeps cats. If it's not an uncharitable suggestion, she seems to keep Smith, too, judging by the amount of money she gave him on demand.' You'd really think the writer was there, wouldn't you?"

"What about Smith's friend?"

"I'm coming to him presently. This man says, 'Here are the numbers of eight pound notes which Smith gave away. I am sending the notes themselves to Dr. Barnado's Homes as I prefer, at the moment, to remain anonymous.' There follows a list of eight numbers. 'I hope you will find these useful. I understand you have means of tracing notes.' "

"Did Dr. Barnado's get them?"

"Don't know yet; the police are enquiring, but I don't doubt it for a moment. The letter ends, 'If I come across anything else which I think will interest you I will give myself the pleasure of sending it to you.' That's all."

Denton began to laugh. "I remember a time when you were driving the Foreign Office mad by writing them anonymous letters. You know now what they felt like."

"Yes, but I couldn't help it; I had a perfectly good reason. I wasn't doing it for devilment like this fellow. Or has he got a good reason too, Denton? I'd like to know what his reason is, if he's got one, wouldn't you? I'd like to get into a nice quiet corner all alone with the writer of this letter," said Hambledon wistfully, "and say to him, 'Now tell me your life's history. Whose baby are you?' "

"What about Smith's friend who was arrested with him? And who, by the way, went with him to that Princes Square hotel, didn't he?"

"Yes, he did. But he didn't write this letter; at least I don't think so. Allen, as he calls himself, is the old-soldier type, talks quite uncultured English, and might be a hotel porter or somebody's servant, according to the police. No, this letter was written, I think, by the man who talked to me on the phone, at which time Allen was at the cinema with Smith. That has been established. But he and Allen are in this together, since only Allen could have told about Mrs. Ferne paying out money. I think they'd do that in private; I wonder they let even Allen see it. And the bit about the little man in the bowler hat—that was Allen's story too, wasn't it? And Smith's alleged brother's address in Ostend."

"So there are two of them in it," said Denton. "No, three."

"Three. There were two of them tying up the Johnsons in Apple Row that night while Allen entertained Smith. They planted Allen on Smith for that purpose, of course. Somewhere, Denton, there are two men, one of whom has a servant whose name probably isn't Allen. They have a down on the Johnsons for some reason, so they break into the house. What for, I wonder? Not the spoons, I'll bet. They find the telephone. Then their servant walks into the trap they digged for another. He was let loose next morning and followed, but he gave the police the slip and hasn't been seen since. I am very curious about that trio, Denton. Why not come out in the open about it? There must be a reason, and I want to know what it is."

"Perhaps he wants to corner the market in sausage skins for himself," suggested Denton sleepily.

"Either that or some other market," said Hambledon significantly. "In our trade we don't always love each other, you know, even if we are on the same side."

"Aren't you jumping to conclusions?"

"Tell me how they knew where to look for the telephone," answered Hambledon.

Marden suggested to Warnford that they ought to get to know some of the Foreign Office people by sight; it would be very useful to be able to recognize them if only to avoid them if necessary. Warnford agreed, and they made a practice of hanging about outside the Foreign Office to see those who entered or emerged, to talk to the policemen on duty outside and watch the cars drive up, wondering which of those who came and went was—Hambledon, Esq. Neither of them ever had the moral courage to ask. They were not so conspicuous as one might think in doing this; there were always groups of people waiting about outside the Foreign Office at the end of August 1938, when the war clouds hung heavy over Europe and the lightning flickered uneasily on the borders of the Sudetenland.

However, there came a day when four Army officers of high rank came walking together along Whitehall with red tabs on their collars and medal ribbons across their chests, and one of them was Warnford's late colonel. Marden heard a sort of gasp at his side and looked round to find his friend had gone. After that Marden usually went by himself; Warnford had something else he wanted to do.

There was a silver-gray Duesenberg rather frequently in evidence among the cars parked along the curb, and one day Marden remarked upon it to the policeman. "That's a nice car. Who does it belong to, d'you know?"

"King's Messenger," said the policeman. "Yes, it's a nice car, and he's not half proud of it either. Always drives himself—well, you'd pretty well have to with a two-seater like that, 'less you wanted your chauffeur in your pocket all day. All bonnet and dickey, those cars are, in my opinion. I'd rather have something I could take the family out in. Excuse me, sir."

The Prime Minister's car drove up, and the policeman went to salute the lean, anxious figure upon whom so great a burden was laid in those historic days. A subdued cheer came from the crowd; Mr. Chamberlain turned to raise his hat in acknowledgment before he went indoors, and Marden strolled restlessly away.

"You feel you can't settle to anything these days," he said to Warnford when he got home. "I think I shall work out a nice juicy burglary somewhere, just to take my mind off Hitler."

"Have a shot at the crown jewels in the Tower," said Warnford with a laugh. He knew perfectly well that Marden would never go on a real housebreaking expedition from the flat they shared together, and he intended to make their partnership last as long as possible, since what had begun as business had continued as friendship. If this should come to an end a time would come when Marden would be short of money, and something would have to be done about it. No burglar can expect to be lucky always, and the thought of that cheerful, sensitive face behind bars in Dartmoor made him shiver.

"As a matter of fact, I don't want any more jewels at the moment, crown or otherwise," said Marden in a slightly more serious tone. "I seem to have rather too many as it is."

"Why? What's the matter?"

"The Desmond diamonds. There were quite a lot of them, you know, and of course I didn't put them all on the market at once. In fact, I've been parting with 'em more or less one at a time; they ought to keep me in modest comfort for years with care. But Palmer is getting fidgety."

"Who's Palmer?"

"My tame fence. He is a prosperous pork butcher and an even more prosperous receiver of stolen goods in Hoxton, where he lives. He knows, of course, that I've got the Desmond diamonds and he doesn't like having 'em doled out in penny numbers. He has to pay more for 'em that way, for one thing. For another, he wants to retire, he says. If he had all the lot to deal with at once he'd make up the amount he's been saving for years to buy a little place in the Highlands, God preserve Scotland. He wants to wear a kilt, he does, and take up shooting and fishing, believe it or not. So he's putting the screw on me."

"Blast him. How?"

"Quite simple. He will inform the police."

"Then he won't get any more diamonds at all," said Warnford.

"I pointed out that jailbirds don't lay golden eggs, but he says it will have such a good moral effect on his other clients. I temporized while I thought things over. After all, I've got a lot more sympathy for the Desmonds than I have for him."

"Don't they want their diamonds back?"

"Bless you, no. The family's desperately hard up and couldn't sell the things; they're heirlooms. The insurance money's set them on their feet for the first time for five generations. Can't let the poor wretches down now—they'd have to pay it back."

"We shall have to deal with Palmer," said the amused Warnford. "We can't have the Desmonds victimized, to say nothing of you. I was just thinking," he went on, "that a little change would do us good. We've been in London all the summer."

"Come down to my cottage," said Marden. "My summer tenants went home in a hurry yesterday; I heard from old Butt this morning. International situation unsettling them, I expect."

"I'd love to," said Warnford. "What I was going to suggest was a run over to Ostend for a look at the Hotel Malplaquet. If war breaks out and Hitler attacks us it mayn't be so easy to get there."

"British understatement," said Marden cheerfully. "If Hitler attacks us now I don't think any of us will ever see Ostend again. I don't see what we've got to stop the German Army with, at the moment. By all means let's go there while we can; Halvings can wait."

But when they reached Ostend their chances of being received into the Hotel Malplaquet or anywhere else seemed remote in the extreme, for the town was packed with people streaming home from all over the Continent and especially from Germany and those countries so geographically unlucky as to be her neighbors. The booking clerk at the Hotel Malplaquet shook her hands in the air and said they had no accommodation, none. Even the bathrooms were occupied. Perhaps in four weeks, or five, if this crisis passed, *"si le Boche ne vient pas,"* they would have room. At present nothing, nothing, nothing.

Marden asked if they could see the manager.

"It is of no use to see the manager. He will only tell you the same as I do, and in any case he is too busy to see anyone. In four or five weeks' time, *messieurs*, if there is no war. If there is—"

"If there is, we'll come back when it's over," said Marden stoutly. "*Au revoir, mademoiselle*."

Warnford had left his friend to do the talking and was leaning against a gilt pillar with a red plush curtain looped against it—for the Hotel Malplaquet was like that—looking at the people. They seemed to be mostly family parties, the elders either sitting anxiously watching the doors or roaming restlessly about the lounge while the children revolved round them asking questions. "Mummy, why are we here?" "Mummy, may I go on the sands?" "Daddy, when are we going home?" "Nanny, when is Mummy coming?" Presently a woman near him said, "There is the manager," and half rose to her feet as a fat little man passed swiftly through the lounge. He was accompanied by a tall man with a black beard whose general appearance struck Warnford as familiar, though he could not remember ever having known anyone with a black beard like that, stiff and pointed at the end. They walked through the lounge too quickly for anyone to stop them and disappeared through a door labeled "Private."

Warnford and Marden had to spend four nights in uncomfortable lodgings before they could board a ship crammed to suffocation and were extremely lucky to get on at all. They landed with profound relief at Dover several hours late and had a leisurely lunch at the Lord Warden, retrieved the Bentley, and drove happily back in the direction of London in a "thank-goodness-that's-over" mood.

"That trip was not one of my brightest ideas," said Warnford.

"Never mind. We've at least seen the Hotel Malplaquet. Would you care to drop in and have a look at my place? It's not much off the road the other side of Maidstone."

"I'd love to; let's go. Have you had it long?"

"Well, yes," said Marden rather diffidently. "It's belonged to my people for some considerable time—it's the last remaining bit; there was a lot more at one time. My people were a Kentish family; in fact, there's a place called Marden not far from here; I expect there was some connection originally. We turn off left just beyond Addington and plunge into the woods. They are not what they were before the last war, but it is still a pleasant spot."

But before they reached Addington they met a large two-seater car being driven in a wildly erratic manner from side to side of the road. Warnford was so justly alarmed that he swung the Bentley into a cart track to get out of the way. They stopped among hazel bushes twenty yards down the lane and walked back to the corner, having heard a crash.

"Feller ought to be in jail," snorted Warnford. "Drunk in charge of a car is practically murder. Feller ought to be hung."

They came into the main road and saw the sports car stopped almost opposite to them with one wheel in the ditch. A big American saloon car had just pulled up behind it, and four men were getting out. "Friends of the casualty, I suppose," remarked Warnford, "following after in case— What's the matter?"

"Back behind these bushes," said Marden, grabbing him. "Don't let them see you. Something funny here."

"Why, what d'you know about it?" said Warnford, retiring as instructed. "Is the binged one a friend of yours?"

"No. But I'll bet he's not binged. That's the King's Messenger with the Duesenberg car I told you about. I thought I knew the car when it came round the bend. Proper toughs those fellows look, don't they? The other car's a Paige-Jewett."

The four men manhandled the Duesenberg out of the ditch and onto the road again; two of them pushed the King's Messenger out of the driver's place and propped him up in the passenger's seat. One of them got into the driver's seat of the Duesenberg, which was apparently unharmed; the other three ran back to the American car close behind and scrambled in. Whereupon both cars moved off with the Duesenberg leading and took the first turning on their side of the road; the whole performance had taken less than three minutes, and during that time the few cars that had passed had taken no notice.

"King's Messengers," said Marden, "don't get drunk when they're—"

"I'll back the car out," interrupted Warnford. "You wait here and give me a clear road, will you? We'll chase these fellows," and he made a dash for the Bentley; Marden came aboard as the car backed out, and they went off in pursuit.

The cars they were chasing were, of course, out of sight, but two cars driven one closely behind the other do not usually travel fast, and Warnford drove the Bentley at the highest speed possible in such a narrow twisting lane, praying to be delivered from farm carts round corners. At the top of a hill the lane dropped steeply away below them to rise again in a long ascent. Near the top of this were two small objects in motion. "There they go!" yelled Marden. "Yoicks forrard!" and he bounced in his seat.

The Bentley shot down the hill like an express lift in the Empire State Building, with the air whistling past the windows; Warnford braked violently when he saw the little humpbacked bridge at the bottom only just in time; as it was, the big car left the ground and it was mere luck that landed them on the road instead of in the ditch. Warnford laughed, and Marden said that so far as he knew there wasn't a hospital along there, though there was a churchyard a bit farther on.

"You know this country, do you?"

"Of course I do. Used to cycle round these lanes when I was a small boy. Hold hard, there's a sharp bend over this ridge."

When they rounded the bend they saw the two cars not too far ahead, and Warnford slowed down. They had no wish at all to get too near. The leading cars turned left and then right.

"Where are they going, d'you know?"

"No idea; might be anywhere. I don't know it so well beyond this point."

Ten minutes later the cars slowed suddenly and turned off up a cart track. "I'll run past the end," said Warnford, "just in case they're watching us. We'll turn somewhere and come back." Sure enough, as they passed the end of the lane the Paige-Jewett had stopped and a face looked out at the rear window.

"Go round that corner and stop," said Marden. "We might be able to see something from there."

The ground fell away from the field gate over which they leaned, and a bare paddock with cows in it ended in a thin hedge through which they caught glimpses of a silver-gray car proceeding with caution and, a moment later, a black car following it.

"Reassured, the pilgrims proceeded on their way," said Marden. "What happens next?"

"Study the lie of the land a little, I think. There was no signpost at that corner, so I think that lane just goes to a house and not beyond. That's the lane, I suppose, that white streak alongside that wood. Yes, there's the Duesenberg. And escort. This is where we exercise caution; they are two to one and, as you said, toughs. Is that a barn of some kind by those ricks? If it is we might be able to run the car in there."

"If it's not locked. It will probably be empty just now," said the country-bred Marden; "the machines will be out harvesting. We could hide the car behind the ricks; there's sure to be a gateway leading in. Let's go."

When they got there down the extremely bumpy lane they found the barn doors only latched and the barn itself empty except for a couple of plows at one end. The Bentley went in easily, and the big doors were closed again. Just past the barn the lane bent sharply to the right between high banks, ran along by the side of a beechwood and across a field. After that it dropped out of sight for a time, to reappear again as a thin streak along a hillside, and came to an end at a gate and a screen of trees; behind these one rose-red brick chimney and the corner of a tiled roof announced the presence of some sort of house. Marden and Warnford found that if they climbed the bank they could see the road nearly all the way to the white gate.

"This is a good spot," said Marden.

"Apart from stinging nettles up my trouser legs and a rose branch down the back of my neck, it is. What happens next?"

"I wish the party would divide. I wonder how long they propose to keep the King's Messenger there."

"I wonder whether they've got enough provisions, or will some of them come out to buy some beer?"

"What were you thinking of doing?"

"Stopping the car," said Warnford, "with a block in the road. There were a couple of plows in that barn; they'd do nicely. Even if they were all four in the car, the moment of impact with two unexpected plows would disconcert them, don't you think? However tough they are. Then, while they're still seeing stars, we can advance upon the car and bat them with something heavy."

"Suppose they don't come out again for hours, or even stay there tonight?"

"If I'd stolen despatches from a King's Messenger," said Warnford, "I'd get 'em away as soon as possible, wouldn't you? All the same, if they don't come to us we'll have to go to them. I wish Ashling was here; he might be useful."

"Would it be a good idea to get those plows out ready in case they come back? We shan't have a lot of time when we see the car coming."

"I think you're right. Have a cigarette and I'll go and get them out of the barn. One of us must do Sister Anne on the top of this bank in case they come upon us unawares; I think it had better be you. You've got a nicer piece of bank than I have, a rail to sit on, I notice, and no stinging nettles."

"I went where there weren't any," said Marden. "I have trained myself to exercise ordinary foresight. While on that subject, could you look round the barn for some weapons of a simple kind? A club or a bar of iron or some such."

"I've always thought what a nice weapon a mace must have been. Not the Lord Mayor's kind; I mean a long handle with a lump of iron covered with spikes on the end. I'll go and see what I can find." Warnford jumped off the bank and walked round to the barn, leaving his friend on the lookout. The barn provided a bar of iron about three feet long, apparently broken off something, a scythe blade which Warnford rejected as being useful but too barbaric, and a couple of scythe handles. He took the iron bar and the heaviest scythe handle outside, put them in a convenient spot, and returned to wrestle with the plows, leaving the door ajar. A plow is not the easiest thing in the world to move about if you are not used to it. Warnford pulled and pushed, got projecting parts caught up in things, and was making a good deal of noise and not much progress when he became aware of the sound of an engine running just outside the door. The next moment the door opened wider and an elderly man with a red face put his head in.

"Oh," said Warnford, feeling thoroughly caught, "er—good afternoon."

"May I ask what you're doing in my barn?"

Warnford abandoned his labors for the moment and explained that he wasn't doing any harm; he and his friend just wanted to borrow a couple of plows for a few minutes.

"Borrer my plows? Whatever for?"

"Oh—er—we just wanted to surprise somebody. That's all."

The farmer looked at him with growing distaste. "Say, you ain't come from Barming, have you?"

"Barming? Where's that?"

"Not far."

"I don't think so. Why?"

" 'Cause if you don't mind I'd rather you went back. Borrer my plows!"

"But why Barming?" asked Warnford.

"County lunatic asylum, that's why. Is this your car?"

"Yes, I—we just—"

"Take it out of my barn. Leave them plows alone; take your car out and get out yourself!"

Appeasement being at that time in the fashion, Warnford thought he'd better try it. "I'm frightfully sorry," he said in a soothing tone, advancing towards the door. "I know it must seem a bit mad to you, but honestly I only wanted to borrow the plows for a few minutes. I'll put them back."

"Come out!" said the farmer, and flung the door wide open. It hit a stump in the ground, bounced back again, and bumped the farmer from behind. This seemed to annoy him more than anything, and he addressed a few remarks to the door. Outside, just in the gateway off the lane, stood a Ford saloon of an early vintage, with buckled wings, a cracked windscreen, and most of the paint missing. The engine was still running.

"I can't get my car out," said Warnford, "till you move yours. It's in the way."

The farmer seemed about to reply when there came a yell from Marden. "They're coming! Look out, quick!"

Warnford caught the farmer by the wrist, swung him forward into the barn, slammed the door on him, latched it, and pegged the latch all in one movement. He leaped at the Ford as Marden came running round the corner and backed the old car right across the lane. "That ought to stop them," he said, getting out hastily. "Weapons here, look. Stick or iron bar for you?"

"They won't see it till they're on it," said Marden, taking the scythe handle; "that corner's perfectly blind from the other side—"

There came from the farther side of the bank the roar of a big car being driven much too fast for comfort on that potholed lane, a slither as it skidded round the corner, the squeal of brakes applied much too late, and a perfectly appalling crash. The Paige-Jewett hit the Ford squarely broadside on and knocked it right across the hedge; the big car appeared to close up in front and slewed round in the road, shot straight into the ditch, hit the roots of a big tree, and turned three complete somersaults, ending up with its wheels in the air. Except for a hissing sound as the water from the radiator poured onto the hot engine, there was silence; even the farmer inside the barn was, for the moment, hushed.

"Good lord," said Marden in awed tones, "you've killed them."

Warnford, white-faced under his sunburn, said hastily, "I didn't expect that. I hope the King's Messenger isn't inside," and ran towards the wreck with Marden beside him.

There were only two men there, and neither of them was the King's Messenger. One of them had been flung out in the road; when he was lifted up his head dropped back like a jointed doll's when the elastic has perished.

"Neck broken," said Marden shortly. "Put him on the grass at the side. Where's the other?"

The other was jammed behind the steering column, and it took some trouble to get him out. He was quite unconscious and breathing noisily, but, apart from some cuts on the head and a broken leg, he was not much hurt so far as they could tell.

"Stunned, that's all," said Marden. "His leg's broken below the knee; he'll be all right again in a few weeks. What do we do now?"

8
Deep Sleep of a King's Messenger

WARNFORD wiped his forehead and looked about him. The farmer inside the barn was shouting remarks fortunately muffled by brick and solid timber and kicking the door with hobnailed boots. The Ford was standing more or less on its wheels astride the hedge; the Paige-Jewett was in the ditch opposite, leaving the road clear. The man with the broken leg still snored heavily, and the dead man in the grass stared blankly at the sky.

"I think we'd better get out of this as quickly as possible," said Warnford. "I suppose a few people do occasionally come along this lane. We'd better go up to the house, lay out the other two, collect the King's Messenger, and leave. I'd like to take the others prisoner and send them to Hambledon, though I don't quite see how at the moment. Perhaps we shall think of something. As for these two, I don't think they're much loss, either of 'em. A more villainous pair of toughs I never set eyes on; the dead one is just like an anthropoid ape with unnatural vices, and this one's more like a hyena."

"Hyena or not," said Marden, slightly horrified, "we can't leave him in the middle of the road."

"No, of course not. For one thing, we should run over him when we come back. Better dump him in the barn, I think, and his late friend too. Then there's the farmer; he doesn't sound too friendly somehow. We can't have him running round telling the world before we're ready."

"Better tie him up and take him with us. Or leave him in the barn to keep the hyena company. By the way!"

"What?"

"Do you think they've got the King's Messenger's papers in the car?"

Marden was quite right; they had. The brown leather satchel had been broken open but still had a number of papers in it; in case any had been taken out search was made through both victims' pockets but without result, except that they each had an automatic which was removed. Warnford concealed the satchel in the hedge for the time being and said, "Now for the farmer. There was some rope hanging up in the barn. You open the door; I'll trip him up, and you sit on him. Then I'll get the ropes and we'll tie him up and put him in the barn. After that we'll come back for these two. We might find a spare door or something to carry them on; easier than just lugging them."

"Hurdles are best," said Marden.

They approached the barn door and proceeded to carry out the first part of the agenda. It did not turn out to be quite so simple as anticipated because the farmer, though elderly, was a strong man, accustomed to manual labor, and he put in a concentrated spell of it before being brought sufficiently under control for Warnford to fetch the ropes. Even then the three of them had quite a lot more exercise before he was tied up like a cocoon and laid in a quiet corner of the barn to cool off.

"Think we'd better gag him?" said Warnford as quiet fled from the corner where the farmer lay.

"Do you think we must?" said the softer-hearted Marden. "He might throw a fit if he couldn't even swear."

"Perhaps you're right. We'll get the others in first, and then I'll talk to him. No hurdles in here."

"Some outside," said Marden. He pulled one out of the ground by the ricks, and they brought the two casualties in, one at a time. The broken-legged one showed signs of returning consciousness, so they tied him up, too, after straightening out his leg and laying him upon sacks; the other man required no consideration.

"You back the Bentley out," said Warnford, "while I talk to the farmer." He strode across the barn and stood over the prostrate farmer. "Listen," said Warnford. "I am most dreadfully sorry to have to treat you like this, believe me; if only I could tell you all about it you'd understand how unavoidable it is. I'll see you're compensated for all this and I'll buy you a new Ford too. I think you'll need one. At the very earliest possible moment I'll send somebody up to untie you. I hope it won't be— What did you say?"

The farmer repeated himself.

"Oh no, I'm not. Neither of us is. As I was saying, I hope it won't be more than an hour at the outside before you're rescued. If you'll give me your name and address I'll see you don't suffer for this." The farmer gave them, and Warnford wrote them down. "These men here," went on Warnford, "won't worry you. One's got a broken leg and a clout on the head; the other's dead. No, I'm afraid I can't give you my name. Think of me as Deadeye Dick from Hangman's Oak. Don't yell too much; you'll only exhaust yourself, and I shall be seriously annoyed. I must go now. Good-bye." He went out, carefully shutting the door after him. The satchel was recovered from the hedge and stowed away under the driver's seat in the Bentley. Warnford collected the weapons, including the scythe handle, and got in. They drove away towards the second part of the business.

As they drew nearer to the place to which the King's Messenger had been taken they could see through the screen of poplars in front of it that it was a small but ancient farmhouse with many outbuildings and that the road ran along the front of it before turning in at the white gate. Warnford pulled the car onto the grass at the roadside well short of the house. "I don't think we'll advertise our coming," he said. "Of course they've probably seen us from afar off and are preparing a hero's welcome with tommy guns. On the other hand, there's just a chance they haven't been looking out of the front windows during the past ninety seconds. We will enter quietly by the farmyard." He led the way over a field gate.

"Nice tall hedges they keep here, don't they?" he went on. "I'd hate to lope along bent double like a kidney-pill advertisement."

"They are very grossly neglected," said Marden severely. They climbed another gate and proceeded quietly since they were nearing the farmyard and there might have been people about. "The place may be stiff with gangsters for all we know," whispered Warnford. "Come in behind this barn."

"There's one chimney smoking," said Marden, looking up, "but I think that fire's only just been lighted."

"Very quiet for a farmyard, isn't it?" murmured Warnford. "Not a sound. You'd expect cluckings and quackings, wouldn't you?"

"I expect the land belonging to this place is being worked by the next farm; this house may be empty. There's grass growing in the cart ruts, look."

"If we get down in the ditch behind this clump of nettles we'll get across to the next shed and work along nearer the house. Come on."

The next building was a cart shed with some derelict farm carts in it; the open front faced the house, and they slipped in at the back and kept in the shadow behind the carts. Before them the cobblestoned yard slept peacefully in the August sun; not a cat or a dog appeared, and the only birds visible were a couple of thrushes hunting for snails in the ivy along the house wall, and then hammering them to pieces on a suitable stone. Only one small window upstairs looked out from this end of the house, and a great chimney projection spoke of an ingle-nook inside. Neglected roses swung loose from the rose-red wall, and the steep roof came down within ten feet from the ground in lovely curves of lichened tiles. There was a small door at one side of the chimney, and about ten yards from it was a cow-tail pump. In the middle of the yard, resplendent in chromium plating and silver-gray enamel, stood the King's Messenger's Duesenberg.

"I think we'll have the ignition key out of that while yet we are alone with it. I don't know what I want it for, but it's good tactics to immobilize the enemy." Warnford sidled round to a spot where the car masked him from the upper window, made a silent dash, and returned with the key. "Nice place, this," he went on in the same low whisper; "brooding peace and all that. Only wants a few pigeons cooing and I'd buy the place."

"Typical Kentish farmhouse," answered Marden. "If you bought the place you could install the pigeons. Hullo!"

The small door opened; a man came out with a bucket in his hand and walked towards the pump. He looked doubtfully at the bucket as he came but put it under the pump and filled it. He looked still more doubtfully at the water, emptied it away, and pumped some more. This time he seemed satisfied, for he picked up the bucket, streaming water from a dozen places, and walked towards the door. Before he reached it there was a sudden gush and a silver flash in the sunshine, and his pail was empty again. The bottom had fallen out. With a gesture of exasperation he swung it round his head and hurled it into the patch of nettles. He looked about rather vaguely for something else which was not there and then went back into the house, leaving the door ajar.

"He's coming back," whispered Warnford. "I'm going to dodge round behind the chimney stack and cosh him with this." He indicated the scythe handle.

"I'm coming. Round behind the car, this way."

They were hardly in the angle of the chimney stack before they heard steps again from the other side of it as the man came out of the door with a shining new tin kettle in his hand. Warnford made a dash at him, cracked him on the head with the scythe handle as he turned, and the man sank to the ground on top of his kettle, which collapsed. Marden took him by the legs and Warnford by the shoulders and stowed him along the house wall beyond the stack where he could not be seen from the door.

"Three out of four," said Warnford. "This is too easy; something'll happen to us next time."

Nothing happened for the next ten minutes, and their prisoner began to stir. "This is awkward," said Marden. "If he comes round and yells just as the next man comes out—"

"He'll have to be coshed again, that's all," said Warnford grimly. "We haven't got any rope here." But the man quieted down again and showed no sign of animation. More time passed in silence till at last they heard footsteps along what sounded like a stone-flagged passage. They stopped at the door the other side of the chimney stack, and a cautious voice said, *"Johan? Wo bist?"*

Johan made no move, nor did his captors, and presently the man took three steps forward and came into their line of vision, a tall man with his back half turned to them, but they could see he had a stiff black beard. He was staring in a puzzled manner at the flattened kettle, and Marden made a dash at him at the same instant that the prisoner uttered a yell, spun round like a released spring, kicked Warnford on the knee with one foot and tripped him with the other. Warnford fell on the man and proceeded to abolish him, hearing at the same moment, with such attention as he could spare, a clean crisp smack from Marden's part of the battle. "That's that one," he thought, and banged Johan's head on the cobbles till he ceased to give trouble and fell asleep again.

Warnford picked himself up, nursing his damaged knee, and looked round just in time to see the tall man emerge from the farther door of the Duesenberg and run like a hare across the courtyard between the barns and away out of sight. Marden was just struggling to his feet, holding his jaw, which appeared to pain him. "You said something would happen to us this time," he mumbled as Warnford limped towards him; "it did. See who that was?"

"I've seen him—yes, I know. That was the man who walked through the Hotel Malplaquet with the manager."

"That's him. He knocked me down and made a dive for the Duesenberg. I didn't catch what he said when he found the ignition key was missing."

"Let's get this fellow indoors," said Warnford. "Blackbeard is probably armed, and we're offering quite good targets if he changes his mind and comes back."

But while they were heaving Johan towards the door Marden stopped suddenly and said, "Listen. What's that?"

"You know what it is," said Warnford bitterly. "It's my Bentley being driven away. Why didn't I take the ignition key out of that one too?"

"At least we shan't be shot at from behind the cart shed now," said Marden. "Need we carry this fellow any farther?"

"Not if we had something to tie him up with. There's a length of wire hanging on that nail; can you get it? That's right. His hands behind his back, so. Handcuffs made to measure for all emergencies. The long end of the wire will go round his ankles if we bend his knees up a bit, since we haven't any wire cutters. I don't think he'll get away now."

"We shall travel in the Duesenberg when we leave, shan't we?" said Marden.

"Certainly. Why?"

"Why not dump him in the dickey now?"

"You have the brains, partner. We must gag him before we start or we shall have wails—ugh, isn't he heavy?—coming out when he revives, and people might not believe it was the cat. Heave him up. Can you hold him like that while I hop in from the other side and stow him? Fine. Let him slide gently to the floor.

I don't want him damaged too much; he's got to talk to Mr. Hambledon tomorrow morning. Now for the King's Messenger."

They entered the house by the same door as the men had used and passed down a stone-flagged passage. The place was plainly uninhabited; cobwebs masked the windows, and it had the stuffy, cold atmosphere of a house which has neither been aired nor warmed for months on end. At the end of the passage an open door admitted them to the farmhouse kitchen, a vast place, stone-flagged like the passage. The only furniture was a couple of boxes, some rugs, and a camp bed with a man lying on it, sound asleep.

"That your friend?" asked Warnford.

Marden looked at the sleeper. "I don't think I've ever seen him, but it must be. He's so obviously respectable."

"So he is. Silver hair, clear complexion, clean fingernails, subdued gentlemanly suiting. Do King's Messengers really wear a silver greyhound badge under the lapel of their coats?"

"Don't know. If he did it's probably in Johan's pocket by now."

"I wish he'd wake up," said Warnford. "I'd like to consult him about— My hat! Do you know what?"

"What is it?"

"His satchel. It's still under the driving seat of the Bentley. Blackbeard has got it."

"Perhaps he won't find it," said Marden consolingly. "You wouldn't expect to find anything under the seats except batteries."

"Wonder what he thought when he rounded the corner and found the Paige-Jewett upside down and his friends gone? He knew the satchel was in that car."

"I should think he'd have a hasty look for it and, when he didn't find it, hop in the car again and drive like blazes," said Marden. "I should. After all, he doesn't know we aren't British Intelligence backed up by the whole of the Kent County Police and, if necessary, the Army."

"Quite true. I only wondered whether he'd come back to see if we'd got it, but, as you say, it's unlikely. I wish—again—this feller'd wake up. Can't we do anything for him?"

"Black coffee? There are some tins in that cupboard, look. The one with the broken door."

"Sardines," said Warnford, examining the tins. "Tongue. Salmon. Biscuits. Coffee; you're quite right. Tinned milk. Sugar. Quite a larder."

There was a fire in the range, struggling bravely against blocked flues, which might boil a kettle though it could not warm the room. "The kettle's squashed flat in the yard," said Marden, "but here's a saucepan; that'll do. Now it's our turn to fetch water."

"I'll come with you. Things are apt to happen to people who fetch water from that pump today."

But nothing molested them, and even Johan still slept in the Duesenberg's dickey. The water boiled on the kitchen fire, made up with the remains of the cupboard door, and there was a pleasant smell of fresh coffee. "I think we might have some too," said Marden. "Can you bear tinned milk? And the tongue also, I think; let us spoil the Egyptians."

Warnford bent himself to the task of inducing the King's Messenger to swallow black coffee while Marden wrestled with tin openers. "I'm afraid of choking this fellow," said the ministrant. "Is there a teaspoon? I'll try that. Come on, old chap. Sit up and lap this down; do you good. That's right, another spoonful. He can still swallow all right, I see. Now some more. Try drinking out of the cup."

When the coffee had begun to do its work the King's Messenger opened his eyes and stared confusedly about him. "Take it easy," said Warnford. "You've been doped, but you'll be all right again soon. You're among friends."

"My—my papers."

"They're all right. They're not here, but I know where they are. Have some more coffee."

"Have a nice biscuit-and-tongue sandwich," said Marden, offering it, but the man refused to eat, though he drank thirstily.

"Who doped me?" he asked slowly.

"I don't know that, I'm afraid. Where did you have anything to drink last?"

"Lunch. At the Green Doors. Roadhouse. On the Dover road. Where am I?"

"In a deserted farmhouse somewhere north of the Dover road; I don't know its name. I should think we aren't far from Meopham, but I don't really know."

"Who are you and how did you come to be here?"

"We saw your car pull up," answered Warnford, ignoring the first part of the question, "and we thought there was something the matter with you. Then a big car came up behind and four men got out, pushed you into the other seat, and all drove off again. My friend here recognized your car, so we followed. That's all. Sure you won't have some tongue? It's dashed good."

"No, thanks. What did—where are the four men?"

"Oh, we managed them. One's in the dickey of your car, tied up; we thought Mr. Hambledon would like to have him."

"Oh—yes. D'you know Hambledon?"

"Not personally, no. Tell me, what would you like to do now? Go back to town?"

"Since I've lost the papers, yes. What did you say about them?"

"I know where they are; don't worry about that."

"My head aches," said the King's Messenger wearily. "I feel awfully stupid still. Perhaps the air will do me good." He lay back on the camp bed and seemed to doze off.

"I think the sooner we get him up to town the better," said Warnford.

"Don't forget to gag Johan before we start," said Marden. "We don't want melancholy noises coming out of the dickey as we drive along. There's a bit of rag here; that'll do. It looks quite tasty."

Warnford slowed down as they passed the barn and put his head out of the window. There came to his ears the sound as of someone chanting one of the less amiable Psalms.

Police-Sergeant Coot had only three more years of service before he retired on his pension, and he was spending them in charge of a small quiet police station in Kent with nothing to worry him beyond a few cases of chicken stealing and sheep worrying, the high spirits of hop pickers in their season, and the deplorable deficiencies of the young constables he had to train.

"One after another," he said, "you comes, you stays a two-three years, and then you goes on somewhere else, and I gets another cub just so like the last I can't 'ardly tell you apart. I don't keep a police station; I runs a college for hinfant constables. You, George 'Uggins, you've been 'ere six months and just left off blushin' when the girls see you in uniform; you think you're findin' your feet, but I tell you you don't know nothin' yet."

"No, sir."

"If you'd started where I did, walkin' a beat in Chatham when I was a lad, you'd learn quick then, believe me, if you didn't want to end up in 'ospital with a face full of broken bottle. Not but what things is a lot better in Chatham now; as people gets more educated they behaves quieter, talks more, and acts about less. I'm not so sure, myself, that it's all that much better. When they was throwin' 'alf-bricks you knowed—knew—what they was up to; now they gets up on soapboxes and talk, talk, talk, and you don't know what it may lead to. Always distrust a man as talks too much, my lad."

"Yes, sir."

"Of course in a place like this you can't expect to get the experience as you would in a dockyard town, or any big town for that matter. It's just the poachin', and we know who's done it if only we can prove it, and sometimes a bit of a bust-up down at the Chequers and that, and that's all. Still, you can learn up your police law here nice and steady, and study yuman nature, too, that bein' the same town and country alike."

"Yes, sir."

"And learn all I can teach you; then when you leaves 'ere and goes somewhere else they'll say, 'You don't know much, but you've 'ad a good groundin'.' That's what they'll say. All the same, I wish sometimes we could 'ave a good case as we could get our teeth into, a nice juicy murder or some such. Make a change, that—" The telephone bell rang, and the sergeant broke off to answer it.

"Yes, sir. … Yes. … Yes, I know Mr. 'Umphreys, the farmer. … Keeps 'is car in a barn? Yes, sir, 'e does, in Frog Lane. … Yes, I know the barn. … Yes, 'e is a rather hasty-tempered gentleman at times. … What? … *What?* … But why tied up? … But why should 'e get into mischief? … Two other men wantin' an ambulance? Why? … Dead? Who killed 'im and 'ow? … Oh, a car accident; I understand. … Broken leg? … Who? Take 'im to who? … 'Ambledon? H-a-m-b-l-e-d-o-n. Thank you, sir, I've got that. … But why is Mr. 'Umphreys tied up? … Yes, of course, but I expect 'e'll tell me without that. … Who is this Mr. 'Ambledon, a local gentleman? … He will let me know? Can't you tell me yourself? … Oh. … Thank you for ringin' up about the accident, sir, but why didn't you untie Mr. 'Umphreys? … Oh no, I shouldn't think 'e'd do that, not if you'd untied 'im, sir. … Where are you speakin' from? … Yes, I know it's the other end of the telephone; I meant—I suppose it's a call box? … My name is not Watson; it's Coot. Sergeant Coot. What is your name, please? … Mr. Early? … Yes, I'm awake; o' course I am. … Oh, poetry. What is your real name? … 'E's rung off." Coot turned a scarlet face upon the enthralled constable. "Get on your bike at once and go—No, it's no use; I must go myself. I shall want somebody to lend a 'and; you'd better come too—can't leave the station. No, you stop 'ere and I'll take Forrest. Get out the motor bike and sidecar; I'll pick him up—Oh, very well. I'll take you, and Forrest can mind the station. Get a move on! To think I was just sayin'—"

9
Dark Deeds in Kent

HAMBLEDON shared a flat overlooking St. James's Park with Reck, the wireless expert, and a stout elderly lady, Fräulein Ludmilla Rademeyer, who mothered them both and was beloved in return. Hambledon had not, therefore, far to go when he was rung up on the telephone and asked to go to the Foreign Office immediately as there was a curious matter claiming his attention. He was in the act of undressing for bed as it was then past midnight, but curiosity would awaken Hambledon at any hour, so he resumed his tie and coat and walked into Whitehall.

Here he found a group of four policemen arranged round a silver-gray Duesenberg which he recognized. The dickey seat was shut and locked, but there was a curious bumbling sound proceeding from it, and occasionally the car rocked slightly as by an unseen hand. In the passenger's seat in front sat the King's Messenger, alone and sound asleep. There was no other person in the car.

"What," said Hambledon, "is all this?"

One of the policemen explained that when he returned from the other end of his beat he found the Duesenberg standing outside the door of the Foreign Office just as it was now; he had not seen anyone get out of it, though presumably someone had driven it up, alighted, and gone away.

"But didn't Mr. What's-his-name—the gentleman inside—drive himself up?"

The policeman didn't think so. He had walked past the car and noticed the gentleman inside; he knew him well, of course. He seemed to be asleep and might have been waiting for somebody. As time passed and no one came the policeman opened the car door to ask if he could do anything and found a label tied to the gentleman's lapel.

"Where is it now?"

"Still there, sir, look."

The policeman shone a torch into the car, and Hambledon read the message written on the label. It ran: "The poor man has been doped with some narcotic. Black coffee seems to help him. Please inform Mr. Hambledon AT ONCE. Further details later."

"Dear me," said Hambledon mildly.

"So I informed the night porter at the Foreign Office, sir, and he—"

"Yes, yes, of course. Well, we'd better get this chap indoors and send for a doctor. What's this?"

It was a key, with another label attached to it, hanging from the dashboard.

"That, sir, would appear to be the key of the dickey, sir, which is shut and locked."

"It would indeed; in fact, it says so. 'Key of the dickey, for Mr. Hambledon with compliments. Open carefully.' Really, anybody would think this was my birthday, wouldn't they? Such interesting presents. Get the King's Messenger out, men, and carry him indoors; after that we'll open the other parcel."

When they unlocked the dickey, a couple of constables standing by with truncheons at the ready, just in case, they found Johan still firmly tied up on the floor, but conscious. He did not speak because he was still gagged, but his face was full of expression. There was yet another label attached to him which read:

"Christian name, Johan; surname not known. Nationality presumably German. Suffering from concussion due to scythe handle and cobblestones, probably cramp also. Concerned in abduction of the King's Messenger."

" 'Little man,' " hummed Hambledon untunefully, " 'you've had a busy day.' "

Hambledon's office telephone rang on the following morning, and the secretary reported that it was some man who wouldn't give his name but who wanted to talk about a Duesenberg car.

"Leave him to me," said Hambledon, picking up the receiver. "Good morning. Thank you for your nice presents. Now tell me all about them."

"The King's Messenger," said Warnford, "was doped somewhere on his way to Dover. Near Addington he ran his car off the road and went to sleep. He was at once removed, car and all, and taken to an unoccupied farmhouse in the Meopham district by four men. One is dead; one has a broken leg; the third was delivered to you last night, but I'm sorry to say the fourth got away. I don't know his name, but he's a tall fellow with a black torpedo beard, and five days ago he was in the Hotel Malplaquet at Ostend, talking to the manager."

"Noted," said Hambledon.

"Blackbeard has the papers but doesn't know he's got them. I will try to get them back for you."

"I sincerely hope you succeed."

"I think that's all, except that I'm sorry about the farmer. A Mr. Humphreys with a hasty temper—I'm afraid I annoyed him. Police-Sergeant Coot will tell you all about it; he also has the man with the broken leg."

"Where is Sergeant Coot?"

"I don't know the name of his village, somewhere near Meopham in Kent. You will be able to find him, won't you? There was a car accident, so I rang him up to report, according to law."

"I like 'according to law' from you," said Hambledon. "Was either of the cars yours?"

"Oh no. One—the Paige-Jewett—was Blackbeard's or his gang's; the other was the farmer's Ford. I'll send you a full account of the affair in writing, shall I? After that I'll see about getting that satchel back."

"Please do both. It would give me great pleasure," said Hambledon earnestly, "if you would dine with me at the Café Royal tonight at eight."

"I am so sorry, I can't manage it tonight. Someday I hope I may. Good-bye."

"Here, stop a minute! Where are you speaking from, a call box?"

"No, as a matter of fact, I'm talking from the Regent Palace."

"Tell me your name," said Hambledon in persuasive tones, but the only answer was a laugh and the click of the replaced receiver.

Hambledon immediately sent two Special Branch police to the Regent Palace Hotel in the remote hope of identifying the man who had telephoned to him from there. In the meantime he ascertained the whereabouts of Police-Sergeant Coot, rang him up, and received from him a description of the scene of the accident and of what he found in the barn.

"The farmer," said Hambledon, "what's he got to say?"

Apparently he had had a good deal to say, but the gist of it was that he had found a dangerous lunatic in his barn who had expressed a wish to borrow two plows for five minutes and, when this was refused, locked him in the barn for ten minutes or so, during which there was an appalling crash outside. The lunatic then came back, bound Mr. Humphreys hand and foot, and left him there with a dead man and another badly injured, who, when he recovered consciousness, talked some foreign language. In fact, he was still doing so when Coot arrived, sent for the ambulance, and had him removed to hospital and the dead man to the nearest mortuary. The inquest would be held next day, which was Friday, and the farmer was prepared to swear that his car was well off the road heading towards the barn. It must have been backed across the road by the lunatics.

"Listen," said Hambledon, "and make sure you get this right. There were no lunatics."

"Sir?"

"Nobody was there at all except the farmer. He—had he been out harvesting?"

"Yes, sir."

"That's it. He had a touch of the sun and suffered a temporary delirium. The Ford's hand brake jumped off—is there a slight slope up to the barn door?"

"Quite a slope, sir, but—"

"There you are, then. The Ford's brake came off; it ran back down the slope and stopped across the road, and the Paige-Jewett came round the sharp bend you describe and ran into it. That's all."

"But, sir—"

"But what?"

"Who rang me up on the telephone?"

"Oh, some passing motorist on a primrosing expedition."

"Not in August, sir."

"Oh, don't be so difficult. Mushrooms, then. I was only trying to account for a strange car wandering about."

"But the farmer was still all tied up when I got there," objected Coot, who saw the case of a lifetime being whittled away before his eyes.

"I have already said that that was an illusion on the part of the farmer. You don't mean to tell me you suffer from illusions too, do you?"

"Certainly not, sir, but—"

"Splendid. Well, that's settled. You know now what case is to go before the coroner, don't you?"

"Yes, sir," said Coot unwillingly. "But who's goin' to persuade Mr. 'Umphreys as 'e's sufferin' from delusions?"

"Don't try. Pass the word round the village that that's what it was and it won't matter what he says. He wasn't tied up when you got there, mind that."

"Yes, sir," said Coot sulkily. "But—"

"Don't keep saying 'but'!" snapped Hambledon.

"Who put the accident victims in the barn? 'Cause they was there when the ambulance came, and I didn't."

"The passing motorist who rang you up, of course; that's simple. By the way! Did you untie the injured man before the ambulance came? You said he was roped up too."

"Only 'is 'ands tied be'ind 'im. Yes, sir, I did."

"Well done, Sergeant. I think you have handled this distressing affair admirably. I congratulate you on your presence of mind and I will see that an official commendation of your behavior reaches the appropriate authority. Good-bye."

Coot put down the receiver, walked round to the back door of the Chequers, and obtained a large whisky for medicinal purposes, since it was out of hours. He needed it.

Presently the two Special Branch policemen returned from the Regent Palace and reported that they had been unable to trace Hambledon's telephone caller but handed in a large envelope addressed to — Hambledon, Esq. They said that after making vain enquiries on the ground floor they had gone upstairs to interview somebody who might know something—he didn't—when the girl at the reception desk came to them. She gave them this envelope and said she had been asked to do so by a gentleman who had just left the building. He told her to tell the detectives that the man they were looking for had gone and asked that the envelope should be handed by them to the addressee, with compliments.

Hambledon murmured something inaudible and slit the envelope open. Inside were a number of typewritten sheets of Regent Palace Hotel paper, headed:

DARK DEEDS IN KENT

CHAPTER I

The Case of the Angry Farmer

Hambledon ran his eye over them. They contained a detailed account of the events of the preceding day and up to the time of the telephone message from the Regent Palace. They ended: "His police have come to look for me; I think I had better leave."

"Did you see the gentleman who left this letter for me?"

"Not to our knowledge, sir. There is a row of telephone boxes at the Regent Palace and people going in and coming out all the time; nobody takes any notice of them."

"Were there any gentlemen there dictating letters to typists?"

"Yes, sir, several. I made enquiries of them all as to whether they had telephoned from the Regent Palace within the past hour, and they all said they had not."

Hambledon thanked the police and told his secretary to ring up the reception clerk at the Regent Palace. When he was connected Hambledon asked if she could describe the gentleman who gave her a note to hand to the detectives that morning. She said he was a tall gentleman with dark hair and dressed in a gray suit.

"Anything else remarkable about him?"

Nothing remarkable except that he was ever so nice and she would know him again at once if she saw him.

"If you ever see him again, anywhere, get to the nearest telephone and ring this number," said Hambledon, giving it; "ask for Mr. Hambledon and tell me all about it."

The reception clerk agreed but privately determined to do nothing of the sort. The gentleman this morning was ever so nice, but this one sounded like trouble.

"You have a typist's office there, I understand," went on Hambledon. He was put through to it and asked to speak to the typist who had typed out the first chapter of a novel called *Dark Deeds in Kent* that morning.

"Speaking," said the voice.

"Oh. Well, I'm a—a publisher. I have received this manuscript, but there's no name or address on it. Do you know who the gentleman is and where he lives? I want to get in touch with him."

"I'm sorry, sir, he didn't say. I expect he forgot to put it in."

"I expect so. He might be someone I know; could you describe him?"

"He was a tall gentleman—I noticed that—and I think he'd got dark hair. He was ever so nice, easy to work for, you know. Didn't get impatient like some of them. He'd got ever such a merry laugh, but his eyes looked sad, as though he'd had trouble."

"Most writers have," said Hambledon darkly, "especially letter writers. What color were his eyes? What sort of face; can you describe it?"

"Dark eyes, I'm sure of that. I don't know how to describe his face; it was very aristocratic, you know; you'd know he was a real gentleman wherever you met him. Well, he reminded me a bit of the pictures of Anthony Eden, only he didn't wear a black hat."

"I see."

"But there, I've no doubt he'll write to you when he doesn't hear, won't he? He's sure to; it's only waiting for it."

"Yes, but I don't like waiting," said Hambledon truthfully.

Denton came into the room while this conversation was in progress; when it was over Hambledon sent his secretary out to lunch and poured out his story.

"It's so dashed awkward," he complained. "You see, I don't suppose he knows how desperately important those papers are. There was even a Cabinet meeting about it this morning; that'll show you."

"What is all this fuss about?" asked Denton frankly.

"Russia. Of course we've been on rather distant terms with Russia for a good many years now, but it isn't going to last much longer. They are beginning to explore stones and turn avenues and all that, to see if we can find a ground of mutual agreement to start talks on. It's all terribly hush-hush, and a week ago a detailed account of conversations in London with representatives of the U.S.S.R.—in code, of course—was flown to our Ambassador in Russia. At least the plane started for Russia but crashed in flames just this side of the Polish frontier; the pilot was killed and the papers burned. That's the story, anyway."

"What actually happened?"

"Well, one of our fellows was floating about in the neighborhood where the plane came down, though he wasn't actually on the spot when it crashed. He says it definitely wasn't burning in the air; he'd have seen it. It was blazing furiously when he arrived on the scene, but not yet entirely destroyed. He says there were bullet holes in the wings."

"Shot down, eh?"

"Presumably. The case, though serious, was not desperate, because they hadn't got the code. Things are different now, because a copy of that cipher was among the papers which the King's Messenger was taking to Paris."

"Oh, ow," said Denton dismally.

"Quite. If they've got the code they can decipher the papers, and the cat will be among the canaries with a vengeance."

"I don't wonder there was a Cabinet meeting."

"No. But can you imagine me explaining to them that I think some young man I don't know is trying to get them back for us? I said the matter was having my sleepless attention and I hoped for results in a couple of days. I do passionately desire to meet this young man; that's why I sent policemen hotfoot to the Regent Palace to try and catch him for me. It was a fool's errand. I only hoped something might happen; it didn't. He just looked at them with his sad brown eyes and walked out on them with a peal of merry laughter."

"What are you going to do about it?"

"I am going down to Kent," said Hambledon, "to try and convince the coroner that my version of the Frog Lane accident is the correct one. It's a much more reasonable explanation than the farmer's, anyway. I shall then interview the tough with the broken leg, though if he's anything like his pal Johan I might just as well talk to myself in the looking glass; I should at least be sure of getting a civil and intelligent answer—if I may say so."

"Johan wasn't much help, then?"

"Johan, like the rest of the Nazi party, is a throwback to the Dark Ages when they tortured prisoners to make 'em talk, and after half an hour's chat with Johan you understand why. I don't think he knows anything important, actually; he is just the useful thug. You may be more fortunate; you are going to the Hotel Malplaquet at Ostend to try and pick up Blackbeard. He may have bolted back there after all this excitement."

"Taking the papers with him, presumably. He has had twenty-four hours' start," said Denton.

"Presumably, but I don't know. Our young friend told me that Blackbeard had the papers but didn't know he'd got them, whatever that means."

"Why don't you put Scotland Yard onto him? All this Boy's Own Paper stuff is all very well for trifles, but this is serious."

"I agree," said Hambledon anxiously, "it is, but I don't like to turn the police onto him. Goodness knows what they'd find. He may be someone they're looking for for something else, and the next thing I'd hear might be that he'd got fifteen years in Dartmoor for coining or something, and he's much more useful to me loose. If he gets the code back he can make all the coins he likes for all I care; there isn't nearly enough money about, anyway."

So Hambledon went into Kent, interviewed the coroner and Police-Sergeant Coot with satisfactory results, and visited Frog Farm, where he found a camp bed, a few picnic necessaries, and an empty tin which had contained tongue. These last were examined for fingerprints, but it was useless, as they had been wiped clean.

Denton caught the afternoon boat to Ostend and failed as completely as Warnford to get a room at the Hotel Malplaquet, for the backwash of international crisis still eddied through its corridors. He did manage to obtain a bedroom in a house near by and arranged to have his meals at the hotel, which was nearly as useful. He settled down and looked round for a tall man with a black beard who was a friend of the manager's. Unfortunately, men with black beards are a common feature of Continental life, and Ostend was thick with them; anyone would think, said Denton bitterly to himself, that the *Société Anonyme des Barbes Noires* was holding a convention in Ostend. Quite a lot of them seemed to know the manager of the Malplaquet.

Eventually he pitched on two as being the least unlikely—that is, provided the right man was in Ostend at all, of which there was no proof—and he kept an unobtrusive eye upon both of them. Denton was strolling languidly along the sea front one morning with, strange to relate, one of the two possibles also strolling along about twenty paces ahead of him, when two obviously English travelers stopped Blackbeard and asked him the way to the head post office. Denton interested himself in a shop-window and heard the man describing the route in English without a trace of an accent. Yet when they were crushed together an hour later in the overfull bar of the Malplaquet and Denton said, "Beastly crowded, what?" in weary tones, he was answered with a blank stare and a brusque *"Pardon? Ne comprends."*

"You want to take up a Pelman course," thought Denton; "your memory's very bad. Either that, or you're a liar." When he discovered that the other Blackbeard was a well-known local dentist Denton eliminated him from the contest and concentrated upon this one.

The following evening Blackbeard went out for a stroll, and Denton also felt that a little fresh air before dinner would do him good. Blackbeard made one or two calls in the course of his walk and arrived back at the Malplaquet to find Denton having an *apéritif* in the lounge and being talked to in an animated manner by a spinster lady of uncertain age who was one of the permanent residents of the hotel. Dinner having been dealt with, Denton was standing in the hall lighting a cigarette for the same lady when Blackbeard came hastily towards the door, bearing a suitcase in his hand, tipped the porter, and passed out into the night. Denton, saying, "Excuse me, I've just remembered a funny story I've got to tell a man," left his companion abruptly and went out after Black-beard, who had just got into a taxi and slammed the door. The car moved off.

There was a second taxi standing by the pavement just behind the first, and Denton, without stopping to think, sprang into it. "Follow that taxi in front," he said, and shut his door also. The driver nodded and obeyed.

"I think I'm a fool," said Denton as the car started. "I'm sure I'm a fool." He looked round the taxi and noticed that the handles by which one opens the windows had both been removed. "I am a drivelling nitwit," he added, and tried the doors, neither of which would open. At the top of the street the first taxi turned to the right while his turned left. "Fancy being had for a mug by this old trick at my time o' life. They will now drive me out into the dunes and bump me off, and it serves me right." He found comfort in the thought of a small automatic in his hip pocket. "In all the best thrillers this is where they introduce a subtle gas into the cab; a bypass from the exhaust would do. Carbon monoxide." The street lights thinned out and ceased, and the taxi drove steadily on into the darkness.

10
Pork and Diamonds

WHEN the typist at the Regent Palace had finished the first chapter of *Dark Deeds in Kent*, Warnford thanked her warmly, paid what was owing, and drifted into the entrance hall. He looked round casually but could see nothing of the two men who had asked him ten minutes earlier whether he had made a telephone call from the hotel that morning. He was convinced they were still on the premises, so he gave the long envelope addressed to Hambledon to the reception clerk to hand to them and walked out.

The first necessity was to find his Bentley, and he went to the police station nearest his flat. There he explained that he had been to a party the night before in the Bayswater Road, had left his car down a side turning, and when he came out at about 2 A.M. the Bentley had gone. He thought the car might have been borrowed by friends, so he had taken no steps in the matter till he had made sure, but there was now no doubt it had been stolen, and could the police kindly do something about it?

Two days later the police telephoned to tell him that the Bentley had been found abandoned on a car park at Dover, one of those parks with a two-hour time limit. When the attendant went off duty the Bentley had been there for six hours already, so he informed the police, who removed it. Warnford would be able to retrieve it on application to the Dover police. He should take his driving license with him and the car's registration book, if available.

"So Blackbeard skipped it to the Continent," said Marden. "We put the wind up him at Frog Farm."

"Yes," said Warnford thoughtfully. "I'm still trying to remember where I've seen him before, but I can't. Well, I'm going to Dover, and I shan't be any longer than I can help."

The station sergeant replaced the receiver after kindly acknowledging Warnford's thanks and looked with awakening curiosity at the papers before him. "Something funny about this case," he remarked.

"Why?" asked the inspector.

"Why, sir, because the car'd been standing on that park in Dover for six hours before the police took it in at 11 P.M., and he didn't miss it from Bayswater till two o'clock the following morning."

"Some party," said the inspector.

"I suppose it is the same car?"

"That's up to the Dover police. Perhaps the party started the day before and just flowed on without his noticing the time. He did look a bit as though he'd had a night out."

At the first quiet spot on the road home from Dover, Warnford stopped the car and looked under the driver's seat. The King's Messenger's satchel was still there; a hasty but thorough search convinced Warnford that the contents had been neither added to nor subtracted from. He drove back to London, singing a little song.

Warnford regained his flat without incident, told Ashling to put the car away and lock the garage doors, and took the precious satchel upstairs to Marden.

"Here it is, all present and correct."

"That's one good thing anyway," said the ex-burglar, laying down a letter he was reading. "I'm very glad to hear it."

"I can now give myself the pleasure of ringing up Hambledon and telling him all is well. I'll do it now." Warnford went to the telephone but returned almost immediately. "He's out; he might be back about six. Well, there's no violent hurry."

"No," said Marden.

"Anything the matter?"

"Yes. I told you Palmer—the fence down in Hoxton—was trying to get me to sell him all the Desmond diamonds at once, didn't I? Here's his Final Notice before taking action; he ought to have written it in red ink like the income-tax people—blast him!" Marden threw the letter across the table for Warnford to read; it was quite short and said merely, "If you do not do as I ask within two days from now you know what I'll do about it and no more kidding."

"Swine," said Warnford thoughtfully.

"I wish somebody'd stick him. I wish he'd get run over. Here am I, just settling down all happy and comfortable, and he sticks his blasted oar in. You see what comes next, don't you? If I sold him the diamonds it wouldn't be long before the screw was put on again to get him something else. I'd like to push him under a bus. I'd like to throw him in the river, tied to a sack of coals. I'd like to take him up in an airplane and drop him into the North Sea. I'd like to blow him up with dynamite—"

"Dynamite," said Warnford. "I've got an idea. Could you break open his safe?"

"If I had ten minutes alone with it, yes. Why?"

"There's your dynamite."

"What? The satchel?"

"If that was in his safe and Hambledon found it there I think you'd have to employ another fence for the rest of your diamonds."

"It's an idea," said Marden. "There might be some other stuff in there too; I shouldn't wonder. I expect he's got, or soon will have, that American woman's rubies that were pinched from the Park Lane Hotel last week. He certainly had the Catherden Manor collection of miniatures—mainly Cosways—he probably has them still. Recognizable stuff like that is generally a slow deal; that's why he pays so little for them. Pearls are the same. Oh, and he had the coins from Barkham Abbey too; Collard told me so last week."

"A careful plan of campaign is necessary," said Warnford. "Tomorrow's Sunday; we've got twenty-four hours to think up something."

On Monday morning Edward Palmer received a letter from Marden. It was a trifle truculent in tone and suggested that the said Palmer was the sort of man who'd poison his grandmother and then sell the flowers off her grave, but it agreed to let him have the balance of the Desmond diamonds all together. Marden added haughtily that it was not convenient to bring them to Hoxton and suggested a meeting at Palmer's c ity office at 9 P.M. on the following day, Tuesday, September the 6th, 1938. A reply confirming the appointment should be sent by return of post.

Palmer read it and laughed. "On your 'igh 'orse, eh? 'Oo'd think you was a jailbird once and soon will be again? Never mind, me lord; I'll twist you for that." He wrote, agreeing to the time and place for the meeting, and Marden received the answer on Tuesday morning. He went out and bought a couple of strong door bolts while Warnford rang up the Foreign Office. He was more fortunate this time; a voice at the other end said, "Hambledon, Foreign Office, speaking."

"Good morning," said Warnford. "It's me again. Do you know Tilmore Street, Hoxton?"

"Not yet," said Hambledon hopefully.

"Forty-seven Tilmore Street—four seven—is the home of one Edward Palmer, a pork butcher. He is also a receiver of stolen goods. He's got some nice stolen goods in his safe," said Warnford with emphasis.

"Oh, has he? Very interesting."

"Only one of the items will interest you, I think, but the police will be definitely thrilled over the rest. In the stately courts of Scotland Yard there will be ceremonial dances."

"I shall look forward to seeing them."

"If you will obtain a search warrant and a suitable posse of police and enter the house at exactly nine forty-five tonight, a happy time will, I hope, be had by one and all."

"At 9:45 P.M.?" repeated Hambledon, making a note on the corner of his blotting paper.

"Yes. I'm sorry if it's an inconvenient hour, but it's the only one possible under the circumstances. Can you make it exactly nine forty-five?"

"I'll make a point of it. Will you be there?"

"Good lord, no," said Warnford in horrified tones. "I'm not a policeman, nor—except in rare cases—a receiver of stolen goods."

"I'm sorry to hear it. I mean," added Hambledon hastily, "I'm sorry you won't be there. I was hoping to meet you. Look here, why be so mysterious? I am deeply in your debt already, and if this comes off I shall owe you more than I can say. I want to talk to you."

"Thanks most awfully; I should like it too. But I don't want you to know who I am just yet. I have a reason for that. I'll tell you all about it someday when I've cleared something up. At nine forty-five tonight, then, you will be at 47 Tilmore Street?"

"I shall attend in person," said Hambledon, and there was a click at the far end of the line. Hambledon rose from his chair, took his hat from its peg, looked at it thoughtfully for a moment, and then flung it up to the ceiling. He then retrieved it from the wastepaper basket into which it fell, avoided his secretary's eye, and went out to find Denton.

"My city office," was the dignified name Palmer applied to one grubby attic room on the fourth floor of a dingy building in a turning off Moorgate Street. Nobody lived there except the caretaker who inhabited the basement; the rest of the house was let off as offices to firms of varying importance; the higher, the less eminent. Most of the tenants went away at five or six in the evening, but there were usually one or two working late for one reason or another, and the front doors were never locked till after ten o'clock or even later. On this Tuesday evening at half-past eight a tall young man came rushing in as one late for an appointment and made for the stairs. He passed the caretaker on the first flight and, saying hastily, "Mr. Green not gone, has he?" dashed on upwards two steps at a time without waiting for an answer. The caretaker merely murmured, "I dunno; 'ow should I know?" and retired to the basement.

Warnford proceeded more quietly as he went up. There was a light showing through glass door panels on the first and second floors, none on the third floor, and none on the fourth. He produced a gimlet, a screwdriver, two bolts, and some screws from his pocket and set to work on a door which had a printed card in a brass frame on it; the name was E.M. Palmer, no profession mentioned. In ten minutes Warnford had finished his job, put his tools back in his pocket, and looked up at the light. It was out of reach of most men, but he had long arms; he wrapped his handkerchief round his fingers and removed the electric bulb. Only a dim light came up the stairs from the lights below and did not illuminate the darker corners of the top landing. He buried the bulb in a sand bucket. "I don't think you'll notice those bolts now," he murmured, and went unhurriedly away without meeting the caretaker again.

Warnford returned to the point where he had left the Bentley with Marden inside and said, "All's well so far, and I've doused the light on the top landing. It is now a quarter to nine; if Palmer's punctual we should just fit the other job in comfortably."

The Bentley was standing at a point not too near the door of the offices, but near enough to see who came in or went out. Marden pulled his hat over his eyes and sat low in the car, watching the passersby; there were very few people about in the city at that hour. The time dragged slowly on, and presently all the neighboring clocks struck the hour.

"Hope he's not going to be late," said Marden uneasily.

"If he comes in the next ten minutes it'll do," said Warnford. "Only just, but we should manage."

"I don't want to sandbag his housekeeper," said Marden. "We want time to persuade her."

"What's he like to look at?"

"Big fat man, pasty-faced blighter—here he comes." Marden bent down hastily as one searching for something dropped, and Warnford watched a large man in an alpaca overcoat and smoking a fat cigar turn in from Moorgate Street and enter the building.

"There's your bird. Give him a minute or two to get well inside; he may mess about trying to switch on the landing light. Just a little longer. Yes, I should think you could go now. Best of luck."

When Marden reached the top floor Palmer's door was ajar; when he heard footsteps he turned towards it.

"You're late," he began, but instead of the door opening wider it was suddenly shut, and the rattle of bolts sounded from outside.

"That's done that bit," said Marden, returning to the car.

"Good," said Warnford. "Just timed it nicely."

The Bentley flashed through the streets and stopped round a corner off Tilmore Street; Marden went first to number forty-seven with Warnford lagging behind.

They were both carrying small attaché cases.

Marden knocked at the door and when the housekeeper opened it asked if Mr. Palmer was in.

"No, 'e's out."

"Not really? I arranged to meet him here tonight; it's very urgent. You know me."

"Yes, sir. 'E's only just this moment gone; 'e said 'e'd be about an hour."

Marden exhibited disappointment and vexation and asked if she had any idea where he'd gone. He knew Palmer never told his housekeeper anything.

"Sorry, no idea."

"I can't possibly wait an hour or more. Look here, I'd better come in and write him a note. There's paper and pens in his room."

The woman hesitated, but Marden overruled her, and they passed upstairs together to the sitting room in which Palmer interviewed clients when he was at home. There was a large desk in the middle of the room and an even larger safe in the corner. Marden sat down at the desk, selected a sheet of paper and a pen, dated the letter, and paused for thought. "Dear Palmer," he wrote, and drummed with his fingers on the desk. "Damned awkward, this is," he said aloud. "I can't think how he came to be out tonight."

"Must be some mistake," said the woman, who was fidgeting round the room instead of going away. He had expected her to insist on staying there. Just as Marden was writing, "There seems to have been some mistake," there came a knock at the front door.

"Now who's that?" said the woman, and moved uncertainly towards the door.

"Another visitor, I suppose," said Marden indifferently, and went on writing.

"P'raps 'e'll go away."

"Maybe," said Marden, but after a short pause the knock was repeated.

"Oh well, s'pose I'd best go and see," said the woman, and drifted off downstairs. When she opened the front door she found a tall man outside who took off his hat politely and said, "Good evening, madam. You have a Hoover, I believe."

"Yus, I 'ave," she said, making to shut the door, "an' I don't want another."

"Naturally not, madam," said Warnford, putting his foot in the way of the door. "I must apologize for calling so late, but I've been delayed—"

"I don't want nothin', I tell you. Take your foot out or I'll—"

"I don't want you to buy anything, madam. The Hoover people have sent me round—" There followed a long story about a new fitting for brushing clothes, a gadget which, in point of fact, Ashling had persuaded Warnford to get only a week earlier. The company did not wish the lady to buy it; they only wanted to leave it with her for a week on trial. If after that time she didn't want to keep it she could hand it back and there would be no argument and no charge. It really was a very useful fitting for furniture as well as clothes.

The woman hesitated, and in the pause a clock in the house struck half-past nine.

"I see your Hoover standing in the corner over there," said Warnford. It always stood there; that was how they knew she had one. "Let me just attach this fitting for a moment and show you how it works. It's really very good. I've just got one myself, and my wife's enthusiastic about it."

"Well, I don't mind you just showin' me, but I'm not promisin' to buy one, mind."

"Of course not, madam." So the banshee howl of a vacuum cleaner rang through the house till Marden came running down the stairs and, saying hastily, "I've left the note," went out. Warnford cut short his patter, left the fitting with the housekeeper, and followed as quickly as possible, wiping his brow and saying, "Gosh! A near thing. Hambledon's due in seven minutes. I thought you were never coming down."

In Palmer's office building it was the caretaker's hour for supper, and, snug in his basement room with a fried kipper, a pot of tea, and an Edgar Wallace propped up against the loaf, he heard no sound of Palmer's yells and bangs. The other tenants who were still there when Warnford screwed the bolts on Palmer's door had gone home in the meantime, and it was a long half-hour before the caretaker laid down his book and told the cat he supposed it was about time he went round to lock up. As soon as he reached the hall he heard muffled noises above and at once jumped to the conclusion that there was a fight going on in one of the offices. "If they don't stop that at once an' go 'ome I'll get the police in; so I will an' so I'll tell 'em. I'll report 'em, too, carryin' on like this," he said, stumping angrily up the stairs, but by the time he reached the second floor he realized it was someone who was locked in and calling for him. "Let me out! let me out! Jackson! Jackson! You — — —, where are you? Jackson!"

"Coming," said Jackson surlily. "All dark up 'ere," he added, trying vainly to switch the light on. "Bulb's blown, I s'pose. Ain't you got your key or what's the matter?" he shouted through the dimly seen door.

"Of course I've got my key, you old fool. The door's bolted on the outside. Undo the bolts!"

"Bolts? There ain't no bolts on the outsides of these doors," said Jackson, peering in the darkness. "Yes, there is though. Well, 'ooever put them on?" He slid the bolts back deliberately, and Palmer fairly bounced out, his usually pasty face purple with fury. "Where've you been all this time? I thought you were supposed to look after these offices, and 'ere 'ave I been yelling my 'ead off this 'alf-hour."

"Eatin' my supper," said Jackson grumpily. "I suppose even a caretaker can eat sometimes? 'Ow was I to know you'd bin an' got yourself bolted in?" But Palmer was running down the stairs and made no answer. He hurried through the streets as fast as his short wind would let him; he hadn't been bolted in there for nothing, and there was all that stuff in the safe at home. That Marden would be sorry if he tried any funny business with Edward Palmer.

He turned into Tilmore Street, which seemed quieter than usual. The inhabitants of Tilmore Street had seen a number of large men arrive at number forty-seven, some of them in the familiar blue uniform, and they had gone indoors at once and stayed there. Palmer put his latchkey in the lock, but the door refused to open.

"The old fool's locked me out," fumed Palmer, referring to the housekeeper. "Don't know what's the matter with me tonight; seem surrounded by blasted old idiots." He pealed the bell violently, anxious about what might have happened at home while he had been decoyed away. Somebody might have tied up the housekeeper and robbed the safe—and other places if they could find them.

Someone fumbled with locks and bolts inside the door, opened it a few inches, and then had to shut it again to undo the chain. Palmer's temper flared up again. "What you mean by it, locking me out? Open the door, you clumsy old fool! Locked in one place, locked out of another—hurry up, can't you? What's the—?"

The door opened; he charged in, and it was at once shut and bolted behind him. He looked round; it was not his housekeeper but a constable in uniform.

"'Ere," said Palmer in a suddenly deflated voice, "what's all this? 'Oo called you in? 'As there bin a burglary, or what?"

Another man in the uniform of an inspector came out of a room on the left and said no, there had been no burglary, and was he Mr. Edward Palmer? Palmer said quite mildly that he was and then drew a long breath and began to storm again. What were they all doing in his house, and would they kindly clear out at once?

"There's a gentleman upstairs who wants to see you," said the inspector. "Will you go up, please?"

"When I please, not before. Once more before I throw you out, what are you doing in my 'ouse?"

"Oh, just looking for something."

"Where's your warrant?"

"Here," said the inspector, and produced it. "Now, will you please come upstairs?"

"No, I'm damned if I do," said Palmer, losing his head, and he turned and charged the constable by the door. There was immediately a scene of considerable disorder; the constable went down with a savage kick on the knee but still clung like a limpet to Palmer's coat while he was trying to open the door and being collared by the inspector from behind. Palmer managed to undo the bolts but was overpowered before he got the door open. He was sat on, handcuffed, and told that if he tried that one again it would be the worse for him. He looked round and saw more police, some of them with their truncheons drawn, and gave up.

"I dunno what it's all about," he complained. "Can't a fellow come 'ome wivout—?"

"Oh, shut up," said the inspector crossly, for his nose was bleeding. "Take him upstairs, some of you. Gibson, you'd better report to the doctor with that knee; sit down over there till the cars come back. Mullins, get the cars back now. You, Palmer, will be charged with assaulting the police in the execution of their duty, if nothing else. Get on upstairs!"

In Palmer's business room on the first floor, the same in which Marden had written his note an hour earlier, he found one man going through the drawers of his desk, another man walking round the room with a sort of clumsy dancing step—in point of fact, he was testing for loose boards—and two men standing by his safe, looking at it. One of these was a short spare man who did not look like a policeman.

"This is Palmer, sir," said one of his escort, and pushed him forward. The short man turned round and stared at him.

"So you're Palmer. This is your safe, isn't it?"

"It is. May I ask—?"

"Not at the moment. Have you the keys of this safe?"

"No."

"Where are they?"

"What's that to do with you?"

Hambledon's jaw came forward and he said ominously, "If I were you, Palmer, I'd try and be civil; that is, if you know how. I dislike impertinence, Palmer."

Palmer tried to stare back but failed.

"Where are the keys?"

"My wife's got 'em."

"Where is your wife?"

"Down at Brighton."

"Oh. Well, I'm afraid we can't wait for that. Better get your experts in, Superintendent; I want that safe opened here and now. It's a pity you haven't got the keys, Palmer; it might save damage."

Palmer hesitated, met that hard stare again, and said confusedly, "I dunno—I b'lieve, after all, she left 'em with me." He put his fingers in his breast pocket and produced the keys; the superintendent took them and opened the safe.

Inside were a number of parcels, one or two little wash-leather bags, and, on top of everything else, a fairly large leather case for papers, something like a music satchel. Hambledon saw it and instantly looked at Palmer, whose face expressed perfectly genuine surprise.

"I never saw that before," he said. "I never put it there. I dunno what it is. I dunno what 'alf this stuff is," he went on imaginatively. "All those little parcels and bits—someone's planted 'em on me."

"Oh yeah?" said the superintendent, opening one of the parcels while Hambledon grabbed the King's Messenger's satchel. "These are the Park Lane rubies, or some of them."

Hambledon ran hastily through the contents of the satchel, and an expression of deep satisfaction spread across his face.

"I never put that there, mister," protested Palmer again.

"Never mind," said Hambledon cheerfully. "I expect you'll have quite enough to explain away without bothering about that."

11

Per Nocte ad Quod

NORMALLY the ways of the civil police lead through more open country than the dark paths followed by the secret service; indeed, the doings of its members do not always meet with police approval. Sometimes the police are called in to help and do so loyally without asking questions, although their natural curiosity must occasionally amount to agony. In the case of Palmer the receiver, however, the functions of police and Intelligence overlapped so much that a certain amount of explanation was necessary, and Hambledon entertained at his office Chief Inspector William Bagshott to receive it. Bagshott was a tall man with thick black hair turning gray, a lean face, and an amused expression which alternately terrified and infuriated evildoers. The more amused he looked, the less they liked it, and generally with reason.

Hambledon told him frankly that he had received a good deal of assistance during the past few months from two men whose names he did not know and whom he had never met. "One of 'em rings me up on the telephone or sends me letters occasionally, but I've never seen either of 'em to my knowledge. This one admitted quite frankly that he had a reason for lying doggo at the moment but promised to tell me all about it someday." Hambledon went on to give Bagshott an outline of the story about the theft of the King's Messenger's satchel, saying it contained papers of the utmost importance, without detailing what they were. He told Bagshott how he had been instructed to raid Palmer's house and had found the satchel in the safe on top of a lot of miscellaneous valuables, "the property of various owners, as the auctioneers say."

"Yes," said Bagshott. "We were very pleased about that. We didn't know that Palmer was a receiver. One receiver put out of commission puts about fourteen burglars out too. It's no good stealing stuff if you can't sell it."

"Quite," said Hambledon. "So I returned the papers to those who so earnestly desired them," he continued, "and collected much credit thereby, I'm glad to say. One tactless individual did ask me how and where I found them, but I merely replied coldly that it was not in the interests of the Service to disclose our methods, and everybody shushed him. Very pleasant."

"Something ought really to be done for the man who actually worked the trick," said Bagshott. "Unless you pass on your O.B.E., or whatever they reward you with, to him."

"I would do quite a lot for him if I could find him. I spent some time last night, when I might have been sleeping, working out how they did it. Palmer told me he'd gone to his city office to keep an appointment with a man and was bolted in. Bolts for the purpose had been affixed to the outside of his office door, and he's sure they weren't there in the morning. Police who went to his office to have a look round report that the caretaker complained that the bulb had been stolen out of the light on the top landing; that's where his office is."

"So they did that job after dark," said Bagshott.

"Yes. Leaving it as late as possible, I imagine, so as not to be seen by the other tenants. Perhaps they did it on their way to Tilmore Street. Because one of them waited till Palmer had left his own house and then gained admittance under some pretext and planted the satchel in the safe. Palmer's surprise at seeing it there was undoubtedly genuine."

"The housekeeper there could tell you something about that, no doubt. Why didn't you ask her?"

"Because the place was buzzing with your men and I thought I'd rather talk to her on that subject when we were alone. In any case, the point that interests me is not the detail of the scheme, but why they had a grudge against this receiver. There's no doubt they had a grudge; they planted the papers there in order to have the place searched, knowing what the police would find. Who has a grudge against a receiver, Bagshott?"

"A dissatisfied burglar, presumably; they are completely in the receivers' hands. They ought to form a Burglars' and Housebreakers' Union to enforce their just claims," said Bagshott. "Motto: *Per nocte ad quod*."

"Yes. Or, 'Nightly but knightly.' I didn't want you police looking for my friend because I was afraid of what you'd find. I think you'd find a burglar, don't you? I think that's why he's so backward in coming forward, burglariousness must be a bit shy-making."

"It looked like a burglar all the time, didn't it, all this aptitude towards safes?"

"He might have been an employee in a firm of safe manufacturers. However, all this means we have got to walk delicately. I don't want them getting scared by the police and running away; they're far too useful to me. Would you mind going down to Tilmore Street and talking to Palmer's housekeeper? I'd like you to go this morning. I can't, and I think she is leaving at once. She was very horrified last night and said she didn't hold with all these goings on. She is rather prim and proper."

"And not very intelligent, I imagine, if she had no idea of what was going on," said Bagshott, picking up his hat.

"Perhaps she merely hasn't got an enquiring mind," suggested Hambledon.

"Same thing," said Bagshott, and departed on his errand.

He returned an hour later, carrying a vacuum cleaner and several fittings. "I've sent a man from Scotland Yard," he said, "along to Tilmore Street at once to get her fingerprints; they'll be all over this and must be sorted out from someone else's. She's leaving this afternoon; she was packing when I was there." He told Hambledon the history of the day before as told by the housekeeper. Mr. Palmer went out; five minutes later a man called, expecting to find him in; said he had an appointment. Yes, she'd seen this man before several times. No, she didn't know his name or where he lived; Mr. Palmer was not one as liked people asking questions about his visitors or any of his affairs. A middle-sized man, neither big nor small. No, not young, but certainly not old, and she didn't think she could describe his face; it was one of those ordinary faces.

Hambledon sighed patiently, and Bagshott agreed with him. The visitor went upstairs to write a note to Mr. Palmer, and she went too; she wasn't supposed to leave visitors alone in that room or, indeed, anywhere in the house. Then a man came to the door and wanted her to try a new attachment to the Hoover.

"So that's how it was worked," said Hambledon. "Very neat bit of timing."

"I asked her if she found the note," said Bagshott, "and she said no, she hadn't seen it. In fact, she hadn't looked for it."

"All the same if she had," said Hambledon. "He didn't leave it, of course. I wouldn't have done, in his place."

"She was a bit better at describing the second man. She said he was about twenty-five, tall and dark; she supposed some would call him good-looking."

"I know, I know," said Hambledon. "With sad eyes and a merry laugh. She'd never seen him before, evidently, whereas she had seen the older man. From this we deduce, Watson, that the older man is the burglar with a grudge against receivers, but it's the younger one who communicates with me. Palmer knows who the older man is, and Palmer is now going to tell me, if you will let me see him. I'll ring you up and tell you all about it this evening; I shall probably want your help again if you don't mind."

Hambledon obtained admission to Palmer's cell, where he was gloomily awaiting the further processes of justice. The receiver was sitting on the edge of his bed, gazing mournfully into the distance, and the sight of his visitor did not seem to cheer him up.

"It's you again," he said. "It's no use your coming trying to worm things out of me; I'm not talking except through my solicitor."

"You're in quite enough of a mess already, Palmer, without making matters worse by truculence. I want some informa—"

"I tell you, I'm not talking to you"—something—"police without my solicitor's here."

"I'm not the police."

"Then that's worse, and I'm not talking to you at all."

"I'm not interested in your filthy past in the slightest," said Hambledon impatiently. "All I want is the name and address of the man who put you here."

"Eh? Oh, 'im. I'll deal with 'im myself, and 'e'll pretty soon wish 'e'd never done it."

"You know," said Hambledon, disregarding this, "the man who sent you a note asking you to meet him at your office. You trotted off like a good little boy, didn't you? Then you were had for a mug."

The man's sallow face darkened with anger, but he made no reply, and Hambledon went on: "You should cultivate observation. Why didn't you see the bolts on your door?"

"'Cause it was dark," growled Palmer. "The bulb outside 'ad gone."

"It had gone because he took it away, you silly mutt. You must have looked a fool, banging the door and yelling for the caretaker to let you out, like a naughty boy locked in the nursery."

"Oh, shut up," said Palmer, wriggling uneasily.

"What's his name?"

"What d'you want to know for?"

"That's my business. What's his name?"

"What's it worth to me to tell you? If I tell you, will you get something knocked off my sentence?"

"Now you're talking. I can't do anything about your sentence for receiving, but I'll tell you what I will do. Do you remember a satchel which was in your safe?"

"Yes, but I don't know nothing about that, mister," said Palmer eagerly. "I never put it there; I never seen it before."

"You say so; can you prove it? Of course not. But that satchel will land you in more trouble than all the rest of the stuff put together."

"Blimy, what was in it?"

"Never mind. Tell me about this man, and nothing more will be said about the satchel. That's worth a lot if only you knew it."

"O.K. Name of Marden—John Marden. Don't know where 'e lives; uses a 'commodation address. 'E's a burglar and a pretty good one. Only been caught once and then got off light, first offense. Doesn't work often; when 'e does it's something big."

"Known him long?"

"Some years."

"What's his accommodation address?"

"I don't know; 'e uses a different one every time. I can't remember the las' one and, anyway, I expec' 'e calls for 'is letters."

"I see. Know any more about him?"

"Not much. Except I s'pose 'e's what you'd call a gentleman," said Palmer scornfully. "Very 'aughty, 'e can be. Got a little place down in Kent somewhere, I believe."

"Down in Kent. Where?"

"I dunno. That's all I do know 'bout 'im."

Further questions having failed to produce any more results, Hambledon left the receiver to his painful thoughts and got in touch with Bagshott at Scotland Yard.

"I want to talk to a man named John Marden who was, I believe, a burglar at one time; he was convicted once, if I've been told the truth. I don't want him arrested, mind—that's very important—I just want to talk to him. It would probably be enough if you could find out his present address. . . . Thank you very much, I'm sure you will. By the way, did you find any fingerprints on the vacuum cleaner?"

"Yes, the housekeeper's and another's. Neither are among our records."

"No? Well, we can't be lucky every time. Good-bye."

"I thought it was a bit odd," said Hambledon to Reck after dinner that evening. "I mean Palmer saying Marden had a little place down in Kent. I immediately wondered who Frog Farm belonged to; I have a suspicious mind. So I rang up dear Sergeant Coot on the telephone and asked him. He told me that Frog Farm belongs to an elderly widow who lives at Hastings. I forget her name, but it isn't Marden. So unless Marden is an elderly widow in disguise or the elderly widow at Hastings is a burglar in disguise, I was barking up the wrong tree. I thought it was just worth trying."

"Talking about elderly widows, is there any more news of the mysterious Mrs. Ferne of Princes Square, Bayswater? The lady with the cats."

"Still leading a sober and upright life. One of her cats died not long ago, and she insisted on having it buried in the hotel garden with a tombstone over it. 'To dear Heliogabala, a blue Persian. Alas, that spring should vanish with the rose, That youth's sweet-scented manuscript should close.' "

"Wunderbar!" said Reck.

Warnford and Marden, very naturally pleased with the outcome of their efforts, decided to have a little celebration. Dinner somewhere—say the Auberge de France or somewhere like that—and a show in tune with their cheerful mood; they dined early in order not to be too late at the theater. Hambledon's instructions to Scotland Yard about picking up Marden had been circulated, but perhaps insufficient emphasis had been laid on the need for tact. Warnford and

Marden were in the act of turning off Piccadilly Circus into Shaftesbury Avenue; there were a lot of people on the pavement who jostled them apart for a moment. Marden, just behind his friend, bumped into a thin-faced young man in a raincoat and apologized. The young man, who was a detective upon his lawful occasions, looked at Marden and recognized him instantly, since it so happened that at Marden's only conviction he had assisted Gunn, now of the Spotted Cow, to make the arrest. For policemen may forget their first love and the house where they were born, but never, while Reason's lamp still shines within them, their first prisoner. He looked, recognized, and acted precipitately.

"Here," he said. "I want you."

Marden immediately fled. He overtook Warnford, dodged through the crowd, and disappeared. Warnford had heard the remark and went into action. As the detective came level with him he tripped him up and fell on him, scrambled to his feet again, holding the detective firmly by the wrist, and yelled for the police. Piccadilly Circus is a good place to call for the police; there are always plenty there. One came, running, and Warnford promptly gave his prisoner in charge.

"This man," he complained, "jostled me so roughly as to throw me down. Of course he was trying to pick my pockets. There is too much of this sort of thing in London, officer. Take him away and tell him not to."

"Have you lost anything, sir?" asked the constable, who did not happen to know this particular detective.

"I am a police officer," said the detective, wriggling in the constable's grasp. "Let me get my card out."

The constable hesitated, but Warnford merely sneered. "Police officer! Hark at him. Hang onto him, officer; don't let him get away with a yarn like that." Warnford stood under a lamppost and turned out his pockets. A twist of string, cigarette case and matches, loose silver in one pocket, loose coppers in another, a slim wallet with pound notes in it, a small brass bolt with a nut on it, half an inch of sealing wax and a tram ticket. During this time the detective was not silent.

"I am Detective-Inspector Marshall from Scotland Yard."

"Says you! How's your brother Snelgrove?"

"If you"—to the constable—"will have the goodness to release my wrist I will—"

Warnford came to the conclusion that this had gone on long enough; Marden was probably a mile away by now. "All right, officer, let him produce it. I'll catch him if he runs away."

The detective produced his official card, and Warnford immediately apologized. He said he was most frightfully sorry, Inspector, but how was he to know? A friend of his had had his pocket picked of a perfectly good gold cigarette case just outside the Carlton, of all places, only last Tuesday, or was it Wednesday?

No, Tuesday, because it was Wednesday when Toots told him about it, and she said "last night," by a feller who bumped into him just like that, and old Bob thought nothing of it till he put his hand in his pocket for the case a few minutes later and, dash it, it had gone. So had the feller, of course—miles away by that time. "Made an impression on my mind, Inspector; it did really. So of course when you came butting into me I thought, 'Ha! Here we are again. Same chap, perhaps.' So I grabbed you. You see, if you had been the same chap I might have got old Bob's case back too, mightn't I? I'm most frightfully sorry, Inspector, but you do understand, don't you? No ill feeling, and all that? Come and have one with me."

But the inspector, who had been trying vainly to edge away, declined with regrets and departed upon his original errand. He had given Marden up as a bad job ten minutes earlier, so he merely reported having seen him in Piccadilly Circus and left it at that.

Warnford took it for granted that the evening's program was canceled and went straight home, where he found Marden waiting for him in a state of some agitation.

"You see what's happened, don't you? This is that swine Palmer's work. He has informed the police about me, and they're after me for the Desmond diamonds and a dozen other things as well, for all I know. I'd leave the country, only I expect they're watching the ports." Marden was walking up and down the room. "The first thing to do is to get out of here; there's no need for you to be dragged into this. You know, I didn't expect Palmer to do this; receivers don't generally squeal. They have to come out of jail sometime and they don't want their late clients waiting for them round every corner with a loaded stick. I suppose he thought he was safe with me; I'm not the murderous type. I'll bet I'm the only one he split on."

"He must have been annoyed," said Warnford thoughtfully. "Does Palmer know you've got a house in Kent?"

"Halvings? I'm not sure; he may. I don't think the police do, though one can never be sure what they know and what they don't."

"Let's chance it," said Warnford. "I'll tell Ashling to pack a couple of suitcases at once, and we'll go down there tonight in the Bentley. It will at least give us a couple of days to think things over. What about it?"

"I don't think that's a good idea," said Marden. "If Palmer told them I'd got a place in Kent—"

"Did he know the address?"

"No, I don't think so, but that wouldn't help. They will circularize the county police to find which of them has a cottage owned by one Marden in his parish, and our local constable's known me for years. He shoots my rabbits for me. He doesn't know I'm a burglar, of course; nobody does down there."

"Pity your name wasn't Smith; it would take 'em longer to find Mr. Smith of

Kent," said Warnford. "What do we do, then, stay here? I think that's your best plan, really. Stay indoors and grow a mustache."

"How long would that take? Three weeks?"

"You can go out after dark, avoiding streetlamps," said Warnford cheerfully.

12

At the Malplaquet

NEXT MORNING, as soon after nine as is considered respectable in government offices, Bagshott rang up Hambledon on the telephone.

"About the man John Marden whom you wanted to interview," he said, "I'm afraid one of my men has made rather a bloomer." He went on to explain that when he saw a report that Marden had been seen in Piccadilly Circus he sent for the detective in question and heard the full story. He repeated it to Hambledon, who made clucking noises indicative of distress, and Bagshott apologized. "I am sorry," he said, "very sorry, and the man who did it is even sorrier. I don't encourage mistakes. Shall I circularize the Kent County Police on the off-chance that it's true Marden has a place in Kent?"

"No," said Hambledon thoughtfully, "no, I don't think so. I'd rather find them in some less official manner."

"There are the ratepayers' lists for that county," suggested Bagshott; "they ought to provide the address. Marden isn't a common name. I'm afraid that'll take some time."

"Never mind, I'll do it; thanks for the suggestion. It's a possible line, anyway."

When three days had passed without a word or a sign from Denton, Hambledon became anxious and asked for news of him from a mutual friend in Ostend. When it was reported that he was missing from the Hotel Malplaquet and that his bedroom had not received him for four nights, Hambledon became more anxious still. He armed himself with one of those peculiar identity cards which Scotland Yard issues to really important officials when they are going upon especially confidential errands and flew to Brussels, where he called upon the Belgian police.

He was received by a roundabout little man with a white mustache and imperial, who glanced at Hambledon's card and asked how he could have the honor to assist his distinguished English colleague.

"A small matter," said Hambledon, drawing up his chair and speaking in low but important tones, "but one in which the utmost discretion is necessary. A certain young man, not himself great, but a member of the most distinguished family imaginable—you understand—"

"Ah," said Monsieur Houys darkly, and nodded several times in a very solemn manner.

"He came to Ostend a week ago for a short holiday and has disappeared. I have been sent over to find him."

"These young men," said Monsieur Houys.

"Exactly. There must be no publicity."

"Of course not."

"He called himself Mr. Smith," went on Hambledon.

"They all do," said Houys wearily. "Or Müller, or whatever is the commonest surname in their country of origin."

"Discretion," repeated Hambledon urgently.

"My dear sir, discretion has become the envelope of my immortal soul," said Houys magnificently. "Where was he heard of last?"

"At the Hotel Malplaquet at Ostend."

"It is a hotel of the utmost respectability."

"He always goes to that sort of hotel," said Hambledon in a resigned tone.

"But, of course, naturally," said Houys enigmatically. "I will charge myself with the enquiry in person," he added.

"You are too good," said Hambledon warmly. "I regret—"

"Not at all. Besides being my duty, it is a pleasure to collaborate with so distinguished—"

"The pleasure is entirely mine and—"

"But the honor is mine alone," said Houys firmly. "A moment to settle my unimportant affairs—can you leave for Ostend in half an hour's time?"

They arrived together at the Hotel Malplaquet, and Tommy Hambledon stood back and left the negotiations to the Belgian. Monsieur Houys began by asking the reception clerk for the manager.

"He is not here, m'sieu."

"Who runs this hotel in his absence, madame?"

"I do."

"I should like a word with you in private; I suggest the manager's office. Here is my card, madame."

The reception clerk was a tall shapely woman with raven-black hair and a remarkably fine complexion. Nevertheless, even her color changed a little when she looked at Houys' official card. She rose to her feet and, saying, "If Messieurs would follow me," swept superbly across the hall with Houys trotting behind and Hambledon bringing up the rear. The manager's office was a stuffy little room which smelt of cigars, hair oil, and brandy and was principally furnished with a large desk and two safes. The lady begged them to be seated and went on to ask in what way she could serve M'sieu.

"This is a matter in which the utmost discretion is necessary, madame. That is why I desire to see the manager. No doubt you can put me in touch with him."

"I—I regret exceedingly that that is impossible. I do not know the manager's address at the moment. He is traveling." She twisted her fingers together.

"Where to?"

"Touring with friends, m'sieu. I do not know where they are going."

"When did he go?"

"On Tuesday."

"That is three days ago, madame," put in Hambledon. "Did he leave suddenly?"

"I—I think his decision was taken rather suddenly. The opportunity offered—"

"Exactly," said Houys. "Who were his friends, madame?"

"I do not know, m'sieu. The manager did not tell me who—"

"I think you are fencing with us, madame," said Houys in a voice which had suddenly become hard. "I am sure of it; your manner does not inspire confidence. I must tell you that it is very unwise to fence with Houys of the Belgian police. Now, when did you know he was going?"

"Not till just before he went," she said sulkily, but her eyes looked quickly from right to left.

"When do you expect him back?"

"I cannot say—"

"There is something very odd here, madame. Good businessmen do not rush off at a moment's notice, leaving no address and without saying when they will return. Did he take much money with him?"

"All the money in the hotel," she answered, giving way suddenly. "It is very worrying—of course there will be the clients' money at the end of the week, but—"

"Now you are more reasonable, madame; that is well. Tell me all about his leaving."

"I came into this office to speak to him," she began, "on Tuesday morning soon after eight, as usual, and I found him with a suitcase packed and his safe door—that one—open; he was taking money out of it. I said, 'What are you doing?' He said, 'I am going away.' I said, '*Mon Dieu*, why and where to?' He said he would write to me; he could not explain then; there was no time. He said something about having been nervous before, but this was too much. I don't know what he meant, m'sieu. Then he said good-bye and went quickly." She dabbed at her eyes delicately with a tiny handkerchief.

"Strange," said Houys, looking at Hambledon.

"Most peculiar," said Hambledon stolidly, but there was a cold feeling about his heart. What had happened to Denton to frighten the manager so much?

"You say this is his safe," said Houys. "Whose is the other?"

"It belongs to a regular customer of ours, a friend of the manager's, a Monsieur Richten."

"Is he here now?"

"No, he left on Monday night. He comes and goes, m'sieu."

"What is he like?" asked Hambledon.

"A tall man," she answered, glancing curiously at Hambledon, "a dark man with a black beard, stiff, pointed like this." She gestured.

"Nationality?" asked Houys.

"German," she answered.

"Richten, you said."

"M'sieu Victor Richten."

"Thank you, madame," said Hambledon with a polite bow. He exchanged a significant glance with Houys, who raised his eyebrows and resumed the enquiry.

"You have the keys of the safe, madame?"

"They are here," she said, producing them from her bag, and immediately broke into elegant sobs. "Find him for me, m'sieu! Find him! I am distracted with anxiety!"

"It is natural," said Houys gravely. "It is humane; it is fitting. What is there in this safe?"

"Only the business books, m'sieu."

Houys opened the safe and found, as she had said, account books, store books, and receipts, all in excellent order. There was also a long envelope, sealed but not addressed. Houys slit it open and looked at the document inside.

"Your name, madame?"

"Yvonne Elise Perigoux, widow." She dried one bright eye with the absurd handkerchief and kept the other intelligently fixed on the document.

"This would appear to be a deed of gift to you of the hotel and all it contains."

There was no doubt about her surprise; she gasped and stared like any schoolgirl. Then, "When was it dated?"

"Last June. Here is a letter to you." Houys passed it over unread, and she took it eagerly. "This is dated last Monday night," she said, read it through, and handed it back to Houys. It began, *"Très chère Yvonne,"* and said that though it tore his heart into fragments to leave her, the time had come when the anxieties of his life were becoming more than he could bear, and he was sailing the next day for South America. His prospects there were too vague for him to take the risk of involving a woman in his uncertain future, and he had therefore made over the business to her as it stood, to ensure her well-being. He thanked her in flowery and passionate terms for her kindness to him and devotion to his interests and added his sincere good wishes for her happiness and prosperity. At the end was a brief postscript, "Beware of R. I do not think he will return; if he does, refuse to admit him."

"It is evident, madame," said Houys, taking off his gold-rimmed spectacles and scratching his nose thoughtfully with the earpiece, "that he foresaw this might happen and prepared in advance as long ago as last June. Who is R.?"

"Richten," she murmured, still being overcome. "Oh, the kindness, the thoughtfulness, the—"

"Something happened on Monday, madame, which made him decide to leave on Tuesday morning. Have you any idea what it was?"

"No, m'sieu, I have not; if I had I would tell you. That Richten, he could tell you, I think. We have been so busy of late, crowded out with people, and food a difficulty; we have had no leisure to talk together, you understand. I did not see him at all on Monday night; I shall never forgive myself—"

"What do you know about him—the manager, I mean, not Richten?"

"He was frightened of something, I am sure, but he never told me about it. Men used to come and see him in private, Richten and others, and then he would be afraid. I could tell it, I who knew him so well, but he always said it was nothing."

"But you had your own opinion, madame," said Hambledon. "What did you think?"

"I think he was a German, m'sieu, though he had lived long in Belgium. He did not much like the Nazis—that I know—but I think they made him work for them. Then they put the screw on too tight and phut! He escaped." She sobbed.

"Accept, madame," said Houys gracefully, "the assurances of my sincere condolences in this sudden and unexpected shock. To have the burden of this business thrown suddenly upon your unaided hands at the same moment, it is hard."

"As for the business," she said crisply, "that will be as it has always been. It is I, Yvonne Elise Perigoux, who am the Hotel Malplaquet, m'sieu. The poor Raoul—he was too sensitive, too gentle—" She wept again.

"Console yourself, madame," said Houys. "Hotels at least do not run away to South America. Now, if I might have a word with my colleague—Have you the keys of M'sieu Richten's safe also?"

"No, m'sieu, no. He kept them himself, naturally. I have never even seen it opened. If Messieurs will excuse me, I have duties." She drifted gracefully away.

"About this fellow Richten," said Hambledon when the door was shut, "we had a hint that such a man as she describes was having a very undesirable influence on our young friend who is missing."

"They seem to have gone away on the same day," agreed Houys. "Together, possibly? I think a glance inside that safe might assist our enquiries." He tried Richten's safe door but without result. "I have an employe in Brussels who will open it for us; I will telephone for him; he will be here in two hours. In the meantime I will call on the police headquarters here. Will you accompany me?"

"I think perhaps if I talked to the people in the hotel I might not be wasting my time," said Hambledon. "I am not the distinguished and famous M'sieu Houys; I shall not alarm them." He left the Belgian issuing orders into the telephone and drifted into the bar. Almost invariably in hotels there is at least one resident whose interest in life is the affairs of his neighbors, and Hambledon was looking for the Malplaquet's specimen. The bar, however, was almost empty, and the few people there were English or American with only one interest in life, a place on a boat bound for England as soon as possible. Hambledon drank a glass of light wine and drifted into the lounge which was filling up for tea. Here were women of all shapes, sizes, and ages, harassed women, excited women, calm women, cross women, hopeful or disappointed women, and here and there one or two captured-looking men; a babble of talk filled the air. "I went down to the shipping office this morning and spoke firmly to the man. I said, 'My good man, my husband is a vice-consul and I Must have a place.' " … "I asked for Du Maurier cigarettes, and the wretched man had sold out of everything except those awful Caporals." … "She told me her children's nurse was absolutely useless traveling; she's always sick in the train." … "A most extraordinary man, my dear; I simply fled!" … "Five drops on a lump of sugar—" … "—four days ago, and she hasn't had a word from him." … "—my dear, simply too devastating."

Hambledon hesitated just inside the doorway and was bumped into from behind by a worried lady with two daughters who had just seen an empty table and wanted to grab it. He apologized, tried to get out of her way, knocked down another lady's umbrella, and apologized again, and a tall thin woman rose from an adjacent table and rescued him.

"If M'sieu would come and sit down here, there really is room if that chair were turned a little sideways, and do forgive my thrusting myself on M'sieu like this, but you did look so lost. The poor m'sieu is a newcomer here, is he not? Such a bear garden this room is at this hour, but tea is not served anywhere else."

Hambledon sank down with a sigh of relief and thanked the lady gratefully. She went on to explain that the Hotel Malplaquet wasn't generally like this; it was usually a quiet, orderly place where a poor lonely little woman could live in comfort and have all her poor little wants attended to, but, she added with a bright laugh, people like Hitler upset the lives of the most harmless people, and one just had to try to be brave. Hambledon nearly rose and fled; he had met lonely women before, but he restrained his natural terror and encouraged her. She was a resident and she had a roving eye; not much would escape that bird-like vigilance, especially if it happened to be a man so personally attractive as Charles Denton.

She told him her life's history. She was the only daughter of a serge manufacturer at Roubaix, a dear kind old man and so good to her, but trade, the atmosphere of trade—she shuddered. M'sieu would understand that to the artistic temperament it was torture. It was starvation; it was exile. In short, it bored her stiff.

She asked him where he came from, and when he told her he was English she practically fell on his neck. English, ah! Once she had nearly been English herself. Quite at the end of the last war she had been engaged to an Englishman, "the dearest fellow; of course I was a mere child then." Hambledon thought that she was now certainly turned fifty but merely mooed sympathetically and was told that they had been parted by unkind Fate. Nevertheless, she bore no malice; the name of England was music in her ears. "I have a gentle, forgiving nature, m'sieu; I cannot help it. It is weak, I know." If she could do anything, small or great, to help anyone English it made her happy for weeks.

Hambledon said that such behavior was not weakness at all but the mark of a noble character and asked whether many English people came to the Hotel Malplaquet.

She said there were usually several English families there during the season and added that though she had found it possible to forgive her Eustace, for that was his name, she found it harder to think kindly of the woman who took him from her.

Hambledon said that in really noble characters a trace of human weakness was merely endearing and asked if she had made friends with any English people who had been there recently.

The lady said that there had been such a rush of visitors of late, not so much visitors as passing migrants, that she had had no opportunity to get to know any of them and asked him whether he knew Mr. Eustace d'Arcy Jones, who lived in London.

Hambledon said he had not that felicity and asked her in turn whether she knew a certain Monsieur Richten who, he understood, often came there. She said at once that of course she knew him, a horrid German and most rude, and did he think it was really necessary to forgive everyone who had ever done one an injury?

Hambledon abandoned the indirect method in despair and, after saying that he was sure impossible perfection was not demanded of fallible human nature, told her plainly that he had come there to meet a friend of his, a Mr. Charles Smith, but seemed to have missed him somehow; did she know him at all? A tall man with a lazy manner, brown hair, blue eyes, rather a good-looking fellow in his way.

"Oh, but Mr. Smith! He and I were the greatest of friends. We would sit in a corner of the hall after dinner and comment upon the people as they went by, very naughty and unkind of us!"

"He was here, then? When did he leave?"

"He did not live here; he had a room somewhere near by and came in for meals. I haven't seen him since Monday night when he rushed off suddenly; it was very strange." She told Hambledon they were together in the hall after dinner when Richten came through with a suitcase in his hand, which seemed to remind Mr. Smith of something, for he excused himself and dashed out of the hotel. She was standing in the embrasure of one of the hall windows and looked out in time to see Monsieur Richten get into a taxi and drive away just as Mr. Smith jumped into another taxi which was drawn up just behind. He said something to the driver, and they went off in the same direction. It was strange he had not returned.

"I expect something delayed him," said Hambledon lightly, and made his escape as soon as possible. He went to look for Houys and found him in the manager's office before Richten's open safe, going through some papers which he had found inside it.

"Sooner than get into a taxi which was waiting behind that of such a man as Richten," said Houys, "especially in places where taxis do not normally wait, I would retire to my own bathroom and blow out my own brains. It would be tidier, quicker, and probably more comfortable. Besides, I might miss myself and I am sure Richten would not." The Belgian paused and looked at Hambledon with one black eyebrow cocked. "Without venturing upon any indiscretion," he went on, "may I admit that I have heard the name of Hambledon before? Would you like to see what I have found?"

"I should be interested beyond all measure," said Hambledon truthfully.

"These—not even to you can I fully display them—are photostat copies of plans of the Belgian fortifications along the German frontier. The latest plans. These others here are similar copies of the frontier arrangements of our friends the Dutch."

"M'sieu Richten has an enquiring mind, evidently," said Hambledon. "The sort of mind which shortens the life of the owner."

"It will if I can so arrange matters," said Houys grimly. "These I will pass over to you, since they appear to concern England. No doubt you will hand them on to the appropriate authority."

"Certainly," said Hambledon, and began to run his eye through them. One was a list of names. "I know some of these worthy people," he went on. "Friedrich Dunck was killed in a motor accident in Kent last week, and Ludwig Haugen had his leg broken in the same crash. Johan Melcher is also in our care. I shall hope to meet some of the others before long." He laid down the list and picked up another paper which contained notes in German; they seemed like memoranda of instructions. "George King, newspaper vendor, Comeragh Road, Hoxton. Becoming suspect; letters appear to have been tampered with. Find substitute," was one. "Somebody's been clumsy," thought Hambledon. "Pity, King was useful. Now we shall have to trace out the substitute." "Mrs. Ferne, Princes Square, Bayswater," began another note. "Good. Increase financial allotment." Hambledon remembered Warnford's comments on the lady and smiled appreciatively. She had been under observation ever since but without result; here was confirmation. There were several other remarks which meant nothing to Hambledon at the moment, but he promised himself that they soon should, then a query. "? defend the Johnsons, P. & S., falsely accused." In another hand was scribbled, "Only Jews, not worthwhile." There were other documents also, one of which would be the subject of almost tearful interest to the Admiralty.

"That's all, is it?" said Hambledon.

"My friend, I have shown you every one."

Hambledon nodded, folded up the papers, and put them away carefully in an inside pocket while the Belgian watched him with an amused expression.

"How we fence with each other, we old ones, do we not?"

"Fence, m'sieu?"

"But yes. Me, I know nothing of M'sieu Richten until today, but you arrive by air from London, and in three hours or so his safe is open and there are the plans. The young man who is missing, he is also the harmless but embarrassing *ingénu*, is he not?" said Monsieur Houys with gentle irony. "They do not send men of the calibre of M'sieu Hambledon"—he pronounced it "Armbeeldo"—"to look for missing younger sons."

"Nor," said Hambledon with a laugh, "do such men as M'sieu Houys of the Belgian police abandon all their affairs to help to look for him. We were, in point of fact, interested in this Richten, though we did not know his name or where he lived. Nor did I expect a haul like this, though I am anxious about my friend, Mr. Charles—Smith."

"As for your friend, since we know now that he left in a taxi, we will talk again with the good police of Ostend. You will come with me, will you not?" The Belgian carefully shut up Richten's empty safe.

"If the manager knew what Richten kept in his safe," said Hambledon in perfectly even tones, "one wonders why he did not expect him to come back, as he said in the letter to Madame here."

An expression of sympathy crossed the Belgian's face. "You are justified in your anxiety about your friend," he said gently, "but I do not think the poor manager would know much. He has for long been afraid, and frightened men believe the worst. Come now and we will enquire."

At the police station they told their story, and enquiries were at once set on foot to find out whether any Ostend taxis had picked up two gentlemen of the descriptions given from the door of the Hotel Malplaquet at about eight forty-five on the night of Monday last. While they were waiting for the information the *Commissaire* of the Ostend police, just by way of making polite conversation, told them that the only unusual happening in connection with taxis which had occurred lately was the case of the lunatic at Middelkirke. "That was on Monday night, too, as it happens," he said.

"Tell us about it, *M'sieu le Commissaire*," urged Hambledon.

It appeared that a taxi drew up outside the police station at Middelkirke, and the driver complained that he had had a lunatic as a fare. He had been told to drive out into the dunes, and when he stopped there in a lonely spot the fare got out and assaulted him with violence, calling him several horrid names. Whereat the taxi driver, who said he was a peace-loving man and no warrior, disengaged himself from the conflict and drove away, though he had not been paid. The fare was definitely a dangerous man, and the police ought to arrest him. While the taxi was being driven away the fare fired several shots after it but fortunately missed each time.

"Was this one of the Ostend taxis?" asked Houys.

"But no, m'sieu, he came from Brussels."

The Middelkirke police accordingly kept a lookout for this man, and in due course he came in from the dunes. When they attempted to detain him the accused became extremely violent, and it took five men to convey him inside the police station, three of the police suffering minor damage. He was accordingly charged with assaulting the police, resisting arrest, assaulting the taxi driver, discharging firearms to endanger life, and generally being a public nuisance. Hambledon was not very interested. Denton had been known to assault people with great effect when there was good reason for it, but this wholesale melee did not sound like him at all, and if he had fired at a taxi at close range he would certainly have hit it. The Commissaire said that the taxi driver's accusations had fallen to the ground since he had not returned to give evidence. Hambledon said, "Really," in a rather bored tone, and the conversation dropped.

It reawoke with a start half an hour later when the Ostend taxi drivers reported that none of them had taken a fare from or to the Malplaquet that night but that one of their number, driving down the Rue de la Chapelle at about that time, noticed two Brussels taxis standing outside the door.

"Did he notice their numbers?" asked Houys.

Yes, he had, and made a note of them. The Ostend taxi drivers were jealously on their guard against Brussels taxis trespassing on their ground; they could not be prevented from bringing fares from Brussels, but they were strictly forbidden to pick up fares in Ostend. The numbers were so-and-so.

"And the number of the taxi involved in the Middelkirke affair?" snapped Houys.

The Commissaire turned it up; it was one of them.

"A car to take us to Middelkirke instantly, please. In the meantime, let enquiries be made regarding both taxis. I will ring up Brussels with the same instructions. Please get me police headquarters, Brussels."

An inspector leaned over the Commissaire's shoulder and murmured something; the Commissaire said, "Indeed," in a surprised tone, and turned over some papers. "You are quite right," he added. "M'sieu Houys, the Middelkirke taxi was found on Tuesday morning abandoned outside the Kursaal here. As it had been reported stolen from Brussels, it was returned there."

"I will see the driver when I return to Brussels. Is that my call? Thank you."

The police car came to the door before Houys had finished his telephone call. At Middelkirke bolts flew back and doors opened before the face of Houys, to disclose a prisoner lounging three parts asleep in a cell. It was Charles Denton.

13

Bells on Their Boots

"I AM GLAD YOU HAVE COME," said the Middelkirke inspector to Houys. "I have been telephoning your office for advice on this case today, but they told me you were out. I am quite sure this prisoner is no more insane than I am, and as for having fired at the taxi, his pistol was clean when I examined it. At the same time, he did assault my police. There is Bastien, who has a jaw of the most painful; Bouget's eye is as you see yonder, and Le Clerc's nose is broken."

"What is all this?" asked Hambledon privately of Denton.

"I was had for a mug," said the tall man gloomily. "An ass, a mutt, an idiot, and a fool—I am all of them. I stepped into a taxi, was driven out miles into the dunes beyond Middelkirke and told to get out there. There was an automatic within a foot of my midriff, so I complied. He then drove away and left me."

"Did you fire at the taxi?"

"Of course not. I couldn't hit his tires in the dark and I've only got a thirty-two, not an antitank gun. I let him go and walked into Middelkirke with my shoes full of sand. On rounding a corner I became aware of a number of dark figures who immediately closed in on me. I thought it was some more of 'em and hit out. I was not in a very good temper. Eventually I was overpowered and borne away, and it then transpired I'd been fighting the police. Why didn't they say they were police? I'd have been pleased to meet them. They ought to have bells on their boots. They ought to have luminous buttons. They ought to have luminous noses and breathe through mouth organs. They ought—"

"All right, all right," said Hambledon. "I'll explain it away." He turned to Houys and told him what had happened, and the Belgian endeared himself to England forever by managing not to laugh. He arranged matters with the inspector in a few swift sentences; Hambledon provided compensation for damages, and Denton apologized all round.

On the way back to Ostend Houys asked if he could describe the taxi driver, and Denton said only in such a manner as to relieve his own feelings, not in any way which would be helpful to the police. The man had a wart on the back of his neck as well as numerous others all over his immortal soul; otherwise there was nothing. Besides, it was dark in the dunes.

"I heard one piece of news just before we left Ostend," said Houys to Hambledon. "I had made a few enquiries about our friend the manager; I wondered whether he had really gone to South America. He did not."

"Where's he gone, then?"

"To heaven, I trust," said Houys piously. "He was found dead in an alley off the docks in Rotterdam with his head bashed in. He had his passage ticket in his pocket."

"He had reason to be frightened," said Hambledon. "Will you tell Madame Perigoux?"

"I think I will write her the sad news; I do not like tears when I am not the cause. If I wish people to weep, that is another matter," added Houys grimly.

When they arrived again at the Hotel Malplaquet, Madame Perigoux met them.

"There is a man who has come," she began, "with a note from M'sieu Richten, authorizing him to open the safe. A M'sieu Albert something—here is his card."

"What have you done with him?"

"I did not know what you would wish, m'sieu, so I told him the manager's office was occupied this evening by workmen repairing the electric fire and asked him to return tomorrow. He said he would come in the morning."

"You have done well, madame. In the morning we shall be pleased to see him. Now, messieurs, a little dinner, yes? And then bed for me. I am used to a peaceful office life, not to rushing about in police cars, interviewing lunatics!"

"I was wondering," said Hambledon, "whether Richten put his gloves on before he wrote that note."

"Fingerprints, eh?" said Houys. "Madame, if you would lend us Richten's note for a short time we will return it—"

"Have it by all means," she said. "It is in the wastepaper basket by the reception desk. I threw it in there when I had read it—his fingers had touched it; I felt a repulsion; you understand? I will go and fetch it." She sailed out of the office.

"I shall hope to hear something tomorrow," said Houys, "of the other Brussels taxi—the one Richten drove away in."

Madame returned carrying a pink wastepaper basket with a gilt rim; it was half full of screwed-up paper, but the lady had a baffled expression.

"It is not here, messieurs. I will look again at all these pieces, but it is not here. I threw it on the top."

"Don't worry," said Hambledon, "to look any further. It isn't there; they thought of that one."

"But the impudence of the most brazen—"

"Madame," said Houys, "we are dealing with the Boche."

Hambledon and Denton were just finishing their coffee and rolls next morning when Houys entered the room, and Hambledon asked him if he had breakfasted.

"At seven-thirty, my friends."

"Then it's nearly time you had another," said Denton. "Getting up early is very uneconomical; one gets so hungry."

"A cup of coffee, perhaps, while we are waiting for the good M'sieu Albert Bertrand—M'sieu Richten's messenger. I rang up my Brussels office this morning to ask what news of the taxi Richten was in; they knew something about it already. On Monday afternoon two taxi drivers complained to my police that their taxis had been stolen. You will guess that these were the two taxis seen standing outside the Hotel Malplaquet in Ostend the same evening. Later that night one of them was found abandoned at the Northern Station at Brussels. This was the one Richten had gone away in, because you remember M'sieu Denton's taxi was found outside the Kursaal here in Ostend on Tuesday morning. My men enquired at the Northern Station whether anything was known about the passenger who arrived in this taxi. By one of those strokes of luck we always deserve and so seldom get, the porter who took Richten's luggage was a friend of the real taxi driver's and was surprised to see a stranger driving the car instead of his friend, though he had no time to ask questions. He remembered all about it; he told us Richten traveled in the same compartment with a Brussels businessman who was also traveling to Köln. He is now back in Brussels, and my police are asking him for everything he can remember about a tall man with a black beard who traveled with him last Monday. He will tell us; he is a good man. I shall hear again in an hour's time."

"It looks as though anyone desiring to interview Richten will have to go to Köln," said Denton casually, with a glance at Hambledon.

"A delightful city," said Houys warmly. "A pleasant trip if one has the time."

"If I ever go to Köln," said Hambledon enigmatically, "I shall have all the time there is between now and Judgment Day. I would rather Richten came back."

Presently a waiter came and murmured something in Houys' ear. He finished his coffee hastily and said, "The gentleman we expected has come. I told Madame to admit him to the manager's office at once. Shall we stroll along?"

The hall of the Malplaquet had several new guests that morning, all men, who stood or sat about, chatting idly of this and that. One was dressed as the Belgian idea of an English tourist, in a loud tweed suit and monumental boots. Houys looked them over with a casual but comprehensive glance, appeared satisfied, and led the way to the office door. The new visitors regrouped themselves in positions conveniently near this door and went on talking; just outside it stood Madame Perigoux in a listening attitude, and Houys and the two Englishmen joined her. From inside the door there came the sound of one complaining in German. "Thieves," he said audibly. "Robbers. Bandits. Jews and the sons of Jews. Rascally double-crossers."

"He seems annoyed," said Hambledon.

"Mrs. Hubbard's dog Albert," remarked Denton.

"Eh?" asked Houys, and Hambledon explained that when she got there the cupboard was bare and so the poor dog had none.

"Shall I ask the 'poor dog' what ails him, messieurs?"

"If you would, madame."

She went in and held the door ajar so that they could hear her asking what it was which distressed him. He replied in angry tones that the safe was empty; the contents had been stolen; there were confidential papers in there and money, lots of money. She had better produce them all, at once, or it would be the worse for her.

"For me, I have not touched your safe," she said indignantly, "and as for you, if you threaten me it is you who will regret it."

"You dare to argue with me, woman? You will find that there is a law even in Belgium which punishes evildoers."

"You probably stole them yourself," she said contemptuously, "and you will accuse me to cover yourself to your masters."

Houys pushed the door open and walked in. "I thought I heard someone invoke the law," he said mildly. "M'sieu Albert Bertrand, I believe." He stared hard at the man and added, "Last time we met you had a beard, I think, prison breaker. I am Houys of the Belgian police, and you are my prisoner, *M'sieu le Capitaine*." He snapped his fingers sharply; Hambledon and Denton found themselves being gently pushed aside, and the new visitors slid into the room. As they entered the prisoner was so ill advised as to produce an automatic, but one kick from the large boot of the pseudo tourist sent it flying before it could be fired.

"Scoundrel, you have broken my wrist!" yelled the prisoner, nursing it and dancing with pain. "You will pay for this when the time comes, you—!"

"Remove the prisoner," said Houys cheerfully. When the party had filed out he turned to Hambledon and said, "You are without doubt my good genius. Here is a man who was concerned with Dombret and Lutger in the theft of the plans of the Albert Canal fortifications. He escaped from jail; at least that is the official story. In point of fact, the escape was connived at by the prison governor, who subsequently regretted it. Bertrand's own government must think very highly of him; the price they paid the governor was colossal."

"He had his share of impudence to come back to Belgium after that," said Hambledon.

"I say again we are dealing with the Boche. Would you be interested to hear his examination?"

"Beyond measure," said Hambledon eagerly. He was provided with a seat in a police car on its way to the police station, and beside him, as it happened, sat the gendarme in the surprising tweeds and mountaineering boots. On the way he appeared to be busied with something on the floor of the car.

"What is it?" asked Hambledon. "Am I in your way?"

"But not in the faintest degree, m'sieu. It is but these boots. They are too big for me outside and too small inside, as it were. I remove them," and he did.

The prisoner, with his arm in a sling, did not take kindly to his examination and only replied to questions with threats of what would happen to them "someday soon" if they did not release him at once, with apologies. Houys wearied of him.

"To quote a neighbor of ours," he remarked, " 'my patience is exhausted.' You are an escaped prisoner, if not worse, and you will go back to jail to complete your sentence." He paused to read a note from Hambledon which was handed to him; it ran, "The prisoner has a wart on the back of his neck like the missing taxi driver." Houys asked privately if there were, by chance, any of the Middelkirke police on the premises.

"There is one who came with some reports."

"Ask him if he saw the taxi driver who made a complaint about his passenger on Monday night."

A gendarme went away to enquire and returned, bringing the Middelkirke policeman with him, who identified the prisoner as the taxi driver in question. Houys nodded at Hambledon and proceeded.

"Albert Bertrand, you will be remanded in custody while certain tests are made with the automatic pistol which was taken from you at the Hotel Malplaquet."

"What folly is this?"

"It is known that you were connected with the murderers of Raoul Delapre, late manager of the Malplaquet, at Rotterdam on Tuesday night. It is desired to ascertain whether the bullet which killed him was fired from that automatic."

"You become more half-witted every minute," said the prisoner contemptuously. "The man wasn't shot at all; he was hit on the head with—" His voice tailed off.

"How did you know that?"

"I—somebody told me—"

"Liar. Nobody knew except the police, and not many of them; it was kept a secret. I am not, Bertrand, the only half-witted fool in this room," added Houys complacently. "You will be handed over to the Dutch to stand your trial for complicity in that murder."

"Who cares?" said Bertrand defiantly. "You will find that I shall not be in prison long, believe me. The day will come—"

"Remove the prisoner," said Houys contemptuously. "How convenient it is," he went on, speaking to Hambledon as the proceedings terminated, "when such men as he commit a murder in the countries they dishonor with their presence. They can then be locked up comfortably without international inconvenience."

"How true," said Hambledon. "We hang them, which is even better. We haven't got any further in the matter of Richten, though, have we?"

"I will try and persuade the Dutch to ask the German authorities for the extradition of a certain Victor Richten, description so-and-so, suspected of being concerned in a murder at Rotterdam. We shan't get him, of course, but it will be amusing to hear what they say."

"They will deny all knowledge of him, naturally," said Hambledon, "but it may earn him a black mark. Such as he are not supposed to render themselves conspicuous, though in point of fact the rule doesn't seem to worry Richten. He had the impudence to try a little kidnapping in England recently—happily he was not too successful; at least he was the only one who got away."

"Impudence, it is the Boche," said Houys once more. "Ah, m'sieu, if you knew the things they do in my poor country which we have not the strength to resent. The intrusions, the insistences, the so-called tourists, the travel agencies, the hotel proprietors—it makes one sick. That prisoner tonight with his threats—This Sudeten business—how will it end?"

"In war," said Hambledon with conviction. "Either now or later, but war in the end."

"That is my opinion also. My poor deluded country—since the Franco-Belgian defensive alliance was given up the government hopes that if we give no offense and swallow all their insults we shall be allowed to remain neutral. The folly, m'sieu! The madness! The Boche plays with the small countries like the big cat with the little mice, just a pat now and again to keep us quiet, but what happens to the mice when the cat is ready? I fought in the last war, m'sieu. Now I look into the future and envy my brother who died last year."

"I cannot reassure you, m'sieu. Your government will not collaborate with ours in the slightest degree; when at last you wish to it may be too late. Still, if it comes it comes; we must beat him harder next time, that is all."

Houys was called to the telephone, somewhat to Hambledon's relief, for what was there to say? The black shadow had grown till it fell across the world, and these people had thrown their chances away.

The Belgian returned, saying that his office in Brussels had reported upon Richten. The Brussels merchant who had traveled with him in the Cologne train had been near him when they passed the customs on the frontier. Richten was evidently expected, for he was met and cordially greeted by three men whom the merchant knew to be Nazi officials.

"He has got away," said Houys. "I will give the Dutch authorities all the data I have, but it will be useless. It may make him a little more careful in his behavior when he comes here again, but I doubt even that. Where the Boche is concerned, it is we others who have to be careful in our behavior," he added bitterly.

"Courage, my friend," said Hambledon. "When the time comes we will change all that, and it will stay changed this time." He took a cordial farewell of the Belgian and returned to the Hotel Malplaquet to rejoin Denton. "Now we return to London," said Hambledon cheerfully, "where I hope to meet one John Marden. It will be a pleasure. Also, I dislike the atmosphere of Belgium at the moment; there is a feeling of impending doom which I personally find depressing."

"Like the farmyard before Christmas," suggested Denton, "if the farmyard knew what was coming. By the way, you remember the fellow who called himself Smith?—I don't mean me but the Johnsons' servant from the funny house in Apple Row."

"Yes. Common names you people do take; I'd forgotten him for the moment. He said the late-lamented manager here was his brother, didn't he?"

"I wonder if it was true," said Denton. "I wonder how much he liked his brother."

"So do I. So much so that I'd like to break the sad news to him myself just to see what happened. I can't, though, by the way; he's been deported."

But the police had no news of Marden for Hambledon on his arrival in London, and two days after his return things began to happen in Europe which drove his unidentified assistants into the background of his mind. On the evening of September the 12th Hitler addressed his faithful party assembled at Nuremberg for their annual congress, and Hambledon, in his flat overlooking St. James's Park, turned the dial of his wireless set to the Berlin wave length to hear him. Fräulein Ludmilla Rademeyer, in an upright armchair on the opposite side of the fire from Hambledon's, knitted a sock for him and listened to the voice of the Fuehrer, her eyebrows rising higher every time the scolding tirade rose to a screech. Reck, sitting by the table near the lamp, put down the photographs he was examining with a magnifying glass—he was an enthusiastic amateur photographer—and listened also, the deep lines in his thin face growing deeper as the speech continued. Hambledon himself sat huddled deep in his chair, staring at the fire, an unlighted cigarette forgotten between his fingers and the muscles at the corners of his jaw working as he clenched and unclenched his teeth. "The misery of the Sudeten Germans is without bounds!" yelled Hitler. "These Czechs intend to annihilate them. They are being oppressed in an inhuman and unbearable manner—"

"Liar," said Reck.

When the speech was over Hambledon sat up and said, "To think there was a time when I could have hit that howling dervish on the head with a brick and dropped him into the Isar, and nobody would have bothered."

"Alas for wasted opportunities," said Reck.

"I always think of him," said Fräulein Rademeyer, "as the funny little man who talked so much and had such dreadful manners."

"He is just the same today," said Hambledon, "except that he is no longer funny."

"I suppose this means war," said Reck.

"War within a week unless a miracle happens," said Hambledon.

"And if a miracle does happen, my dear?" asked the old lady.

"It might be postponed for a year, not more."

But Chamberlain flew to Berchtesgaden on the fourteenth, and the miracle began to appear. The British and French governments put pressure on the Czechs to come to terms, and as they did, so Hitler raised his terms. Another flight, to Godesburg this time, with Hitler demanding the cession of the Sudetenland to Germany. "The last problem which must be solved, and which will be solved, confronts us," he said in another speech at Berlin, and added, "This is the last territorial claim which I have to make in Europe."

"My dear, can one believe him?" said Fräulein Rademeyer doubtfully.

"No," said Hambledon promptly. "Does it sound as if anyone did? They are calling up the Army; they have mobilized the fleet."

"There is a notice outside the underground station about where we are to go to receive our gas masks," she said, "and I hear they are sending thousands of children away from London."

"They are digging trenches in the parks," said Reck.

"I never ought to have left Germany," said Hambledon gloomily. "I might have been able to do something if I'd stayed; I'm helpless here."

"Goebbels would have had you assassinated," said Reck. "He tried hard enough."

"I ought to have bumped off Goebbels, but I didn't even try. I have no excuse; I knew this was coming."

"My dear, that would have been murder," said Ludmilla Rademeyer.

"Nothing of the sort. Killing vermin isn't murder; it's an imperative duty, and I failed in it," said Hambledon savagely.

Fräulein Rademeyer glanced at Reck, who merely raised his eyebrows and said nothing. There was no arguing with Hambledon in this mood.

On September 29th Chamberlain flew to Munich, where in company with Daladier and Mussolini, for the time being on the side of peace, Hitler was prevailed upon to sign an agreement on the Sudeten problem.

" 'Peace for our time,' " said Hambledon, quoting the prime minister. "I don't believe he said it; he must know better. He said, 'Peace for *a* time.' That's what he said. I give it a year."

"I hope you're right," said Reck. "It might be a lot less."

14
Mrs. Ferne's Guest

MARDEN took his friend's advice and lay low at the flat, growing a mustache, practicing card tricks, and being bored stiff. The fact that as the mustache grew it became more and more evidently ginger made it funnier but not more exciting.

"I can't think why it's this color," he said, inspecting it in a mirror. "My hair's brown; why doesn't it match?"

"I've never seen a mustache which looked so obviously false," said the amused Warnford. "You'll have people pulling it to see if it comes off."

"Even that would be a pleasant change from staying indoors for weeks on end. How long is this going to take to pass the unshaven stage?"

"Oh, not long. Only another fortnight or so," said Warnford unkindly. But the next fortnight was filled with the Sudeten crisis, and anxiety replaced boredom as the historic days dragged by.

"I shall go back in the Army, of course," said Warnford.

"I expect they'll recall me to the colors," said Ashling. "If so be as they don't, I'll recall meself."

"I suppose they'll have me?" said Marden. "I'm turned forty."

"You've no need to tell 'em so, sir. There's many a man in the Army whose birth sustificate's got the wrong year on it."

But Munich came and postponed the war, and Marden's mustache grew from shadow to substance.

"I've been thinking," he said. "Something ought to be done about Mrs. Ferne. Blackbeard has apparently gone abroad from Dover and stayed there; the Johnson brothers have got fifteen years for drug trading. I don't think I'd better go to the Spotted Cow just now, even for the pleasure of talking to Gunn, and Mrs. Ferne is our only chance. We know she's in with 'em, whoever else isn't."

"Carried," said Warnford cheerfully. "What shall we do about it?"

"I think I'll go and spend a few days at her hotel. It will be a change too. If I wear glasses and brush my hair straight back I shouldn't be too readily recognizable, even if the police are still snooping round her. Isn't there some stuff you can brush into your hair to make it white? What do they powder footmen with?"

"Isn't it just flour? I don't know. A theatrical makeup shop would be the place. I'll go down to Wardour Street tomorrow morning if you really want something. You can't have white hair with a ginger mustache, can you?"

"I can powder the mustache too; it'll tone it down a bit. I don't want white hair all over—merely that suspicion of silver at the temples which always looks so respectable; I can't think why. It's nearly as good as a bank reference and much easier to produce."

So Mr. Marchmont arrived at the hotel in Princes Square one evening in time for dinner. The dining room was set out with many small tables, some to accommodate two people and some four; Mr. Marchmont shared one of the smaller ones with an elderly colonel since the place seemed rather full. The colonel was very inclined to be friendly.

"Sit down, sir, sit down. No, that place doesn't belong to anybody; I shall be glad to have a stable companion at feeding time."

The next table remained unoccupied for some time until a lady came in late, an elderly woman, softly stout, unfashionably dressed in trailing draperies. She greeted the colonel in passing, and he rose to his feet to answer, calling her Mrs. Ferne.

"Charming woman," he told Marden *sotto voce*, "charming. Only got one weakness, cats. Got about half a dozen of the beasts here. One's a hulking great particolored brute, tortoiseshell tabby or something. Came into my bedroom the other morning and started prowling round. I soon booted it out. Can't stand cats. When I was at Ahmedabad in '08 my bearer kept cats, and they were all over the place. Cats in the bathroom, cats under the verandah, cats everywhere. I soon thinned 'em out. I could shoot in those days."

"I wonder the management allows it," said Marden. "Hotels don't generally like pets, especially London hotels."

"Oh, she's privileged. She's lived here I don't know how long. She's got a pull with the management—owns some of the shares, I shouldn't wonder. She's given up bringing the cats down to meals; people objected to losing their Dover sole off their plates if they took their eyes off it for a second. But she's got a pull all right. Feller came here one evening with a bull terrier. Nice well-behaved beast. I like bull terriers. But Mrs. F. came downstairs with her half-dozen beauties trailing after her, and he forgot his manners. Never laughed so much in all my life. Cats everywhere: cats up the curtains, cats behind the pictures with their heads sticking over the top, believe it or not, even a cat on the top of that grandfather clock in the lounge, and the dog leaping from one chair to another after 'em. Laugh! I was helpless. But the feller had to go. Left next morning after breakfast. Oh, she's got a pull."

"She must have," said Marden, "though I don't mind cats myself. I rather like them."

"You can have 'em, for me," said the colonel.

Mrs. Ferne found the new visitor quite delightful, especially after he had helped her to bandage a long slit in Persephone's hind leg. Persephone had had a night out and had apparently fallen into low company.

"So foolish, is it not, Mr. Marchmont, the way most men seem to think it's manly to dislike cats? I blame Kipling very much for encouraging the idea in small children—in the *Just So Stories*, you know. 'The Cat That Walked by Himself'—of course you've read it. Why shouldn't cats walk by themselves if they want to?"

"Why not?" said Marden. "In fact, it's just as well. Be a bit awkward if they expected us to romp over the rooftops with 'em in the moonlight, what?"

He got on very well with Mrs. Ferne, who kindly asked him to have tea with her in her sitting room. It was a pleasant sunny room on the first floor with the bedroom beyond it and a small iron balcony overlooking the dusty laurels and smeary grass of the hotel garden. He found her an amusing woman who had traveled extensively and observed what she saw; if she tried to pump him occasionally about his past, his connections, and his interests, that was only to be expected of a hotel acquaintance, and she did it unobtrusively and with dignity. Had it not been for Ashling's account of the curious interview with Smith, the Johnson servant, when Mrs. Ferne not only paid out money on demand but apparently treated the man on terms of equality, Marden would almost have taken her for the ordinary hotel type of retired globetrotter, only distinguished by her cats—almost. For there was something about her, as Ashling had said, which was not quite right. The stout figure, the trailing draperies, the stick she used in walking, all suggested the inertia of advancing years, but something in her carriage contradicted that and suggested dynamic energy instead, as a cat's lazy stretching suggests the tigerish leap in reserve. "A dangerous woman," said Marden to himself, and became even more friendly than before.

She told him one day that she was expecting a guest to dinner that evening. "Such a dear fellow, and I have known him ever since he was in the nursery. His mother was a school friend of mine, poor Emmie! She died, you know—why do I say 'you know'? Of course you don't—about three years ago. He is very polite to an old woman; he always comes to see me when he is in town."

Marden had intended to go out that evening, but he changed his mind. When Mrs. Ferne trailed graciously across the dining room to her table she was followed by a tall man whom Marden did not see very well at first because he passed behind his chair. After the stranger had sat down Marden looked casually at him and was glad he himself had had the forethought to arrive early to dinner. One is so much less conspicuous as one of a crowd of seated diners than when one walks alone across a room. The visitor had a black beard, and Marden remembered distinctly the crisp stiffness of it against his knuckles when he hit it at Frog Farm. The man was Blackbeard.

Marden looked away quickly and reminded himself firmly how much spectacles, graying hair, and a mustache had changed his appearance. A man is apt to remember another man with whom he has fought. When the stranger's eyes did meet his, however, they did so without a sign of recognition in them, and Marden breathed more freely.

Snatches of conversation floated across from Mrs. Ferne's table. She was telling him at one time about a letter she had had from somebody called Vera, and Anna was quite a big girl now, nearly sixteen, and getting more like her father every day. At another time he was telling her about a visit to some mutual friends. "George practically runs the place now, you know; the poor old man's getting a bit doddery. Well, he's turned eighty, isn't he?" It all sounded so kindly and natural, Marden blinked for a moment and looked again. It was Blackbeard all right.

The old colonel at his table leaned across and said in a low tone, "Mrs. Ferne's boyfriend's here again."

"Oh?" said Marden. "Does he often come, then?"

"No, not often. Seen him two or three times. Can't stand the fellow. One of those standoff mind-your-own-business-damn-you wallahs." From which Marden concluded that the colonel had displayed a too kindly interest in the visitor and been snubbed. "I tell you what," went on the colonel. "I don't believe the fellow's English."

"Oh, really," said Marden, surprised by an acuteness he did not expect. "What makes you think that?"

"Oh, I don't know. One senses these things when one's knocked about the world a lot, you know. Fellow's name's Richards—that's English enough—but I bet his mother was a foreigner. I know he was educated abroad, anyway."

"Did he tell you that?"

"Not exactly. Asked him what school he was at, and the fellow bit my head off. Well, if you've been to a decent English school, why not say so, what?"

"Perhaps he was chucked out," suggested Marden uncharitably. "I was at Tonbridge myself," he added with a laugh.

"There you are. You were at Tonbridge and you say so at once. I was at Haileybury. Besides, one can tell. This fellow, pah! Can't stand him."

The hotel guests repaired to the lounge for coffee, and Marden found a seat within earshot of Mrs. Ferne. Unfortunately the other half of his little settee was immediately occupied by a lady who seized the opportunity to tell him all about the prophecies embodied in the design of the Pyramids and the layout of their passages and rooms. She was adept at the practice of dodging interruption; possibly she had come to expect it, and her voice flowed on and on, drowning the conversation of Mrs. Ferne and Mr.—what was it?—Richards. As the only words he caught were "Persephone" and "smoke-gray," he did not seem to have missed much. Not, of course, that they would have said anything significant in such surroundings, but he did not want to miss anything they said, good, bad, or trivial.

"As no doubt you know," said his tormentor, "the main passage in the Great Pyramid is at first level, then rises gradually, and finally quite sharply. This is where the British races, in which I include, of course, not only the dominions but the United States of America as well, have their destinies clearly marked out for them so plainly that a child could understand. The length of the level portion—"

Mrs. Ferne rose to her feet, saying, "Come and see her for yourself; I shall be glad of your opinion," and led the way upstairs, followed closely by the affectionately deferential Mr. Richards. Now, if only Marden were sitting on Mrs. Ferne's little iron balcony all in the dark instead of on this ridiculous sofa being talked to by this absurd woman, he might do some good. As it was—

"You remember the inverse parallel I mentioned just now," she said.

"What? Oh, ah, yes, of course."

"The seventy-five cubits."

"Yes, yes."

"There is a considerable divergence of opinion upon the exact significance of this seventy-five cubits—"

"I heard a very interesting explanation of that the other day," said Marden, feeling that something had got to be done about this. "You know the width of the Ark was fifty cubits?"

"Yes, but—"

"And seventy-five cubits is half as much again?"

"Yes, but—"

"That is a ratio of three to two, is it not?" he went on firmly. "You must admit that."

"No one would deny it, but—"

"Which proves that if the peace of the world is to be maintained the size of the British Navy must exceed all the other navies of the world in the ratio of three to two."

She stared at him.

"There is only one obvious conclusion to be drawn from this very striking coincidence," continued Marden impressively. "Do you know what it is?"

"Er—no—"

"Join the Navy League."

He rose to his feet with an air of subdued triumph and stalked solemnly up the stairs before the lady had time to think of an answer.

At the head of the stairs a passage ran straight ahead for a short distance and was then crossed by another running right and left with doors on both sides of the corridor. Mrs. Ferne's room was the third door along the turning to the left. Marden turned left and was annoyed to find an electrician upon a flight of steps near the third door, doing something to one of the passage lights. Very tiresome. However rightly absorbed in his duties an electrician may be, the spectacle of a gentleman listening intently at the keyhole of someone else's door must strike him as odd. People seldom listen at their own. Marden pulled a handful of letters out of his pocket and dropped several of them. It took him some time to pick them up because he was clumsy and dropped two of them again. There was no sound of talking inside Mrs. Ferne's door; he had an idea there might not be. If they had anything very private to say they would be safer in the bedroom beyond. He straightened up, opened the door quietly, and walked straight in, with an excuse ready if there had been anyone there. The sitting room was empty, with the light on, and the murmur of voices came from the bedroom beyond.

Marden left the door ajar behind him, walked across the room, and listened intently at the bedroom door.

He heard Blackbeard's voice, which was easy to recognize, and then the voice of another man, which surprised him. "How many more have they got in there?" he thought. "Committee meeting, or what?"

Then he distinctly heard Blackbeard's voice again, and he was describing somebody.

"About five foot eight inches tall. Slim build, rather broad shoulders. Brown hair parted on left, turning gray at temples. Short face, deep cleft in chin, thin nose, brown eyes, thin eyebrows, brown complexion, reddish mustache, left ear protrudes more than the right—"

"My golly," said Marden to himself, "he's describing me!"

"Eyes set rather deep, strong hands, signet ring left little finger. Dressed in dinner jacket, boiled shirt, overcoat probably—what color's his overcoat?"

"Oh, one of those nondescript gray things," said Mrs. Ferne. "Dark gray."

"Dark gray overcoat. Got all that? ... Well, bring the car round here—where are you exactly? ... Behind the church? Good—"

"Oh, I've got it. Portable wireless again," said Marden, inaudibly addressing himself.

"—car round to the front door; keep the engine running. He always walks out at the front door for a few minutes before turning in, they tell me. When you see him you know what to do. Don't make a fool of yourself and bump off the wrong man."

Indignation took possession of Marden and drove out any natural fear which would otherwise have seized him. If this fellow thought he could sit in a respectable London hotel and issue orders for assassination as quietly as though he were ordering a dozen of beer from the local wine merchant, he was wrong. He was very wrong. Who the devil did the half-bred mongrel think he was? Hambledon would be very interested indeed and should receive a report at the earliest possible moment. In fact, probably the most sensible thing Marden could do would be to walk straight out of the room and ring up the Foreign Office then and there. Sensible, but not satisfying. What he really wanted to do was to take the man firmly by the beard, punch the more outstanding portions of his face out through the back of his head, and throw the debris down the stairs. While he was hesitating he heard Mrs. Ferne say she had seldom been so surprised. "I thought him quite harmless. Rather a nice little man, in fact. Are you sure you're not mistaken?"

"Perfectly sure. I know I'm right. His childish attempts at disguise did not deceive me for a moment."

"But you only saw him for a moment, you tell me, and under such different circumstances."

"My good woman, when a man has suddenly attacked you without warning you remember his face forever after."

Perhaps being called "my good woman" annoyed Mrs. Ferne, or perhaps it was merely the domineering tone he used. Whatever the reason, she persisted.

"I shall go and call him up here," she said, opening the bedroom door as she spoke. "I think you ought to make quite sure. He was kind to Persephone, and it won't make any difference, if you are right."

The balcony window, which was close to the bedroom door, had long curtains drawn across it, which reached to the floor. Marden was behind these long before she finished her sentence. She walked across the room and paused to pick up her stick; Marden had a moment's fear that one of his feet was showing and moved it back.

Instantly there was a bloodcurdling yell and several sharp points sank into his ankle; he had trodden on the tail of one of the cats, and the beast had turned on him. Marden abandoned concealment and made a dash for the door; it should be an easy matter to push past the old lady.

"You!" she cried, and sprang at him as actively as one of her cats. She caught his arm in a jujitsu hold for which he was unprepared and threw herself back. Marden felt himself falling when there was a loud bang from behind him.

Mrs. Ferne released his arm, leaned against the wall by the door, and slid slowly down it, switching off the light in her fall. Marden, on the floor, shot backwards and under the table and lay still. Blackbeard leaped out of the bedroom door, stooped over Mrs. Ferne, and immediately straightened up and walked quietly out. The electrician, who must have been startled, came quickly down his stepladder, staring at Blackbeard as he approached, and began to say something. Blackbeard promptly hit him hard under the jaw, and the electrician ceased for the time to take any more interest in these curious happenings.

Blackbeard turned the corner towards the stairs and met the manager coming up.

"Is everything all right, sir? I thought I heard—"

"Perfectly all right, perfectly," said Blackbeard soothingly. "My fault entirely; I banged the door when I came out." He slipped his hand under the manager's elbow, and they went downstairs together. "It is a foul habit of mine, slamming doors; I must break myself of it." Still apologizing cheerfully, he took leave of the manager and walked out of the hotel. There was a car standing outside with the engine running; he got into it and was driven away.

Marden lay still for a moment, expecting to hear sounds of running feet and cries of alarm, but everything remained perfectly quiet. None of the other inhabitants of the passage were in their rooms at the time, and the electrician was lying quietly along the floor with his nose pressed against the skirting board.

Marden got up, dashed into the bedroom and locked the door behind him, turned hastily, and was nearly thrown by another of the bereaved cats who got under his feet. Marden bumped heavily into the wardrobe door, said something uncomplimentary to the cat, and started feverishly collecting all the papers he could find lying about; he had no time to search the room. There was a loose-leaf notebook near the wireless set, a couple of letters on the table, and a long envelope on the settee. He stuffed these hastily into his pockets, opened the window, and stepped out onto the sill. It was wide enough to stand on, so he closed the window carefully behind him and felt along the wall for the down pipe from the eaves of which he had previously taken particular notice. He had had an idea it might come in useful. He slid carefully down it and landed in the hotel back yard among dustbins and empty packing cases. There was a door in the rear wall of this which led into a narrow alley between the houses; he went out this way, not knowing that the car which had been waiting for him had already left with Blackbeard inside. Marden emerged at the end, stopped the second taxi which passed empty—he thought there might be something funny about the first—and drove back to Warnford's flat as fast as the driver would take him.

The pyramid-obsessed lady in the lounge had found another listener after Marden left her who seemed much more reasonable, not to say intelligent.

"I have a very interesting little booklet upstairs," said the lady, "which puts the matter in a very clear light. I should so much like to show it to you—I will run upstairs and get it. No, no trouble at all, a pleasure. I won't be a moment."

Her room was at the far end of Mrs. Ferne's passage, so she turned left at the top of the stairs and found the unconscious electrician still on the floor.

"Oh, the poor man," she said aloud; "he must have fallen off the steps and hurt himself. Are you much hurt? I'd better ring for help. No doubt that was the bump we heard just now."

She saw an open door almost opposite, which was Mrs. Ferne's, and entered it, meaning to ring the bell. She switched the light on and looked down.

Mrs. Ferne was lying on the floor just inside the door with a little blue hole in her temple, and the great gray cat Persephone, walking round and round the body, rubbed her head against her mistress's every time she passed it.

Marden, in the yard below, heard the shriek and broke into a run. The manager heard it and came up the stairs two steps at a time; all the guests heard it and rushed up, headed by the old colonel. Waiters, tidying the dining room, heard it and ran up; chambermaids in their mysterious lairs heard it and joined the throng; everyone heard it except the electrician, who still took no notice, even when people tripped over him.

"Murder!" shrieked the lady. "Murder!"

"What is all this?" said the manager.

"Murder!"

"For goodness' sake, stop yelping," said the colonel. "Get the police, man, at once."

"What's this man doing in the passage?"

"Who's murdered him?"

"He isn't murdered," said the colonel after a brief inspection.

"Then why is he dead?" said someone in the back row who couldn't see properly.

"Ladies! Gentlemen!" appealed the manager. "Quiet, please. Let me—"

"Nothing must be touched," said the colonel authoritatively. "Lock the door, put the key in your pocket, and send for the police."

15
And the Manager Fainted

THE MANAGER rang up the nearest police station and reported the affair. He was told that they would send somebody round at once but was mildly surprised when a short gray man with an official manner walked in thirty seconds later and said he was Detective-Inspector Barnes from Scotland Yard.

"Dear me," said the manager, "you have been quick."

"Naturally. I understand there has been a death here."

"Yes—upstairs—"

"Take me up at once, please."

The manager led the way upstairs at a smart pace, for that was the effect the gray man had upon him. "Will you wish to question everyone?" he asked nervously.

"Naturally. When I have examined the scene of the crime—if it is one. No one must leave the premises under any pretext whatever."

"No, sir. Certainly not."

They passed the still-unconscious form of the electrician, who was receiving first aid from the colonel, the hotel porter, and a couple of chambermaids, but the detective barely glanced at him.

"This the room? Is that the key? Give it to me, please. Thank you."

The detective opened the door for himself, went in, taking the key with him, and shut the door again at once. The manager, left outside in the passage, heard the key turn in the lock.

"Well, I think that is rather— No doubt detectives are busy men, but—"

Mr. Barnes wasted no time on Mrs. Ferne or on Persephone but walked straight across and tried the bedroom door. It was locked, which surprised him, but he produced a small lever from his pocket and forced it open. He looked hastily round the room, then again more thoroughly with a puzzled expression, and turned over one or two cushions.

"Where the hell did he put them, then?" he said aloud.

Nearly two hours earlier, as soon as Blackbeard had arrived at the hotel and asked for Mrs. Ferne, a telephone call went through to Tommy Hambledon from the hotel porter who was new to the place, having only been there a few weeks. The previous one had left for a better job for which, if he had only known it, he had to thank the Foreign Office. Hambledon had found the description of the visitor so interesting that he rang up Chief Inspector Bagshott about it, and both men had come to the hotel while the residents were at dinner. They were at once taken upstairs by the porter during the manager's temporary absence. Bagshott was the electrician in the corridor, wearing a shabby suit with the pockets bulging with tools. Hambledon went straight into Mrs. Ferne's bedroom and looked round for a place of concealment. Unfortunately for him the bed was of the divan type and would not receive him underneath; the only place available was the wardrobe. Hambledon got into it, left the door ajar, and waited upon events. He took great interest in everything Mrs. Ferne and her visitor had to say to each other and was enjoying himself thoroughly up to the point where Marden trod on the cat's tail.

Hambledon took the risk of opening the door wide enough to peep out while the excitement was going on but could see nothing of what happened in the farther room. Blackbeard fired one shot from an automatic and immediately left; Hambledon was just about to step out and take an active part in the proceedings when a middle-aged man with brown hair turning gray bounced into the room, locked the door, tripped over the cat, bumped into the wardrobe door, and slammed it shut. Hambledon just got his fingers out of the way in time.

After that things became, for Hambledon, a trifle confusing. Wardrobe doors have no handles on the inside, so he could not open it again. He assumed from Blackbeard's references to Frog Farm that the newcomer was probably either Warnford or Marden—Marden by the description—but he could not be sure; it might be someone else altogether. Mrs. Ferne did not come back, which, if she had received the shot, was not surprising, but where was Bagshott? Someone fell when the pistol was fired. Why was everything so quiet when one would have expected shrieks and rushings about, and what was this fellow doing?

At that point Hambledon heard the window being pushed up; a slight scuffling sound followed, and then the window closed again. Silence, more profound than ever, settled on the scene.

"He dropped something out of the window," said Hambledon to himself, "in order not to be seen with it on him, whatever it was. He will now open the door, walk downstairs with a calm unruffled countenance, and pick it up outside." No door opened, however, and no movement was to be heard.

"He didn't drop anything out," said Hambledon; "he got out—"

There was a piercing shriek, followed by cries of "Murder! Murder!" Hambledon relaxed a little. This was what one expected; this was natural; now things would begin to move, but what was Bagshott doing all this time? Voices were heard, many voices.

A door shut—that was when the manager locked the outer one—and once again quiet descended. "They are sending for the police," said Hambledon. "I am tired of being in here." He began to feel along the panels and push here and there, but the door resisted firmly. He braced his feet against the back, put his shoulder against the lock, and was just going to break out when a door opened and shut again. He stopped to listen.

The bedroom door was tried; the handle rattled again. “It’s locked, old boy,” said Hambledon softly, hoping it was Bagshott but waiting to make sure. There was a sort of splintering crash, and someone walked hurriedly in.

“If this is Bagshott he knows where I am and he’ll let me out.”

But the newcomer took no notice of the wardrobe, and presently Hambledon heard an aggrieved voice, perfectly strange to him, asking where the devil somebody had put something. There was a click, as of a switch, and a deep voice said, “Hullo?”

“Blackbeard,” muttered Hambledon. “Where did—?”

“Heinrich here,” said the strange voice in German. “I can’t see any notes; where did you put them?”

“Oh,” said Hambledon to himself, “the wireless, of course.”

“Right in front of your nose, you fool. A notebook on the wireless set and a long envelope on the settee or a chair or somewhere. Get a move on; the police will be there in a minute. Perhaps they’re on the floor; those damned cats may have pulled them down. Get them and come out.” Click.

Heinrich sighed audibly and could be heard moving chairs about and conducting a thorough, if rapid, search. “If he opens this door,” thought Hambledon, “he’ll find something he doesn’t expect. He’ll give it up in a minute and leave by the window like the other chap, and I haven’t even seen him.” He braced his feet against the back again and leaned his shoulder against the door, ready to burst out at the first sound of the window opening, but at that moment Heinrich, trying in despair the last hiding place he could see, flung the wardrobe door open wide.

The manager, still smarting under Detective-Inspector Barnes’s snubs, had hardly sat down again in his little office when two more men walked into the hotel, followed by a constable in uniform who took his stand by the front door. The manager came out to meet them.

“Good evening,” said the older of the two in a pleasant voice. “Are you the manager here? Good. I am Detective-Inspector Egan of Scotland Yard, and this is Detective-Sergeant Knight. I understand you have had some trouble here.”

“Yes, sir, we have indeed. A lady has been found shot—a Mrs. Ferne, one of our oldest residents. You would like to see—”

“Thank you, we should. Where did this happen?”

“Upstairs, sir; this way if you’ll follow me.”

“Carry on, please. I’ll leave a constable on the door if you don’t mind, just to see that nobody goes out. When did all this happen?”

“We only heard of it about ten minutes ago,” said the manager, pattering up the stairs, “but I think it occurred about five minutes before that—this way, gentlemen—when I heard a bang—"

They rounded the corner in the passage and found Bagshott still being efficiently tended but not yet responding.

"Great Scott," said Egan.

"That, sir," said the manager, "is a man from the electricity company, I understand. I don't know how he hurt himself, unless the shot startled him and he fell off the ladder. I told my people to look after him. This is the room."

"There will be a doctor here in a minute," said Egan, and left his superior officer for the time being. "This door's locked; have you the key?"

"No, sir. Inspector Barnes has it. He took it and locked himself in; he's still in there."

"Inspector Barnes? Did you say Barnes?"

"Yes, sir. Detective-Inspector Barnes from Scotland Yard, he said he was. If you knock, sir, he'll hear you."

"When did he come?"

"About ten minutes ago, sir. Just after I'd rung up—I'd only just left the phone. I said to him, 'You have been quick,' and—"

The sergeant stooped down and looked at the keyhole. "He's left the key in the lock, sir."

"Break the door in, sergeant."

"Break the door!" said the horrified manager. "Why don't you call to him?"

"Because he— What's that?"

"That" was a cry of astonishment followed by stampings, thudding noises, and exclamations of wrath. When the wardrobe door flew open Hambledon shot out as though propelled by a spring like a jack-in-the-box. He saved himself from falling by pushing Heinrich in the chest and immediately hit him hard on the nose with satisfactory results. Heinrich reacted extraordinarily promptly, when one considers how astonished he must have been, and caught Hambledon a crack in the eye which closed it for him. In spite of this he went on hammering at his adversary even if some of his blows were rather wild, and the German jumped back and pulled out an automatic. Tommy saw that quite plainly even with one eye and kicked him violently on the wrist, whereupon Heinrich dropped the gun with one hand, caught it with the other, and started shooting. He was not a left-handed shot; a picture on the wall and the wardrobe door suffered accordingly. Hambledon produced his own Luger, but it is nearly as difficult to shoot with the wrong eye as with the wrong hand. The police outside, charging the locked door with their shoulders, counted eight shots before silence supervened and the door gave way at last.

They rushed in and met Hambledon staggering out considerably war-worn, with a bullet through the top of his shoulder and the beginnings of a wonderful black eye.

"Good evening," he said. "What, another corpse in here? What an evening.

There's a dead German in the bedroom too. Where's Bagshott?"

Bagshott came to the door and stood there, holding onto the doorpost. "Thought I heard shooting," he said unsteadily. "Anyone hurt? Who shot the lady, did you?"

"Not unless it was a ricochet," said Tommy, and sat down heavily. "What is all that noise outside?"

The old colonel came to the door and said, "Excuse me, but the other guests are a little agitated; could you give me a message for them?"

"Tell the manager," began Egan, but the colonel shook his head.

"He's no good," he said. "The poor chap's fainted. These civilians, you know. No nerve."

"Tell the guests," said Hambledon, pushing a handkerchief over his shoulder under his coat, "that Mrs. Ferne and her visitor were shooting the cats and accidentally shot each other."

"Certainly, sir," said the colonel. "Did they mistake you for one of the cats?"

Hambledon stared for a moment and then grinned. "Possibly. No, tell them it was a suicide pact. Tell them this second fellow—the dead one in the bedroom—was jealous of Mrs. Ferne and her earlier visitor, so he shot her first and then himself."

"Taking eight shots to do it," commented the colonel. "Persevering sort of chap. All right, I'll tell them the police are investigating the matter and will issue a statement later, shall I? Right." He turned to go.

"I am really very much obliged to you," said Hambledon. "When the manager revives I should like to see him."

"I'll tell him," said the colonel, and went out, shutting the door behind him.

When the police doctor, who had been attending to Bagshott, had strapped up Hambledon's shoulder—it was a trivial flesh wound—Tommy and Bagshott interviewed the manager in his office. He apologized for his pitiable weakness in fainting. He had never, he said, had very strong nerves, and if the gentlemen could have heard the guests—! Then there were the police breaking down the door, and that dreadful outburst of firing; he really began to wonder if it were the I.R.A. and whether the next thing wouldn't be bombs exploding here and there on his premises.

"You have had a trying evening," said Hambledon sympathetically. "I prescribe a mild restorative—"

The manager sprang to his feet and rang the bell, apologizing again for his lack of manners. "My wits must be woolgathering. What will you have, gentlemen? Whisky, or—"

"Thank you."

"Bring the Haig," said the manager when a waiter appeared. "Now, gentlemen, anything I can tell you—"

There was, in point of fact, very little the manager could say that Hambledon did not know already about that evening, and he turned his enquiries to the past. This Mrs. Ferne, now …

Mrs. Ferne had been a resident in the hotel for a number of years, longer than the manager himself, and he had been there nearly seven years. She was a very nice lady and never gave any trouble, though other guests sometimes objected to the cats. But they were very well-behaved cats. . . . Yes, she was a lady who had a good many friends, men and women, yes, but mainly men, though the gentlemen would understand there was never the faintest breath of—oh, quite so. Sixty at least, if not more. He had occasionally put up one of her friends for the night, but usually they just called, or stayed for a meal like the gentleman tonight. Well, not noticeably foreign, though he had thought that some of them were not English.

As this didn't seem to be getting them anywhere interesting, Hambledon switched over to Blackbeard. The gentleman who visited her tonight—did the manager know anything about him?

"Richards," said the manager. "Mr. Richards." He said it in a tone of heavy irony, and Hambledon lifted his eyebrows. Mr. Richards apparently was the one dubiously colored splash on an otherwise unblemished career. "She thought I did not recognize him, gentlemen, but she was wrong. She told me the first time he came, with his beard, 'A Mr. Richards will be lunching with me today,' she said. 'A very dear friend. His mother was at school with me. Show him up to my room when he comes, and send up your best dry sherry. He does not like cocktails.' So I said, 'Yes, madam,' naturally, and when he arrived I looked at him. She thinks I do not know him again because he wears a beard and calls himself Richards. Am I a child? Two—three years ago he was a young man with a small mustache in the Tank Corps, and his name then was Rawson."

"This is very interesting indeed," said Hambledon truthfully. "Rawson, eh? In the Tank Corps."

"Yes, sir. He came here twice, possibly three times, in uniform. Mrs. Ferne said then that he was her nephew, her only sister's son."

"We ought not to speak ill of the dead," said Bagshott, "but either Mrs. Ferne had a very bad memory indeed, or she was a liar."

"Yes, sir. As for the bad memory, she thought I had one. She was wrong."

"Evidently," said Hambledon. "What happened then? Did he leave off coming here for a time?"

"Yes, sir. There was a scandal in the Tank Corps at about that time, something about some missing plans. We were all interested—the hotel staff, I mean, and some of the guests too—on account of knowing this Captain Rawson in the Tank Corps. It wasn't Captain Rawson who did it, though; it was another young officer. I can't remember his name. There was a trial—a—what do they call it—?"

"A court-martial?"

"That's it, sir. Captain Rawson gave evidence."

"In the prisoner's favor?"

"No, sir. Against him."

"Oh. What had Mrs. Ferne got to say about all this?"

"Much the same as everyone else was saying: wasn't it dreadful to think a British officer could sell his country's secrets for money, but perhaps the poor boy had got into financial difficulties and was tempted. So horrid for her nephew Victor to be mixed up with that sort of thing and have to give evidence against a brother officer. It upset him very much, she said."

"Shows a nice feeling, doesn't it?" said Hambledon. "Don't you agree, Bagshott? Well, well. Thank you very much for all you have told me. It's been most helpful; it has really. I think I'll push off now; shoulder aches a bit, you know. I expect Chief Inspector Bagshott has a few more questions to ask you. He's got to catch the blighter, you know. Good night, and thank you very much indeed. I'll be seeing you in the morning, Bagshott, I expect."

As soon as he arrived at the office next morning Hambledon sent for files of the papers of about two or three years earlier giving any account of a court-martial in the Tank Corps. When they came he read them through carefully and gave a summary of the case to Denton when he came in.

"It may be all right," said Hambledon. "Of course I wasn't there, and evidence sounds more convincing when you hear it in court instead of reading extracts from it in the paper. Also, I don't know anything about courts-martial. All I can say is that it doesn't particularly impress me."

"I think you're missing the point," said Denton. "This chap what's-his-name—Warnford—was court-martialed because confidential documents in his charge had disappeared, and they had. He wasn't charged with selling them to the agents of a foreign power. Though our dear Victor did his best to suggest he had, nobody seems to have taken any notice of the suggestion. He wouldn't have got off with merely being dismissed from the service if they'd believed that."

"I expect you're right. Our other friend sticks to the name of Victor, doesn't he, whether he's being Richards, Rawson, or Richten at the moment. Perhaps he does it for luck."

"I hope it defeats him," said Denton callously.

"It will if I can manage it. By the way, I had a telephone call from our anonymous friend this morning, telling me all about what happened last night. I heard him out and then said I thought it was an excellent account and that the description of him interested me very much. Of course he'd left out that bit. He asked how I knew, and I said I also was among those present. He said, 'Good lord, where?' I said, 'In the wardrobe,' and he said, 'Gosh,' in one of those awed tones you read about in books. I said I was glad to hear he had avoided being bumped off, and he said so was he. He is sending to me by post all the papers he picked up in the room. He went out of the window and down a drainpipe. Stout fellow."

"Did you tell him you saw him?"

"No. The one I saw was evidently Marden, got up in spectacles and a false mustache. I'm sure it's false; it's the wrong color. I shall find both these men one of these days. I wonder, Charles, I wonder—"

"What?"

"Whether Marden's partner might possibly be the innocent victim of that court-martial stunt. It's a long shot, but it would explain a lot of things if it were right. It would account for his chasing Rawson—Richards—Richten. It would account for his unusual bashfulness. There's a photo of him in these papers which is very like the descriptions we've had of him."

"What was the name again?" asked Denton.

"Warnford," said Hambledon. "I wish you'd go and look up the Tank Corps and see if you can find out where he lives now and anything useful about him."

Denton went, and had an interview with the man who had been Warnford's major. He said that he always thought there was more in the case than met the eye, and as for the putrid suggestion that the boy had sold the stuff to the Germans or the Wops, that was all my eye and nobody believed it. "The man who made the suggestion," said the major, "subsequently resigned his commission. Fellow named Rawson. Curious chap. Not popular."

"Indeed," said Denton. "Where is he now, do you know?"

The major said coldly that he had no idea at all. As regards Warnford, the court-martial judged on the evidence; they had no alternative. No, he didn't know what had become of Warnford either; none of their lot had seen or heard from him. Probably gone abroad; fellows generally did in cases like that. Nice fellow. Everyone would be delighted if he could be cleared and reinstated, particularly one young fellow, man named Kendal. "Always a great friend of Warnford's; in fact, we used to think at one time that they were going to be related. His sister, Miss Kendal, don't you know. Charming girl. I'd take you to see Kendal, only he's not here now. He might know a bit more about Warnford than I do, though he doesn't know where he is now. I asked him myself recently, as it happens, and he said he had no idea."

"Is Captain Kendal away on leave?"

"Yes. Long leave. Indefinite leave. He's an expert on armor-piercing projectiles and he's experimenting on some new idea he's got. The pundits thought it good enough to give him indefinite leave to work it out. I disapprove, myself. I don't think it's a good thing to allow young officers to get out of touch with their regiment. Suppose we all did that, what? Impossible situation."

"Oh, quite. I quite agree," said Denton, who had been on leave from his own regiment ever since 1916. "Where does he live?"

"Got a place in Hampshire. Marybourne House, Marybourne. Lives there with his sister. Why?"

"I suppose there'd be no objection to my going down there to see him?"

The major hesitated for the first time. "Go and see him, eh? Well, I really don't know. He can't tell you any more than I've told you already."

"He might remember a few details, sir, such as would only be known to an intimate friend of Warnford's. As you rightly guessed, sir, there is more in this than meets the eye, and we know a bit more about things than was known at the court-martial."

"I see. Yes. But it's a frightfully sore point with him. Personal friend and all that, you know. Hates talking about it."

"Naturally. But if it's a chance of clearing Warnford—"

"I'm afraid that's not very likely after all this lapse of time, is it? Why, it must be nearly three years ago. No, I shouldn't worry Kendal about it if I were you. Tell you what I'll do; I'll write and ask him to write out a full and complete account of the affair with every detail he can remember, what? More satisfactory, having it in writing. I'll send it on to you."

"But there are some questions," began Denton.

"Tell me what they are and I'll ask him. I shouldn't advise you to go down there. Hell of a journey, all on branch lines, and getting the train stopped for you at Marybourne Halt. Besides, he's a frightfully busy man; if you went down there he might be away or anything."

"It does sound rather a wild-goose chase," said Denton, yielding gracefully.

"Exactly, exactly. I knew you would see that. Now, is there anything else I can do for you?"

"Just one thing, if I might trouble you. Have you got a photograph of Rawson?"

"Of Rawson, eh? Oho, is it like that?"

"You understand, of course, sir, that all this is not only confidential; it's very secret."

"Of course, of course. My dear fellow, I've been keeping official secrets for years, and damned tosh most of 'em were. Photograph. Just a moment." The major took down an album of regimental photographs and turned the pages over. "Some groups here, dating from that time. Here's one. Rawson is in the second row there, but he seems to have moved. Here's another. Some silly ass has got in front of him; the photographer ought to have seen that. Here's another, but the fellow's looking down. That's Warnford at the end there, poor chap. No, we don't seem to have a good one of Rawson; I'm sorry."

"No," said Denton significantly. "You haven't, have you?"

"What? What? You don't mean to say—Well, Gobbless my soul," said the major. "Crafty devil!"

Denton reported to Hambledon, adding, "I noticed the photographer's name and address and the date; the photograph of Warnford is quite good."

"We will get a copy," said Tommy Hambledon. "It might help. Rawson would, of course, keep out of the limelight." He paused and added thoughtfully, "You know, whenever it appears to me that there is any particular place where somebody doesn't want me to go, I can never rest until I've been there. I think we'll go to Marybourne, wherever it is, if only to find out why the major didn't want us to. Something funny about all this. Not tomorrow. I've got that French fellow coming to tell me his troubles. The day after, Tuesday, will do. We'll drive down in your car and you can do the driving; my shoulder still wants resting. How far is it, seventy-five miles? Good. We'll start at eleven, lunch at the local, have a look round, and return in time for dinner. 'A little fun Just now and then Is relished by The wisest men.' That's why I like it. Good night, Denton. See you on Tuesday."

16
Disappearance of an Experimenter

WARNFORD'S LIFE being what it was, his doorbell only rang for tradespeople, postmen, and persons who read meters. He therefore took no notice when it rang on Monday morning, the day after Denton's visit to the Tank Corps Depot. Ashling passed the sitting-room door to answer the bell; Warnford heard without interest his footsteps on the stairs and the sound of the door being opened. The next moment it shut again, and there were voices on the stairs. Warnford threw down his paper and sat up. Ashling's voice, pleased and excited, saying, "Yes, miss," and "No, miss," and "This way, miss, please," and another voice so quiet as to be almost inaudible except as a gentle murmur. Warnford rose slowly to his feet as Ashling opened the door and announced, "Miss Kendal to see you, sir."

She came in shyly, as one not certain of a welcome, a tall fair girl with gray eyes and a sensitive mouth. "Jim. I hope you will forgive me for coming—"

"If only you knew," said Warnford, stammering a little, "how much I have wanted to see you—"

"I would have come long ago," she said, giving him her hand, "but you wouldn't answer my letters and I didn't like to hunt you down."

"I know. It's all my fault. I couldn't bear to see anybody at first, and later on I was ashamed to write. Jenny, can you understand, d'you think? I'm so glad you've come at last."

"I wish I'd come before, then. Roger wanted to hear from you too, you know, but he didn't know where you were. He thought you'd gone abroad."

"How did you find me, then?"

"Oh," she said, looking rather confused, "it's quite simple—I'm not going to tell you; it's my secret."

"Oh, all right. So long as you've come I don't care if you employed black magic. Sit down, won't you?" he said, awakening to the fact that he was still holding her hand. "Sit here; this is the nicest chair, I think. What's all the news; tell me what you've been doing."

"The news," she said, and her eyes darkened with anxiety. "I'm in great trouble, Jim. Roger is missing."

"Missing! What d'you mean?"

"Just that. He was working in that outside laboratory of his in the gardens—you remember that silly sort of pavilion place beyond the tennis courts? He had it altered and adapted for a sort of workshop when he started all these experiments. He was working there late on Thursday night. He often worked late; there was nothing in that. Only in the morning he wasn't there, and nobody's seen him since."

"That was Friday morning."

"Yes. The lights were all on, and things left standing about—you know, all his jars and things; I don't know anything about his work. But he wasn't there."

"You wouldn't know if there was anything missing?" said Warnford thoughtfully.

"No, I couldn't tell you. Well, I waited all day Friday; I thought perhaps he'd suddenly wanted something and dashed off to get it, only I didn't see how, as the car hadn't gone. But there might have been some explanation of that. I didn't want to get into a flap and make a fuss when he might have come back or rung me up at any moment. Nothing happened. I don't think I slept at all on Friday night. I kept on thinking I heard the telephone and dashing out of my room, but it was just imagination. On Saturday I couldn't stand it any longer and went to the police about it."

"What did they say?"

"They—it was our Constable Leggatt at Marybourne I went to, of course—he said he would have enquiries made. I must try and not worry; no doubt the captain would turn up in a day or two; the police would do all they could, and things would be sure to turn out all right—all that sort of thing. He was very nice about it, but I could see he thought I was making a silly fuss about nothing."

"Probably thought Roger'd gone off on a binge," said Warnford.

"Yes—as though he would, leaving all his work about and the lights on! Silly. If he wanted to go away he'd have had his things packed and gone in the car. Why not? Besides, he'd never go off without a word and leave me worrying; it would be so rude as well as unkind."

"Of course. It's out of the question. Did he take much money with him, d'you know?"

"I don't. The bank would tell me if he'd cashed an extra-big check lately, I suppose. We never kept an awful lot of money in the house; it wasn't necessary. I paid the bills by check, you know, and all that sort of thing; I don't know what Roger had."

"No. What do you think about it, yourself?"

"Jim, I don't know what to think," she said, her eyes shining with tears. "Friday, and now it's Monday, and not a word. It's not like him; he's always so considerate. One hears of people losing their memory; do they really? I thought they generally just pretended to, and I can't imagine Roger doing it, anyway. Of course he has been working very hard lately; I suppose it's possible. What do you think?"

"Oh, it's possible, all right. There are genuine cases, plenty of 'em; it's not always a music-hall joke."

"I hope it is, because they always remember themselves again suddenly, don't they? Or at least they are about somewhere and can be found," she said nervously.

"Jenny. What are you thinking about?"

"I'm almost afraid to say it to myself; it sounds so silly, like people in a thriller, and I would have said things didn't happen like that in real life, not to ordinary people like us," she said, pouring her words like a torrent, "but it happened to you, didn't it? I mean somebody stole your papers and the model; they didn't just melt away; somebody thought our tanks worth scheming and plotting to find out all about what we were doing. And Roger's work was definitely very important; his major told me that. I said to him how keen Roger was on his experiments, and he said if they were successful it looked as though all the other nations would have to rebuild their tanks, and he wasn't joking. Well, if somebody got wind of that they wouldn't stick at anything to find out what he was doing, would they? Jim, I don't know what to believe, but I'm frightened. Jim, where is he and what are they doing to him? Here are we just letting the days go by and not doing anything; I don't believe the police are worrying a bit, and all the time what is happening? Oh, Jim—"

"Steady, steady," he said. "It's frightfully worrying for you, but try not to get too upset over it. The loss-of-memory idea may be the right one, you know."

"Yes," she said with a violent effort at self-control. "That's why I've come up to town, to see if I can find anyone among our friends who's seen him anywhere this weekend. Because they don't want it advertised, for some reason."

"Who is 'they'?"

"The Army people. I've been ringing up his major—you remember, Major Distin—and he's all hush-hush about it. And nobody's doing anything! Oh, Jim, d'you remember saying once that if I were in any sort of trouble you'd help me?"

"Of course. I mean it; I'll do anything."

"Yes. Please do something at once—but what?"

"Let me think," said Warnford, and put his head in his hands. "Tell me," he went on after a minute, "have you noticed anything out of the ordinary just lately? Strangers about, that sort of thing?"

"No. Summer visitors driving about the country—most of them come from Winsbury—but not more than usual. Roger did tell me he'd engaged a couple more keepers, and I asked him why, as the shooting is all spoiled with his explosions in the park. The pheasants have gone for miles, you know. He said they were to help patrol the place and keep people off; he didn't want people nosing about; besides, it wasn't safe when he's firing his guns; there might be an accident. I've wondered since whether they were brought in more as guards."

Warnford nodded. "Where do they live?"

"In the cottage where old Meek used to live. He died—oh, more than a year ago—and his daughter's gone away into service."

"That's on the edge of the park, not far from the pavilion, isn't it? They ought to have heard if there was any sort of a schemozzle in the night."

"Yes. I asked them, but they hadn't heard anything. I expect they sleep soundly; men like that generally do."

"I think," said Warnford, getting up to bring cigarettes from the mantelpiece, "that I'd better run down to Marybourne and have a look round. I've no idea what to look for, but it seems the obvious place to start. I'll stay at the Seven Stars, I think, not at the house."

"Will you go alone?"

"I've got a friend who'll go with me, man named Marden. You'll stay in town, will you, and see if you can run across anything? Where are you staying?"

"At my club," she said, and gave him the address and telephone number. "I thought I'd be freer there than staying with Aunt Pamela."

"From what I remember of your aunt Pamela you certainly would be. What's the time? Nearly twelve. I'll go down to Marybourne this afternoon, I think. I'd ask you to lunch with me somewhere, but I think you'd rather I got going. I'll get hold of Marden and talk to him; he's out at the moment, but he won't be long. Keep your heart up and try not to worry more than you can help. I'm awfully glad you came; sensible thing to do. I'll let you know how I get on, of course."

She rose to go. "I'm much happier since I've seen you," she said frankly. "At least we can try to do something now, and, besides—I don't think you realize how much we both missed you. Don't vanish again, will you?"

"I shouldn't be such a fool again."

"No. Good-bye, Jim. I'll keep my fingers crossed till I hear from you again."

When he had seen her off he returned upstairs and met Marden coming out of his own room.

"Oh, hullo, old chap," said Warnford. "Didn't hear you come in. I've got something to tell you."

"Had some letters to write," said Marden, who, in point of fact, had been kindly but firmly headed off the sitting room by Ashling. "What's happened?"

Warnford told him the story, adding, "I know the place pretty well, stayed there several week ends in the old days. Roger Kendal and I were always good friends. It's about eight miles from Winsbury, all among the Hampshire downs. Open rolling country for the most part, chalk hills with clumps of beeches; you know the sort of thing. Marybourne itself is in a valley and fairly wooded, but part of the park is like moorland with heather and bracken and pine trees. The house is on the far side of the park from the village; I should think it's two miles or more, so it's pretty lonely, apart from gardeners' and keepers' cottages and the home farm beyond the gardens. I remember this pavilion place she talks about quite well; I think their grandfather built it. It's something between a large summerhouse and a small ballroom, with Corinthian pillars up the walls and lots of windows. When the old people were alive they used to use it for teas and things when they gave big garden parties, but a more useless place normally you couldn't imagine, too far from the house to be convenient and not far enough for picnics. I should think it would make an ideal laboratory for a shy experimenter."

"How far from the house?" asked Marden. "Would you hear a yell from there, for example?"

"About a quarter of a mile, and you can hear a yell a long way on a quiet night if you're awake to hear it. But there are walled gardens between and then the tennis courts and a screen of trees, sort of shrubbery business, rhododendrons and that sort of thing. I shouldn't think a yell from there would wake anybody at the house. The keepers' cottage she spoke of is much nearer, just round the end of the shrubbery; they don't seem to have heard anything."

"I suppose one must start by going down there," said Marden, "though frankly I don't know what you expect to find. If Kendal was kidnapped, the kidnappers would be extremely careful not to leave any traces, you'd think."

"I agree. I'm only going there because I can't think of any better place to start. There is this about it: if the trick was worked with the help of anyone employed on the estate or a local visitor, they would be very careful to stay on for a time so as to avoid suspicion."

"I'll pack a bag and get the Bentley out."

"No, don't," said Warnford thoughtfully. "The Bentley is rather too well known in some circles. I think we'll go by train."

"Surely," said his friend, "you don't think Blackbeard is in this business too, do you? The damn fellow's getting on your nerves. He can't be everywhere at once."

"I'm not thinking one way or the other," said Warnford. "I'm just taking precautions. Pass the Bradshaw over, there's a good chap. Ashling! Ashling!"

"Sir?"

"Pack my small bag for a couple of nights, please. Toothbrush, pajamas, shirt, socks, shaving tackle. Only for country pub."

"Very good, sir."

"And Mr. Marden's the same. Now then. Waterloo to Marybourne Halt. They don't seem to have heard of Marybourne Halt. Yes, they have. Page 168a. No, it's not here. Yes, among the notes—"

"Oh, let's get to Waterloo and ask there," said Marden. "They're more used to Bradshaw than we are."

They snatched a couple of sandwiches and a glass of beer at Waterloo and caught the two-ten. It was a long and circuitous journey, involving a change at Guildford, with twenty-five minutes to wait; another at Alton, where they waited half an hour, and a third at Winsbury, where the local to Marybourne Halt was held up for twenty minutes, waiting for some trucks containing prize cattle from a West Country show.

"I've never come by train before," said Warnford when they found an empty compartment. "We always came by road from wherever we were stationed. In fact, I don't think I've ever come here from London before." The train started at last, crawled through the Winsbury Cutting deep in the chalk, and came out among wide rolling fields and patches of woodland glowing in the yellow light of an autumn sunset. The fields came up close to the train on both sides, and Marden, looking out of the windows, said, "Why, it's a single line. This is real country."

"Yes," said Warnford, staring out of the window, "it's real country all right. It used to be very pleasant coming here in the old days. We used to ride on the downs or go out shooting or just go out. There are trout a bit lower down the Marybourne River, not on Kendal's place, but the old squire used to rent a stretch of the river the other side of Stoke Bourne. I'm beginning to recognize landmarks; that hill over there with the clump of trees on the top is Gallows Hill; there's the upright of the gallows still there. The last people hung there were a man and a woman who murdered a sailor in 1795; he lost his way on the downs at night and knocked at their door to ask the road. They took him in, found out somehow that he had a good bit of money on him, and cut his throat. I don't know how it was discovered, but they were hung all right."

"Hanged in chains, I suppose," said Marden, "as a warning to others."

"Oh yes. Roger told me that when he was a boy an old woman showed him one of the man's finger bones. She kept it as a cure for rheumatism or toothache or something. Roger said he earnestly wished to own it himself, but the old woman wouldn't part, so he went up to the gallows and scratched round in the turf to find another one. He did and kept it for years till somebody told him it was a sheep's foot bone, then he threw it away. He was about eight at the time. Ghoulish little beasts boys are."

"He was born here, I suppose," said Marden.

"Oh yes, and always lived here except when he was away at school and afterwards in the Army. He's wrapped up in the place. Marden, I don't believe for a moment that he went away of his own accord, all of a sudden like that; it wasn't like him. He never did stupid, inconsiderate things to leave people wondering. I never knew anyone so reliable; if he said he'd do a thing he'd do it; if he believed in anything—after adequate proof—you couldn't shake him. At my court-martial he came up and volunteered to give evidence of character. He said he didn't know anything about the event itself because unfortunately he was away at the time, but he said that the stuff must have been very expertly stolen and not through my carelessness because I wasn't careless and that was that. I can see him now standing up addressing the court. 'Men act according to their characters,' he said. 'You don't find habitual liars becoming suddenly trustworthy, or born misers throwing money about. Warnford was conscientious to the point of absurdity; to suggest he left the keys about for anybody to find is simply damned nonsense, sir.' Of course his evidence didn't cut any ice for me; it only showed what a good chap he was. Obstinate, yes, but not impulsive and silly. I don't believe he just walked out, Marden."

"Unless he had some sort of brainstorm," said Marden. "Overwork."

"It takes an awful lot of overwork to turn a fit man's brain when he's interested in what he's doing. Jenny hadn't noticed anything wrong. I haven't seen him since the court-martial," said Warnford, harking back again. "He wrote to me care of my bank and said he wanted to see me, but I refused. I wish I hadn't, now; if he'd had any suspicions of any dirty work about he'd have told me. The last I saw of him was walking out of that room after he'd given his evidence; he turned in the doorway and looked at me. But Rawson's evidence had done it for me. Funny, he turned round, too, when he'd got— Marden!"

"What on earth's the matter?" said Marden, for Warnford was staring at him like one who sees a ghost.

"I've just remembered," said Warnford slowly.

"Remembered what?"

"When we were in the Hotel Malplaquet, you know, while you were talking to the girl at the desk. Blackbeard walked through with the manager and I said he reminded me of someone, but I didn't know who."

"Well?"

"Blackbeard is Rawson. I can see him now, walking down the room after he'd said his little piece. Rather a stiff-legged walk he had, very ultra-military. Blackbeard had too; d'you remember? And the shape of the back of his head. What a fool I've been."

"Are you quite sure?"

"Of course I'm sure. I knew him from the start, only that beard of his misled me. Rawson, eh? Very funny. You said I'd come across him somewhere, didn't you? Now Kendal's disappeared. Well, we've made a long step forward, Marden; we know what we're looking for."

"But you're jumping to conclusions," objected Marden. "There isn't a shred of evidence that Rawson had anything to do with Kendal's affair."

"No. But will you bet on it?"

"No, I certainly won't," said John Marden.

17
The Old Barn

Dusk was falling by the time the train reached Marybourne Halt, which consisted of one platform, one shed, one garden seat, and one porter, who looked at the two strangers with interest. The only other passenger to get out there was a young girl who wheeled a cycle out of the shed to the road outside and pedaled quickly away. Warnford looked about him, but the station was shut in by a hazel copse on one side and a rising fold of ground on the other. The porter took their tickets, and they stood in the road outside and heard him rattling keys and locking the shed behind them. The noise of the train died away in the distance; somewhere among the hazels a rabbiting dog barked excitedly; farther down the lane to the left a cock pheasant cried, and against the amber glow in the west one large star hung like a lamp. The air smelled of damp moss and the Michaelmas daisies in the Halt's one flower bed, and there was nobody to be seen anywhere about, nor sound of any traffic.

"What a gorgeous evening," said Marden, inhaling long breaths of the cool air.

"Yes, isn't it? Here," said Warnford suddenly, "this won't do; I don't know the way. Where's that porter gone?"

"I bain't gone, sir, yet," said the porter, and emerged from the shadows wheeling a cycle. He shut the platform gate and locked it behind him. "Where did you genelmen want to go?"

"To Marybourne Village."

"Well, there's two ways to Marybourne; there's the road an' there's the footpath."

"How far is it?"

"Matter o' three mile by road, sir; 'tis shorter by footpath, naturally."

"Path, I think," said Warnford; "it's getting dusk already."

"'Tis that, sir; evenin's be closin' in on us now. Still, there'll be moon up presently; it won't be dark not yet awhiles. You goes down this road," he said, pointing to the left, "till you comes to the river. There's a bridge over, but you doan' cross it; you goes over stile just this side of it on your left 'and. You keeps on alongside the river through three fields, what we calls the water meadows, till you comes to a wood. Path runs alongside wood—you can't miss un—till you comes to a farm. Bear left there down a sort o' lane, like, till you comes to them 'igh-tension cables an' the lane turns left, but you keeps straight on over another stile you'll see there till you comes to a wall. That's the park wall, like, an' there's a gate in it an' a short cut across corner o' park to the village."

"Ah, I remember that bit," said Warnford.

"Ah, you've bin 'ere afore, sir?"

"Yes, but I never came from this side before."

"No, sir, I see. Well, you do just as I've told you an' you can't go wrong. Thankee very much, sir; much obliged, I'm sure. Good night, genelmen."

The porter put the shilling in his pocket, climbed onto his bicycle, and rode leisurely away.

" 'And left the world to darkness and to me,' " quoted Marden.

"The twilight will last some time on such a clear night, and it didn't sound far. Three fields, a wood, farm, bit of a lane, field, park wall, and so home. Come on."

They walked through the meadows and found the wood, but it was wedge-shaped, with the point towards them and the path divided to pass up either side. They decided after discussion to take the right side, since the park must lie on their right somewhere, and wherever they found the wall they could walk along it to the gate. But the wood petered out on rising ground into patches of gorse and juniper bushes among which the path weaved about, divided, rejoined again, and lost itself. The darkness deepened; the moon lingered behind the hill, and the two men disentangled themselves from blackberry trailers and came to a stop.

"We're lost," said Marden cheerfully. "Look, there's an owl; he passed quite close."

"This path," said Warnford, "wasn't a path at all; it's just cattle tracks. We'd better go back to the end of the wood and up the other side."

But the wood, when they got back to it, had either changed its shape or else it wasn't the same wood, and Marden stumbled into an unexpected depression in the ground and tore his trouser leg on a branch of thorn.

"What is this I've fallen into?" he asked. "It's a foot or more deep and seems to be round."

"Hut circles," said Warnford. "Abode of prehistoric man. I know where we are now; this is War Down. Where's north—? Oh, that way. We go south, come on."

They were, however, fortunate in meeting an elderly agricultural laborer on his way home who put them on their right road in such broad Hampshire that it was difficult to understand him.

"I'd love to hear him discussing politics with a Clydesider," said Marden. "I don't believe either would understand a word the other said. Bit tough on an invading force who'd learned their English at school, trying to gather information from him. I see lights ahead; is that your village? It's been a nice evening for a walk, but we seem to have missed the park altogether."

"Never mind, we'll attend to the park tomorrow. There's a church tower against the sky; the Seven Stars is just across the green, and I hope the landlord's got bacon and eggs."

The landlord said yes, there were bacon and eggs if the gentlemen would like to have them, but they could have dinner in a quarter of an hour if they would prefer it. Soup, kidneys on toast, roast pheasant, sweet omelet, and a nice piece of Cheddar.

The visitors said they would much prefer it, but they had not expected to find catering of that standard in a small village inn. How on earth did the landlord manage it?

The landlord smiled proudly and said it was due to his having had the common sense and good luck to marry the cook from the big house in the park, one who really was a cook and took pride in it. Not but what he would probably have married her all the same if she hadn't been able to boil an egg, but there it was, and he knew when he was well off. Rooms for the night? Certainly. Perhaps the gentlemen would like to see their rooms while the dinner was cooking. This way, please. "Lizzie! Dinner for two more, please."

"You have other guests staying here?" asked Warnford.

"One old gentleman who's been here before—several times this year, in fact—old Mr. Quint. Professor of botany, we understand. This is a great part of the country for wild flowers, he tells me; I don't know much about that sort of thing myself, haven't got time to study it. He walks miles all over the place, carrying tin boxes for his specimens, as he calls 'em, and has 'em spread all over his room on sheets of blotting paper, and it's as much as the housemaid's life's worth to touch 'em. Now, there's these two rooms, gentlemen—"

They dined excellently in a room panelled in oak with a log fire on the hearth whose leaping flames were reflected from the rosy faces of several copper warming pans hanging on the walls. The professor of botany was also dining at a small table across the room, a short wide man with grizzled hair, bushy eyebrows, and a stoop. He was very inclined to be friendly and asked if they took any interest in his particular hobby. "For I am one of those happy few whose profession is their hobby. If I were not a botanist I should want to be a botanist."

Warnford merely knew some of the more familiar flowers when they were brought to his notice but would never think of looking for them. He left the conversation to Marden, who was quite capable of being enthusiastic over *Lycopersicum barbarum* in Hampshire. "In Norfolk or Essex, now," said Quint, "one would not be surprised, but here—"

"I've seen it in East Kent," said Marden. "The Duke of Argyll's tea tree to you," he added to Warnford.

"Why?"

"I don't know," confessed Quint. "I imagine there must be a story attached to such a strange name, but I'm afraid I've never heard it. This district is a botanist's paradise; I have found no less than ten varieties of orchis within a three-mile radius of this place, and even the very rare *Spiranthe aestivalis*."

Marden admitted that he had never even seen it; the *autumnalis* species, now, that was common enough if you knew where to look for it. Intercepting an imploring glance from Warnford, he disentangled himself with difficulty from the old botanist, and the two friends retreated towards the bar.

"I suppose," said Warnford, "that sort of thing is frightfully interesting if you like it."

"Yes, it certainly is," said Marden. "At the same time, I thought it wasn't a bad idea to find out if the old bird really is a botanist or not. He is."

"Good for you; I couldn't have risen to those heights."

"Botany was my father's hobby," said Marden. "I had it pumped into me daily when I was a boy."

They entered the bar which was comfortably but not overly filled with clients and were greeted by a slight pause in the conversation while everyone glanced at the newcomers and immediately went on with what they were saying. A game of darts was in progress at the far end of the room which was attracting most of the attention; Warnford looked round to see if there were present any of the few estate servants who might have remembered him, the head keeper, the head groom, possibly a gardener, and certainly the butler, but none of them was there. He leaned against the bar, ordered whisky for himself and Marden, and opened the ball by saying that this was a lovely part of the country.

The landlord said he didn't believe it had its match in England, of its kind, and supposed it was the gentlemen's first visit.

Warnford said no, as a matter of fact he had spent a week end there some years ago at the invitation of Captain Kendal, and, finding himself again in the neighborhood, thought it would be a good idea to look him up. But it appeared that he was away from home.

The landlord, with a certain reserve in his voice, said yes, he understood the young squire was away just now. From which Warnford gathered what he would have known if he had ever lived in real country himself; namely, that Kendal's unexplained absence was known all over the village, however quiet Jenny thought she had kept it. No comment would, of course, be made to a total stranger, but several men looked at him with curiosity in their glances.

Warnford said it was very disappointing; he'd looked forward to renewing the acquaintance. No doubt there had been a good many changes since Captain Kendal's father died. And what was the landlord having?

The landlord said his was a port, with many thanks. Yes, there had been changes, of course. "Your health, gentlemen. Captain Kendal was a very clever gentleman, by all accounts—was, I said—is, I mean, of course. He's very busy all the time inventing some new explosive or some such for the Army. Anyway, there's some fine bangs goes on in the park now; frightened all the game off the place. That pheasant you had for dinner, now, I'll bet that was one of the Marybourne House pheasants, for all it was shot on old Leonard Scrubbs' land three miles away."

"I've heard Captain Kendal has a great reputation as an expert," said Warnford casually. "Seems a pity, though, to spoil the shooting here; it used to be so good. We had a day with the pheasants when I was here, I remember."

One game of darts came to an end and another started; a few people went out, and there was something of a space left round the bar when things settled down again.

"I was really looking round, wondering if I might recognize anybody in here," went on Warnford, "keepers principally, but I suppose they've been paid off since there's no game."

"Well, no," said the landlord. "There's been changes, of course; some gone and others come, but on the whole there's more than there used to be. Very funny sort of keepers some of 'em are, too; my old span'el here knows more about game than the likes of them. Funny speech, too, the last new ones; come from Sheffield, they tell me. They say quite openly they don't know much about the country and don't like it much, either, but they was out of work, and the job offered and they'd try anything once. Fact is, sir, in my opinion they aren't keepers at all, not ordinary gamekeepers; more what you'd call park keepers to see folks don't trespass where they ain't wanted. Well, stands to reason all them explosions must be dangerous; why, they shakes our windows sometimes, just like guns. May be guns, for all I know. Well, they wouldn't want people wandering about getting hurt; young Squire wouldn't want that. Quite right too. He's got a six-foot wire fence around part of the park, over towards the warrens, and no matter when you happen to go by near there'll be one of these fellows warning you off. Why, only yesterday my two little nieces went in after sweet chestnuts, as children will, and were told to run away. Excuse me a moment, sir. Yes, Lizzie, what is it?"

"Marvelous man," said Marden in an undertone. "Runs on and on like a dripping tap."

"Very nice too," said Warnford. "Gasbags have their uses. Hullo, I wonder if these are the two new keepers; they don't look like countrymen."

Two newcomers entered and came up to the farther end of the bar, one a fat pasty-faced man and the other tall, with a long nose and eyes set too near together, both of them reddened but not browned with the sun.

"I think you're right," said Marden. "Not long accustomed to an open-air life. What is more, they've been drilled at some time or other; look at their shoulders."

"Ex-Army, possibly. Not last war; they're too young."

The newcomers ordered beer, and somebody in the room called out some jesting remark about a badger. The tall one laughed, and the landlord came back to tell Warnford a long story about their meeting a badger one morning before dawn and thinking it was a wildcat, if you ever heard the like. A square man with the air of a seaman came up to the bar and engaged the pasty-faced man in conversation. Warnford and Marden had their glasses refilled and listened without appearing to do so.

"Mr. Owen," said the landlord quietly, indicating the square man. "Retired mercantile marine. Mate, I believe."

Apparently navigation was the subject, for Mr. Owen said something about a sextant and "shooting the sun." The pasty-faced man said something about the stars which made Owen laugh but persisted, mentioning "astral navigation." Then came something which was lost in a burst of laughter in the room, and then "artificial horizon." Marden pricked up his ears.

The landlord returned from another errand, leaned upon the bar, and said in confidential tones, "Those are the two new keepers I told you about. Now, what do you think?"

"I wouldn't have said they were brought up to it, certainly," said Marden cautiously, and Warnford asked where they lived.

"Up near the gardens. In a cottage where an old man used to live who was keeper here years ago and pensioned off. Old Meek; you wouldn't remember, I expect. He was bedridden some time; he's dead now."

Warnford nodded. These were the same two keepers of whom Jenny had spoken, the only two near enough to the pavilion to have heard if there was any disturbance on the night when Roger Kendal disappeared. "Have another, Marden?"

"Just time for another round, gentlemen," said the landlord, glancing behind him at the clock on the wall.

"One more for the road to bed," agreed Marden. "Doesn't Professor Quint ever come in here in the evenings?"

"Hardly ever. Has whisky and a siphon taken up to his room after dinner; he says that's when he does his work. Arranges his specimens, I suppose, and does his writing. I believe he's writing a book."

"Botany, I suppose. He seems a man of one idea," said Warnford, who found Mr. Quint a bore.

"He's a very quiet gentleman," said the landlord loyally. "Time, gentlemen, please!"

Marden came into Warnford's bedroom for a moment and shut the door behind him. "Did you hear the conversation between that pasty-faced feller and the Ancient Mariner? The keeper is, or has been, a flying man and a navigator at that."

"And not an out-of-work from a Sheffield slum," said Warnford. "I think we'll look them up in the morning."

They entered the park on the following morning by the public footpath which ran across a corner of it, not wishing to be asked their errand at the lodge gate. There was an inconspicuous track which turned off, twisting through the shrubbery; Warnford led the way through it without interruption except once, when a cheerful whistling sent them to earth behind a clump of oaks while a boy went by with letters in his hand. Presently the track bent to the right while on their left the trees thinned out to a screen. Warnford turned left through the trees which ceased suddenly; there was a steep drop of a hundred feet or more, and there below them was a small white cottage backed up against a shrubbery which curved round towards another building farther off, a white building with windows flashing in the sun.

"This is old Meek's cottage where those men live," said Warnford. "Keep back under cover; don't show yourself. The building beyond is the pavilion, and behind that again are the tennis courts. Those walls farther back are the walls of the gardens, and there's the house, farther round to the right. Got the lie of the land now?"

"Perfectly. I don't see anyone about."

"Nor do I. Let's sit down under that clump of bushes there and contemplate Nature for a bit; something might happen. Have a cigarette; we're well hidden."

"There's a barn or something down there," said Marden when they had settled down. "This side of the cottage—look, against the trees."

"Oh yes, but that's never used now; it's quite derelict. The roof was beginning to go when I was here last."

Some time passed before anything happened, then suddenly the cottage door opened and two men came out, by their build the same two who were in the bar of the Seven Stars the night before. They stood outside the cottage, talking, then one of them walked away round the edge of the shrubbery towards the pavilion and disappeared in the distance. The other went round the cottage towards the back, was gone for a few minutes, and returned carrying something heavy in each hand.

"What's he got?" murmured Marden. "Looks like square boxes."

"Cans," answered Warnford excitedly. "Petrol cans. Now what?"

The man walked along to the disused barn some fifty yards from the cottage and put his cans down. He then opened one of the doors, not without effort, picked up his cans again, and went in.

"Well, well," said the interested Marden. "What d'you know about that? Derelict, eh? Perhaps they've had it done up since you were here."

"They may have, of course. It's their barn. I wish he'd opened the door a little wider; we might see what's inside. Now what happens?"

There was a short wait while the man busied himself within the barn, then he reappeared again.

"The cans are now empty," said Warnford. "See the debonair way he swings 'em."

"He returns to the cottage," said Marden, lying flat on the ground and sticking his face through a tussock of grass. "He is going round to the back where he got those cans from. Perhaps he's been brought up to be tidy and is now putting the empties away. No, he returns with two more. Full ones."

"Eight gallons," commented Warnford. "He rather toils along, doesn't he? I don't think Augustus really likes work. Now what happens? Same again?"

It was the same again, except that this time the man shut the barn doors and appeared to lock them also.

"Twelve gallons," said Warnford. "Must be a big car. One would almost think it was being prepared for a journey, wouldn't one? Round the back of the cottage again to put the empties away. Now which way? Up towards us? Make up your mind, Augustus. No, away across the park; he's going towards the warrens where the barbed-wire enclosure is, according to our host. Now what do we do? Go and look at the barn? Right, come on.

"In the old days," went on Warnford as they reached it, "these walls were full of chinks you could see through, and the dogs used to squeeze in and hunt rats. I don't find any chinks now."

"There is something hung up inside; looks like a rick sheet," said Marden. "The ivy's been cut round the doors, and there are tire marks in the grass. You work round that side and I'll take this."

When they met again behind the barn he found Warnford pulling at a shutter which had been nailed up, but the wood was rotten with age and broke away from the nails. "They won't notice this from inside," he said, "thanks to the rick sheet; they've hung them all round the walls. You heave that side, Marden. Come off, you—got it. Throw it in the bushes; I'm going in. Coming?"

They slid in through the gap and under the rick sheets into a dark space smelling of petrol; a faint light filtering through the roof showed the outlines of a big American saloon car painted black.

"I wish I'd brought an electric torch," said Warnford. "I want to look at this; there might be something interesting in the pockets."

"If I hold up this—er—glittering arras," said Marden, "you might be able to see a little. Aren't rick sheets heavy? This one is heavier than usual—with cobwebs. That any better?"

"Much, thanks. Let's try the driver's side first. All right, you can let go; here's a torch in the cubbyhole. Now what have we? An empty matchbox, a screw driver and a spanner, a dirty duster, and a copy of *Men Only*. In the pocket of the door one map and a piece of paper containing a ham sandwich. The map—Hullo! It's marked, look. There's a pencil line leading to Marybourne."

"Where does it come from?"

"Winsbury—it's very faint—Alton, Guildford, Reigate, Westerham. I don't think it goes beyond Westerham."

"They wouldn't start it from their front door, you know," said Marden. "Of course they may live at Westerham, or it may be the place where they join the main road."

"I've got a feeling," said Warnford, "that we'd better not linger here. I'll put the map back where I found it; have a look through the other pockets while I fold it up, will you? Nothing in any of 'em? Then either they haven't owned the car long or they aren't human. We'll shut the doors and go. 'By the pricking in my thumbs Something evil this way comes.' I'll give you a leg up; are you through? Anybody about? Splendid. I am with you."

Looking back from the ridge from which they had first seen the cottage, they saw two men returning across the park, and one had a gun under his arm and was swinging something.

"Rabbit for dinner," said Marden. "Just in time. They might have had us."

18
Hambledon Listens In

At about the time that Warnford and Marden were breaking and entering the barn, Hambledon and Denton arrived at the Seven Stars and asked for lunch. While preparations were being made Hambledon talked to the landlord, asking a few casual questions about Marybourne House and its owner.

"Captain Kendal is a very nice gentleman indeed," said the landlord warmly. "Of course he owns all the property round here. He is very well liked indeed."

"I've come down here to see him," said Hambledon, "though actually I've never met him."

"Then, sir, I'm afraid you'll be unlucky; the captain is away from home."

"I'm sorry to hear that. I suppose you've no idea when he will be coming back?"

"I couldn't tell you, sir."

"No. Well, perhaps they'll be able to tell me at the house how to get in touch with him."

"That will be your best plan, sir, to ask at the house. Very unfortunate, the captain being away just now; as it happens, there's two other gentlemen staying here who've come on purpose to see him, and they've been disappointed too."

"Oh, really? Perhaps they are mutual friends. What are their names?"

"Mr. Warnford and Mr. Marden, sir."

"Oh," said Hambledon with assumed indifference. "No, I don't know them. Are they here now?"

"They are out at the moment but will be back presently; they are staying here tonight. Excuse me, gentlemen," said the landlord, "lunch is served."

They entered the dining room; a short thickset man with bushy eyebrows, who had been sitting in a corner of the lounge reading *Country Life*, rose and went in too. He sat alone at a small table not far from theirs, and Hambledon heard the waitress call him "Mr. Quint, sir." Hambledon and Denton got through the meal quickly and went out to their car; they did not, of course, discuss Warnford's presence till they were alone.

"I still want to find out," said Hambledon, "why your Tank Corps major didn't want us to come. If he knew the man Kendal was away, why not say so? So we'll just run up to the house and try to find that out and then return to the Seven Stars, hoping to find Messrs. Warnford and Marden, for my soul desires them. I did say one of them might be Warnford, didn't I?"

They drove in at the lodge entrance of Marybourne House just as Warnford and Marden were emerging from the public footpath a hundred yards farther down the road. "We are late for lunch," said Marden; "our hostess will look reproachfully at us."

"We're not so late," said Warnford, "and, anyway, I want to see a map while that route is still fresh in my mind. I thought it better to put the other one back where we found it in the car."

They walked into the lounge and met the landlord, who said that lunch was served.

"Let it wait just a moment," said Warnford. "I want something else first. Can you find us a map covering the country between here and Westerham in Kent via Alton and Reigate?"

"Between here and Westerham," repeated the landlord. "I think so. Let me just look in the office."

There came a clatter from the dining room next door as though someone had dropped his spoon and fork hastily on a plate, followed by the sound of an outer door opening and shutting. The dining room at the Seven Stars had a separate entrance from the street. The next moment a thickset figure passed hastily by the window, and as the landlord went to his office Marden watched Professor Quint hurrying up the street and diving into a telephone box at the next corner.

"Curious," said Marden to Warnford. "Why so much excitement?"

"He's forgotten to back Buttered Toast for the two-thirty," suggested Warnford, and the landlord heard him.

"Professor Quint is not a betting man," he said, returning with a map. "He disapproves of it. Will this be the one you want, gentlemen?"

"Thank you, this'll do very well," said Warnford, and laid out the map on a table. "Here we are—Alton, Guildford, Reigate. Where was the last place? Westerham?"

"Westerham, yes," said Marden, still looking out of the window. "Quint hasn't got his call. He is standing outside the box looking impatient."

"He has left his pudding unfinished," said the landlord, returning from the dining-room door. "Very unusual. He's particularly fond of boiled-treacle pudding."

"He is pacing round the box all same like tiger in zoo," said Marden.

"I hope he hasn't had bad news," said the landlord. "Come to think of it, he couldn't have, not since he started lunch. He couldn't have heard any."

"Heard," said Marden slowly, and Warnford looked up from his map. "Tell me, do you happen to know whether he knows those two odd keepers you pointed out to us last night?"

"Know the keepers?" said the puzzled landlord. "Why, no, I'm sure he doesn't. I've seen him pass 'em by more than once. He's not one to talk much with the folk about here. Come to think of it, it's queer him going up to that box when we've got a telephone back of the lounge here; why go out?"

"Where's your telephone? Through that door? Right." Marden dived towards it, followed by Warnford asking what the idea was.

"He heard us asking for the map to Westerham," murmured Marden, hastily turning up Kendal in the telephone directory and lifting the receiver. "Marybourne 67, please. This is Marybourne 43. ... Yes, thank you. ... Oh, is that Marybourne House? ... Would you put me through to the keepers' cottage, please? The two new keepers in Meek's cottage."

"They are still out, sir," said a voice from the other end in slightly reproachful tones. "I will ring you back, sir, as soon as they return, as I said just now."

"Thank you," said Marden, and replaced the receiver. "Quint did ring them up. He is in the swindle. He did hear us ask for the map. He is waiting at the telephone box for the call. Something is going to occur."

"Perhaps he's going to tell 'em to clear out," said Warnford. "I think we'd better get back there as quickly as possible. Something might be done about that car of theirs, if only a potato in the exhaust pipe."

"But your lunch, gentlemen," said the hospitable landlord as they passed him in the lounge on their way out.

"'Fraid it'll have to wait," said Warnford; "we're busy," and they left the inn at a smart pace.

In the meantime Hambledon, in the car driven by Denton, arrived at Marybourne House, and the butler opened the door.

"I have come from town," began Hambledon, "on purpose to—"

"Oh," broke in the butler, recognizing an official voice, "did Miss Kendal send you?"

"Not exactly," said Hambledon, realizing from the man's agitated manner that there was something very much wrong. Such butlers as this do not break into the opening remarks of visitors without very good reason. "I haven't seen Miss Kendal, but I've come down to—er—you understand." Hambledon hoped so, anyway, since it was more than he did at the moment.

"Yes, sir, of course. Please come in."

"You'd better come too," said Hambledon to Denton. "Now," he went on to the butler when they were inside, "perhaps it would be best if you just told me yourself exactly what happened, then I can ask you again about any point that isn't quite clear."

"Yes, sir. This is the morning room, if you would care to sit down." The butler went on to tell them much the same story that Jenny Kendal had told Warnford twenty-four hours earlier. "Of course we in the house didn't know exactly what the master was doing, but we knew it was something important for the government. … Came down on Friday morning, and when we went to call him he wasn't in his room and the bed not been slept in, then the head housemaid said to me it looked as though the lights was still on in the pavilion. Well, it's difficult to tell, sir, by daylight, so I hurried across there, wondering if there'd been an accident, and the lights was all on, but no sign of the master. … Miss Kendal went up to town Monday morning early, saying she'd see somebody who would do something about it, as the police didn't seem to worry. So when you came, sir, I thought you'd seen her."

"Tell me exactly what happened the evening before—When did you last see Captain Kendal?"

"Well, sir. To start with, whenever he was going to work late he'd tell me after dinner. Then about ten o'clock I used to take him coffee in a thermos flask, and sandwiches, over to the pavilion, and put out whisky and a soda siphon and a glass as was kept over there in a cupboard. I did this Thursday night as usual. He was working there then, very busy; he just looked up and said, 'Oh, thank you, Vokes,' and I said, 'Good night, sir,' and came away. That's the last I saw of him, sir."

"Hear anything in the night?"

"Well, I wouldn't like to say. Something woke me up in the night, but I didn't hear anything when I was awake. It might not have been anything, but I don't awake between two and three as a rule. I woke up with the idea I had heard something, if you understand me, sir. I got up and opened my bedroom door, but all was quiet in the 'ouse—house. I then put a coat on and had a walk round, but all was as it should be, and the dogs was asleep in the hall. So I went back to bed and, looking out of the staircase window as I went up, I saw the lights was still on in the pavilion. It might not have been anything, sir."

"No, it might not. Is there any house or cottage nearer the pavilion than this?"

Vokes told him about the keepers' cottage and that they had said they had heard nothing. Hambledon noticed that his tone in speaking of them was rather cold and asked, "Reliable men, are they?" Vokes answered that he could not say; they were new men, only taken on a month ago, and were complete strangers, not men off the estate or even from the immediate— A bell rang, and the butler said, "Excuse me, sir, the telephone."

He went into the hall, and they heard him say, "I will ascertain, sir." There followed subdued clicks and a pause, then the butler's voice saying, "They are not in. If you will give me your number I will ring you back. Thank you."

Vokes came back to the morning room and said that of course the master's absence might have some perfectly natural explanation, but it was not like him to rush off like this without telling anyone, not even Miss Kendal. He was always thoughtful and considerate even as a boy, when you might expect— The telephone bell rang again. Vokes excused himself and went out hastily; they heard him say, "They are still out, sir. I will ring you back, sir, as soon as they return, as I said just now."

He came back again looking a little irritated and said that of course every time the telephone bell rang he hoped it was some news of the master instead of somebody wanting to speak to those keepers. Some people had no patience.

"You have a private switchboard in the house here, have you?" said Hambledon.

"Yes, sir. With extensions to some of the cottages so that we can ring them from here and they can also have calls from outside put through."

"And both those calls were for the keepers? The same person each time?"

"I thought the voice was the same, sir; I may of course have been mistaken."

"Very odd. He is in a hurry, isn't he? Do you get a clear line here when anyone is speaking from outside to one of the cottages? I mean can you listen in to what is being said?"

"You could, sir, easily. Not that one would—"

"Of course not, normally, but the circumstances are unusual. When they do talk to each other I should like to listen, if you don't mind."

"But, sir—"

"Look at this," said Hambledon, and showed the man his official card.

"Indeed, sir. Thank you, sir; that is another matter. In that case I will call up the cottage now to see if they are back and connect them with the number the gentleman gave."

"Half a minute. You said 'gentleman.' Did you really mean it, or was it just politeness?"

"The voice sounded like that of a gentleman, sir."

"Did you recognize it?"

"No, sir."

"And do you know whose number he gave—was it a local call?"

"Yes, sir, but I don't know which house it belongs to."

"Pity," said Hambledon. "He is waiting there—wherever 'there' is—and we could have dived down and looked him over. However. Try them again, will you?"

The butler led the way across the hall to an alcove in which there was a telephone and a small switchboard. He rang up a number on his board, and a deep voice could be heard answering.

"Hold on a minute," said the butler; "there's a call for you." He telephoned the exchange, asked for the number Quint had given, said, "Is that you, sir? … The men have returned and I have put you through. … Thank you," and handed over the receiver to Hambledon.

"That you—er—Jones?" said one voice.

"Jones speaking," said the other.

"Gut," said the first voice, relapsing into German. "There are two men at this hotel asking for a map which covers your route. They seem excited. They have found out something; it is possible they have seen your map. You have probably left it lying about, dunderheads that you are."

The second voice uttered noises suggestive of protest, but the first voice swept on unheeding.

"Clear out at once. Take the car and clear out. And beware of two men somewhere along the drive; I saw them going that way. Get out."

One receiver was slammed down, and a click followed when the second was replaced. Hambledon put down his receiver and repeated the conversation to his enthralled audience of two.

"Good gracious, sir, you don't mean to say so," gasped Vokes. "I never did take to those two men."

"Definitely suspicious characters," drawled Denton, "definitely."

"Did you say they were talking German, sir?" went on Vokes. "Then the poor young master—"

"Your master has got to be found," said Hambledon. "Denton, get outside and have a look round. Vokes, will you point out to him where the keepers' cottage is? And which way they are likely to go."

"They must pass the house," said Vokes, leading the way to the front door, "if they are going by car. But where did they keep the car?"

"Try to stop them," said Hambledon rather dubiously. He picked up the receiver again and rang the local exchange. He was answered by a woman speaking in a pleasant country voice and asked her if she would be so good as to tell him where that last call came from.

"From the telephone box in Marybourne Village," she said at once.

"Thank you very much. I suppose you didn't recognize the voice? The gentleman forgot to give his name."

"I didn't recognize the voice, sir, but I saw the caller. This post office be just opposite telephone box."

"Oh, is it? How very convenient. Who was it?"

"Excuse me, sir, the gentleman was speaking to you, was he?"

"He was," said Hambledon truthfully, adding, "though he didn't know it," to himself.

"And forgot to give his name? Well, then, it was that old professor of botany, or whatever he is, that's staying at the Seven Stars. Quint, the name is."

"Thank you so very much," said Hambledon gratefully. "That is most helpful." He replaced the receiver. "But not to Quint," he added grimly. "I'll hinder him." He strolled across the hall to the front door, humming a tuneless little song.

In the meantime Denton stood on the two broad steps outside the front door with the butler. The drive up which they had come stretched away in front of him straight as a line for half a mile till it disappeared into a wood. In front of the house there was a wide expanse of gravel; on the right side of this two other drives led off; one, said the butler, towards the gardens and the keepers' cottage, while the other went round the house to the stables.

"They must come up there, sir," said Vokes, "and pass us in front 'ere—here. That is, if they are driving, though I cannot think where they would keep—"

"Listen," said Denton. Away to the right beyond the gardens the roar of a high-powered car came to their ears. "Jones has been quick," said Denton, and leaped for the driving seat of his own. He swung the car round on the gravel, stopped it right across the top of the main drive, and got out, with his right hand in his coat pocket, just as a big black American saloon came fast up the road from the gardens and straight at him. Denton yelled at them to stop, first in English and then in German, but the big car took to the grass verge and slithered past with a scraping crash of mudguards. Denton just managed to jump clear, pulled out his automatic, and fired at their tires but missed. A hand and arm came out of a side window of the American car together with a face, scarlet with fury, and Denton ducked too late; a bullet caught him in the left arm and threw him back against his own radiator.

Hambledon leaped the steps at the sound of shooting and ran across the gravel, but two men who burst panting out of a clump of bushes were quicker still. "Much hurt, old man?" gasped one of them, and removed him from the radiator. "Excuse us if we borrow your car, won't you?" They dived into it and drove violently away; the gravel kicked up by the back wheels fell upon Hambledon as he arrived. Probably they never noticed him, for farther down the drive another drama was being played.

Constable Leggatt was cycling up from Marybourne to enquire into the matter of a dog license which ought to have been taken out by the coachman's family if their puppy was as old as he looked. He was a quarter of a mile away, but he saw the affair of the two cars quite plainly and heard the shooting. Here was a large car apparently intent on leaving the neighborhood; they must stop and explain themselves. So he threw his bicycle on the grass, stood in the middle of the drive, and held up his hand.

Almost he stood there too long; if he had not been young and active he would never have escaped. As it was, a projecting corner of the damaged mudguard ripped his tunic, and a loud bang made his head sing as a bullet tore through his helmet and jerked it off his head. Also, the chin strap caught under his nose and made it bleed.

He was just picking himself up as another car skidded to a standstill beside him, and the rear door opened ready to receive him. "Come on," said a friendly voice. "After 'em!"

"I'm after 'em," said Leggatt, scrambling in as the car moved off again. "Under the Firearms Act of 1937, Section 23, Subsections (1) and (2), it shall be an indictable offense, punishable by penal servitude," he went on between gasps, "for any person to use or attempt to use a firearm with intent to resist or prevent the lawful arrest or detention of himself or any other person, or to have same in his possession when committing many offenses under several other acts. The offenses against the Person Act of 1861, Section 14, would apply here."

He stopped for a moment and dabbed delicately at his nose.

"Any person riding any horse or beast or driving any sort of carriage, riding or driving the same furiously so as to endanger the life or limb of any passenger, may be arrested without warrant by any person witnessing the occurrence under the Highways Act of 1835, Section 78. Though as I'm only a constable they might get away with that."

"Great Scott," said Marden, "why?"

"Because a constable is not a passenger on the road for the purposes of the—Mind this corner, sir."

The car slowed slightly for the turn out of the lodge gates and leaped forward again; half a mile ahead the tail of the American saloon disappeared round a bend.

19
Arrest of a Botanist

WARNFORD was never one of those drivers who impede the traffic by loitering upon the highway, and on this occasion he did his best, but the road was strange to him and so was the car. Also, the pace of the saloon in front was excessive. The voice of Constable Leggatt floated forward to Warnford's ears.

"Driving a motor vehicle on a road recklessly or at a speed or in a manner which is dangerous to the public, having regard to all the circumstances of the case, including the nature, condition '—it was covered in places with wet leaves—' and use of the road, commits an offense under the Road Traffic Act of 1930, Section 11."

However, Denton's car was a good one, and Warnford gradually reduced the lead from half a mile to a quarter, to three hundred yards, to two hundred. The road swept down a long valley in a series of curves; happily it was unfrequented, but such other persons as happened to be using it at the time spoke of the chase for weeks afterwards, and all the way the voice of Leggatt in the back seat recited the offenses of the first car in a steady monotone.

"Any person riding or driving so as to endanger the life or limb of any person or to the common danger of the passengers in any street (including any highway, road, county bridge, etc.), not being a street within the Metropolitan Police District, may be arrested without warrant by any constable who observes the occurrence under the Public Health Act of 1925, Section 74 (2)."

"I say," said Marden, turning round in his seat, "you do know the law, don't you?"

"Sitting for my examination for sergeant," said Leggatt, "next week. Been mugging up police law."

"I hope you pass with honors," said Marden appreciatively.

Warnford reduced the two hundred yards' gap to seventy-five; once again a hand and arm, followed by an angry face, emerged from a window of the leading car, and several shots ensued. Fortunately the aim was wild, owing to the pace at which the cars were traveling, and though the top of Denton's windscreen was starred there was no real damage done.

"Discharging firearms within fifty feet of the center of a public highway," said Leggatt in horrified tones, "as laid down in the Highways Act of 1835, Section 72. I dessay they haven't got a gun license either. Being in possession of firearms——"

The American car went round a sharp bend, and there was an eldritch shriek plainly audible in the second car. When they in their turn rounded the corner two seconds later there was an enormous pig lying at the side of the road, just giving its last kick, and beside it an elderly farm laborer shaking his fists in the air and shouting loudly. The car ahead was proceeding in a series of increasingly violent swerves; eventually it hit the bank, rolled over, and stopped. Warnford jammed his brakes hard on and came to rest alongside it.

They dragged out the two keepers who appeared to have got off rather lightly. The driver had been winded by the steering wheel; he sat down in the road, both hands over his diaphragm, and made crowing noises. The other had hit his head on the windscreen and was partially stunned.

"Got any handcuffs?" asked Warnford.

"Two pair, luckily," answered Leggatt, producing them. "There was one pair just come back from being repaired—"

Warnford took them and passed one pair to Marden, who handcuffed the two prisoners together while Warnford put one handcuff on the other wrist of the stunned one.

"Here," said Leggatt, noticing this, "you aren't doing it right; you don't want to join 'em round in a ring like ring o' roses."

"Oh," said Warnford blankly. "You've got the keys, haven't you?"

"Here they are," said Leggatt, and bent down to unlock the handcuffs. The next second the keys were tweaked out of his fingers, and the free handcuff clicked round his own wrist.

"Here, what's all this?" said the outraged Leggatt. "A joke's a joke, but this isn't. Unlock me at once, please."

"Sorry, old chap," said Warnford, and pushed a pound note into the constable's tunic pocket. "I hate doing this, but there might be an attempt at rescue, and I think this'll cramp their style. Get the map out of the car door, Marden."

"I have," said Marden, showing it.

"Unlock these handcuffs at once," said Leggatt, "and I don't want your money, either. Here, come back; where are you going? Assaulting and impeding the police in the execution of their duty, contrary to the—"

But Marden and Warnford got back into Denton's car and drove rapidly away.

Outside Marybourne House, Hambledon grabbed Denton and said, "You're hit. Are you much hurt?"

"Nothing much," said Denton, exploring carefully. "Bullet through my left arm. Missed the bone completely. Don't think it's even bleeding much."

Vokes arrived, running. "Gentlemen—sir—are you hurt? What happened? Who took your car away? They have taken Leggatt away too," he added, staring down the drive.

"Oh, they're all right," said Hambledon; "they're friends of ours—I think. Have you got a first-aid outfit handy?"

"At the house," said the butler, "if the gentleman can walk across the gravel sweep. Or shall I bring it here?"

"No need," said Denton. "I could take any number of gravel sweeps in my stride." In fact, the injury proved upon investigation to be merely a flesh wound.

"You'll have a stiff arm for a few days," said Hambledon, bandaging competently; "after that you'll be all right. Now then, we want to get back to the village in rather a hurry; we have a little job to do there. Is there anyone there who'd bring out a car for us? I don't think my friend wants to walk a couple of miles just now."

"No, sir, of course not. I regret there is no hire car available nearer than Winsbury, but I could run you down in the Ford myself, if that would be agreeable. We keep a Ford for utility purposes, sir; Miss Kendal took the Rover up to town with her."

"Perfect," said Hambledon. "Very good of you."

"Not at all, sir. A pleasure."

They proceeded towards the Seven Stars at a pace which the butler considered appropriate to the transport of wounded, and Hambledon fidgeted slightly.

"If that fellow Quint's got any sense, he's packing," he said. "In his place I shouldn't even wait to pack."

"If he hasn't got a car of his own," said Denton, "he probably can't get away at once, unless of course he runs."

"I should run," said Hambledon with conviction.

However, when they approached the Seven Stars they saw Professor Quint going towards it from the telephone box. He appeared to be in a hurry. He was not in the lounge when they entered, and Hambledon asked the landlord where Mr. Quint was.

"Professor Quint has just gone upstairs to his room. I'll send somebody up to tell—"

"Please don't trouble; we'll go up. Which is his room?"

The landlord stared a little, but people did not argue when Hambledon used that tone. "Number seven, sir, up the stairs and turn right."

"You cover him when we go in," said Hambledon to Denton in a low tone. "If he begins to romp, take appropriate action. With my shoulder and your arm, to say nothing of my black eye, neither of us wants to gambol."

Hambledon opened the door of number seven and walked straight in without knocking, immediately followed by Denton with his hand in his pocket.

"Mr. Quint, I believe," said Hambledon, walking quickly towards him. "Put your hands up, please; you are my prisoner."

Quint hesitated momentarily, and the automatic in Denton's hand immediately came into view. The professor of botany put his hands up at once, and Hambledon, being very careful not to intrude upon Denton's line of fire, removed a very serviceable Luger from one of his prisoner's pockets and three spare clips of cartridges from another.

"Curious instrument for a botanist to carry," said Hambledon blandly. "Though no doubt it would be useful for shooting down specimens otherwise out of reach."

"To what am I indebted," said Quint furiously, "for this unspeakable outrage?"

"Cheese it. I am Hambledon of British Intelligence, that's what. I see you were actually packing your shirts—I thought you would be. Go over into that corner, sit on that chair, and don't move till I give you permission. Here's a chair for you, Denton; I am going to telephone to the police."

Hambledon was in the act of asking where the Seven Stars kept its telephone if it had one, when a small saloon car pulled up outside with a screech of brakes; a large man scrambled out of it and fairly bounced into the lounge.

"I say, Pitt," he said, addressing the landlord, "let me use your phone, there's a good chap. I've just seen the damned funniest sight I ever have set eyes on in all my puff. There's a policeman down the road handcuffed to two prisoners, and he can't let himself go because somebody's pinched the keys. For a picture of dignity mingled with embarrassment—well! I've got to ring up the police at Winsbury to run out and release him."

"I was just going to ring them up myself," said Hambledon, "about another little matter. You tell your story first and then perhaps I might—"

"I'll hand the doings over to you," said the large man, "if you'll stand by. Just a minute while I find the number." He retired to the back of the lounge where the telephone was kept.

"Who is this?" asked Hambledon quietly of the landlord, who replied that the gentleman was a commercial traveler in groceries. "He generally has lunch here on Tuesdays; he's late today."

The commercial traveler could be heard explaining to the Winsbury police that Constable Leggatt was at a point on the Marybourne–Martyr Worthy Road, about two and a half miles from Marybourne, handcuffed to two prisoners. Would the police please bring keys for handcuffs, as his own had been taken away, also the police ambulance, as the prisoners had been injured in a car crash? "There is also a dead pig," went on the traveler, "if that's of any interest to you, and Constable Leggatt is having his work cut out, fending off an infuriated yokel who wants to beat the prisoners with a large stick. . . . No, I am not romancing, and I'm perfectly sober." He gave his name, address, and occupation, and went on, "Leggatt asked me to go on to the nearest telephone—I happened to be passing and pulled up when I saw the crashed car. I am speaking from the Seven Stars at Marybourne. Hold on a minute; there's another gentleman here who wants a word with you."

Hambledon took over the telephone, introduced himself authoritatively, and said, "I've got another prisoner here for you; better bring another police car besides the ambulance. It is advisable these prisoners should not meet or know that the others are in custody. It is an important case. Thank you."

He returned to the lounge and found the landlord and the commercial traveler looking at him round-eyed and in silence. The Seven Stars' telephone made no attempt at aural privacy, and they were both of them plainly thrilled to the backbone. Hambledon smiled amiably and said, "Thank you very much," to either or both indefinitely, leaned one shoulder against the mantelpiece, lit a cigarette, and looked at the landlord.

The commercial traveler stared at Hambledon, opened his mouth to ask a question, thought better of it and shut it again, and shifted his feet. The landlord met Hambledon's look squarely, raised his eyebrows, and glanced at the traveler. There was an awkward little pause which the traveler eventually broke.

"I know I'm frightfully late today," he said, addressing the landlord, "but I'd still like some lunch. Can you do something about it?"

"Certainly, sir," said Pitt, shepherding him towards the dining room. "Cold game pie, cold beef, ham and tongue—"

"Had a spot of ignition trouble just this side of Alresford; that's why I'm late. Hung up for an hour at Ropley—"

When the landlord returned Hambledon told him he was sorry to have to remove one of his guests. "Professor Quint—rather a bad lad, actually."

"Indeed, sir. A rather unusual type of guest, Professor Quint."

"One hopes so," said Hambledon solemnly; "one hopes so. Your other guests, have they returned yet? What were their names, now, Warnford and Marden?"

"Not yet, sir. I saw them pass the house the best part of an hour ago, driving a car which I thought was the one you and the other gentleman came in, but I was probably mistaken."

"Not at all. They borrowed our car, but I did not quite gather how long they wanted to keep it. However, they have evidently gone on."

"Yes, sir," said the landlord doubtfully.

"You did not happen to hear them say where they were going?"

"As a matter of fact, sir, yes, I did. At least they mentioned a route and asked me for a map to look it up. Here's the map; they left it behind. They left the house rather hastily, sir, the last time. The route was Alton—Guildford—Reigate—Westerham."

"I am very much obliged to you indeed," said Hambledon sincerely. "May I use your telephone again?"

He rang up the police, the A.A., and the R.A.C., giving the number and make of Denton's car and asking to have its position, direction, and time of passing reported to him directly at Marybourne 43. On no account was the car to be stopped or hindered, whatever happened; on the contrary, the drivers were to be assisted in every way they might require. Hambledon, Foreign Office, speaking from Marybourne 43.

He had hardly finished telephoning before the police arrived from Winsbury, relieved Denton of his guard, and took away Professor Quint in an unobtrusive saloon car.

"Removed in a plain van," said Denton, watching their departure.

"The ambulance went by a few minutes ago," said Hambledon, "to bring in the others." He repeated the commercial traveler's story.

"Those two fellows," said Denton, referring to Warnford and Marden, "are certainly men of resource. They didn't mean the constable to lose his prisoners and they took a most sensible course to ensure he didn't. Where have they gone; d'you know?"

"Westerham, I think," said Hambledon, and told him what the landlord had said. At that moment the telephone bell rang, and thereafter a series of messages began to come through, reporting the car on the expected route. The commercial traveler finished his lunch and passed through the lounge on his way out, saying genially, "Good afternoon to you, sir, good afternoon," to Hambledon as he went. The landlord's wife came in, asked the gentlemen if they would like tea, and brought it. The sun went down and lamps were lit in the Seven Stars, and still the messages continued to arrive. The car reached Westerham, and then came a message from the police saying that the driver was asking to be directed to the local house agents.

"This is odd," said Hambledon. "They're looking for something and they don't know where it is."

"It's particularly odd," said Denton, "their doing that in that neighborhood."

"Really. Why?"

"Several slightly mysterious occurrences have taken place in the Westerham district in the last half-dozen years. You, being abroad, naturally haven't heard anything, but one or two of our people who disappeared were last seen near there, or going in that direction. Poor Finnis, for example; perhaps you remember him—yes, I thought you might. He was last seen leaving Westerham Station on his own flat feet and has never been seen since. Then there was a man named O'Dare who did very well in Russia and round the Baltic generally; you wouldn't know him. He was supposed to be meeting somebody off a ship at Southampton and never turned up. A friend of his reported having seen a man he thought was O'Dare driving through Orpington in the back seat of a car— There's your phone again.

"But he admitted he might have been mistaken," went on Denton when Hambledon returned. "Still, it's the same neighborhood. Another pin?"

Hambledon had spread out on a table the map which the innkeeper had lent to Warnford and was sticking pins into it at every point whence the passage of the car had been reported. A thin line ran from Marybourne to Westerham; one stood alone a little way down the Eastbourne road, but this last one was on the road to London.

"Perhaps they're packing up for tonight; it is getting late," said Hambledon. "Be dark before long; we shall know when the next call comes through. Yes, it's odd what you were saying."

"The oddest of all," continued Denton, "was the case of an elderly man from America who was a professor of conchology at some university or other. I am never sure whether conchology is shells or bell ringing; I never saw the man, but I'm told he was almost too lifelike to be real. Thick mane of grayish hair which he continually combed with his fingers, glasses so strong that his eyes popped at you, and a passion for delivering lectures to everyone he met. There's the phone again."

"Farther up the London road," reported Hambledon. "I think this expedition is drawing to its close for the time being. Well, what happened to him?"

"He disappeared from his Bloomsbury lodgings for three days, though I can't say anybody worried much at the time. I mean he might have gone anywhere; he was his own master. Then the police found him, dressed in pajamas several sizes too small for him, asleep in a dry ditch on Epsom Downs. He said a man came and told him that a fellow countryman from his own home town was ill at a certain address—they'd got the name right and the fellow was in Europe—and would he come? So he started, and that's all he remembers, except grinding up a long hill with a bus just behind them, and the bus had 'Edenbridge' on the destination indicator. Well, here's Edenbridge, all in the same district, you see. My theory is that these people, whoever they are, didn't believe in him and roped him in for investigation. Then they found he was all right and threw him back. He doesn't remember anything about his stay or anyone he met."

"Doped, I expect," said Hambledon, returning from the telephone again. "I am getting tired of all this hopping up and down, but they are in London now; a little longer and we can go too, I hope. Yes, it looks as though there was some funny business going on near Westerham; you never found anything, I suppose?"

"Not a thing, and I hope our friends are more successful."

"You know," said Hambledon, "I was expecting a biggish house on a tidal estuary somewhere, with a natty boathouse containing a fast cabin cruiser or two. I can't think what they're doing so far inland."

"A country house, a good flat park—not too many trees—you could put an airplane down in a spot like that. And take off again if you weren't too heavily loaded," suggested Denton.

"It's an idea, certainly. In fact, if I don't hear some definite news from our friends tomorrow I shall look for it myself. Surely it would be easier to spot it from the air? Can't one hire an air taxi of sorts from Croydon?"

"Oh, certainly. I think it's a very sound idea now that we've some idea where to— The phone again."

This time Hambledon came back laughing. "We can go home now," he said. "Your car's been deposited at the door of the Foreign Office. Two men corresponding to the familiar descriptions got out and asked for me. When told I was not yet returned the tall one wrote me a note, after which they both walked unhurriedly away. I am going back to read that note as soon as possible."

"How did they know," said Denton, "that the Foreign Office was the right place to leave the car?"

"I haven't the faintest idea," said Hambledon. "Perhaps they just thought I'd like it. It's quite a nice car."

20
Police Car Vanishes

WARNFORD drove Denton's car when they left the Marybourne constable indignantly handcuffed to the two alleged keepers; Marden studied the map and dictated the route.

"I was sorry to handcuff that good chap," said Warnford. "Right fork here? But it had to be done. We don't know how many more of the gang are hovering about; they might have been released in ten minutes."

"Exactly. Left here and then right. You shouldn't have given him that quid, though; that's bribery and corruption."

"Nothing of the sort; it was compensation for inconvenience. He can charge me with assaulting and impeding the police in the execution of their duty—if he can catch me."

"Go easy, this must be the main Alton-Winchester road. Yes, it is. Turn right. What exactly do we do when we get to Westerham?"

Warnford paused to arrange his thoughts before answering. "In the first place, I was very surprised to find it was Westerham. I should have expected people like that to have a place on the coast somewhere, a quiet inlet like Bosham Harbor—or quieter—or some backwater on the Broads. There is no possible doubt now that poor Kendal has been abducted by German agents who want to make him talk." Warnford shivered suddenly. "That's why we're in such a hurry. But people like that want a quick and unobtrusive getaway; they don't pass through the customs at Dover every time they come and go, not they. Especially if they've got an unwilling traveling companion. So I should have thought a fast cabin cruiser at the bottom of the lawn which sloped gently down to the water, as in all the best novels. I don't think, though, that a cabin cruiser would be much use near Westerham. So I think we are looking for a property with a sufficiently large expanse of flat land to serve as a private aerodrome, and enough private property round that to make sure that even the doings on the aerodrome are not in the public eye. What do you think?"

"If you ask me, I think it's a dashed good thing we are looking for something large. Don't you think Hambledon ought to know about this?"

"I do, indeed. In fact, if we can find out anything useful—or even if we can't—I shall ring him up this evening and tell him the whole story. This is a nice car, you know; I wonder who it belongs to. I wonder who the lanky bloke was who was pipped in the arm by the keepers."

"There might be something informative in the pockets," said Marden. "Maps in this one, no name on them. A shopping list in a feminine hand: bacon, butter, 5½ yards pink celanese, whatever that is, and a scrubbing brush. The owner has, perhaps, a wife. Here's something screwed up at the bottom, an envelope addressed to Mrs. Chas. Denton, Woodside Avenue, Blackheath. Does the name of Chas. Denton convey anything to you?"

"Nothing whatever."

"Not informative to us, though we know now an address to return the car to. I'll put these things back and try the rear door pockets." Marden put the maps back and twisted round in his seat to reach the rear door pocket nearest him. "Hullo, there's something slipped down between the seats. A long envelope, empty, with the route from London to Marybourne scribbled on the back, and it's addressed to—who d'you think? You won't believe it. T. E. Hambledon, Esq., Foreign Office, London."

"Good heart alive," said the startled Warnford, "you don't mean to tell me we pinched— D'you suppose the long man was Hambledon? I hadn't thought of him as being like that. So they've called in Hambledon on this job," he went on more gravely. "They must think rather seriously of poor Kendal's disappearance if a man like Hambledon comes down in person to look into it. I wish I'd known he was at Marybourne; it would have paid us to have a talk with him about it. However, it's too late now; he's probably left again—if he can get another car. I say, what a nerve we've got. D'you suppose he'll put the police onto us? He didn't know who we were"—in which Warnford was mistaken—"I can't think what he thought when we just brushed him aside and pinched his car—" His voice tailed off in horror.

"I should think it's all right," said Marden consolingly. "He was after those keepers, too, or they wouldn't have been firing at each other."

"It does suggest a certain coldness between them, certainly," murmured Warnford.

"Well, we got them for him. I mean it's obvious we're on his side, as it were. He may have guessed it was us. Anyway, you can explain when you ring up."

"Not much good ringing up when he's in Hampshire, is it? I should think he'd be pretty late getting back, especially without his car. I say, what a frightful *gaffe;* I go hot all over whenever I think about it. I've dropped some pretty resounding bricks in my time, but this—"

Marden thought it kinder to change the subject. "How are you going to set about it when we get to Westerham?"

"House agents," said Warnford promptly. "Westerham's a sizable place; there'll be sure to be some there. We'll ask a policeman."

They did this, and the policeman was most helpful. He not only showed them carefully where all three house agents were, but went straight to the police station when he left them and reported it. In ten minutes' time Hambledon, at Marybourne 43, heard about it and was very interested indeed.

The first house agent was out, and the office was in charge of a thin boy with pimples who didn't know much. He was very sorry Mr. Bickerstall was out; if they would call back in half an hour when Mr. Bickerstall would be back—

The second house agent was just the sort of man whom Warnford was hoping to find, friendly, talkative, and very well informed about the neighborhood. He told them about the height above sea level, the soil, the subsoil, the water supply, the drainage system, and the train service to London. He took a short flight round the local notables and back to the Conservative Club, the Cricket Club, and the British Legion. He admitted the rates were a bit on the high side, but you got value for your money in Westerham. The electricity supply—

"I gather from some names you mentioned," said Warnford, "that there are some pretty large properties in the neighborhood."

There were; yes, there were. But that only added to the amenities of the district, because none of the gentlemen concerned were at all exclusive as regards their properties. There were public roads across all of them, besides bridle paths and footpaths; there were some delightful walks in the neighborhood. "In fact, there's only one place near here which is closed to the public, and you wouldn't want to go there anyway," said the house agent, laughing pleasantly.

"What's that?"

"Morley Park. It's about two miles out on the Eastbourne road. It's a private mental home."

"I say. That's not too pleasant, is it?"

"Never had any trouble from there, my dear sir, never. In fact, from what I hear, it's such a marvelous place that it's quite a privilege to be a lunatic. Huge great house, not picturesque, but comfortable, excellent gardens, and a very large park. And a high stone wall all round with barbed wire on the top. A gilded cage, in fact—quite the gilded cage."

"Oh. Who's it run by?"

"The mental specialist in charge is a Dr. Goddard. I have an idea the place is financed by someone else, but I don't know who. That may not be true. I should think it's a paying proposition, the prices they charge. But why are we talking about lunatic asylums when what you want is a perfectly sane cottage with some rough shooting? I will make out orders to view the three places I mentioned to you, and perhaps you'll have a look at them and tell me what you think of them."

When they eventually got away from the house agent it was nearly seven and already getting dusk. "We can't do much tonight," said Warnford. "Suppose we just run down and have a look at the place to be quite sure where it is. After that I think we'll drive back to town, return this car to the Foreign Office, and come again tomorrow morning in the Bentley. Two miles out on the Eastbourne road, he said."

They came first to a high wall with three strands of barbed wire on the top and followed this to the entrance gates, tall iron gates, very strong and heavy, with matching lodges on either side. The gates were shut, and inside were two men lounging against the wall of one of the lodges.

"Remember the taller of the two keepers?" said Warnford softly. "These men might be his brothers." He pulled the car round, drove up to the gates, and hooted. The men inside came up to the gates but made no move to open; one of them looked between the bars and shouted, "What d'you want?"

Warnford leaned from the side window and said haughtily, "My good man, mend your manners. Is His Grace at home?"

"Who?"

"His Grace the Duke."

"We've got no dukes here as I know of."

"What place is this?"

"Morley Park Mental Home. No admittance except on business," added the man impertinently, and the other grinned.

"We've come to the wrong place," said Warnford to Marden in a tone audible to the gatekeepers. "I might have known the duke would never employ louts like that." He backed the car away from the gate and moved away again towards Westerham, Marden watching the gatekeepers, who had turned their backs on the gate and were strolling slowly up the drive.

"Those men also have been recently drilled," he said. "Look at the set of their shoulders."

"The gentle Nazi to the life," said Warnford, "and heaven help the poor lunatics. This place is big enough in all conscience. I think we go back to town now and report to Hambledon."

"I wonder if there really are any lunatics there."

But when they reached the Foreign Office and asked for Hambledon they were told he had not yet returned. Warnford looked conscience-stricken but said nothing in reply, only asking if he might leave a note. He was given the necessary materials and wrote hastily: "Dear Mr. Hambledon, I can't apologize enough for having pinched your car; I didn't know it was yours. We have our very serious doubts about Morley Park, Westerham, which is alleged to be a lunatic asylum. We are going there tomorrow morning to look for Kendal; if you don't hear from us again soon you will know we were right." He sealed up the envelope, told the Commissionaire to be sure to let Mr. Hambledon have it as soon as he returned, and walked out to find Marden waiting for him with his back carefully turned to an adjacent policeman.

It was late that night when Hambledon got back to the Foreign Office, but he read Warnford's note, tossed it across to Denton, and rang up Scotland Yard.

"Is Chief Inspector Bagshott still there? … Good. Could I speak to him, please? … Bagshott, this is Hambledon speaking from the Foreign Office. I'm sorry to bother you, but could you come round here? I've got something important to tell you. . . . I know, I haven't had dinner myself yet. . . . Never mind, you can go to bed early tomorrow night—perhaps. And perhaps not. … Right; thanks very much." He replaced the receiver. "He says he wants to go home to supper and bed. Poor man, how little he knows me. Let me see, Butler Vokes said, didn't he, that the police didn't seem to be worrying much about the young master? I'll worry 'em. You'd better go home and get your arm tied up properly; I'll ring you up in the morning and tell you what's happening. You'd better take three days off and see the doctor. My regards to your wife."

Chief Inspector Bagshott arrived, and Hambledon unfolded the whole story of Kendal's disappearance, his own visit to Marybourne, and Warnford's intervention. "I've got an important appointment at eleven," he said, "but I'm going to Westerham as soon after that as I can. You'd better come, too, with all the police you can muster, and the bigger the better."

Bagshott said that the police did not as a rule leap immediately upon the trail of young gentlemen reported recently missing by their loving female relatives. They usually turned up again with a much better story than anything the police could think up. This case, however, was obviously different, and he would take any steps in the matter which Hambledon suggested. Also, he would enquire what was known about Morley Park Asylum. "These places all have to be licensed, you know, and are open to inspection by the proper authorities."

"Yes. I expect it seems all right, but we'll see. Any other news about anything interesting?"

Bagshott was just in the act of saying that an atmosphere of humdrum virtue appeared to have settled deeply over the British Isles, when Hambledon's telephone rang. He said, "Excuse me," and lifted the receiver. "Yes, he's here. Hold on just a moment. … Call for you," he added to Bagshott, handed over the receiver, and strolled tactfully out of the room.

When he returned the telephone conversation was over and the chief inspector was staring into vacancy with just the concentrated expression of one completely foundered in *The Times* crossword puzzle. He looked up when Hambledon came in and said, "I spoke too soon just now about nothing happening. An odd event took place half an hour ago. At eleven-thirty, to be exact; it's just on midnight. A police car containing a prisoner, escort, and driver have disappeared entirely from the Kingston bypass; car, escort, and prisoner all complete, and they can't be found anywhere."

"But that's silly," said Hambledon.

"Silly or no, it's happened. You know the prisoner, by the way, one Palmer, a pork butcher from Hoxton, convicted of being a receiver—"

"I remember perfectly. I found some missing documents in his safe and I'll swear he didn't know they were there. However, he wasn't accused of having 'em, so it doesn't matter. What happened exactly?"

"Well, we discovered that Palmer was a fairly rich man, and, human nature being what it is, rich prisoners are more difficult to keep caged than poor ones. In fact, a rumor got about that an escape was being arranged. A little matter of smoke bombs lobbed into the exercise yard and a rope ladder thrown over at a convenient spot. So we arranged to move him to another jail, and the move was as close a secret as possible. But—"

"I know these close secrets," said Hambledon sympathetically.

"Don't we all? Anyway, he was taken away by night—tonight, that is, after dark—in a police car. He had one police escort who was attached to him by a handcuff—"

"Remind me of that again when you've finished and I'll tell you a funny story," said Hambledon.

"If it's about the police, I heard it when I was a constable," said Bagshott.

"No, it's not that sort of story. But go on."

"Palmer had this one escort, and there was also a police driver. Constables on point duty throughout the route—they were going to London—were warned to look out for the car. It was duly noted passing the Ace of Spades crossroads at 11:25 P.M., but it never reached the Ewell–Surbiton crossroads. There is no turning off between the two. There was nothing much on the road at the time: a lorry or two, a furniture van—that sort of thing—but nobody reported having seen anything unusual. We have searched all the garages of all the houses between those points but entirely without result."

" 'Like snow upon the desert's dusty face,' " misquoted Hambledon, " 'they glimmered for an instant and are gone.' "

"It's not a laughing matter," said Bagshott rather sharply.

"I know, I know. But I have learned to laugh at things that aren't. Cheer up, there is doubtless a perfectly simple explanation if only we knew what it was. It is true that I have heard that remark made about the Indian rope trick, but this can't be in the same class as that."

"It's worse, because I've never heard of the Indian rope trick being performed by policemen."

However, Hambledon was perfectly right; there was a simple explanation. The date and time of Palmer's removal to another jail had leaked out to interested parties and the route they would follow correctly deduced. As the police car entered the stretch of the Kingston bypass between the Ace of Spades crossroads and the Ewell–Surbiton crossroads, the driver saw ahead of him a furniture van pulled up not very near its own side of the road. There was also a group of people more or less in the middle of the road who were gathered about a prostrate form being apparently tended by one of the group.

"Accident," said the police driver to himself, and slowed down a little.

A man in the uniform of an R.A.C. scout ran forward and signaled the police car to stop, and though a tiny warning bell rang in the back of the driver's subconscious mind, he obeyed automatically.

"I say," said the R.A.C. man, coming up to the driver's open window, "I wonder if you'd mind—" With that the scout hit the driver on the chin with all his strength, and the policeman closed his eyes and slumped unconscious in his seat. At the same moment another man opened the rear door behind the driver and dealt similarly with the police escort. The driver was pushed over into the other front seat, the man who had hit him got in and drove slowly towards the furniture van. Two more men were flinging open the van's rear doors and letting the ramp down; the police car was driven up this into the van, and ramp and doors were instantly closed again, with several of the group who had been round the casualty inside as well. The others melted away, including the casualty, who got up and ran for it. The furniture van moved sedately on its way.

"Well done," said Palmer in a voice shaking with excitement. "Now one of you look through this copper's pockets for his keys and unlock this—handcuff."

When the policemen came dizzily to their senses again they were lying on the floor of a small room, handcuffed to each other and to a staple driven into the wall. They blinked at each other and their surroundings, and the light of recollection dawned on the driver's face.

"I am a fool," he said, and repeated the remark several times in different terms with lurid embroidery.

"Why?" said his mate.

"Because R.A.C. men go off duty at sundown, and I ought to have known that fellow was phony. I'll be dismissed the force for this, and serve me right."

In the meantime things were not going too smoothly with their captors. Palmer's rescuers, most of whom knew him quite well, naturally wanted their pay on the nail before they parted from him, and Palmer, of course, had no money on him, having just come from prison. One of the gang whom he mistrusted less than the others was accordingly sent to London with instructions where to find the receiver's little nest egg and to bring it back with him. "There's bearer bonds there, and notes, mostly fivers," said Palmer. "Bring the lot."

The man grinned, fully aware that this was to ensure that none of it stuck to his fingers on the way. He departed for Hoxton on a rather elderly motorcycle at its best speed, since the time was already nearly 2 A.M., and there was a little burglary to be done in the course of his mission. Palmer had hidden his money in the false bottom of the refrigerator in his Hoxton pork shop, which was still carrying on a normal and legitimate business with a manager in charge. Neither the manager nor any of his assistants had any idea that there was anything in the refrigerator besides pig products, and it was therefore necessary to break into the premises and get clear away again before they opened for business. If the job was neatly done no one need ever know that the place had had a visitor during the night at all. Palmer, who was too excited to sleep, spent the time chatting pleasantly with such members of the party as were also awake. He knew them all by repute, but there were one or two among them whom he did not know personally; they had been gathered together from various sources for this enterprise. One of these was a dark bullet-headed man with a condescending manner towards the others, as of one who asked himself what a man of his calibre was doing in this galley.

"Of course," he told Palmer, "I shouldn't usually be bothering myself with this sort of stunt, only I hadn't much on and I thought it might be a bit of a lark. It was too. Very neat idea that of yours, the furniture van," he added kindly.

"Ah," said Palmer, expanding comfortably. "Thought that one up years ago when I was reading one of them silly books about convicts escaping from Dartmoor and running like beetles all over the country, 'iding under bushes and living on turnips. If a chap 'ad a fast car 'anging about at the right spot to pick 'im up at the start, I says, well, somebody's sure to see the car and report it. Well, who cares? Drive it into a furniture van in a quiet spot, and puzzle, find the monkey!"

"What were you in for?" asked the man idly. "Forgery?"

"Good lord, no," said the horrified Palmer. "I was framed; that's what it was. Framed. Well, I useter buy some bits of things second'and; I always wanted to be an antique dealer reely, only there isn't the money in it that there is in pork. Not the turnover, if you get me. Tie up your capital for years in some of them fancy bits, you can, before you gets it back. Still, if I saw a nice bit going I didn't seem able to keep me 'ands off it. Silly, perhaps, but you know how it is."

"Just a hobby," said the dark man, and attended to his fingernails with a pocket file.

"Just that, and a fine mess it's landed me into. Well, it seems some of my little bits 'ad been stolen some time or another. Well, 'ow was I to know that? Been through four or five 'ands, maybe, before they reached me. Somebody spotted one of these bits and went to the police about it; I reckon I know who it was too: man I've done many a kindness to," said Palmer with virtuous indignation.

"Oh, yeah?"

"Yes, and I'll tell you one thing," said Palmer impressively, leaning forward and tapping the table. "When the police come and opened my safe there was one thing in there I never 'ad seen before, and it was not there the las' time I went to it. Sort of paper case, like."

"Oh, ah. What'd it got in it? Money?"

"I tells you I don't know, mister. Never seen it before. There was a plain-clo'es man there made a grab at it pretty quick; it's my belief he knew it was there. Sort of brown leather satchel thing, it was—"

"Here," said the dark man, suddenly displaying interest. "What did you say it was like?"

"Flat brown leather satchel case, like what you'd carry papers in, with a brass lock on it."

"Oh. And the plain-clo'es man grabbed it, did he?"

"P.D.Q. Yes, and I don't believe he was a busy, either. Not big enough for a copper, for one thing, and 'e 'adn't the look of one of them gentry, if you get me. Not but what 'e was sharp enough."

"Listen. Very queer this is, your telling me this. My boss—you wouldn't know him—had a case like you describe stolen just about the time you were shopped. Got most important papers in it. Private papers. My boss was no end upset about it—went to Scotland Yard and all that," went on the dark man romantically, "but he never saw hide nor hair of it again. Now if you were to go to him and tell him about this it'ud be a good job for you. He's always one to help those as help him.

Might get you clear out of the country if you could put him on the track of his satchel—if it was his."

Palmer, who had been wondering how on earth he was to get out of the country, seized upon this but did not show it. "I'm one as is always ready to do a man a good turn," he said modestly. "It'ud be a queer thing if it was your boss's case that was in my safe. I don't see 'ow I'm to get to tell him, though; shall have to be careful 'ow I move about for a bit after this."

"He lives not far from here; in fact, I took this little place to be handy to him. This is my little place you're at; we had to stay the night somewhere while things were being fixed up," said the man, tactfully referring to Palmer's payment for results. "Keeps a big private loony-bin; Morley Park's the name of it. He's got a well-known loony doctor in charge; Goddard, his name is, Dr. Goddard. You'd be surprised the people he's had there."

"Goddard. And where's this place, d'you say? Morley Park, is it?"

"'Bout two and a half miles that way," said the dark man, indicating the east. "Cross the railway line and you're there. Big park and all that."

"Oh, ah? Might pop across there later on when we've finished 'ere. What sort of a chap is this boss of yours?"

But the dark man was evasive in his replies, and the conversation languished. The time lagged heavily; Palmer became sleepy and dozed in his chair. The dark man did not sleep but sat alert, glancing at Palmer occasionally with a mixture of curiosity and contempt.

21
The Place Where Things Happen

At the time that Palmer was arrested the police went through his private house with a thoroughness which left nothing to be desired but failed completely to find there any such traces of wealth as a bank passbook, bearer bonds or other securities, or even notes to any substantial amount. There were the accounts of his pork business, all open and aboveboard, and that was all.

"He's got some stowed away somewhere," said Chief Inspector Bagshott. "There are some more of the Park Lane rubies somewhere too. Go down to his pork shop and don't come back till you've found something."

The police sighed patiently and went along to the pork shop, which they dissected into its component parts. The manager hovered round and wrung his hands while they took adrift the sausage machine and looked inside each separate part of it. He became so distressed when they uprooted the bacon slicer from its bed that they told him to go away and have a nice cup of Ovaltine somewhere. Consequently he was not there when they gathered round the open refrigerator and stared helplessly at it.

"Nothing in here but pork of sorts," said the detective-inspector in charge. "Better have those cupboards right off the wall, George; there may be a space behind them."

"Come to that," said a young constable diffidently, "there's a lot of space to spare at the bottom of that fridge."

The detective-inspector looked at the refrigerator again and pulled the bottom shelf right out once more. Underneath was a nice sheet of white enameled iron fastened down by chromium-plated screws.

"I expect it's only the works under here," he said; "however, we'll see. George, the screwdriver."

The white enameled sheet came up and disclosed a space the whole size of the refrigerator and about four inches deep. There were several large and fat envelopes in it containing, as Palmer had said, bearer bonds to a considerable amount and bundles of notes, mostly fivers. There was a small notebook or two, and that was all.

"Very nice," said the detective-inspector, "as far as it goes. One up to you, my lad," addressing the constable, who blushed hotly. "We still haven't found the rubies; he may have passed them on. Now then, look sharp and tidy the place up again. I'll take this stuff along to the chief."

When Palmer had escaped from custody and two policemen vanished with him, Chief Inspector Bagshott said, "He'll be wanting his dough soon. Put a man onto the pork shop, and if anybody comes for the money don't stop him. Follow him. Where Palmer is our men are. Put a good man on."

Accordingly, when Palmer's messenger made his quiet entry into the shop between three-thirty and four that morning he was unobtrusively observed. A telephone call went through to Scotland Yard, and the Flying Squad turned out. The messenger on his homeward way on the elderly motorcycle did not drive the machine so hard as he had done on the way up, so he was not surprised to be overtaken several times by things like a fruiterer's van with a rattling body and wobbling rear doors and an ancient taxi. He was having a little trouble with the ignition and was too busy to notice that it was the same van and the same taxi which kept on overtaking him and then waiting, down side turnings, until he had gone by. It did not even dawn on him that, considering their appearance, they had a remarkably good turn of speed. Nor did he know that behind these two, but in wireless communication with them, were several other police cars loaded with muscular and athletic Special Branch constabulary. "Take plenty of men," said Bagshott. "There must have been quite a gang on that job, and you don't know how many of 'em you'll meet. All of them, possibly, if, as I suspect, they are waiting to be paid. Else why the hurry for the cash?"

Palmer, dozing in a wooden armchair, awoke with a start at the sound of a stuttering motorcycle coming up the lane. "Here's our man," he said. "Good. What's the time?"

Before the dark man could answer the door burst open and the motorcyclist came violently in. Other members of the party, who had been resting, also heard the arrival and came yawning and stretching to meet him; the small room filled with men staring at Palmer and the motorcyclist, who stared back and did not speak.

"Well," said Palmer, "have you brought it?"

"There wasn't anything there."

"Don't be a fool," said Palmer irritably. "You can't get away with that. Out with it."

"I tell you," said the motorcyclist truculently, "there wasn't anything there. The place was as empty as a poor box in a work-'ouse."

The men who had been staring at the motorcyclist looked at Palmer instead, and those who had been staring at him before went on doing so. He found it most distasteful.

"Then why were you so long getting back?" he asked defiantly. "Where've you been on the way 'ere?"

"Nowhere. 'Ad ignition trouble."

"Ignition trouble my foot. You've been and—"

A large unpleasant-looking man in the group lifted up a loud unpleasant voice and said, "Freddy's all right. If Freddy says the stuff wasn't there, it wasn't."

Palmer found himself involuntarily backing towards the inner door of the room. "Listen," he said. "I put that stuff there myself, and nobody else knowed anything about its being there. I was arrested most unexpected one night as I got 'ome from business—I didn't 'ave no chance to move it if I wanted to," he added pathetically.

"You double-crossing old twister," said the motorcyclist.

Palmer found the door open behind him and backed into the doorway.

"'Ere," said the large unpleasant man, "you ain't gettin' away with this. You gotta—"

Palmer felt someone behind him draw him back and press something hard and cold into his right hand. "You may need that," said the dark man who had talked to him about Morley Park, and immediately melted into the shadows. Palmer, with some idea of getting reinforcements, darted back along the passage, unlocked the door of the room where the two policemen were, sprang inside, taking the key with him, and locked it again from the inside. He switched on the electric light and looked round.

The two policemen were sitting up on the floor, still attached to each other and to the wall. Palmer rushed at them with some idea of breaking open the handcuffs; these men looked like old friends to him compared with the toughs outside the door.

"Help," gasped Palmer. "They're going to murder me—"

There was a rain of thunderous kicks on the door which leaped in its frame and shouts of "Open this door, you—" Palmer spun round, looked dazedly at the revolver the dark man had given him, and fired all five shots through the panels at a yard range. Yelps and curses outside indicated that this had taken effect on somebody, and there was a momentary pause in the uproar which allowed another sound to be heard, heavy knocking on the front door of the house and a deep voice demanding admission.

"Police," said an awed voice in the passage. "Scram!" And there were sounds of departure merging at once into sounds of strife.

Palmer switched out the light and backed towards the window which suddenly showed a square of November dawn as somebody opened the outside shutters. The lower half slid up quietly; a pair of strong arms came in and grabbed the receiver, who uttered a squawk of terror and struggled violently.

"Don't be a fool," said the dark man hoarsely. "I'm trying to help you. Come on out of it and we'll buzz off to Morley Park. This place is too hot for comfort."

Palmer scrambled eagerly out of the window, and both men disappeared at once; the two policemen left behind looked at each other.

"Morley Park," said one. "Where's that?"

"I don't know yet," said the other, "but you bet we shall. It's a place where there'll be things happening very shortly."

Three hours later the superintendent of police at Westerham arrived at Morley Park with an escort of constables and overawed the guardians of the gates into admitting them. At the house the superintendent asked for Dr. Goddard, who came hastily, a worried-looking little man with a ragged white mustache.

"Sorry to trouble you, sir," said the superintendent. "The fact is, there's been a prisoner escaped from custody near by here last night, and there's reason to think he's hiding in the neighborhood. We have accordingly been given instructions to search all the houses in the district; I have a search warrant if you wish to see it."

"Not at all," said Dr. Goddard, "please—"

"Thank you, sir. Of course it's a mere formality in your case, but it's got to be gone through. Are there to your knowledge any clothes missing? Or any food? Those are the two things he'd go for."

"I will have enquiries made," said the doctor, "at once. I'll send someone to show you round the house."

The superintendent thanked him, and the search began. The doctor wondered what, if this search were a mere formality, a real one would be like. There were men on guard at every exit door from the big house, overlooking every side of it. Other men stood about on staircases and in passages while the superintendent and two more searched every room, every cupboard, wardrobe, alcove, and recess from ground floor to attic, to the pleased surprise of some of the inmates, who offered helpful suggestions.

"Doesn't seem to be here, sir. Have you any cellars?"

The police were conducted through coal and coke cellars and "my simple wine cellar," which appeared to the superintendent to be more than well stocked, through the basement furnace room for the central heating, but all to no effect. Palmer was not to be found.

"This is absolutely all there is to see, sir?"

"I think you've looked into everything in the house above the size of a boot box, Superintendent."

"Thank you, sir—"

"Tell me, Superintendent, is he at all likely to be lurking in the grounds? Before I let my patients out for exercise I should like to be sure they will not be molested."

"I have some more men outside who are having a look round. Unless he can change himself into a rabbit they'll find him if he's there. I will just enquire how they're getting on," said the superintendent, walking outside the front door. "Sanders!"

"Sir?"

"Any luck?"

"No, sir."

"There you are, sir. You can let your patients out with perfect confidence. I am sorry to have had to give you so much trouble. Good morning, sir."

"Good morning, Superintendent."

The police got into their cars and drove away, and Dr. Goddard watched them till they were out of sight. When it became obvious that they were not coming back he walked across the hall to a large cupboard in which coats were hung, opened it and stepped inside as the superintendent had done, and opened another door at the back of the cupboard which the superintendent had not opened. It was not at all noticeable. Inside it was the head of a flight of stone stairs, leading down. Dr. Goddard leaned over and called down the stairs that it was all right now; the police had gone. Several men who were waiting rather anxiously at the bottom thereupon came up the stairs; the first of them was a tall man with a stiff black beard.

When the superintendent arrived back at the Westerham Police Station he rang up Bagshott at Scotland Yard.

"Nothing out of the usual in any place open to inspection, sir. There is no place aboveground to hide anybody that I could see; you gave orders the place was not to be pulled to pieces—"

"Quite right," said Bagshott.

"But I think there are some cellars they didn't show me. There are no cellar windows, but there are ventilators at ground level such as are put in houses to keep the foundations dry. One of my men was standing outside one of these and he smelled cigar smoke, sir. That was exactly behind the hall; I would say there was a room or so under the hall."

"No obvious entrance, of course?"

"No, sir. But there is a large coat wardrobe in the hall; I looked into it, and the back might possibly be false. I did not tap it, sir."

"Quite right. I shall be with you in about an hour and a half."

"Very good, sir."

When Hambledon returned to the Foreign Office at about half-past eleven from his interview with the Home Secretary which, incidentally, was about quite another matter, he found Bagshott waiting for him, bursting with news.

"I never heard of this place Morley Park in my life till you mentioned it to me last night, and now it's cropped up again," he said, and repeated what the two kidnapped policemen had heard, that Palmer was going there. "Your two gentlemen, Marden the burglar and his friend, were quite right. I thought I'd give the Morley Park people a chance to show they were all right, but they're not." He told Hambledon what the Westerham superintendent had said.

"Good man, that," said Hambledon.

"Yes, and the man outside the ventilator wasn't too dull, either."

"I suppose they really do have loonies there, do they?" said Hambledon doubtfully.

"Oh yes, no doubt about that; I've had the place looked up. It's properly licensed and all and has a very good reputation."

"Very valuable asset, a good reputation," said Hambledon. "That's why I'm always so careful about mine."

Warnford and Marden reached Westerham that morning later than they intended, but it was perhaps as well, since otherwise they would have encountered the police at Morley Park. As it was, they met quite a procession of cars about a mile beyond Westerham, and Marden ducked when he saw that they were all filled with police, headed by the superintendent in full uniform in the leading car.

"My golly," said Marden in awed tones, "did you see that? What on earth can have called out that parade?"

"Somebody's been doing something naughty," said Warnford, "unless civil war has broken out between the Men of Kent and the Kentish Men. There's the wall ahead of us; I shall pull the car off the road here and put it neatly away among those bushes."

The road here ran unfenced across a stretch of common, rough and sandy, patched with heather and tall clumps of gorse, which was due for burning. Ahead of them the wall of Morley Park, ten feet of stone with barbed wire atop, came from the left and curved round to follow the road. Warnford turned the Bentley into a rough track on the left and bumped gently along for fifty yards till the track dropped into a hollow, and he stopped the car behind a patch of gorse, tall and straggling, but still bearing a spur or two of golden bloom even in November. It was a lovely day for the time of year, windless and sunny, smelling of fallen leaves and wet turf. The two men got out, carefully removed the ignition key, locked up the car, and looked round.

"I am a fool," said Warnford. "We ought to have brought something to help us over that wall. I was hoping for a tree with overhanging branches we could drop from."

"They'd take good care there wasn't one, wouldn't they," said Marden, "in a lunatic asylum? I ought to have thought of it too. We couldn't drive the car close up, could we?"

"Stand on my shoulders," said Warnford, "and see if you can do any good."

Marden said he never was a cat burglar but would try anything once; Warnford hoisted him up, and there was an interlude of effort.

"No good," gasped Marden. "Down. The wall is about eighteen inches wide at the top; I can't reach the farther edge, and it's too smooth to get a grip anywhere."

"What about the uprights for that wire?" suggested Warnford, thoughtfully rubbing his left shoulder.

"They've thought of that one; they are wound round with barbed wire. Otherwise this is a good spot; there's a clump of trees between us and the house, so they wouldn't see us hopping over."

"It's a pity," said Warnford. "Once inside, we ought to be able to get away with that gas-meter story; they would think we must be all right if the gate guards let us pass. It's only to get on the drive somewhere and walk up, and here we are stumped by a mere wall. This can't be our lucky day. Let's have a walk round and see if we—"

"Look," said Marden. "What's that?"

One short length of the Westerham road, where it topped a rise, was visible to them through the bushes, and upon it there was a small depressed-looking figure wheeling a handbarrow. Mr. Mullins was a painter and decorator in a small way; he had been busy on a job at home in the earlier part of the morning and was now on his way to paint the outside woodwork of a cottage just past the gates of Morley Park. He had with him the tools of his trade, several paintpots, a tin containing putty under water, several brushes in a jam pot, a canvas bag holding two hammers, a putty knife and a tin of the small nails called "sprigs," and, what had attracted Marden's attention, a twelve-foot ladder. He was always depressed because that was his habit of mind, but on this morning he was more miserable than usual. Yesterday's dead certainty, on which he had put a whole ten shillings instead of his usual bob each way, had come in among the also-rans, and he was wondering how on earth he could keep the news from his wife. She was not a patient wife, and when she heard this he looked like being the patient. Better not tell her while she was rolling pastry. . . .

Two men emerged hastily from among the bushes and came up to him. The taller one held a piece of paper towards him and said abruptly, "Ten bob for the loan of your ladder for half an hour."

Mullins hesitated. One does not lend one's ladder to total strangers, but ten bob—just what he wanted.

"Come on," said the tall stranger. "You shall have it back in half an hour."

Mullins made up his mind. The tall man looked and spoke like a gentleman, for one thing; for another, Mullins was a nervous little man, and these people looked as though, if they did not get the ladder, they would take it, and finally there was the ten bob.

"Awright," he said, and took the note. The two men untied the ladder from the handcart, lifted it off, and ran with it back into the bushes they had come from. "Be careful with it, mind," Mullins called after them but got no reply.

He scratched his head, staring after them, then sat down on the handle of his cart and lit a cigarette. Last time somebody borrowed his ladder it was to get in at their own bedroom window which happened to be open. They had gone out in the garden to pick a few peas, and the door had slammed and locked them out. Half-a-crown he got that time. But there was no house just here; what would two gentlemen be wanting his ladder for?

He turned this over in his mind, got slowly to his feet, and walked into the bushes the way Warnford and Marden had gone. He was just in time to see them standing on the top of the wall in their shirt sleeves, because their coats were laid over the barbed wire. They were standing astride the wire and hauling the ladder up. While Mullins watched it tilted over the top like a seesaw and slid down the other side. The tall man descended a few rungs of it, lifted his coat off the wire, and disappeared. The shorter man followed him, and there was nothing to be seen but the ends of the ladder standing up against the wire, silhouetted against the soft blue sky. At least Mullins knew where it was; it was quite safe. He went back to the cart and waited. Stroke of luck, getting that ten bob.

He waited for a considerable time, smoked another cigarette, and then looked at the Ingersoll watch he carried. Good watch, that; bought it at a Jumble Sale for a tanner, and it went perfectly. Somebody made a mistake sending it, most likely. More than half an hour; they ought to be back.

He wandered into the bushes again and looked up at the spot where the two men had got over. There was nothing there but the wall and the wire; even the ends of his ladder had disappeared. Why? This was the wall of Morley Park, the loony asylum; perhaps those were two of the loonies, though they seemed all right. But whoever heard of two loonies trying to get into an asylum?

He sat on his barrow till one o'clock, which was an hour and a half, occasionally getting up to look at the wall and returning unsatisfied. At last he picked up the handle of his barrow and started disconsolately to walk the two miles back to Westerham, looking smaller and more depressed than ever.

22
Most Irregular

HAMBLEDON AND BAGSHOTT were sitting in the superintendent's office at Westerham Police Station, discussing ways and means, when Mr. Mullins walked into the outer office and spoke to the desk sergeant.

"Good afternoon," he said.

"Good afternoon, Mr. Mullins. And what can we do for you this fine day?"

"My wife sent me," said Mullins dismally.

"Want to give yourself in charge for something?"

"No. I've lost my ladder."

"What d'you mean? Had it stolen?"

Mullins embarked on a long story about two men who borrowed his ladder for half an hour, disappeared over a wall with it, and didn't come back, though he waited and waited and then went home and told his wife, who told him to come along to the police at once if he ever wished to see it again.

"Well, perhaps it's come back by now if you go and have another look."

"It's a long way," grumbled Mullins, "trailing out there and maybe not finding anything and having to come back."

"Where is this place, then, where you lent the ladder?"

"Morley Park."

"Morley— Here, wait a minute."

The sergeant carried the story into the superintendent's office and was listened to with rapt attention.

"I've very little doubt these are the two men I told you about, Superintendent," said Hambledon. "Can this fellow describe them?"

But beyond saying that one was taller than the other, Mullins was not helpful.

"Did they have a car there?"

There might have been a car there, but Mullins hadn't seen one. There were some bushes about there; if there was a car behind them he wouldn't have seen it. He was looking for his ladder, not a car.

"Do you generally lend your things to total strangers?" asked Bagshott.

"No. And I wouldn't have done these, only they gave me ten bob. But the ladder's worth much more than that."

He was dismissed with words of hope and comfort, and the superintendent said it looked as though something might have happened to the two gentlemen.

"Yes," said Hambledon. "They've got away with a lot of things, but they may have slipped up this time. Something must be done about it at once."

"We could go up again," said the superintendent, "and pull the place to pieces. We know where to look now—under the hall."

"I'm a little nervous of doing that," said Hambledon. "We want to rescue our friends alive, not fish them up out of wells. One of us has got to be there before you start operations, only it does seem a little difficult to get in. However, some method will doubtless present itself. They really do have bona fide lunatics there, don't they? Are they all locked up in rooms?"

"Oh no," said the superintendent. "Apparently there are more or less three sorts of patients there: those who are dangerous all the time; they're more or less locked up in rooms, but even they come out for exercise, under supervision. Then there are the ones who have bad turns and are all right in between; they go about the grounds as they like in their better moments, as you might say. Then there are the harmless ones; they're about all the time. Like the one who thinks he's St. Francis—his name happens to be Francis—and wanders about in a monk's robe, talking to the birds. He was a stockbroker actually, and a very keen amateur racing motorist; he was injured in a crash at Brooklands. Then there's the one who doesn't like groundsel and wanders round the garden all day with a—"

"Just a moment," said Hambledon. "This man Francis, what's he like to look at?"

"Oh, medium height, hair thin on top—he calls that his tonsure—inclined to be a bit tubby—"

"Not too unlike me in a monk's gown or frock or whatever you call it?"

Bagshott and the superintendent stared at Hambledon, who went on, "Any chance of finding a monk's dress in Westerham? Do you run an amateur dramatic society here or anything like that?"

"We do," said the superintendent with a slight gasp. "One of my constables fancies himself an actor." He got up and opened the door. "Where's young Verrall? I want him."

Young Verrall had not been long in the force but had an unhappy knack of getting into trouble. He arrived hastily, tightening his belt and asking himself what on earth it was this time; it couldn't be those apples.

"Sir?"

"You belong to some sort of acting club, don't you?"

"Yes, sir."

"Do you think any of your members has a monk's robe—you know, hood and all"—the superintendent gestured—"they would lend us for a few hours?"

"There's one belonging to the society, sir. When we produced *Romeo and Juliet*—"

The superintendent snorted, and Verrall stopped.

"Who's got it now?"

"Miss Gallagher, sir. She looks after the wardrobe."

"Oh lor'. You can go and interview Miss Gallagher. The superintendent's compliments, and could she oblige us—all that sort of thing. Get a move on."

"Yes, sir," said Verrall, and fled. "What's in the wind now?" he asked himself, pedaling violently along the road. "Super getting up a fancy-dress dance?"

"But how d'you propose to get in?" asked Bagshott.

"Over the wall, like our friends. Only with two ladders, one up and one down. And a couple of constables to heave them about for me."

"You'll be seen and nabbed, like the others," said Bagshott.

"Oh no, I shan't. Everybody will be running to see what the loud bang is a quarter of a mile round the circumference of the wall."

"And what will it be?" asked the superintendent nervously.

"A two-pound slab of guncotton hurled over the wall at an appointed moment by some of your fellows. You've got a man or two who served in the last war, haven't you?"

The superintendent nodded. "I did myself, for that matter."

"And you can get hold of some guncotton?"

"I could, I think. But look here, this is all highly irregular; I should—"

"So is Morley Park," said Hambledon, "and we are going to regularize it."

The patient who thought he was St. Francis was sitting under a tree in the afternoon sunlight, engaged in what he called his meditations. He did this because he knew it was his duty to meditate, though he much preferred talking to the birds. It is difficult to meditate without letting one's mind wander back, and it hurt him that his mind would not go back beyond a point where there was a loud bang and a flare of flame. This memory frightened him so much that it made him shake; he would get up hastily, abandoning his meditations, and go across to the warren and watch the rabbits playing about. It was very sad that they always ran away when they saw him coming; they ought to know he would not hurt them. If he meditated more, perhaps he would get the power of not frightening the rabbits, but there was always that terrible moment when one remem—

There was an earsplitting roar quite close to him, a shower of clods and stones; and a small oak sapling sailed past his head and came down to earth with a crash. Francis leaped to his feet and ran like a hare. Run, run, there is danger. Why couldn't he run faster? He used to be a good runner, only he didn't have these skirt things hampering him. Why was he dressed up like this?

He dodged round a clump of rhododendron slap into the arms of another monk who was advancing cautiously with his hood pulled well forward and his hands in his sleeves. Francis seized him by the arm.

"What am I doing in this—this monastery? I'm not a monk; I'm a stockbroker."

"My dear fellow," said the other monk.

"I'm not even an R.C.; I belong to the Church of Scotland," babbled Francis. "I ought not to be here; I've got a wife and child at home. Oh, let me get out!"

The other monk took him by the arm and piloted him behind a group of hollies.

"See that ladder?" he said, pointing to one which leaned against the wall. "There's another the other side. Over you go. You'll find some police outside; they'll see you're all right."

"You're a pal," said Francis, and shot up the ladder, overcame the connection between his robe and the barbed wire with a rending sound, and disappeared. The other monk pulled his hood forward again and advanced towards the house with measured strides. Two men came towards him, running, and one of them called to him. "What's happened? Are you all right?"

Tommy Hambledon turned his back on them, gazed dreamily up into a tree on which a starling was sitting chattering to itself about the bang. "Poor little brother," said Tommy softly, "sing your lovely song for me."

"He's all right," said the other man. "Come on." They ran on in the direction of the explosion, and Hambledon quickened his pace towards the house. He walked into the hall, which happened to be empty, and immediately recognized the large cupboard of which the superintendent had spoken. He tried the door, but it was locked.

"Damn," said Hambledon softly, and looked about him. He was in a square, ugly hall paved with black-and-white-marble squares; a large room furnished as a sitting room opened off one side, and a long passage, with doors at intervals, off the other. Hambledon looked round for some tool with which to force the door, but there was nothing, not even fire irons in the grate. "I suppose they don't have fire irons in loony-bins," said Hambledon. "Funny there doesn't seem to be anybody about."

Down the long passage somebody was shouting and somebody else knocking from inside a door. Hambledon felt horribly conspicuous all alone; it only wanted someone who knew the real Francis to come along and look at him hard, and the game would be up. Create a diversion. He turned abruptly and walked down the long passage, opening all the doors. They were not locked; they merely had no doorknobs on the inside.

For a long minute nothing happened; Hambledon reached the end of the passage and turned, and cautious faces began to appear in doorways. One tall man who looked like a soldier said it was most irregular; he'd already had his exercise. He went back into his room and sat down again, but the others drifted out into the passage and followed Hambledon into the hall.

He looked them over as they came in; they might be prisoners and not lunatics at all; certainly they looked sane enough to him. Hambledon had never seen Kendal and had only a fleeting glance at Warnford and Marden outside Marybourne House. Then there was O'Dare whom he had never met either, and Finnis whom he remembered rather vaguely, though it was hardly likely the last two were here or, indeed, anywhere except in heaven, thought Tommy. Nobody there resembled Warnford or Marden in the least, though there was one young man who might conceivably be Kendal. He looked more like a spring poet than a Tank Corps officer, but one never knew.

"Excuse me," said Hambledon, addressing him. "Is your name Kendal, by any chance?"

The young man turned an abstracted gaze upon him. "My name is Benvenuto Cellini, and I am also a cousin of all the Doges. I am a goldsmith of some small repute."

"Oh dear," said Tommy inaudibly.

"Your face reminds me of a pickled onion," said the young man thoughtfully, and drifted away.

A fat man with a good-tempered face came up to him and said, "It was extremely civil of you, sir, to open my door for me. I have been ringing for the servants, but nobody came."

"There ought to be some servants about, surely," said Hambledon. "I have been wondering that, myself. There are generally people about here, aren't there?"

"As a rule," said the fat man, "the attendants are assiduous in their duties, but perhaps they have all gone to the fair. Do you like clocks?"

"Very much, thank you."

"Have you got one you could give me? I take them to pieces and repair them, though Marie says it is not suitable employment for one of my rank. But surely a king may choose what amusements he pleases?"

"Certainly, Your Majesty," said the tactful Hambledon. "Isn't there one on the drawing-room mantelpiece?"

"Where? In there? Sir, you are perfectly right, and I am much obliged to you." The fat man made him a slight bow and trotted off into the drawing room, which was adorned with a large marble clock with gilt figures on it. The king tried to lift it and failed, so he levered it off the mantelpiece with a piece of wood from the unlighted fire; it landed in the fender with a satisfying crash and broke into a dozen pieces. The king picked the works out of the wreckage and retired to a corner with them; the others took not the faintest notice.

"I have certainly let out the wrong ones," said Tommy anxiously to himself. "I sure have," he added fervently, and dodged out of the way as a tall thin man came loping in with an axe he had found somewhere and attacked the grand piano.

"Ha," said one of the others. "Firewood, eh?" and went to help him.

There were quick footsteps in the hall, and the two men who had spoken to Hambledon in the park came to the door and looked in.

"Gott im Himmel," said one, "the lunatics are loose."

Hambledon turned his back on them and examined a picture on the wall.

"Where are their proper attendants?" asked the other, speaking in German.

"Locked up upstairs," answered his friend in the same language. "They threatened to call the police back after that row when Goddard bolted, so we locked 'em up."

"Let 'em out again, I say. Police are bad enough, but raging lunatics are worse. *Allmachtige*, they've started on the chairs now."

"We can't have the police here yet; it's only another hour or so and we shall all be away; the Herr is arranging it. I will speak to them firmly; perhaps they will go back to their rooms." The man, who certainly did not lack courage, advanced into the room, stopped, and suddenly yelled at the top of his voice like a drill instructor in a barrack square.

"Attention! Back to your rooms, all of you. You have played long enough."

The man with the axe turned like a flash and swiped at him, hitting him a glancing blow on the head with the back of the axe, and the German dropped where he stood. The other lunatics, who were standing apathetically about, brightened up at this and began to close in on him, making unpleasant little growling noises, but the axeman merely started on another chair. The second German sprang into the room, menacing them with a revolver, but they took no notice of it. The tall soldier who had returned to his room suddenly appeared in the doorway, surveyed the scene, and said, "Most irregular," in a disgusted voice. He saw the revolver in the German's hand, picked up a long bar of wood from the ruins of the piano, and hit him hard on the wrist with it. The German dropped his gun, nursed his wrist with the other hand, cursing, then suddenly seized his unconscious friend by the feet and towed him out of the room. He slammed the door after him, but Hambledon could hear him in the hall outside yelling for somebody called Alberich. "Alberich! Come up! The lunatics are loose, and there's hell to pay."

The tall soldier threw down his piece of wood, said, "Most awfully irregular," and stalked out of the room, leaving the door open behind him. Hambledon saw him cross the hall, walk down the passage opposite, and turn into his own room again.

"Got a one-track mind, that fellow," said Tommy aloud, and moved near enough to the door to see into the hall. As he did so the door of the big cupboard opened and a fat little man emerged. He took in the situation at a glance, said, "The official attendants instantly released must emphatically be," and bolted upstairs. The undamaged German heaved up his battered friend and bore him away somewhere into the back regions, and the hall was, for the moment, empty.

"Now for it," said Hambledon, and glided with artistic dignity tempered by haste across the hall and into the cupboard. He shut the door after him, noticing that it had a spring lock on the inside. A light was switched on in the cupboard by the shutting door, and he saw that a panel at the back had been slid open; through it he saw stone stairs leading down and another electric light at the bottom.

"I wonder how many of the gang are down here," said Tommy plaintively to himself. "I shall present a singularly easy target walking down these stairs. Oh, why wasn't I a stockbroker like Francis?"

He pulled his hood well forward again—the wretched thing kept on slipping back to display his face—and walked steadily down with a measured pace and his automatic, with the safety catch off, in his hand under the wide sleeve. At the bottom was a short stone-flagged passage with three doors on either side; the first door was open to a room with a table, a couple of chairs, and a good fire in the grate. The room was unoccupied.

"The guardroom," guessed Tommy correctly. "Then it's just possible I've chosen the right moment. The other doors all have bolts on the outsides, and they're all bolted."

He unbolted and opened all the doors one after another, and four men came out; the fifth room was empty.

"You all prisoners?" asked Hambledon briskly. "Yes—I thought you might be. If you can get across the hall and down the drive unseen, lie doggo near the gate. The police will be here shortly. Don't talk, go."

Three of the men murmured, "Thanks awfully," and departed up the stairs; the fourth hung back and said, "Police?" in a doubtful tone. Hambledon looked at him attentively.

"Hullo," he said. "We've met before. Your name is Palmer."

"Yes, and I don't know as I want to meet the police."

"Please yourself," said Hambledon. "There are worse people than the police, you know." He turned and led the way upstairs, with Palmer following irresolutely behind.

"I think this is where I ring up the superintendent," said Hambledon to himself. "I wonder where they keep their telephone."

The cupboard door was open when he reached it, and he caught sight of the other three prisoners peeping out of one of the passage rooms till recently occupied by the genuine patients.

"Young idiots," said Tommy crossly, "why can't they do what they're told?"

He was delayed in his search for the telephone by the young man who thought he was Cellini. He came across the hall with his arms inconveniently full of bottles, gave Hambledon two of them to hold, and pushed him firmly into the drawing room. He appeared to have been exploring the house, for he had several bottles of eau de cologne, one of salad oil, one of methylated spirit, and a cut-glass decanter of whisky. The wreckage of the furniture had been loosely cast in a heap, and he emptied the contents of his bottles over it. Hambledon watched with horrified fascination while he struck a match and set fire to it.

There was much stuffing out of chairs in the heap, and the bonfire was an immediate success.

Hambledon dropped his bottles and bolted out of the room to find the telephone. "Probably somewhere just off the hall," he muttered, and tried a door opposite. It was a small room furnished rather like an office, with a desk, a couple of leather armchairs, a grandfather clock, and a telephone. He sprang at it, dialed Exchange, and asked for the number of the Westerham police. While he waited for the call to go through he heard sounds of running feet on the stairs and someone saying, "But who let them out?" in an unmistakably English voice.

"The official attendants instantly released have evidently been," said Hambledon. "That you, Superintendent? … Hambledon speaking from Morley Park. Come along as quick as you can; there's—"

"Drop that receiver at once," said a voice behind him.

Hambledon turned and saw behind him a man whom Denton had described in detail, and he was holding a revolver very competently.

"Blackbeard!" said Hambledon in a loud voice, hoping the superintendent would hear, and dropped the receiver, but not onto its hook. "Herr Richten, I should say."

"I think you had better put your hands up," said the tall man with the black beard. "It is always done on these occasions in the best novels. I am pleased to meet you at last, Mr. Hambledon; I have heard much about you, but I hardly know what to do with you now I've got you. Since our countries are still at peace—officially—I can't very well shoot you. I can't even stay and have much of a chat with you either, because I am leaving almost at once. My usefulness here has come to an end for the moment; I suppose I have you to thank for that. I have a very good mind to shoot you after all; you know too much about me, I think."

"I am not the only one," said Tommy mildly.

The fat man who thought he was a king strolled into the room and said, "Hullo, here's another clock."

"Run away, there's a good chap," said Blackbeard quite good-naturedly. "There's a much nicer clock on the stairs." He kept his eyes fixed on Hambledon and the gun quite steady.

"But this is such a nice big one," said the king, and opened the door in the case.

"If only he'll get between us," thought Hambledon, "I'll rush Richten and chance his gun."

"Listen, Your Majesty," said Richten, "if you'll just go and call Alberich here you can have this clock all to yourself."

"I thank you, sir," said the king statelily, "but I already have it." He put his arm inside the clock case, and there was a sound of a chain rattling.

"I really must go," said Richten, and took a step back; Hambledon at the same moment stepped forward. "No, don't do that, otherwise I shall have to shoot you."

For a wonder the king noticed this remark and resented it. "Sir," he said, addressing Richten, "we cannot have this tone used to a friend of ours. We are obliged to this gentleman for several courtesies already."

"Oh, go and boil your head," said Richten irritably. "It might do it good," he added under his breath, and Tommy bit his lip.

The king withdrew from the clock case with a heavy weight on the end of a chain and examined Richten critically. A cloud of smoke rolled in from the doorway and made him sneeze, which added to his annoyance.

"We do not like men with black beards," he announced, and walked round behind Richten. The German half turned, but Tommy moved, and Richten faced round again instantly. "Clear out of this; get out!" he said in an authoritative voice, and the king snarled.

"We find you lacking in respect," he said, showing his teeth like a dog, and a little foam appeared at the corners of his mouth. He was staring at the back of Richten's head, and Hambledon had the utmost difficulty in keeping his eyes off him over the German's shoulder.

"Wonderful world these people must live in," said Tommy conversationally, and found it an effort to keep his voice steady. There was a clatter of feet in the hall outside; somebody shouted something in German; an English voice answered angrily, and someone else screamed in a high-pitched shaking voice.

"Alberich!" shouted Richten. "Ernst! Here to me," but there was such a noise outside that no one answered him. The lunatic who thought he was a king, still fidgeting about behind Richten, swung his clock weight and hit himself on the leg with it. He looked down to see what had touched him, held the weight up, and looked from it to Richten's head and back again, over and over again. The German was plainly uneasy, though he dared not take his eyes off Hambledon.

"Look here, old chap," he said. "Your Majesty, I mean. There are lots of other clocks in the house waiting for you to mend them. Go and have a look round; don't stand there." But the king did not seem to hear him.

"We seem to have reached something of a deadlock, don't we?" said Tommy cheerfully. "In the meantime, the police—"

"I am going now, and if you move I will shoot you," said Richten, and took a step back. "Damn you"—to the king—"get out of my way."

The king also stepped back, and his face was like nothing human. He swung the clock weight round and round on the end of its chain and brought it down with frightful force on the back of the German's head. He dropped like a log, and the gun in his hand went off; Hambledon felt the wind of the bullet as it passed his ear. The king looked down and giggled.

"Is that funny stuff his brains?" he asked.

"Yes, Your Majesty," said Hambledon, walked hastily out of the room, and was uncontrollably sick in the hall. When he had recovered a little he realized that the place was full of smoke, growing thicker every moment, and that there was a series of fights in progress. It seemed to him that everyone was fighting everybody else and that a lot more people had arrived and joined in. Just in front of him a tall man with brown hair, one of the released prisoners, was hammering a large square man who was swearing in German. Eventually the Englishman knocked down the German, who hit his head on the marble pavement and ceased to offend. The tall man turned round, and Hambledon asked if his name was, by any chance, Warnford.

"Yes," said Warnford, panting. "Curse this smoke."

"I'm Hambledon. What is all this strife?"

"Oh. Er—how d'you do? We didn't have a nice time down in those cellars—especially Kendal. So whenever we see a German we hit him. The others are the loonies fighting their keepers. Gosh, what a brawl. There's another," gasped Warnford, and sprang at a man Hambledon recognized as Alberich.

"I think I'd like some fresh air," said Hambledon, and stumbled towards the front door, averting his eyes from the open door of the telephone room. In the doorway he met the lunatic who had once been a soldier.

"Most irregular," he said gloomily.

"I couldn't have put it better myself," said Hambledon.

23
Conversation Piece

"When we got there," said the Westerham superintendent, "smoke was pouring out of the windows. It looked to me as though the place was well alight, but nobody was taking the faintest notice of it. The loonies were popping in and out like a lot of jackrabbits in a bury and fighting the attendants who were chasing about trying to round 'em up. Then there were three husky fellows busy knocking hell out of half a dozen bullet-headed toughs who were—well, they weren't English. I gather that is all frightfully hush-hush and confidential, so we'd better forget it. The loonies were joining in that too; in fact, it was a real free-for-all. Then round the corner of the house came that poor boob Palmer chased by a lunatic with an axe. I never saw a man run like it; I didn't blame him. He threw himself at me, clutched me round the knees, and said he wanted to go back to jail; it was safer. I said I thought we could oblige him."

"And the lunatic with the axe?" asked the chief constable.

"One of my fellows downed him with a truncheon, and the loony keepers collected him. Another of my constables saw a man in one of the rooms, so he rushed in to rescue him. The next minute my man—young Verrall it was—came flying out through the window backwards and landed in a flowerbed. A cloud of smoke came out through the broken window, and a face appeared for a moment—a long melancholy face. It said, 'Most irregular,' and disappeared again. They got him out later. Young Verrall picked himself up, came up to me, and said, 'Excuse me, sir, may I make a suggestion?' Always very polite, young Verrall. I said, 'What is it?' and he said, 'Wouldn't it be a good idea to send for the fire brigade?' "

"Hadn't you?" said the chief constable.

"I didn't seem to have had time, sir; there were so many things happening at once. I did then. It was really rather awkward for us police; we knew from Mr. Hambledon of the Foreign Office that we'd got to arrest some spies, but even he didn't know how many there were, and we didn't know which were lunatics, their keepers, the spies, or the prisoners they were supposed to have locked up there somewhere. Especially as the place was so full of smoke you couldn't see anything properly and, as I say, they all seemed to be milling round, fighting anybody they met. It was a proper picnic."

"How did you get them sorted out?"

"Mr. Hambledon was very helpful, and we knew the head mental attendant. When we'd got everybody out, including a corpse with its head bashed in, there was still one lunatic missing. Besides Mr. Francis, I mean, he who recovered his wits and came over the wall at the outset. They found the missing one eventually outside the gate among the crowd there was there. I don't know where all the people came from in the time."

"One never does," said the chief constable, "but people always do arrive."

"There they were, all craning their silly necks like a lot of geese, and the loony in the middle. I don't think he'd got the silliest face, either. As I say, sir, it was a proper picnic."

"I shall regret to the end of my days," said the chief constable, "that I didn't attend it."

"In the course of my dubious career," said Hambledon, "I have killed people in various unpleasant ways, but I think that was the nastiest. It seemed to go on for hours and hours, waiting for that poor lunatic to make up his mind to strike."

"I don't see what you could have done about it," said Denton consolingly. "If you'd said to him, 'Whip behind,' or something like that, he might not have believed you."

"No. But I didn't even try—quite the reverse, in fact. It was one of the most difficult things I've ever done in my life, managing not to look interested in what was happening behind him. It had to be done, you know; he'd have given us a lot more trouble if he'd lived. Quite an able fellow, Richten."

"What I don't understand," said Denton, "is why they'd locked up Palmer. Wasn't he in with them?"

"Oh, that was simple. He came along with one of the gang who told him Richten'd get him out of the country in exchange for information about that diplomatic satchel I found in his safe. As a matter of fact, Richten's man slipped up; Richten'd lost interest in the satchel, and here was somebody totally unreliable who'd learned too much about him. Palmer was quite right; he is safer in jail. He was going to be taken up in that airplane they kept in the park, and I expect they'd have dropped him out over the Channel. I don't know, but I'm sure they wouldn't have preserved Palmer."

"Richten left it rather late if he was going to escape by plane," said Denton. "What about warming up the engine? He would probably have crashed taking off, anyway."

"He made a mistake coming to talk to me; he ought to have fled when he heard me telephoning. Perhaps he thought it might be useful in the future to know what I look like. I thought it would be more useful if he didn't. Have a future, I mean, once he knew me."

"One final point. The real head of the lunatic asylum—what was his name? Goodwin? Where did he come in?"

"Goddard. The unwilling accomplice. He'd blotted his copybook at one time, and Richten was blackmailing him. He really is an expert on mental diseases, and most of his work there was perfectly genuine. The place was financed by Richten, of course, as a cover for other activities. It's a pity Goddard has disappeared; he might have claimed a cure in the case of Francis. Recipe, one two-pound slab of guncotton complete with cap and fuse. Ignite, throw, and pray."

"We got over the wall all right," said Marden, "but they must have been watching us. Captain Warnford went down first and held the ladder for me; I came down backwards and didn't see anything happening. They must have clouted him when his back was turned and me as I came down. The next thing we knew was when we woke up in those basement cells with bumps on our heads."

"Of course," said Ashling, "the captain 'asn't 'ad any experience of real war or 'e'd know better than to turn 'is back on the enemy. Now, when I was on the Somme—"

Young Constable Verrall was standing outside Westerham Police Station wishing it was lunch time, when a depressed little figure came along the road pushing a handbarrow.

"Morning, Mr. Mullins."

"Morning."

"So you got your ladder back all right."

"Oh, ah. Got me ladder back."

"So you're ten bob to the good."

Mullins merely looked at him sourly.

"Aren't you?"

"I put it on Roast Potato yesterday," said the painter reluctantly, "for the four-thirty."

"Oh. Hard luck. What did Mrs. Mullins say?"

"She don't know yet. She was making pastry this morning," said Mullins, and passed on his way.

"Pastry?" said Verrall thoughtfully. "Oh, rolling pin, of course. Poor old Mullins."

The convicts, carefully spaced out, were taking their daily walk round and round the exercise yard, and one of them was talking. He did not move his lips and he desisted whenever he neared a warder, but the convict behind him heard what he was saying. He was giving his opinions of prison and its warders, its exercise, its food, its accommodation, and everything about it.

"Oh, there's worse places than this," said the second convict, also without moving his lips.

"What?"

"Loony-bins," said Palmer, the receiver.

The first convict was so startled that he shied visibly. "What! You been in a—?"

"No talking there," said the warder. "Silence. And space out. Keep step, you there."

The convicts went on shuffling round and round the exercise yard, but every now and again one of them glanced nervously over his shoulder.

Mr. Gunn, landlord of the Spotted Cow, was having a quiet glass with his friend Captain Butler, who had spent so many years of his life on the Hooghly. Gunn was looking with interest at a picture in a newspaper; it was a photograph of some entrance gates with a lodge on either side and a group of men in the act of getting into cars. "Morley Park, Westerham," said the caption, "the sumptuous private mental home which was yesterday set on fire by escaped lunatics. Police had to be called in to assist in restoring order, and in spite of the efforts of the fire brigade the place is a total ruin."

"You police do get some queer jobs," said Butler. "Dealing with lunatics, now; that is awkward."

"There's something behind all this," said Gunn. "I'd dearly like to know what it is."

"Why? Wouldn't you expect 'em to call in the police if the loonies got out of hand?"

"The local police, if necessary, yes. But not Chief Inspector Bagshott of Scotland Yard and a small army of Special Branch men. There's Sanders there; I've known him for years, and several of the others I know, too—Dicky Rice, for one, him on the left there, always called Birdseed."

"D'you mean to say," said Butler, "that they got men down from Scotland Yard to deal with a few escaped lunatics?"

"Doesn't sound very likely, does it? That's what I said; I wonder what's behind it. There's another man there, that short man—he's not a policeman, but Bagshott is standing back to let him get into the car first. He must be somebody pretty important, but I can't see his face; it's turned away from the camera."

Thomas Elphinstone Hambledon always turned his face away from cameras.

"Of course I'm going on with my job," said Roger Kendal. "What d'you take me for? I'll be a bit more careful whom I engage as keepers in the future."

"I wish you'd do your work in the house," said his sister anxiously, "instead of in that silly place on the far side of the gardens. There's plenty of room in the south wing."

"All right, I'll move the things up. It will be more convenient, really. I wish Warnford took more interest in my line; we might work together."

"He's so happy," said Jenny, "to be back with the regiment, I don't think he'd leave it even to work with you. I have some news for you, Roger. I'm going to marry Jim quite soon."

"If you think that surprises me," said her brother, "you're wrong. I knew this would happen. Find me a good housekeeper before you go, won't you? Dear old Pieface, I hope you'll be awfully happy. Jim's had a rotten time; he deserves all the best."

"I'm going to try and make him forget it."

"He won't do that, but you can make it unimportant. How, exactly, does one give the bride away? I suppose there's a drill for it; I must find out."

Tommy Hambledon gave a little dinner at the Café Royal at which Warnford was unable to be present, owing to his regimental duties, but Denton was there, and Marden.

"I miss him frightfully," said Marden; "I must find something to do. They won't have me in the Tank Corps at my age."

"Terribly good for the liver, I hear," drawled Denton, "bouncing about in a tank. Counteracts middle-aged spread, and all that."

"You won't have far to look for a job," said Hambledon. "You are coming on my department."

Marden fixed his eyes on Hambledon and seemed about to speak, but the Intelligence man swept on without waiting for an answer.

"I think you will be very useful. I hear you have a way with safes, and that is a valuable accomplishment in our line. I understand you can walk about a house without disturbing the inmates; I have often longed for a trained and obedient ghost. At least it won't get you into jail in this country, though it's true that

Continental prisons are not too comfortable. Endeavor to keep out of them. Though I'm afraid that on your new job you may have to do many things without lawful authority."

THE END

About the Rue Morgue Press

"Rue Morgue Press is the old-mystery lover's best friend, reprinting high quality books from the 1930s and '40s."
—*Ellery Queen's Mystery Magazine*

Since 1997, the Rue Morgue Press has reprinted scores of traditional mysteries, the kind of books that were the hallmark of the Golden Age of detective fiction. Authors reprinted or to be reprinted by the Rue Morgue include Catherine Aird, Delano Ames, H. C. Bailey, Morris Bishop, Nicholas Blake, Dorothy Bowers, Pamela Branch, Joanna Cannan, John Dickson Carr, Glyn Carr, Torrey Chanslor, Clyde B. Clason, Joan Coggin, Manning Coles, Lucy Cores, Frances Crane, Norbert Davis, Elizabeth Dean, Carter Dickson, Michael Gilbert, Constance & Gwenyth Little, Marlys Millhiser, Gladys Mitchell, James Norman, Stuart Palmer, Craig Rice, Kelley Roos, Charlotte Murray Russell, Maureen Sarsfield, Margaret Scherf, Juanita Sheridan and Colin Watson..

To suggest titles or to receive a catalog of Rue Morgue Press books write 87 Lone Tree Lane, Lyons, Colorado 80540, telephone 800-699-6214, or check out our website, www.ruemorguepress.com, which lists complete descriptions of all of our titles, along with lengthy biographies of our writer